THE LOST AND THE DEPARTED

THE CRACKLOCK SAGA: BOOK 2

C. A. DEEGAN

The characters and events portrayed in this book are fictitious. Any similarity to actual persons, living or dead, is coincidental and not intended by the author. Names, characters, businesses, organisations, places, events and incidents are the product of the author's imagination or are used fictitiously.

For information, contact www.thecracklocksaga.com

ISBN: 978-1-7399081-2-6

This book is dedicated to Tony, who's enthusiasm for my writing came as a total surprise to me. Thanks Dad!

THE LOST AND THE DEPARTED

THE CRACKLOCK SAGA: BOOK 2

C. A. DEEGAN

"False words are not only evil in themselves, but they infect the soul with evil. "

\- Socrates

THE STORY SO FAR...

Terrible news! Children all over the globe are coming down with some strange sickness that seems to age them almost overnight. And nobody has any idea what it is or how to cure it.

Jack is a boy from a single-parent family on the poor side of town who has no idea of his past, having been glamoured to hide him when he was four. Two subsequent accidents in close succession break the glamour, which includes a fight with the local bullies (the LaFey twins) when he tries to help his friend Jimmy Owen and an attack by the indomitable Mr Binks who, not knowing who Jack really is, tries to harvest Jack's life force, or 'grackles' with a tube-like device that is being used to drain the life force from younger children. Jack resisted Mr Binks but is blinded in an accident during his escape; his loss of sight is the last-ditch magical attempt of the glamour on him to stop him from seeing the Faery folk. His Great Aunt Elsie Cracklock comes to look after him and, after much heart searching, removes the glamours remains, restoring Jack's sight and his ability to see Faeries. She helps him understand his past and abilities with an introduction to the Faery realm and family history, with help from old family friends, Fermerillion (Fermy) (a Feeorin) and Dorcas (a Brownie). Jack is a Cracklock, a family able to see the little folk due to their unique ancestry.

Meanwhile, other Cracklocks (Malchiah, Anastasia and Benedict) have learned what has happened to Jack and, believing him to be the family member they have been trying to locate for years, initiated a search. Jack visits Faery to learn more about his history via Timothy Tattingmouse (a Fae Scholar and Myomancer). Whilst he is there, Jimmy is attacked by the LaFey's but is saved by Dorcas. She was forced to reveal herself to Jimmy following her actions, and he learns about the hidden world his friend has been suddenly thrust back into.

Upon learning about the strange tube during the discussions in Faery, Fermy resolved to steal it from Mr Binks so they can investigate it further. But he was subsequently captured, and Jack, Jimmy and Elsie rushed to his rescue. Fermy needs urgent help, forcing Elsie to return to Jack's home to tend to him. Elsie didn't know that Anastasia and Benedict had already arrived there and were harshly interrogating Jack's mother, Sammy, and Dorcas to find Jack. Only the arrival of Elsie managed to save them, but the ensuing battle resulted in Elsie's hospitalisation.

Following Fermy's rescue, Jack and Jimmy discover captured Faeries at Mr Binks's house and remained to release them, stealing the tube whilst they do so. Mr Binks pursues them before setting his Lisovyk, a type of Faery forest demon, onto them. Following a showdown at the school with the monster, the stolen tube is revealed to be a strange lifeform from another realm, a place that none of the friends knows anything about.

And now, Fae friend, please read on...

CHAPTER 1

Sammy sat with Elsie in a quiet side ward of the critical care unit, or CCU, as the ambulance staff had called it. The old woman was sleeping now and seemed comfortable despite being attached to heart monitors and other equipment. Some colour had returned to her face now, and her lips were no longer purple, which Sammy took as a good sign. The chair that Sammy sat in was uncomfortable, and she fidgeted as she sipped the stewed sweet tea that the healthcare assistant had brought for her. She was patting Elsie's hand gently, more to reassure herself than anything.

Sammy thought over the madness of the last few hours. The maniac blonde and the man who had forced their way into her home, demanding Jack and David. And the thing that had appeared; the Dorcas thing. It was all too crazy for her to think about, but as she sat there clutching her aunt's hand, it all whirled around in her mind. The things that they could do. And Elsie! She could do them too; magic spells or whatever it was. The flashes and bangs glittered in her mind's eye. She wanted, no, needed to talk to Elsie about it all, to try and make some sense of it. And where was Jack? That worried her the most, and she looked at her phone again. Hardly any battery. If Elsie was safe for now, she would maybe see if she could find a payphone. But she was so tired, fighting to keep her eyes open.

The heart monitor beeped rhythmically. Another instrument took Elsie's blood pressure at regular intervals and gave a warning if it became abnormal; it had sounded once since they had been admitted, but for now, it was quiet as it did its job. The consultant had said that it was more likely to be chronic angina than a heart attack. He had given Elsie some painkillers through a cannula that had been quickly inserted; the results easy to see as her chest pain had eased, and relief had flooded the old lady's face. Now she slept, and Sammy was close to nodding off herself. She sat back in the chair, the steady *swish-swish* of the machine's white noise lulling her as she started to nod and stretch towards dozing off.

A shadow falling across her snapped her awake, opening her eyes and sitting up with a jerk. At the foot of Elsie's bed stood an elderly gentleman, impeccably dressed in a grey suit and cravat. In one hand, he held a grey bowler style hat, and in the other, a gold-topped cane that he leaned on as he studied the slumbering Elsie. A blue jewel set in an ornate pendant was visible just above the suit jacket's buttons, winking in the dull yellow of the ward's overhead strip lighting. As Sammy studied him, a single tear rolled down the man's face, and he patted the blankets at the foot of the bed gently as he wiped it away.

Registering that Sammy was awake, he gave her a sad smile and said, "Samantha. How is she; how is Elsie?"

"Who are you?" asked Sammy, a little bewildered and foggy at waking so suddenly.

"An old friend. Malchiah Cracklock, Doctor Malchiah Cracklock," said the man, holding out his hand, which Sammy took and shook, caught off guard as she was. Then as the name registered in her brain, Sammy recoiled, yanking her hand back as she did.

"Cracklock? The last Cracklock I met put Elsie in here. Get out before I scream the place down," she spat, looking around for something to defend herself with.

"Please, I am here only out of concern for my cousin. Nothing more; I want no trouble with anyone here."

"You've seen her; she's doing as well as can be expected. Now get out. I mean it."

"You don't remember me, do you, Samantha?" the stranger said quietly.

"Of course I don't; I have no idea who you or those crazy psychopaths that came to my home earlier today are. They said they were Cracklocks and that they wanted David and Jack."

"Yes, I understand that they were a little heavy-handed in their approach, for which I apologise. That is, unfortunately, Anastasia for you. The unfortunate product of many marriages between cousins over the years. It has to be said that we do not like outsiders, and it causes some quirks. Other members of our family, myself included, do not have such 'issues.'"

"You know that evil woman?"

"Yes. Yes, I do." Malchiah examined his fingers as he looked away from Sammy's forthright glare.

"And do you know...know about those hidden people, those brownies?" Sammy was hesitant to ask.

Malchiah's eyes darkened, and his hand went unconsciously to the pendant around his neck.

"Yes, I know only too well of the devils amongst us," he said to Sammy, his mouth set. "I know how they bewitch people and how they have divided our family over many years. I know what they have done to Elsie and David, and presumably Jack and yourself by now with their deceits, devilry, and glamours. And I know that they must be stopped."

"From what I saw, it was your people that were at fault, not that brownie."

"Are you bewitched as well? I sense a glamour upon you, and it is strong." Malchiah continued to handle the blue gem.

"I have no idea what you are talking about. I am not bewitched, nor have any idea what is going on here. All I know is that some people claiming to be relatives showed up tonight, asking after David and Jack. When they didn't hear what they wanted, they went berserk, and could do...they could do 'things.' And this dear, sweet lady here was the main victim of this whole incident. Then you show up, a complete stranger, who Elsie has never mentioned even once in passing, claiming to be a cousin. And I have no idea where my son is; he hasn't called me, and I am worried sick and too tired to deal with this rubbish." Sammy's cheeks were high in colour now, fists clenched as her tears filled her eyes.

Malchiah's face was inscrutable. "And you really don't remember anything? Nothing that David told you?"

"David is dead!" Sammy shouted and then covered her mouth in shock, remembering where she was.

"He is not dead, just absent," said Malchiah quietly.

"How dare you? How dare you presume to know my family and me?" Sammy took a step towards the man, the anger that Jack had inherited from her now building.

"Tell me about David's funeral."

"No."

"You can't, can you? You don't remember. Because there was no funeral."

"There was. We had a ..." Sammy tailed off as she strained to remember. The details of the funeral weren't there. She was sure that there had been one; it has been the worst day of her life. But thinking about it, there was no substance to the slight memories, just clichés. 'He'll be sorely missed' and 'Taken too soon.' No recollection of who was there, where it took place; even the damn wake was absent.

"You look puzzled, my dear," said Malchiah.

"It's been a long day, and I'm tired," said Sammy defensively.

"No. You look puzzled because you know that I am correct. David is not dead."

"I don't believe you. How could you know that?"

"That is for another time, Samantha. I am here to see my dear cousin only, not to reminisce. But I will tell you; I need to see Jack. And you will tell me where he is, the next time that we meet."

"I will not. My son is not part of this...this...madness. And my husband is dead, goddammit!"

"David is not dead. And Jack is part of this 'madness' as you so eloquently put it. If our suspicions are correct, he will be a great boon to the cause in more ways than you can imagine. We will know more once Mother has had a chance to examine him."

"*Leave my Jack alone*!" screamed Sammy, frustration in her voice.

The door pushed open, and an enquiring nurse's head appeared.

"Is everything okay, Mrs Crackley?"

"This gentleman needs to leave. Right now!" Sammy panted.

The nurse looked around, puzzled, staring straight through Malchiah.

"What gentleman?" she asked.

Sammy stared at Malchiah, who lowered his head, a sly smile on his face.

"This gentleman," said Sammy, gesturing.

"Mrs Crackley, are you feeling okay? What happened to your aunt was a shock, I know. Do you want me to call someone?"

"This man, here, look," said Sammy, stabbing her pointed finger at Malchiah's chest.

"Mrs Crackley," said the nurse gently. "I think that you should perhaps think about heading home, get yourself some rest? It has been an emotional and traumatic day for you and your aunt, and she is in safe hands here. We will call you if there are any developments."

Sammy slumped in defeat.

"Okay, okay. Just give me a few minutes, and I will think about it. I'm sorry; I've just woken up."

"No harm done," said the nurse reassuringly. "But you do need to keep yourself well for when she comes home. She'll need you."

Sammy gave a sad smile, and the nurse left, closing the door quietly behind her. She turned on Malchiah.

"What the hell? How did you..."

He interrupted her. "Another glamour, Samantha, my dear; the devils aren't the only ones who can make things to their will. And to avoid any further interruptions to my visit, I think that we had better stop twitching ears." He gave a complex series of gestures and then nodded.

"You may be as loud as you wish now, Samantha; a veil of silence is over this room."

"Just who are you?" demanded Sammy.

"Malchiah," a croaky voice, muffled, said quietly.

The two turned to Elsie, who lay there, her eyes open, studying the two people at the foot of her bed.

Sammy went straight to the old woman and clasped her hand.

"Elsie, thank goodness you're awake. How are you feeling?"

"Help me take this damn thing off," said Elsie, gesturing weakly at the oxygen mask over her mouth and nose. "And no arguments Sammy. Take it off."

Shaking her head, Sammy gently lifted the mask and slipped the elastic from the back of Elsie's head. Elsie fixed Malchiah with a steely look.

"What are you doing here, Malchiah?" she said hoarsely.

"Elsie, I was concerned after I heard what Anastasia had done. I wanted to see for myself that you would pull through."

"Your concern is noted, cousin. Now get out."

"Elsie, please. Despite all that had been, I still care. Please let me help in whatever small way I can."

"You cannot rewrite the past, Malchiah," Elsie gave a slight cough and gestured to the glass of water, cool drops beading its surface. Sammy passed it to her, and she took a sip. "You have done terrible things, terrible. What you did, what you made them do, it shattered David. It destroyed him, along with everything he had with his father and Nancy. I will never forgive you for that."

"Elsie, please. I had no choice. I did it for you, for us. You had to see the truth, as did Andrew and Nancy. I had to save you and David, too, before it was too late."

"No, what you did, you did for your witch of a mother. And destroyed everything, including what we had, when you did."

"Please, Elsie, please. Your bewitchment is still..."

"Just stop, Malchiah. Stop and get away from us. The only bewitchment is the fool tales that your mother, her mother, and all the rest have forced upon your lot over the years. If you want to help, then just stay away from me, stay away from Sammy and Jack, and stay away from all of the Fae, friends of ours or otherwise."

"I can't do that, Elsie. Not while there is still hope to end this, to stop those devils. And we intend to finish what our forebears started." There was a zealous look now in Malchiah's eyes. "You could be part of it, Elsie. You could come with me; we can find the boy, and then we can stop those things once and for all."

"Oh, Malchiah," said Elsie sadly. "You poor deluded fool. You continue this war with our friends, but to what end? The Fae will never fall to a group of deluded lifers like the family, and it is foolish to think that they ever will."

Malchiah's eyes darkened again, the anger apparent on his face. He glared at the two women, and Sammy took an involuntary step backwards at the malice he radiated.

"So be it, Elsie Cracklock. I came here to help you with an offer of friendship, and perhaps more, and once again, you scorn me. Reject me, in favour of those…those…things." Spittle flecked his lips. "Well, no more. Out of respect for what was, I will allow you your time to heal. But the next time we meet, it will be under less favourable circumstances. And you," he pointed at Sammy, his arm jerking out with whip-like speed. "You need to get wise and quickly. We want the boy, and by the grace of the Lord, we will have him. Do not stand in our way."

"Over my dead body," said Sammy defiantly, folding her arms.

"We shall see. Now get out," said Elsie firmly.

Glaring, Malchiah gave a stiff little bow, plucked his bowler hat from the foot of Elsie's bed, and stormed out of the room. As he left, he wheeled around one last time.

"You are making a mistake, Elsie. If you realise this before it is too late, then you may contact me. I urge you to do so. The end is coming, and, despite everything, I do not wish you ill. And Samantha, if you see the error of your ways and wish for your son to see the truth, please also get in touch. At any time." He placed two small cards on the chair next to the door, turned, and pulled the door shut behind him.

Elsie blew out a long breath and gave a little suppressed shudder. Sammy seized her hand and looked at her.

"Who was that? He said he was Doctor Malchiah Cracklock, but who was he really?"

Elsie stroked Sammy's hand and looked at her.

"My dear, would you be so kind as to go and get me two cups of strong sweet tea, please. And something chocolatey from the vending machine?"

"I'm not sure you're allowed it, Elsie. Let me get the staff nurse; I'll see if you can…"

Elsie cut her off. "Sammy, I'm feeling much better. Really. And I will need the sugar, my dear."

"Why?" asked Sammy. "Because if you think you are leaving here tonight, you are very much mistaken."

"I need the energy, Sammy, because I am going to have to help you remember. We will need all the help we can get if we are going to find David and help Jack. And to do that, I need to take off that damned glamour that has been on you all this time."

Sammy's jaw dropped, speechless. Seeing the old woman's determination, she left the room to get Elsie what she had asked for.

THE FOUR FRIENDS, Jimmy still slumped on the floor, stood stunned, staring at the talking tube as it looked around at them with its bright blue eyes. Its spindly arms tucked onto its hips as it glared up at them.

'I repeat. Who are you, and where am I? Don't stand there gawking like dummies; answer me. This instant.' The voice echoed in their heads again, like a chime, and the little tube stamped one foot on the ground as it stared at them. It was challenging to tell facial expressions without any visible face, but its eyes certainly looked angry.

Jack, Jimmy, Dorcas and Fermy stared agog at the tube, not that they looked much better themselves. All four were covered in mud from their battle with the Lisovyk, and Jack's face was a mess with the blood from his abused nose; the fallen Fae-daemon he had destroyed lay slumped beside them further up the corridor. Broken bottles of chemicals lay strewn around, winking in the dim overhead lighting of the school corridor. A flash of white in the muck showed the plastic tub that had contained the iron filings, discarded from where Jack had dropped it when the tube had begun its strange resurrection.

Fermy was the first to step forward; the little Feeorin in the mud-stained suit still loomed over the tube, and he was careful not to get too close. He held up his hands in a placatory gesture and smiled.

"I'm sorry, friend; we mean no offence. It is just that we have never met your kind before, and while we are always pleased to meet new friends, your appearance came as a bit of a shock to us."

The tube's posture seemed to relax, as did its bright eyes. The voice came again into their heads.

'Well, that is all well, but what is this place? And who are you? The big ones, you, and the pretty one, these are new faces to me.'

Dorcas blushed at being called pretty and giggled coquettishly behind her hand. Fermy shot her a look and then turned back to the tube.

"Well, friend, my name is Fermerillion or Fermy to those who know me well, and I am a Fae from the Feeorin cast. The lady is my good friend, Dorcas, a Brownie. And these two young gentlemen are Jimmy and Jack."

'Well met then, Fermy, Dorcas, Jack, and Jimmy,' echoed the tube, giving them each a little bow in turn. *'I am...'* and their heads filled with a strange whooshing noise, like the leaves of a forest rustling in the wind. The friends looked at each other, bemused.

'Well?' said the tube. *'Why the looks?'*

"I'm sorry," said Dorcas. "But I is afraid that we's did not get your name. We were's not able to understand."

The tube turned its bright blue eyes onto Dorcas.

'Understand? Was I not clear? You are not fools, are you?'

"Not really, no's. I's don't think's that we can speaks the language of your name, not even Fermy here, who is one of the cleverest Fae that I knows."

'Stranger and stranger. This truly is an odd place. And you speak with the sounds, which is an old way. Older and not efficient.'

"We can hear you clearly in our heads when you speak, just

not your name. It sounded...well, it sounded like the wind in the trees."

'The wind in the trees? Unusual. A strange notion for an odd place. I wonder how I came to be here. And where are my brethren?'

"If we can't understand your name, what shall we call you?" said Jimmy. "I mean, 'tube' is a little rude, I think. As is loo roll."

'Lou roll? What is 'Lou Roll'?' chimed the tube, fixing Jimmy with its stare.

"Well, it's..." began Jimmy before Jack cut him off.

"Look, it doesn't matter. Perhaps we can call you by a nick-name or something? We really need to be going; the police will be here shortly, and I don't fancy having to explain to them or the caretakers about us being here or this mess. Trespass and vandalism are what they will say."

"Agreed," said Fermy. "We need to leave. I need to speak with the Council to rescue these poor folk trapped amongst this muck; they can do this without fear of intervention from the law bringers I would think, as they will not be seen. But they will need to come soon, for surely the body of this thing will be removed shortly?"

"And I needs to see to poor Jack's nose and Jimmy's heads, plus the mess back at home," added Dorcas.

"What mess?" said Jack.

Fermy gave him a brief overview of what had happened; about Anastasia and Benedict attacking Sammy and Elsie. The colour had drained from Jack's face by the time he had finished.

"Are Elsie and Mum okay?" he questioned the two, his voice quavering.

"I's don't knows," said Dorcas. "They tooks her away in the ambulatingerabance with the blues light." She then slapped her head. "I was supposed to's ask you to rings poor Sammy when's you got home. She was worrieds about you."

"I'll do it as soon as we get back home, but we need to get out of here now," said Jack.

"Well, let's go. Roly, are you coming? We can explain a little more to you once we're away from here," said Jimmy, getting to his feet.

'Roly? Your name for me is Roly?' chimed the tube.

"It'll do for now. Now come on, let's go," said Jack.

He went over to the noticeboard in the hall and grabbed the sign-up pen that hung there, suspended on a piece of string. A quick yank, and he was over to the door closest to them, sketching the travel glyph.

"Back to mine," he said, slapping the glyph and pushing the door open to reveal the dancing blue flames.

"After you, Roly," said Fermy, gesturing towards the door.

The little party trooped into the blue-flamed room, and the door swung shut behind them.

SAMMY RETURNED to Elsie's room with two sweetened teas and two Kit-Kat chocolate bars, which she handed over to the old lady.

"Oooh, I love these," said Elsie, tucking in. Sammy shook her head at the fact that Elsie just bit into the bar without snapping the fingers off but decided to let it go. She knew that David's aunt was strange anyhow.

"Mmmfff, ggod," said Elsie with her mouth full. "Pooolll ofer the chir."

Sammy did as she was bid, pulled the chair closer to Elsie's bed, and plumped herself down into it.

Elsie gulped tea and unwrapped the second bar.

"That's really good. I sometimes forget how much glamouring takes out of you. Let me get this one down, and then we can look at getting that thing off of you."

Sammy looked at her, puzzled. "I'm sorry, Elsie, but I don't understand what you mean. Not that I actually understand very much of anything that happened tonight, if I am honest. Why do these people want Jack? And why do they think that David is still alive? He's been dead now for eleven years."

Elsie patted Sammy's hand. "Look, my dear, everything is not what you think, and I am so sorry that it has been kept from you for so long. All I can tell you is that David may not be dead. We don't know for definite because we have no idea where he is. I cannot answer why they want Jack so desperately because we don't know that either. They just do and have been searching for him. For the past eleven years, we have been trying to keep Jack safe from those people, and this was done at both yours and David's request."

"*What?*" Sammy was on her feet now. "That Malchiah said that David wasn't dead, and now you're confirming it?" She wrung her hands together, eyes glancing around the room. "Are you telling me he's not dead? And what request?"

Elsie gave a sad smile. "Yes, it was agreed, and you were party to it all. Look, it will be much easier if you can remember past events. The memories you have aren't, shall we say, strictly true."

Sammy stared at the old woman. "You mean to tell me that everything I can remember about David is a lie?"

"No, no," said Elsie with a placatory wave. "It's just that some of the things are hidden from your mind's eye. To keep you safe. Your memories of David are quite correct and true. My nephew is a kind and loving man, and what has happened was not deserved by any of you. I intend to see if we can start to put all that right. Now, sit forward in that chair for me; I need to be able to touch your head."

"Will it hurt?" implored Sammy.

"No, my dear. I took it off Jack, and he was fine, although he got a bit of a shock when he saw Fermy."

"When he saw the ferret? Why?"

Elsie laughed aloud at this. "All will become clear, my dearie. Now, sit forward for me."

Sammy leaned forwards, and Elsie put her hands onto Sammy's head, taking a deep breath as she did so.

"I can feel it here, but it's a little more embedded than Jack's was. This may feel strange," she said to Sammy. "Close your eyes."

Sammy closed her eyes. She felt Elsie's hands clutching her head firmly, and then suddenly, they were gone. Sammy felt a strange stretching sensation, like the mental equivalent of pulling chewing gum from your mouth. She felt it stretch and stretch and could hear Elsie panting in the small room like a steam engine. The stretching sensation continued to tighten until she felt something begin to tear.

"*Come on, come on, come on,*" she heard Elsie chanting, muted like she was speaking through gritted teeth.

Sammy's head felt like it was wrapped in paper now; she could almost hear it rustling in her mind. A ripping noise filled her head; whatever it was peeling away more and more until she felt it go entirely, unravelling from her mind.

"*Yes!*" came Elsie's triumphant cry, and Sammy heard her slump back in the bed.

All was dark in Sammy's head for a moment, and then it was like someone had shone a bright light into her memories. All of a sudden, a deluge of thoughts and visions swept in like a flood, washing over her and bringing clarity.

She opened her eyes and stared at Elsie.

"I remember everything," she said.

THEY HAD BEEN SEEING each other for a few months when David first brought up the subject of Faeries. Sammy's affection for the handsome (if easily distracted) man had grown with each date until she was sure he was the 'one.' There was something about him, a kindness that was not easily fathomable, but just part of him, running about after his dotty old aunt who had raised him. He was sweet and attentive, good company, and had a dry wit, although he did have a habit of 'going off with the fairies' as her mother would say, sometimes losing the thread of a conversation and staring off into space. Nonetheless, the two of them had said the 'L' word and were comfortable in their relationship; the only thing that niggled at Sammy was these lapses in concentration. It was during one of those episodes, a picnic at the park on a brilliantly sunny afternoon with them both curled up comfortably on the blanket, that Sammy decided to tackle it head-on. David was once again staring off into space, a smile etched on his face when Sammy had nudged him and said, "Penny for them."

David, startled out of his apparent daze, turned to face her, blinking a little before smiling.

"Oh, sweetie, I am so sorry. I just noticed something there that got my attention. I didn't mean to be rude. What were you saying?"

"I wasn't; just enjoying the sunshine. However..."

"What is it?"

"These episodes you have; you just seem to 'go away' somewhere, and it happens fairly regularly. Are you alright? Seriously?"

"Alright? I'm fine, Sam, really."

"It's just that these fugue states, well, I'm a little worried about them. They could be an indicator of something else, and I saw this program on them a few days ago. It could be that..."

David threw back his head and laughed. "Sweetie, seriously, I'm fine. It's difficult to explain if I'm honest, but I am excellent. As I am sure you will agree!"

Sammy sat, looking into his smiling face and thought, 'God, I love him. I really do!' To David, she said. "Please try."

"Please try what?" said David, puzzled.

"Please try to explain why you're not worried about these episodes and drifting away."

David shifted uncomfortably on the picnic blanket and looked at her.

"Well, I know how I appear, but it's really nothing to worry about; I am still 'in the room' if you will. But I've always struggled with multitasking, and sometimes my attention goes elsewhere. That's probably the best way to explain it."

"But, there's nothing there to multitask!" exclaimed Sammy. "Not a lot of the time, anyway."

David gave a small smile. "There is; it's just that you can't always see."

"See what?" said Sammy. "What are you saying?"

"You'd never believe me if I told you."

"What are you? Some sort of psychic? Because my granny thought she was one of those, and she ended up upsetting no end of people."

David put his hand on Sammy's knee and gave it a slight squeeze. "No, I'm not psychic, although it would be helpful to know the Lotto numbers, wouldn't it?"

"Don't joke, Dave, seriously. I am worried about this drifting business, and I want to help you."

"It's not a problem, Sam."

"It is a problem if I think it is," said Sammy, her blood starting to rise now. "Sometimes, it's like you're not here at all. We have precious little time together as it is, and what time we do have, I'd like to spend it with you properly."

David looked at her for a long time, so long in fact that Sammy started to feel uncomfortable. He finally gave a small smile and said. "Do you love me?"

Sammy smiled at him. "You know that I do. You're my beau."

David grinned from ear to ear. "Okay then, good enough. Now, do you think that you can keep a secret?"

"Yes. Provided it's a good one."

"Oh, it's a good one, alright. But before I tell you, do you promise to hear me out completely and do exactly what I say?"

"Oookkkayyy," Sammy drew out her agreement, a puzzled look on her face now.

David stood up and held out his hand. "Come with me."

Feeling a little bewildered, Sammy allowed David to pull her to her feet and held his hand as he led her across the small park to one of the flowerbeds. The flowers were in full bloom at the height of the glorious summer, and the roses and hydrangeas nodded gracefully in the warm breeze.

"What do you see?" asked David.

Sammy was still bewildered, but she squatted down to look at the flowerbeds. The fragrance was subtle but delicious.

"I see flowers, roses mainly. Some aphids on them, though. Leaves. David, what am I supposed to be looking for?"

David put his hand in his pocket and pulled out an object. "Here," he said, and dropped a smooth flat stone into her hand, a worn hole through the top end of the egg-shaped piece of rock. The stone was warm from David's body heat and fit snugly into her palm.

"Look again. But through the hole this time."

Shaking her head slightly, Sammy raised the stone to her eye and looked through the hole. She gasped, sat down firmly on the ground, and stared at David. She then raised the stone to her eye again and looked through it again.

Through the smooth hole, she could see, well... fairies. Tiny people, about six of them, fluttering around in the flowers on gossamer wings. They were swift and chattering away to each other in a high pitched tone that Sammy struggled to make out. One of the tiny fairies noticed her attention and swiftly flew over to hover in front of her. Its face looked agitated as it hovered there, bobbing on its wings like a hummingbird.

From behind her, she heard David say. "It's okay; it's okay. She's a friend of mine. You can trust her."

The fairy nodded to David and then doffed its hat to Sammy. It then flew back to the others and continued with whatever it was they were doing.

Sammy turned to David, a look of amazement on her face. She turned the stone over in her hand and poked the tip of her finger through the hole. No lens or anything, and it appeared to be just a stone. She shook her head.

"David. What the actual... Did I just see that?"

"I'm sorry, sweetie, but I didn't want just to tell you; you'd think I was mad. Better to show you. Can I trust you?"

"Of course. David, this is amazing! But how...how can you see these things?"

"I just can. The Cracklocks are blessed with the ability to see the Fae, and we don't need any gimmicks or hagstones to do it," he said, gesturing to the stone in Sammy's hand.

"But fairies aren't real."

"I can assure you that they are. I have several terrific friends who are Fae; that's what they call themselves, rather than 'Faeries.' And I can see and speak to them, as can everyone in my family. Sometimes I get a little distracted by them. That's why I am like I am."

Sammy slumped backwards on the floor.

"But how?" she said.

"Oh, that is a long story. One best told over a drink or two. Fancy it?" He gestured across the road to the pub, one with a large beer garden.

Sammy stood up and threw her arms around David. "*Yes. Yes, I do.*"

Six years later

'If only there were a laundry fairy, a real one, not just me,' thought Sammy, blowing errant hairs away from her face as she folded what seemed to be the umpteenth shirt. Dorcas was only too willing to do it, she knew that, but she felt guilty about asking the brownie; she did enough around the house, as well as acting as nursemaid and playmate to Jack. She glanced out of the patio windows to the garden, where she could see Jack playing, gesturing in the air as he did so. Dorcas sat on a blanket watching the four-year-old, a tub of something next to her. 'Biscuits', Sammy thought, 'she does love to spoil him so'. Sammy couldn't see who Jack was playing with out there, and she grubbed in her pocket for a hagstone. Locating one, she raised it to her eye and saw a plethora of the little folk dancing around Jack, tinkling laughter filling the air as the hagstone revealed the other world to her. Sammy smiled and went back to her folding.

The sound of the front door banging shut bought her out of her revelry, and she turned to see David rushing up the hall, an anxious look on his face.

"Where's Jack?" he panted to her.

"In the garden with Dorcas, and goodness knows who else. He's having a whale of a time. Are you okay?"

"Go upstairs and get some things together quickly. Throw as much stuff as you can into the suitcases and bring them down here. We need to go."

"What? Why?" said Sammy, picking up on David's anxiety.

"We need to get out of here. Right now. Please, just do as I ask; I'll get Jack. I'll explain once we're away from here."

Sensing that her husband wasn't playing some sort of elaborate prank, Sammy grabbed the washing basket and went upstairs as quickly as she could. She pulled their battered suitcases out from the top of the wardrobe and started to pull clothes from hangers and out of drawers and toss them into the cases at random, not caring what she was packing nor making any attempt to do it neatly. She was interrupted by a loud childish scream from the garden, making her heart jump into her chest. Jack!

Sammy flew down the stairs and through the kitchen to the back door. Halfway down the garden, she could see David throwing bright glamours at unseen targets, offensive glamours judging by their deep red colour. Dorcas was herding Jack up the garden towards her, turning now and again to lash out with her favourite rolling pin. Sammy fumbled the hagstone from her pocket and, with a trembling hand, raised it to her eye. She gave a panicked gasp as the air seemed to leap out of her chest.

At the bottom of the garden were what seemed to be a horde of goblin-like creatures, red hats on their heads, and they were battling the faeries that Jack had been playing with earlier. Streaks of coloured light whirled around, sparking in the sunlight as the Fae tried their best to stop the advance of the creatures that kept coming through the hedge. As she watched, one of the faster ones caught up to Dorcas and Jack as they dashed towards the house. Dorcas turned around in a flash, parried the jab from the creature's spike-like spear with her rolling pin as it lunged at her and then rapped the creature hard on the top of its head, dropping it to the floor.

Seeing Sammy at the door, she shouted, urgency in her voice. "*Sammy. You take's Jack and gets to the car. I will help's David. Start it ups; we will be there. Go! Now!*"

Jack ran to Sammy on his short little legs, sobbing. "Goblins, Mummy. Goblins. They want to get me." Sammy gathered him up in her arms, his little body trembling against her. Taking one last look at her husband and her friend Dorcas sprinting to his aid, she ran for the front door, scooping the keys out of the bowl in the hall as she did so. She yanked open the front door, and leaving it open behind her, ran for the car, clicking the unlock button as she did so. She pulled open the back door and dropped Jack into his seat, clicking his seatbelt into place with trembling hands. She then jumped into the driver's side, put the keys in the ignition, and started it. Panting, she sat, her hands on the wheel and eyes on the front door, willing David to come through it.

A minute passed, and nothing. Jack was sobbing in the back seat and kept saying, "Daddy. Where's Daddy? Where's Dorcas? I want my Dorcas!" repeating himself over and over again. Sammy was on the verge of getting out to see what was happening when David suddenly burst through the doorway, Dorcas in his arms. He yanked the door shut behind him and ran for the car. As he ran, Sammy heard a huge bang and watched the front door visibly shake. David yanked open the passenger door and jumped in, Dorcas still in his arms. Close up, Sammy could see the brownie was bleeding through her flowery dress.

"*Go, just go!*" screamed David. In the back seat, Jack was screaming at the sight of Dorcas, who lay in David's arms, motionless.

Sammy jammed the car into reverse and got moving as fast as she could. She cleared the bend on the drive, and as she did so, the front door burst outwards on its hinges, flying away from the house to land in the shrubs that lined the drive.

"*David, what is happening?*" Sammy screamed back. "*I can't see; what are those things?*"

"Redcaps. And they want all of us. Drive, drive, drive."

"But, Dorcas..."

"She'll be okay; she's breathing, but we need to get to someone who can help. Just drive. Quick...Oh, my!"

There was a thud on the bonnet of the car as Sammy reversed out of the gate, and the bonnet in front of Sammy's eyes visibly buckled as if something huge had landed on it. The car hitched but carried on backwards, the fan belt squealing slightly as it did so.

"David?"

"Keep going, but swing the car about if you can, try and dislodge it."

"What is it?" shouted Sammy over the noise of Jack's terrified screams.

"Hobyah, I think. Never seen one before. Whatever it is, it means business." The panic in David's voice was evident as he tried to manoeuvre himself free of Dorcas.

Sets of holes punctured themselves into the metal surface of the bonnet, and Sammy gasped.

"It's got its claws in now. You need to shake it off, Sammy."

The car cleared the drive's end, and Sammy swung the wheel to the left at speed, narrowly missing a parked car. She was rewarded with a dull thud, and more of the bonnet on the right-hand side buckled.

"How big is that thing?" she yelled at David.

"You do not want to know. Swerve, swerve, swerve!"

Sammy weaved the car up the road, accelerating as she did so and then screamed as holes punctured themselves into the windscreen. With a wrenching screech, the windscreen pulled itself free, and Sammy swore she could smell the sourness of the creature, despite it not having revealed itself to her. David gestured, and a bright light left his hands, coalescing around the creature, freezing it into place. Sammy was shocked at its size, although she could only make out the outline of a human-shaped form, but far more bulky.

Dorcas suddenly sat up on David's knee and shook her head. She glanced at the thing on the bonnet and at the panicked faces of David and Sammy as they weaved the car at speed, trying to shake it loose. David grasped her.

"Are you alright?"

"Hurts, David, but I's be alright. We need's to get rid of that," and pointed at the Hobyah as it struggled against David's glamour. She turned to face Jack and raised her finger to her lips in a 'shush' gesture.

"Shhh, Jacksie, sshh. Dorcas is here, and Dorcas will makes the nasty monster goes away."

Jack stopped his screaming at the sight of his playmate and put his thumb into his mouth.

"Holds me, David, please," said Dorcas in a matter of fact tone, indicating her flowery belt. David grabbed it, and Dorcas stood up, swaying slightly on David's legs as the car's seesaw motion on the road caused her to lose her balance a little. She held out her hand, and her rolling pin zoomed into it from the footwell.

"When I say's so David, you hits it with whatever glamour you has. We are getting that things off the car." David nodded his understanding.

Though Sammy's vision of the creature was limited, she could see that the creature was holding onto the bonnet with one arm only; the other was raised above its head to strike before David had paralysed it. Even now, its outline was juddering as it fought against the glamour.

Dorcas leaned out of the missing windscreen and swiped at the arm that held the creature to the bonnet. Her pin hit the arm with a thunk, but it didn't move. She hit it again, with the same result. She turned back to David with a resolved look in her eye.

"David, I's want you to release the glamour on it. But only at the moments I swings. Do you understand?"

"Are you sure? That thing will be through that window like a shot the minute I do."

"It won'ts. Trust me. And Sammy, I will swing's from left to right. You must turn the car left to help."

They both nodded, and David gasped, "Okay. When you're ready."

Dorcas shuffled further forward and, looking back at David, said, "Holds me tight. I's not wanting to goes as well."

A left turn was coming up, and Sammy tapped the brakes slightly. She felt she was going too fast.

"Don't slow down, Sam, don't. I'm struggling to hold this thing; it's so strong." panted David, beads of sweat standing out on his forehead as he gripped Dorcas's belt. The brownie was almost entirely out of the windscreen now, her eyes on the left turn that was coming up rapidly. Only David's tight grip was preventing her from being thrown clear. And then, all of a sudden, the turn was there.

"Now," shrieked Dorcas, and David let the glamour go, the shuddering outline disappearing from Sammy's view. The Hobyah, suddenly freed from its struggles, overcompensated, and as it stumbled, Dorcas swung the pin with all her might, Sammy yanking the wheel over as she did. The combination of the three factors had a devastating effect. The pin connected solidly with the creature's jaw, tumbling it to the right as it saw stars. The centrifugal force from the cars screeching turn tore it free from the car, and Sammy felt the car's front lift as the Hobyah's weight left it.

"Has it gone?" Sammy screamed, wrestling with the steering wheel as the car clipped the opposite curb, again narrowly missing a parked car. Jack screamed, and the angry horn of an approaching car bellowed as she pulled the wheel with all her might to get it back onto the right side of the road, her heart hammering in her chest.

"No. It's still after us!" screamed back David, looking out of the rear window as the creature loped towards them. *"Drive, drive!"*

Sammy pushed the accelerator down and noted a *thud thud* sound from the wheel that had hit the curb.

"I think we've got a flat," she gasped.

"Don't care. Just go. Faster. Faster."

The next couple of minutes were taken up with them all concentrating; David and Dorcas on the diminishing loping figure behind them, and Sammy on keeping the car straight on three tyres, her knuckles white on the wheel.

Eventually, David said with a sigh of relief. "We lost it. Pull over. You did fantastic, darling."

"But what if it..."

"It's gone. As do we need to be; they know the direction we are travelling in, and we need to throw them off the scent. Pull over; there will do; that pub carpark."

Sammy pulled into a small carpark adjacent to a run-down pub.

"Right," said David. "Let's go find a door and get to Aunt Elsie's."

CHAPTER 2

Sammy gave a deep breath and opened her eyes. Elsie lay back in the hospital bed, her eyes on Sammy, a look of expectation on her face.

"Well?" she smiled.

"I remember! I remember it all. David is not dead, is he?" Sammy yelled as she gave a little jig on the spot, her eyes bright with happiness at the memories now singing in her mind, overlaying the false ones and driving them away.

Elsie couldn't help but smile at the woman she loved so much. "We hope not, but as I said, we don't know. He's been gone a long time."

"But there's hope?"

"There's always hope, Sammy dear, always. It is what keeps us going and is what will keep you strong with whatever happens next, come what may. Now my dear, tell me the rest."

Elsie was in her cosy little living room, her slipper-clad feet up on a pouffe and nodding nicely when a tremendous clatter jerked her from her near sleep. She was on her feet before she knew it and called out a brave "Who's there?"

"It's us, Aunty, just us," came back David's voice from the kitchen. "Sorry about the noise; it's a little tight."

Elsie bustled through to the kitchen and gave a gasp. A dishevelled Sammy was holding Jack close to her, and David, his hair a mess and clothing torn, was supporting a staggering Dorcas who had what appeared to be blood all over her dress. The brownie's face was pale, her eyelids drooping.

"Oh my grockles, whatever has happened?" shrieked Elsie, her hands clutching to her chest.

"Later, Aunty. I need your help with Dorcas; I'm not sure how badly she's hurt."

"Of course, of course. Take her through to the living room, put her onto the sofa." Turning to Sammy, she said. "Why don't you make us some tea, dear? And there are some biscuits in the tin there for Jack-Jack, if he'd like one?" Lowering her voice, she continued. "I don't want Jack to see Dorcas. Not yet." Sammy nodded her understanding.

David half carried the little brownie through and laid her gently onto the sofa. Elsie, her medical kit in hand, arrived a few seconds later, and she placed her hand on Dorcas's forehead.

"What happened?" she asked David again.

"Redcaps attacked us, a whole horde of them. And they sent a Hobyah; at least that's what I think it was; it was pretty big, scaly, with those yellow eyes they talk about and huge claws. They were after Jack and me; I heard some of them slathering on in that strange dialect of theirs. Everyone else...well, they weren't needed. I think that Dorcas may have been on the receiving end of one of their spears; I didn't see."

"Those evil little swines. They must have come from the Unseelie Courts, but why? They have no argument with us; they know the different lines of the family."

"I don't think it was the Courts. Dorcas, Aunty, please."

Elsie tore Dorcas' dress near the main bloodstain area and peeled it back gently. The brownie winced as she did so and then settled again. Elsie tore open an antiseptic wipe and gently wiped the area, ignoring Dorcas's hiss.

"Its stings. Stop," bleated Dorcas.

"Not till I see what the damage is. Now hold still," said Elsie firmly.

Elsie's gentle fingers probed the area and located a puncture that was weeping blood. She wiped around it gently and then patted it with a dry swab. She got close up and peered over her glasses at the hole before sitting back again with a smile.

"Well, my dear, it appears that there are some advantages to being on the large side. It looks to be a neat hole, but not too deep; your belly fat stopped it, I think. It bled a lot because it nicked a vein, but it's clotting nicely now. I am going to clean it up, and I want no wriggling while I do so. A bandage, a little rest and a hot sweet drink, and you will be fine. And no exertion."

"Buts they have rips my dress. I look a fright," said Dorcas, happier now that they were all safe.

"Well, I'm afraid that you'll have to have one of my blouses for now. It'll do as a dress until we can get you back to David's for a change of clothes."

"We can't go back there, Aunty. Not now," said David quietly. "They'll be watching it."

"Who will?" said Elsie. "What is happening, David? What have you done this time?"

"I'll try and explain, Aunty, but please attend to Dorcas first. You may want to get the brandy out for the telling. But tell me, are we safe here?"

"Yes, yes, of course," said Elsie with a wave of her hand. "The whole place is untraceable to Fae."

"But what about other family members? Do they know how to find it?"

Elsie looked at David and shook her head slowly. "No, it's a safe place for our friends. It's hidden from the other family members out of necessity, purely for that reason. Only one has been here, and that was many years ago; the hiding glamour will still be working on him." *'I hope'*, she thought to herself.

David sighed. "Good enough for now. I'll go and help Sammy make some tea; plenty of sugar for our brave friend here." He smiled down at Dorcas, who blushed. "Then I'll tell you what I know."

Elsie nodded, her expression a little puzzled, but she trusted her nephew. She unravelled a bandage and turned back towards Dorcas.

Twenty minutes later, and everyone was in Elsie's living room supping cups of hot sweet tea, even Jack, who did not normally drink hot drinks, was dunking biscuit after biscuit into his drink and slurping up the resulting mess. The brandy bottle stood on the little coffee table, the lid still on for now. Once everyone was settled, Elsie turned to David.

"Okay. Now, what is going on? Who is after you? And who is watching the house?"

David drummed his fingers on his chin and muttered, "Where to start...where to start?" He then sat back and cleared his throat.

"Okay. We all know about the other side of the family, and their, shall we say, less-than-friendly attitude towards our Fae friends?"

"Yes, yes," said Elsie, exasperated. "But that has been going on for centuries. What have they done now?"

"It's not just what they've done. It is what I suspect they are going to do. And I emphasise, at this stage, I only suspect. We are in the process of checking; Timothy is trying to get me something that I need in order to confirm my suspicions. But after today, I'm nearly certain that something is going on."

"Well, what are they going to do?" asked Elsie.

David took a deep breath. "I think that they have found a way to destroy Faery once and for all," he said quietly.

There was a stunned silence. Then both Elsie and Dorcas started laughing. David sat there, not joining in, waiting for them to stop. After about a minute or so, the laughter subsided.

"Oh, David. It's nots a problem's. How's could they destroy's Faery? We have enough glamours and things to stops anything from the lifer's realm, likes the bombs and things. Do not worry about's it," Dorcas chuckled.

"I know that, Dorcas," replied David. "But I think that the Cracklocks have found another way. A different way."

"Poppycock," said Elsie, wiping a little tear from her cheek. "There is no way that the Cracklocks could destroy the Faery Realm. No way whatsoever."

"I disagree," said David patiently. "I believe that they have found a way and that they have already started."

"Why?" asked Elsie. "I understand that you must believe that this is a real thing, but it's just not possible to destroy an entire realm, and particularly a magical one. Even if you had all of the nuclear weapons in the world and could get them there. Which the Cracklocks don't and, despite their wealth, never will."

"It does sound a little unbelievable, David," said Sammy. "I mean, the wonders that come out of Faery are far beyond what any of us here could ever understand. It's unlikely that a bunch of malicious people would ever destroy such a magical place."

"I know that it sounds ridiculous, but I have my reasons. I hope that I am wrong on this and can join in the laughs once proven that I'm a fool. As I said, I am not a hundred per cent sure."

"Oh, David, come on," said Elsie. "It's just not possible." She sat back and folded her arms. "Okay, then. Convince us. How are the Cracklocks going to wipe out an entire realm?"

"As I said, I don't have all the facts yet. But I think that they've found a way to destroy the basis of the realm itself."

"Whatever do you mean?" said Elsie.

"I think that they've found a way to destroy the Faery realm without having to go there. And I think that they've already tried to do it with another realm to test their theory."

"Another realm?" said Elsie, sitting forwards.

"Yes. You know that there are more realms than just here, Fae and the departed. The Courts archives have all kinds of theories on them."

"How do you know? That area's restricted."

"Eermm...let's just say that Timothy has ways and means of getting in there. Secret ways."

"So that's what you've been spending your time doing, is it, rather than fixing up the house? Poking around in dusty old archives?" chimed in Sammy.

David held up his hands and smiled. "Yes, sometimes. Not always, but sometimes certainly."

Elsie flapped her hand at Sammy. "Well, what made you start thinking about this? I'm confused."

David tapped his teeth, something he did when he was thinking, as Sammy well knew.

"Well," he said. "What really got me started was something that Fermy's friend said, you know, that elfin Kaia. She said that some of her friends had gone missing; they could not be found anywhere in Faery or here. They just vanished, apparently. She was worried enough to go to the Seelie Court about it, and they sent out folk to look but didn't find anything. I mentioned it to Timothy in passing, and he said that some of the Curiosity Sanctuary folk had disappeared as well, which was very unusual. There was no evidence of them fading from existence or anything; many of them were in their prime. So, it was a little odd; Fae do go wandering, as you know. But they always come back, and other Fae can normally find them, regardless of where they are. It was a good old fashioned mystery."

David took a gulp of tea and continued, gagging a little as it had gone cold.

"Anyhow, it got me wondering as to where they could have gone." Elsie started to speak, and David held up a finger. "And yes, I do appreciate that there are Fae locked places, usually those where our family is and that they do extinguish Fae whenever they can. But those that had disappeared had no real reason to go anywhere near any of our family, and as a group, they were too diverse. It's not like a bunch of Nymph friends had wandered off together; Fae were missing from all manner of the Faery sub-realms. Timothy has a clerk friend at the Court who confirmed the disappearances. But it was the only explanation we could think of, and as a friendly Cracklock, the Courts asked me to look into it and see if we could find out if the missing folk met their end at the hands of our family members."

"Risky," said Elsie.

"Not as risky as you might think, Aunty. True, the family has no love for our position on things and would rather we did not harbour our friends, but they generally treat us as the 'poor cousins'; to be mocked and pitied. The intention was for me to see one of the family and scope out the lie of the land. Which I did."

"How?" said Elsie.

"And why would missing Fae prompt you to think that all of Faery was in danger?" asked Sammy.

David rested his hand on Sammy's knee. "I'll get to it, I promise, but let me fill in the gaps first."

Replying to Elsie, David said. "Do you remember cousin Mephias?"

"The drunk?" said Elsie scornfully. "You spoke to drunk old Meffy, and he told you that the family is going to destroy all of

Faery? Really, David, I thought that you would have had more sense! And why would he talk to you anyway?"

"No, no, he didn't say that at all. Truth be told, he thought that I was somebody else from the family; all that liquor has addled his brains, but he was happy to talk to me if I was buying. After I bought him a few, well, more than a few drinks to loosen his tongue, he ran his gums like nobody's business. But he didn't say anything like that."

"So?" Elsie said. "What was the great revelation?"

"He asked me if Malchiah had approached me about procuring, but not extinguishing, some Fae for him. The 'big ones' was how he put it. Meffy said that Malchiah wants the big ones, as those are the ones that he could use to 'catch children.' A number of the family were already on board with it. I went with it and said that I was indeed involved."

"Catch children? Whatever do you mean?"

"I don't know. But he asked me what I thought of Malchiah's new artefact, the one that he could control Fae with. Apparently, he uses the captured Fae to catch the children; 'less chance of being seen' was how he put it. He offered quite an incentive in cash if Meffy would do it; he asked me how much I was 'on' for the works, but I played coy. He was keen to point out in his ramblings that he was hesitant at first; he did not want to be involved in abducting children or anything, but Malchiah had said that the children are not removed from their parents. It was something else that he was trying to catch. Using these Fae."

"Sounds like a load of nonsense to me," snorted Elsie.

"I don't know," said David. "It is larger Fae that have been going missing, so as far as that goes, it makes sense."

"Yes, but that doesn't mean that he is going to destroy Faery," said Sammy.

"Not on its own, no. But I got talking with Timothy, and he was interested in this artefact that could control Fae; he'd never heard of such a thing, a Fae being controlled by a lifer, as it's normally the other way around."

"A friend of mys brother, Grasky, got's in trouble for controlling lifers, making them's do silly things," said Dorcas matter-of-factly. "But I's never hearing of lifers being able to control's Fae. We's too magical."

"I know, I know," said David. "But that's not where it ends. It intrigued me enough to want to check further. I wanted to see this artefact for myself. The difficulty was that the Malchiah and Agatha both know me, and it was doubtful that they would tell me anything or even let me into the house; you know how paranoid they are of the Fae and of us by proxy. I could not see any way of getting close to them. They'd rip through any glamours that I used to disguise myself, and anyhow, that mansion of theirs is too well protected."

Elsie's interest was piqued now. "So, did you get in then?"

"Yes," said David, and a dark look passed over his face. "I got in and saw this artefact. It's an amulet, a blue jewelled amulet. Malchiah wears it. And I was unfortunately seen, which is why I think that they sent those things for us. They must be under Malchiah's control; there is no reason for Redcaps to come after us otherwise; we are on reasonable terms with them, despite the Unseelie aspect."

"How did you manage it? And when?" asked Sammy, a worried look on her face.

"Just a couple of days ago. I am a fool; I thought I'd get away with it. As to how I did it, well, you can thank Gordon for that."

"Gordon?" said Sammy, with a raised tone in her voice. "Gordon? That idiot? What the hell, David?"

"I know you don't like him, Sammy, but..."

"But nothing. We agreed that you weren't going to see Gordon anymore; he's trouble. Always in and out of prison."

"I know, but he's one of my oldest friends. And a few pints with friends never hurt anyone."

"Not if he's helping you break into people's homes, regardless of the reason!" Sammy said, her voice raised now and colour in her cheeks. Elsie looked at Dorcas, who was wincing.

"Sweetie, calm down. It was nothing like that. I didn't 'break into' Cracklock Manor; there was no way I'd get past all their security anyhow."

Sammy relaxed a bit. "So, how exactly did Gordon 'help'?"

"Well, I asked him what he thought about theoretically getting into a big house like a mansion where breaking and entering was not an option. And he said 'People gotta eat.'"

"What?"

"He meant that a lot of people have food delivered nowadays; it's getting more popular. And those big houses have had deliveries for years, if not centuries. The staff don't go shopping; they order in. If you want to get in somewhere without suspicion, deliver the groceries."

Elsie clapped her hands together. "Genius. So how did you do it?"

"That part was easy," said David. "I just called around all the local supermarkets near Cracklock Manor, claiming to be wanting to add to the order. Stupidly, I left Waitrose until nearly last; I should have known, really, the snobs. The person at Waitrose was very pleased to help me out and confirmed the delivery date, time, and everything. After that, I just hung around in the lanes near Cracklock Manor, flagged down the van while wearing a little old lady glamour – actually looked a lot like you, Elsie – and then glamoured the two staff into letting me switch with one of them. Easy peasy after that; just drove straight in."

"And didn't they see you?" asked Sammy.

"Hiding in plain sight, darling. The Cracklocks aren't interested in humble delivery staff, and besides, it was mainly the staff that I dealt with. I did see Agatha briefly, criticising a member of the household, but she was in the main kitchen and paid me no attention while we were bringing the boxes into the pantry."

"Then what did you do?" asked Elsie.

"Waited until we were leaving and ducked into a side room off the kitchen. I put a mirror glamour on my co-worker that activated when he got inside the van. It made it look like two people were leaving together to any casual observer. I didn't know if I'd get away with it or not, but it seemed to work. And there I was, in Cracklock Manor, with no real plan other than to do a bit of snooping."

"David Cracklock, you are an idiot," said Sammy angrily. "What would have happened if they'd caught you? I doubt very much that they'd have called the police."

"I know, but I was caught up in the romance of the mystery of it all," said David sheepishly. "I just wanted to find out more."

Sammy was about to say more when the group was interrupted by a rich voice calling out, "Hello? Anybody home?"

"In here, Fermy," called back Elsie. "In the sitting room."

The little Feeorin strolled into the room, his hat in his hands.

"Hello all, how are...whatever has happened?" he said, his eyes fixed on Dorcas and the dishevelled Cracklocks.

David bought Fermy up to speed about the visit from the Redcaps and the Hobyah, as well as his suspicions. The Feeorin listened the whole time intently without interrupting, pondering what was being said. When David had finished, he gave a little nod.

"Well, I must say I agree; it's a little difficult to believe that the Cracklocks can destroy Faery. But please, tell me more of the amulet again if you would. It sounds to be something not of either realm if it can control Fae."

"Where was I?" said David, tapping his teeth again. "Ah, yes; the Mansion. Well, I got rid of my fluorescent shop vest, and, as fortune would have it, the room I was in seemed to be the servants changing area. There were all kinds of overcoats and things hanging up. I availed myself of a housecoat and a cap, picked up a bucket of cleaning things and went off into the house. A duster in your hand is almost as good as an invisibility glamour where the rich are concerned. The staff were no issue; the place is so big, all I got asked was 'are you from the Agency?' and I was pretty much left alone. I guess that they must have people in to help all the time. I reckon they must glamour them or something."

David paused and looked at the brandy on the table.

"Aunty, could I trouble you for a glass of that? The next part gives me the shivers just thinking about it."

Elsie got up, got some glasses from the sideboard, poured four large measures and one Feeorin sized one. Swirling the amber liquid in his glass, David took a swallow and smacked his lips. Setting the glass down, he continued.

"I worked my way around until I heard voices I recognised. The door was closed, so I pressed my ear to the door and heard Malchiah talking; as you know, his voice is quite distinctive, but it was difficult to make out what he was saying. And then I heard Agatha's quavering voice as well, answering in response."

"What were they saying?" asked Elsie, in hushed tones, entirely enthralled by the story now.

"Well, I checked out that nobody else was in that part of the house and then went and pressed my ear to the keyhole. As I said, it was difficult to hear it all; I think that Malchiah was walking about whilst he was talking, but the gist of it was as follows."

David swallowed and then gave an eerily good impression of an old woman's quavering voice, cracked and high pitched.

"I trust that that little treasure of yours is doing what the ledgers and their legends reported?"

David's voice lowered and became more masculine.

"Yes, mother. The legends are quite correct. This gives us

what we need; the devils are completely in our thrall now, and the stone works as we anticipated."

"Difficulties?"

"No, not really, once I had mastered the...the differences that the Stone of the Lost bestows on its user. But I am well again and able to exert the dominance we need."

"And the creatures you took from their realm. They are also within our thrall?"

"Completely. The stone was central to their existence. When we took it, they fell to the wishes of the bearer of the stone and are now in torpor. They are working as well as we thought."

"They extract the grackles?"

"Yes, mother."

David paused and took another swallow of the brandy. Continuing now in his normal voice, he said. "I heard the old lady clap her hands and cackle in glee. She then said what has got me all bothered about this. She said, 'When you took it, was its container destroyed as we surmised?' And what Malchiah's replied chilled me to the core. He said, 'Yes, and it was felt across the realms. Here it was the Sichuan earthquake, but there was a similar response in Fae. It will work, mother; it will work. We can destroy the devil's realm once and for all'. And then they both started laughing."

There was silence, and then Sammy said. "Am I missing something here? I don't understand."

David picked up his glass again, saw it was empty, and put it back down. He smiled sadly at Sammy and said.

"The Sichuan earthquake in China on the twelfth of May lasted for around two minutes, causing over eighty-seven thousand casualties across nearly a hundred cities. It was also the largest on the scale for a long time. And the Cracklocks caused it with whatever they did. And I think that they are looking for ways to do it again."

The others looked at David, dumbfounded. They had all

seen the terrible earthquake on the news, of course, and it was certainly an unusual event. But the fact that it was something more than a naturally occurring event shocked them, despite how unlikely it might seem.

Fermy shifted in his seat and looked at David.

"What do you think they are going to do next?" he said. "I remember there was a glamour explosion in Fae around that time, in the realm of the stars. It was unusual, but none of the folk were hurt as it took place away from anywhere with a population, so it was put down to similar happenings; probably someone dabbling with things best left alone. But if it happened here as well..."

"I don't know, really, I don't," said David. "But I have an idea about where they found this stone thing, and I'm going to check there if I can find the travel glyph. I need to see it and see if I can figure it out."

Sammy held up her hand and looked at David. "Why you?" she asked, her lips pursed.

"Because I need to stop them from doing whatever it is they have got planned."

Sammy shook her head at David. "I repeat. Why you?"

David lowered his head and then looked back up at his wife. "Because of what they said next."

"Which was?"

"They said that they needed Jack for the next phase. They said that because of 'Sammy's uniqueness,' that was how they put it, that 'Sammy and David's boy is what we need, he is the only one that can go.' I need to stop them, Sammy, for your sake, and Jacks."

Sammy gasped, and then anger contorted her face.

"What the hell David? What do they mean? Why the hell do they want Jack? Over my dead body." Her fists were clenched as she stared at her husband, and he lowered his eyes, but Sammy wasn't done.

"And what do they mean about 'My uniqueness'? I'm not unique; I have never been. You and Jack are, as are our friends here, and you, Aunty. You are all special. I am just along for the ride and believe me, I am fine with that."

David held up both hands in supplication.

"Again, I don't know, sweetie, I really don't. But I intend to find out."

"And I intend to help him," said Fermy.

"And me's," said Dorcas.

"We'll all help," said Elsie.

Sammy glared around at them all, red spots high on her cheeks now. When she spoke, her anger was unmistakable.

"Well, that's very kind of you all, I'm sure, but it seems that 'I Don't Know' is David's favourite phrase at the moment. And I'll be damned if you all go off on your adventures and leave Jack and me at the mercy of those, those..." Sammy hitched and buried her face in her hands, her sobs starting.

David moved over and wrapped his arms around her. "Do you think for one moment that I would leave you and Jack in danger? Come on, darling, you know that would never happen."

"I kno...know," said Sammy, between sobs. "But the fact that they are talking about Jack and me. I...I've never...never even met them. Those evil, evil people. Faeries, both good and bad, I can deal with. But why are they so interested in my baby?"

"We'll find out, and while we do so, we'll find a way to keep you safe, I promise," said David, gesturing to Elsie for a handkerchief, who pulled one from her sleeve and handed it to him. "Now, come on. We need to figure out what we are going to do."

Sammy gave a few more snorts and scrubbed at her eyes with the handkerchief.

"Okay," she said. "We'll figure that part out if you're sure that you need to do this. Finish your story."

David blinked and said. "I was pretty much done."

"No, you weren't," said Sammy, laying her hand on top of

David's. "How do those Cracklock's know it was you and to send those things for you and Jack?"

Elsie leaned over and poured a splash more brandy into David's glass. He took it gratefully and swallowed it.

"They didn't see me, not up close. I had my ear pressed to the keyhole, and then, unfortunately, one of the other staff came into the corridor. They saw me crouched down and called out to me. Well, it did make me jump, I can tell you! The voices behind the door stopped at the shout, so I left my cleaning stuff lying on the floor and fled down the corridor as fast as I could. I heard the door open and Malchiah calling after me, not by name, though, more of an "*Oi*." I glanced back and saw the blue stone amulet on his chest. But I didn't hang around; I just went around the corner and through the first door I could find. It was a bedroom, not that that matters. I was panicked; I won't lie to you. I didn't know what to do, so I did what we always do. I tried a travel glyph, and it worked. To be honest, I was surprised when I opened the wardrobe door and saw the flames, but the relief...well, it was huge. It would seem that travelling from out of Cracklock Manor is not a problem; it's the going in that is."

"But I still don't understand how they knew it was you?" said Sammy.

Fermy shook his head and said, "It would have been easy enough to figure out; a simple glamour on the things David left behind would have revealed quite nicely who had held them last."

"Damn it," said David in exasperation. "I should have thought. Anyhow, it is done now, and there's nothing that we can do. I guess that they spent a couple of days gathering those Redcaps and then sent them after us. It was only because of the note that I got home in time when I did."

"The note?" said Elsie

David nodded. "Yes, a note. I stopped to get petrol on the way to work this morning, and when I came out from paying, it was tucked under the windscreen wiper. I thought it was one of those flyer things until I saw my name written on it."

"What?" said Sammy and Fermy together; "Do you still have it?" Fermy continued.

David fished around in his jacket pocket and pulled out a single piece of paper, which looked like it had been torn from a notepad. He handed it over to Fermy, who took it, peered at the scrawled name on the front, and then opened it. It was contained only eight words, scrawled in capital letters in crooked handwriting:

GO HOME NOW. THEY ARE COMING. GET OUT.

"There were plenty of people milling about on the forecourt, but nobody I knew, and I don't recognise the handwriting. But it sent enough shivers down my spine to make me turn around and come back home. You know the rest. Whoever wrote it saved our lives."

Fermy sniffed the paper and then placed it flat on the coffee table, moving the glasses to make room for it. He performed a complex gesture over it and then sat back. The others sat looking at him as a puzzled look came over his face, and he sat forward and performed the same gestures again. He then turned to the others, perplexed.

"I tried the Reveal glamour on it to see who our unsung hero is. But...nothing. It's not revealing anything."

"Could they have masked it?" asked Elsie.

"If they had, then there would be some trace of the masking on it. At least that would tell us that someone with significant powers and knowledge of the Fae had left it. But there is nothing, absolutely nothing. It's like the person who wrote this does not exist. I have never, in all my years, seen anything like this."

The others looked at each other in amazement.

"Something else to add to the 'I Don't Know's,'" said Sammy drily. "And there are entirely too many of those for my liking."

"I guess that will have to take a back seat for now. We need a plan on how to keep Sammy and Jack safe while we start the search for this realm that was destroyed."

"Oh, that's easy, dear," said Elsie. "They can stay with me, of course. Nobody will find them here."

"Are you sure, Aunty? They are obviously keen to get their hands on us if they sent a Hobyah; those things are not easy to control."

"I've already said, this place is glamoured to hide it from Fae; always has been. It's supposed to be a sanctuary for the Cracklocks and the Fae. Only the people I invite know of its location, and only those can find it. It'll be perfectly safe for Sammy and..."

She was interrupted by a loud banging on the front door; loud booms emanating as a fist beat hard against the sturdy wood. David looked at Elsie with panic in his eyes.

"Who can that be? Are you expecting someone?"

"No," Elsie replied. "And that's not the postman's knock, either. I think that you three had better go upstairs. You too, Dorcas as well, please. Now."

David ushered Sammy, Jack and Dorcas ahead of him, casting a fearful look at the solid front door as he did so. Elsie waited until they were out of sight, removed the various locks and pulled the door open. Standing on the front step was a tall pair of elves. Tall and graceful with their blonde hair and deep green almond-shaped eyes, these two still looked forbidding. They were dressed in the golden armour of the Courts, with belted swords at their sides. Patterned livery fluttered in the slight breeze, and each wore a stern expression as they appraised the old woman before them.

"Elsie Cracklock?" the taller of the two enquired.

"Yes, that's me, gentlefolk. How may I be of assistance?"

"Elsie Cracklock, on the orders of Queen Tatiana and King Oberon, we are commanded to attend here to bring the fugitive David Cracklock before the Seelie Court to answer for charges levied against him."

"What the grock are you going on about?" said Fermy, coming into view. "We haven't seen David and the family for days. What has he done now?"

"Master Fermerillion," said the second Elf, dipping his head in acknowledgement. "David Cracklock is wanted for gross destruction within the Realm of the Stars. The Courts have it on good authority that David Cracklock is responsible. He must answer these charges."

"Oh, what rot," said Elsie. "On whose 'good authority' are these charges made? I find it difficult to believe that David would do anything to damage Faery, even if he could do so. And how did you find my home; I take great pains to preserve my privacy?"

"The sources are not for Lifer's ears, and the Courts know of you, Elsie Cracklock," said the first Elf pompously. "We understand that he is here, and he must come with us. Stand aside, please."

"For goodness sake, he's not here," said Elsie indignantly. "Where did you get this information?"

The Elf didn't bother to respond; he simply pushed past Elsie and entered her small hallway.

"Now, wait a minute," said Fermy, standing in the way, his arms folded. The second Elf entered and glared down at him.

"Master Fermerillion, out of respect for the services you have rendered, I will not arrest you this instant. Nevertheless, if you persist, then you will also be taken. We do not hold with the harbouring of fugitives. Now, for the final time. Stand aside."

Seeing that there was nothing more that he could do, Fermy stood to one side and gestured for the Elves to enter.

"Go ahead; search the place. You will be apologising to Mrs

Cracklock here shortly for your impudence in entering her home uninvited."

The Elves quickly scouted the downstairs, starting in the kitchen, before moving through to the sitting room. Here they paused.

"The drinking vessels. Why so many, Elsie Cracklock?"

"Whatever do you mean?" said Elsie.

"Why so many used drinking vessels? I count six. For two folk only."

"Oh, they are dirty ones. Fermy and I can't abide to use the same cup twice, can we, my dear? And we've been having a good old natter here," said Elsie, her face straight.

"Nothing worse than a dirty cup," agreed Fermy.

"And if I were to check these drinking vessels, we would find no trace of David Cracklock?"

"Be my guest," said Elsie and gestured to the table.

The Elves fixed her with a firm look, and then the first one picked up one of the brandy glasses. He started to perform a reveal glamour when suddenly from upstairs came a resounding crash.

"Just two people?" said the second Elf, a grin forming on his face. The two of them dashed to the stairs and were three steps up when a sizeable patchy cat with stubby ears came streaking down the stairs past them and out through the open front door.

"Oh, Snuggles!" said Elsie in a scolding voice. "What have you done now?"

The Elves glared at Elsie and then walked at a more sedate pace up the stairs.

"When did you get a cat?" whispered Fermy to Elsie.

"I didn't," whispered back Elsie.

"Nice cover-up," said Fermy, with a big smile.

The two Elves came back into view and stamped dejectedly down the stairs. One of them raised his hands and performed a complex gesture. A pulse of green light washed out in all directions, and the caster stood, eyes closed. After a few seconds, he opened them and nodded to his colleague, who frowned.

"We have checked your abode, Elsie Cracklock, and nobody is indeed hiding here. Whether David Cracklock was here before, we cannot say, but it is clear he is not now. However, I would caution you about keeping fugitives from the Courts. If he comes here, you will contact a Court representative straight away. Are we of an understanding on this?"

"Of course, of course," said Elsie, with a wave of her hand. "Although if he comes here, he will be on for a good telling off anyhow, bringing the Courts to my door."

"Our apologies for disturbing you, Elsie Cracklock. We will take our leave now."

Without a further word, the two Elves walked through the front door and down the path. As they approached the small garden gate, they faded from view.

Elsie blew out a massive sigh of relief and turned to Fermy.

"Where have they gone now, then?"

Fermy was about to answer when the creak of the garden gate grabbed their attention. Turning to the still-open door, the two friends saw the diminutive figure of Dorcas enter the garden, cautiously glancing about her as she did so. Spying her friends, she called out, "Everything alrights here?"

Fermy gave a relieved laugh and called back, "Yes."

Dorcas beckoned behind her, and David and Sammy followed her through the gate, Sammy carrying Jack in her arms. His thumb was in his mouth, and his mussed-up hair and sleepy eyes made Elsie's heart break a little.

"Come in, come in, quickly. Let's get that little boy to bed for a bit. Then we can decide what to do next," she called in a loud whisper.

The four sprinted up the path, and Elsie slammed the door shut, engaging all of the locks. She then bustled into the kitchen and turned on the kettle. Sammy took Jack upstairs to the small spare bedroom, speaking quietly to him as she went.

"Where did you go?" Fermy asked David.

"Pub down in the village. Gave an old man quite a fright as we walked out of the toilets together; Dorcas almost knocked him over with the door, not that he could see her. We gave it ten minutes, figured that would be long enough, and then sent Dorcas up to spy out the lie of the land for us."

"And the cat?" called through Elsie.

"Well, Jack knocked over a lamp; don't worry, he didn't break it, but it kind of gave the game away. I was already setting the travel glyph when he did it, fortunately. I thought you'd need a reason, and glamoured the cat as a cover as we all climbed into your wardrobe. Tight fit, but it worked. And as an aside, Aunty, you do know that people don't use mothballs anymore, don't you?"

"I like the smell," said Elsie defensively. "Anyhow, people always come and go via the pantry; I don't encourage people to go rummaging through my smalls upstairs."

They all laughed, including Sammy, as she returned from the spare room, the tension of the moment draining away as their narrow escape sank in.

"Well, I guess that we know that we can't stay here," said David with a sigh. "And I am guessing that Faery is also out of the question. I have no idea what to do or where we can go. No parents to hide us apart from Sammy's dad, but he won't be able to keep us in his tiny house, plus it's the first place they'd look if they haven't already."

As if on cue, Sammy's mobile rang. She looked at it and mouthed the word "Dad" to the others, before leaving the room to take the call.

"There must be somewhere?" said Elsie.

"We could rent somewhere, I guess, but what if they find us? I won't be able to work, for obvious reasons. Plus, there's Jack to think about. He is too young to not react to Fae Folk when he sees them; he has played with them all his life. People will talk if they see him with any of the folk; it'll look odd. And we can't hide indefinitely, not that we'd need to if I can prove that Agatha and Malchiah are behind all this." David was tapping his teeth again as he thought things through.

Sammy came back in, looking pale.

"Dad has had some 'funny' people 'round, as he put it. He said they were police, but he thought they seemed odd; they wanted to know where we were. When he refused them entry, they pushed past him and searched the place anyway. They were polite enough and didn't make any mess, but were very thorough. They said that they would be back to check up on him."

"Is he okay?" asked David.

"Yes, just a little shaken up at having had strangers go through the house, even if they weren't threatening. And he's worried about us, of course. I didn't know what to tell him other than that we were fine."

"Well, that decides that. We're stuck then; we have to get away from anyone who knows us while I straighten this out, including our friends amongst the folk. We will need somewhere where the Fae won't get to Jack as well, which is nigh on impossible; they're everywhere. And if he sees them, he'll want to talk to them; it's what he's always done."

Fermy had been looking thoughtful while the discussions had been going on. He looked up at David.

"How long do you think you will need to prove this matter that has got the Courts so flustered?" he asked.

"A few weeks, a couple of months at the most, I would think."

Fermy continued to look thoughtful.

"Okay," he said. "What about if we just hid Sammy and Jack until you're done? We could put them in some town, way away from where you are, with a whole new life and background. That would be easy enough to fix in the short term."

"Like one of those witness protection programmes?" said Elsie, rubbing her hands together. She loved those shows.

"It doesn't solve the problem with Jack, though," said David. "He will always talk and play with Fae; it's how he is. Sammy would be fine; she won't see them without a hagstone, but Jack, well, you know how he loves his friends. He's four; he won't be able to act as if he can't, nor would I ask him to; it's not fair to expect that. However, the Courts aren't my main concern. It's the Cracklocks and their bloody minions. We can't leave Sammy and Jack where they can find them; I can't lose them. And the Cracklocks have plenty of informants amongst the Fae, despite their prejudices. Money and power still talk."

Sammy interjected. "And while I will be able to avoid our friends amongst the folks, if those Cracklocks turn up, what could I do? They could glamour what I know out of me in no time and take Jack and me away to goodness knows where."

"But if you didn't know anything..." said Fermy, tailing off into thought. He then looked up at David and snapped his fingers.

"I've got it. We relocate Sammy and Jack somewhere but give them an entirely new life and background. But we also glamour them with an illusion charm to make them believe they are someone else entirely. If we used a powerful one, with a few of us to instill it, then it would be practically unbreakable. Sammy and Jack would not know any difference so that they would be immune to any Cracklock interference; they don't know Sammy and Jack after all and would struggle to find them. We could make sure that Jack couldn't see the Fae as part of the charm; that would solve that problem. Then, when you're back, and this is all straightened out, we take it off, and everything goes back to normal."

David tapped his teeth again, looking at Fermy as he did so.

"Yes...yes; that could work. For the short term, anyhow. We have enough savings to rent somewhere for a couple of months, and we could work up a cover story. Elsie could keep an eye on them while I'm not about. And we can explain things to Sammy's dad about an extended holiday or something, so he doesn't worry. Yes, I think it would work."

"David, are you sure?" said Sammy with fear in her voice. "It's a lot to ask. What if it were to take longer than a few weeks? Are you sure you can clear your name and get the Cracklocks off of our backs in that time?"

"I think so, yes. I only have to check a couple of things, get the proof, and then go to the Courts. And I'll make damn sure I am confident that you'll be okay before I go. It'll be fine; they'll never find you."

"But what if it takes longer?" Sammy was insistent.

"There is another option," said Fermy, quietly, "Although I'm not sure you will like it." The others looked at him quizzically, Sammy with her eyebrows raised. The Feeorin fiddled with his cup before looking back up at the others.

"We could make you believe that David has passed away. That way, if it takes more than a few weeks, the story and the glamour can stay in place until you're back."

"*No way,*" cried Sammy, her cheeks instantly flushing. "I won't pretend that you're dead, David. Leaving us with horrible untrue memories of what has happened. Absolutely not."

David nodded slowly, thinking it over. After a few seconds, he leaned over and took Sammy by the hands. He stared his wife directly into eyes that shimmered with held back tears.

"The idea has merit, Sammy. If everything goes to plan, it won't matter; we can soon remove the glamour, and everything goes back to normal. But if we try to make you think that I'm just away, say on a works outing or something, and I don't come back soon enough...well, the glamour is bound to weaken as your subconscious fights against it. It'd be like those hypnotist victims we saw on that programme; their brains were fighting against those commands. As the story started to fail to stand up, the glamour would break and then you'd be confused with contradictory stories. Plus, the glamour would then need to go on again, and I have no idea if that would be dangerous. And think about Jack-Jack; goodness knows what would happen to him if his memories kept being messed with. This really needs a single glamour on you that we can take off when I'm done."

"But it seems so final," Sammy replied, and this time a tear rolled down her cheek. "I don't want to think that you're no longer with us, regardless of how long it is. A few weeks is too long."

"I know," said David softly, "And I don't like the idea any more than you do. But if we do it this way, you will be safe for as long as it takes. You won't need to be repeatedly glamoured."

Sammy wiped her cheek with the back of one hand and sniffed. It did make sense, regardless of how bad it felt.

"Okay, then I'm willing to do it to protect Jack. But you better be sure. And when we 'come back,' I want things to be how they were." Sammy stared at David, who well understood the meaning in her eyes. He nodded.

"Well then," said Fermy. "We had better get started. I think that we'll need Timothy Tattingmouse for this; he will help, I'm sure."

The friends looked at each other with some trepidation at what they were about to do.

SAMMY LOOKED at Elsie in the hospital bed with tears in her eyes.

"David never came back, did he?"

"No, sweetheart, he didn't. And the Cracklocks never gave up looking for you; their desire to get their hands on Jack for whatever reason is still there as you have now seen. So we had no choice but to leave you alone where you were safe."

"But the rest…how did we get to see Dad again? We had five good years with him before he passed."

"Well, we had to glamour him too and get him to move. It wasn't easy, but we owed you the support; we didn't want you to be on your own. "

"I should be angry," said Sammy. "But I just feel relief. And fear, a little anyway."

"I know, I know. For what it's worth, I'm sorry that we didn't tell you sooner. You deserved better than that. But we didn't know what to do; we'd promised David, and we were too few to hide you again successfully from the Cracklocks. Nobody regrets those missing years more than Dorcas, Fermy, and I."

Sammy nodded her forgiveness. "So, where the hell is David?" she said.

"We don't know, dear," said Elsie gently. "But now that you and Jack are back with us, we will do our level best to find out. Now, go and see if you can get me checked out of here; we need to find Jack and the others. I just hope that they're okay."

CHAPTER 3

Jack exited the travel room ahead of the others into the house's front room and gasped in shock at the state of the place. The coffee table was upended, as was the sofa. Glass from broken photo frames littered the floor, and the television, probably the most expensive thing that they owned, had a massive hole in the middle of the screen.

"What's happened here?" he said, rounding on Dorcas. "I know you said it was a mess, but this? *Mum? Aunty?*" he shouted at the top of his voice, poking his head through the lounge door and into the hall.

"She is alright's Jack; she wents to the hospitals with Elsie like I says," said Dorcas.

"Hospital?" shouted Jack back at Dorcas. "What actually happened, Dorcas? You said some mess, but this...this is destruction."

"There was some troubles with the bad Cracklocks, and Elsie's has some troubles with her hearts," said Dorcas, trying to pat Jack's hand. He snatched it back and instead fumbled his phone from the pocket, punching the number for his mother. He jiggled about with nerves as it rang, pacing back and forth over the devastation. When it was finally answered, he almost sobbed with relief.

The others watched him talking on the phone as they surveyed the damage. Dorcas tutted to herself and then left for the kitchen. Roly studied the mess with his bright blue eyes, plucking at fragments from the floor.

'I think it's strange that you live like this,' he chimed into their heads. 'Such a terrible muddle.'

"It isn't supposed to be like this," said Jimmy, as he gathered up pieces of a broken vase and dropped it onto the upturned coffee table. "It looks like there was a right set to in here."

"There was," said Dorcas, coming back into the room carrying a dustpan and brush. "Bad Cracklocks come's to take Jack. But we stop's them, Elsie, poor Sammy, and I. And now's poor Dorcas has to clean up the mess. I do's this first, and then looks at Jack and Jimmy when Jack's finished with his tellybone thing."

She set to, sweeping the glass up when Roly chimed in, *'May I help you?'*

"It's okays," replied Dorcas, busying herself with the glass. "There's only one's pan here, and glass doesn't glamours so well. Always little pieces missed. Better to do's it by hand."

'But it will be quicker if I do it,' chimed Roly.

"I don't see's how," said Dorcas, a little irritated that someone was pushing in on her cleaning.

"Let him help if he wants to, Dorcas," said Jimmy. "Many hands. I'll pick up these bits..."

He was interrupted by the chiming in his head as Roly stood, his eyes closed and tiny fists clenched in concentration. A bright blue light was starting to glow in the hollow of his tube-like body.

Jack walked back into the room. "I've just spoken to mum, and she and Elsie are fine. They are on their way back here in a taxi; apparently, those Cracklocks were arrested, so it's safe enough. So all's well that...what is Roly doing?"

The others were silent, watching the tube as the blue light within it grew brighter and brighter. The chiming in their heads grew louder and louder until it started to verge on painful, a buzzing sensation that they could feel in their teeth and bones, like an angry wasp's nest.

"Roly," said Jimmy and received no response.

"Roly!" shouted Jimmy. *"Stop. It's hurting us!"* No response.

And then a blue light erupted out of the top of the tube, in the shape of a whirlwind, and the chiming in their heads faded. The thin end ended at the top of Roly's head, the thicker part touching the ceiling. It probed around the top of the room, and when it touched the light shade, there was a small *'whumpf,'* and the light winked out. The flickering blue light of the whirlwind lit their faces as the top of it swooped down to the floor and flicked over the broken glass, which vanished. As did the coffee table and cracked vase as it touched them, along with vast swathes of the lounge carpet. Roly stood there; his eyes screwed tight shut as the top of the funnel moved around the friends, over the detritus, sucking up anything that it met.

"Roly, stop!" shouted Jack as loud as he could. *"You're destroying the room."* No response.

Fermy stepped over to the little tube and put his hands on him to shake him. Roly's eyes shot open the minute the contact was made, and the whirlwind winked out of existence. The room stayed in darkness, the lightbulb and shade missing from their place on the ceiling. The little tube surveyed the room and raised his hands, covering his eyes. In their heads, his voice chimed.

'I am so, so sorry.' And the sound of sobs started to fill their heads, as the tube appeared to start to cry.

Fermy made a gesture, and a ball of light shot from his hands and hovered where the lightbulb had been, giving off a bright light. The friends surveyed the room, which was now completely free of all the broken items. As well as several things that hadn't been broken, including a number of the sofa seat cushions.

"What the hell was that?" asked Jimmy, looking down at his shoes that were now missing their laces. In their heads, the sobbing continued.

"Roly," said Fermy gently. The tube continued to shake, with his hands covering his eyes.

"Roly," repeated Fermy, a little more forcefully. "What just happened?"

The tube removed his hands and opened his eyes to peer fearfully at the group of friends. He blubbed a few more times and then said. *'I am so sorry. I am not supposed to transfer yet; I have not yet finished my studies. I just wanted to help. To impress, if the truth is told.'*

"But where has everything gone?" said Jack. "Mum is going to go mad!"

'Away,' said Roly. *'But it can come back. It's just, well, I'm not too good at that part yet.'*

"But where?" insisted Jack. "Did you just vacuum it all up?"

'I sent it away,' chimed Roly. *'It's what I, well, we do. My people. Our place in the scheme of things.'*

The little tube stood up proud and chimed in a monologous voice, *'We are the keepers of the lost, the missing and the unwanted. We keep all things for when they may be needed again.'*

Fermy was studying the little tube, a distant look in his eyes.

"That is very interesting. Us Fae can glamour things away and back again, but it takes many grockles to do it, even for small things. May I ask, these things that you 'keep'? You can retrieve them again whenever you wish?" he asked.

'Yes,' chimed Roly. *'Well, we're supposed to be able to. I'm just not that good at that part yet; it means finding the things first, and I haven't had a lot of practice.'*

"Finding them?" said Fermy.

'Yes. In the Cartulary. It's where they go.'

"The cartulary?" asked Fermy.

'Yes,' chimed Roly in an annoyed tone. *'The Cartulary is the record. If you can find it in the Cartulary, then you can retrieve it. But, it's so difficult to find things; there are soooooo many.'* The tube rolled his eyes at the memory.

Fermy pressed on. "And the things that you send away and are added to the Cartulary. Are these just physical things, like the broken bits, or can you send anything away?"

'Anything. I did the sky power once, the lightning in training; that was fun!' chimed Roly, jigging a little at the memory.

"And what about grackles? Could you remove grackles from someone?"

'What are grackles?' asked Roly.

"Life-force, I suppose, would be the best way to describe them," said Fermy.

'Why would we want to take someone's life away from them?' asked Roly, genuinely surprised at this.

Fermy nodded in acknowledgement. "It was just a question. And where is this Cartulary?" he asked.

'In here,' chimed Roly, tapping what was presumably his chest. *'Not really in here; it's elsewhere, by the Focus, but we are all linked to it. My people, I mean.'*

"The Focus?" asked Fermy.

The tube put his hands where his hips would be and turned his blue eyes onto Fermy in further exasperation.

'The centre of our realm. Yes, I know all about your realm, Faery man, and some of the ones where these short-lived folk reside, although I thought I'd never actually come here. And I have no idea how I am here now. We don't travel between realms, as we have too much to do. But there are other places to go, you know, other than these; we study them from afar. My place is at home, where the lost and missing are,

not here. We take good care of them, mark my words, or otherwise they'd be gone for good.'

"And are people there, I mean, in the Cartulary?" said Fermy, the excitement evident in his voice.

'Sometimes,' said Roly, with a shrug. *'But it's difficult to keep people 'away'; they don't stay so well when they go there. It's not a place for the living.'*

Fermy looked at Jack, who was staring at the little tube. The boy was clearly excited, his face holding a vast smile. "Dad," he said, at the same time as Fermy said, "David."

Roly looked at them, both bewildered, unsure as to what they were saying.

"I would hear more about your home, Roly, and the cartulary if you would tell the story?" said Fermy. "But I would like to ask your permission to have a friend also listen. He would be very interested in your tale."

'Of course, I would be happy to tell you of our history,' said the tube, obviously flattered. *'And to whoever would listen. But it may be easier for me to show you.'*

"We can go to your home?" interjected Jack. "How? We don't have the travel glyphs,"

'I can return home, I think. I was shown but have never done it,' said Roly. *'But I would be happy to take you all if you would come. I think that you could return here yourselves perhaps? My people would be most pleased to welcome you, I think.'*

"Well met then," said Fermy. "Now, please excuse me while I fetch Timothy to accompany us. I would also suggest waiting for Elsie and Sammy, of course, so that we can all listen. This could be the answer that we are looking for about our missing friend."

As Fermy turned to leave, the sound of the front door opening snapped them out of the conversation, as they heard Sammy's voice call out a 'Hello?'

Jack dashed from the room and into his mother's arms.

Hugging her tight, she said, "Jack, your nose! Is it broken? Whatever has happened?"

"It's a long story, mum. Elsie, are you alright now?"

"Just a little murmur, Jack, nothing to worry about," said the old lady, looking a little worn out.

"Sammy, Elsie. Are you's alright?" said Dorcas, bustling through from the lounge. "I will makes's tea, and while the kettle is boilings, Jack and Jimmy come with me. Let Dorcas make you's better again."

"Dorcas, where's Fermy?" asked Elsie anxiously. "Is he okay?"

"He's is fine. He has gones to get Timothy. We have a new friend's who might help us finds David."

"A new friend?" said Elsie.

"In here, Elsie," called through Jimmy. "Come and meet Roly."

ANASTASIA SAT in the drawing-room of the mansion, raging at herself. Post battle with the Cracklocks, she hadn't had the time to berate herself; she'd been a little stunned, her head aching from that damn Sammy, and things had happened very quickly with the police and ambulance arriving. She hadn't had time to process it all until she was safely in the back of the Bentley, Nigel cruising the car gently, looking for somewhere away from prying eyes where they could all travel safely back home. As such, she hadn't dwelt on what had happened to them until they were back.

Now, having had time to stew on it, she was furious. Mainly at herself, allowing a stupid old woman and a devil to get the better of her. And they'd attacked Benedict as well, her little boy. For that indiscretion, there was no end to the ways she intended to punish that family. She now had reason enough to hate them all, not just David, and she would have her revenge.

Benedict, on the other hand, had no such regrets; he'd shrugged off the episode with barely a second thought, although he had muttered 'Dorcas' a few times under his breath and twitched when he did. *'The bag full of Fae that he caught in the gardens and a new police taser to play with probably has something to do with that,'* she thought and gave a bitter little laugh. Benedict disappeared off to his workshop as soon as they'd got back, and if she strained to hear, she thought she could hear his cackling laughter at the other end of the house.

So Anastasia sat gently rocking in her chair and chewing on her hair braid, as she did when she was deep in thought. She knew one thing; she was going to deliver that brat, Jack, to her Aunt Agatha, and whilst doing it, she was going to cause as much distress to David and Sammy as she could. And the old bag as well, Elsie had it coming. If it was the last thing that she did, then so be it.

A light tap on the door roused her from her contemplations, and she looked up as Nigel padded into the room.

"Ma'am, your Uncle has arrived. He is requesting to see you," he said, his eyes downcast. He was well used to his mistress's rages.

"I am in no mood to receive visitors, Nigel. Tell him I will see him tomorrow at that damn Cracklock hovel. I only spoke to him a short while ago by telephone."

"He was very insistent, Ma'am."

"I said no!" screamed Anastasia, vaulting out of her seat and spinning to face the manservant, her fists clenched.

"I will deal with this, Nigel. Please bring us through some tea," came a voice from behind the door, and Nigel obediently stepped aside to permit Malchiah to enter the room.

"Anastasia, please calm down," he said and gestured to the seat she had just vacated.

"Not now, Uncle. I am in no mood at this time to discuss our arrangements. Not until that beglamoured brat is safely tucked away with Great Mama and those...those...those damned Fae lovers are..."

"*Silence!*" yelled Malchiah, and Anastasia shut up in shock at the tone of her Uncle's voice.

Malchiah continued. "Now listen to me. I saw what you did at that house, you damned fool! Put them on their guard against us, as well as trying to kill Elsie! What, in the Lord's name, do you think that you were doing? You have destroyed any chance of convincing Jack to come over to our cause now. There is no way that the boy will willingly help us, assuming that he can actually do what Mother presumes. We will have to employ other methods."

"They were disrespectful to Benedict and me," said Anastasia in a small voice.

"Disrespectful?" Malchiah's tone was unbelieving. "Forcing your way into their home, glamouring them and trying to kill one of their friends? What the hell were you thinking? I gave you that information to help me track them down; I did not expect you to go to war with them."

"David killed Rudolph. David left Benedict without a father and this house without a master." Anastasia had spots of colour in her cheeks now, and her fists were clenched again. "I had every right, the Lord himself states so in Leviticus 24, '*And if a man causes a blemish in his neighbour; as he hath done, so shall it be done to him; breach for breach, eye for eye, tooth for tooth: as he hath caused a blemish in a man, so shall it be done to him again.*'"

"I am aware of the scriptures, Anastasia," said Malchiah quietly. "And I prefer, in this particular case, Luke 19:27. *"But these enemies of mine, who did not want me to reign over them, bring them here and slay them in my presence."* They have a purpose in our plans, and your actions this evening have made it ten, no, a hundred times more difficult."

"I will have my revenge on them, Uncle. In that, you will have no say."

"I agree. But you must hold your temper until we have what we need. We need the boy, and I would rather he was able to act as he is required to do so. His friends and family may be needed for, shall we say...leverage, in that respect."

"And when you are done? And the boy has fulfilled whatever tasks Great Mama has in mind?"

"Then they will be yours to do with as you will. You and your son; I will not stand in your way."

Anastasia was a little more subdued now. "I have your promise on that?"

"Yes. They will be yours once we are finished with their role in our plans."

Anastasia nodded her agreement.

"So, Uncle. What are the plans for tomorrow? I assume that we will return to that delightful little town and procure the boy?"

"I will return with some friends of mine," said Malchiah. "You will remain here. I do not want any more mishaps until I have them in my custody."

"You will not require our help?" said Anastasia, the disappointment clear on her face. "Benedict is keen to have the Brownie."

"Once they are in my custody and have served their purpose, you can have the Brownie. Call it a down payment on our agreement. Now, I understand from my brief conversation with Nigel that you have some assistants in the town who are familiar with the boy?"

"Those doltish twins? They are useless."

"But they can be put to task. Have them watch the house and follow if they leave via conventional means. I do not want them getting away; I have others watching for them in that damn filthy realm if they go there, as well as Elsie's home."

"I will call them now. I hope that you know what you are doing, Uncle; that family is not to be underestimated."

Malchiah handled the blue gem pendant around his neck.

"It will be fine, Anastasia. It will be fine."

TYLER AND MASON were engrossed in a particularly violent video game when the mobile phone started to ring. They ignored it. The phone cut off and then immediately started ringing again. This time, the volume was louder. Mason reached over, grabbed the remote, and turned up the sound on the game before getting stuck straight back into the carnage. The phone rang out, went quiet, and then started again. This time, the ringing was deafening, far beyond what the speakers were capable of producing.

Tyler paused the game and turned to the phone just as a bawling voice came screeching up the stairs, *"Whose phone is that?"*

"I'm sorting it, Ma!" he hollered back before answering it. He listened for a moment, and his face fell. Mason watched with interest.

"We're done," he heard Tyler say.

"But you said..."

"No. Ain't doing it."

"You can't make..."

"Leave them alone. You do that, lady, and I'll..."

Tyler hung up, his face pale.

"We've got to go out, Mase. Watch that Crackley's house for that mad woman."

Mason grunted.

"I know, but she's threatened Ma. Reckon we're right in bother if we don't."

"'Nore it," said Mason.

The phone started ringing again, its volume deafening. Tyler picked it up again. He listened quietly and finally said, "Okay."

Turning to Mason, worry unusually etched on his face, he said. "We're going. End of."

Mason grunted again and turned off the game.

DORCAS WAS SERVING a mountain of sandwiches to everyone when Fermy returned with Timothy in tow. Roly was watching them all eat, his bright blue eyes moving from person to person as they spoke, but had refused anything himself.

'I don't need to take those things. My people take our sustenance from the Cartulary and our realm,' he chimed into their heads, as the others ravenously devoured the sandwiches.

When Timothy entered the room with Fermy, the chewing stopped long enough for the greetings to happen and then started again. Timothy looked down at Roly, who stared back, unblinking. Timothy spoke first.

"Hello, fellow, and well met. You are Roly, I presume, that Fermy here has told me about? A bit of a mystery by all accounts?"

'That is the name I was given, yes, by the young gentleman there,' chimed Roly, pointing at Jimmy. 'The mystery is how I came to be among you, for which I have no recollection.'

"I am Timothy, Scholar of Fae and friend to these people here. Your manner of speaking, with the mind, is unusual. Do your people all communicate in this way?"

'Yes,' chimed Roly. 'My people and my home, I can recall. My purpose also. My reason for being here, I do not know. The first I knew of it was when I was awoken by the young gentleman there.' This time he pointed at Jack.

Timothy looked at Jack, taking in his dishevelled state and bloodstained clothing. Jack swallowed a mouthful of sandwich and nodded at Timothy.

"I want a word with you, Timothy. Your oscillator machine said that the mission would be successful. It was anything but; we all got attacked by various things, and Fermy here was captured."

"And yet here you all are, together, with the object we sought," said Timothy simply.

Jack looked puzzled for a second and then nodded.

"But it could have warned us," he said.

"I'm afraid that the theriomantic oscillator isn't so specific. I have been working on this aspect for many years and still have much work to do. It is the best that it can be for now," said Timothy haughtily.

Jack held up both hands in surrender.

"It's great, Timothy, really. I'm not criticising it."

"I appreciate that, Jack. One can get rather protective of one's life work."

"Gentlemen, we can debate the benefits of the oscillator at length another day if you wish. However, for now, we are here to listen to our new friend here, who has kindly offered to take us to his realm. None of us is familiar with his people, and I, for one, would be interested to hear his story and see this new place." Fermy stood, looking at the both of them, with his arms folded.

"Of course, of course. Friend, you must think me rather rude," said Timothy to Roly.

'Of course not,' chimed the tube. *'Your conversations have allowed me to think about how to explain about my people. I will try to show you something of interest. I will take you to the Focus, I think. Would you come with me?'*

"Of course. Would it be possible to see the Cartulary list? We have an interest in a friend of ours who is lost. We would like to see if he could be there."

'I would have to seek assistance from my teachers for that,' chimed the tube. *'As I explained, I am not so good at retrievals.'*

"We would be most grateful if you could," said Fermy. Timothy cleared his throat.

"And we would be interested to learn how you are able to extract grackles," he said.

Roly spun to face him, his eyes angry.

'*Why would we take life-force?*' he chimed, an angry note in his voice. '*We are not thieves of such precious things.*'

It was Timothy's turn now to hold his hands up in a placatory manner.

"I am sorry; I mean no offence. It is just that we heard of tubes that are able to take life force. Indeed, you were used by your captor on young Jack here, we believe for just that purpose."

Roly's eyes looked puzzled. '*Whatever do you mean?*'

Jack explained briefly about his first encounter with Mr Binks and the use of the tube. He finished with, "But don't worry, nothing happened to me."

Roly still looked puzzled. '*But I do not recall this, and besides, we are forbidden to take lives. So I do not think it could have been my people, even if they could be bewitched, which I doubt. And how did I end up with this 'Binks' you talk of?*'

"We don't know," said Fermy. "But perhaps we can find some answers in your realm? We need to start somewhere, after all."

Roly nodded his agreement. '*Then, I shall try to open a portal for us to return there. Please allow me a little room, as I have not done this before. All of my people are able to return home in this manner, and whilst we are taught it, I have never had to use it. We are not travellers.*'

The tube moved away from the others and closed his eyes, fists again clenched. The blue whirlwind again rose from inside the hollow of his body, but this time, it was more controlled, less erratic in its movement. It bent over at a right angle, and the top of the funnel focused onto the wall next to the living room door. The shape changed from a spinning circle to that of a spinning oval as it touched down. As the others watched, the colour changed slowly, from the bright blue, through a glorious green to pale yellow. It twitched and became transparent; an oval hole cut into the wall. Through it, the others could see a reddish light, like at sunset, but this one pulsed to an unseen rhythm, like a heartbeat.

'Please step through the portal,' echoed Roly's voice in their heads, quiet this time, like the tube was not there.

"Is it safe?" asked Sammy anxiously, looking at the others.

"I have no idea," said Fermy. "But, I am hopeful that if we are trapped there, we can realm travel back here or to Faery. I say we go."

"And me," said Jimmy, who was staring at the oval hole with a look of wonder in his eyes. "I have never seen anything like this."

Jack got up and walked over to the hole. He hesitated and then pushed his hand into it.

"It's fine; it feels like a warm wind, but not unpleasant. I say we go if there is any chance that Dad could be there." With that, he stepped through the oval and into the other realm. The others could see him, slightly shimmering through the portal, and he turned to look back at them.

"Well, that decides it," said Jimmy, strolling through the portal to stand next to Jack. The others quickly followed through until the little party stood, huddled together, with the warm wind blowing around them in an otherwise featureless landscape. Behind them came a popping sound, and they turned to see Roly, standing slightly bent on the other side of the portal. The popping sound came again, and then he stood with them in the same position but facing away, the portal still in existence. It was like a mirror image had come into play on this side of the hole. The whirling portal continued for a few seconds, and then Roly opened his eyes. The whirlwind and the portal winked out of existence.

'It worked,' chimed the tube in their heads, dancing a little jig. *'It worked, it worked, it...'* He then stopped, conscious of the eyes of the others on him, as they smiled down.

'I'm sorry, it's just I've never done that before. The teachers would be impressed. You will tell them when we meet them, won't you?' he implored the others, the chiming clear in their heads.

Elsie chuckled. "Of course we will, Roly, of course we will. And they will have to believe us because we are here, aren't we?"

The tube nodded frantically and then gave a little jig again.

"Roly," said Elsie. "May I ask you a question?"

'Of course,' chimed Roly.

"You talk about these teachers a lot. They must mean a lot to you. May I ask, are you at school?"

'School?' chimed back the tube.

"A place of learning. For children. In our realm, our young people attend school to study and learn. When they leave, they are considered to be almost adults."

'We learn from our teachers,' replied Roly. *'From when we are foundlings until we are ready to become keepers. We learn to use the Cartulary in all its aspects. And I am still learning; I am not yet ready to become a keeper.'*

"And how long have you been learning?" asked Elsie.

'Not long. I have only seen four darknesses.'

"What do you mean?" asked Fermy. "What are darknesses?"

Roly turned his eyes onto Fermy.

'Here, we have the light,' he gestured at the red sky, which was strangely cloudless. *'We do not have the fast darkness all the time, like in your realm. The darkness comes only after a long time and stays only briefly. It is a time of joy and merriment.'*

"So, it's how you measure time?" asked Jimmy.

'Time has no real meaning here,' chimed Roly. *'But, we measure our spans here by darkness.'*

"So you're just a wee bairn then?" said Jimmy, in a mock Scotch accent.

'I do not know what you mean,' chimed Roly, a puzzled expression in his voice.

"Never mind," said Timothy. "I think that he is joking with you, Roly. Shall we go? There seems to be little here for us, other than the ground and the sky."

'We shall go to the Focus,' confirmed Roly.

"Is it far?" asked Sammy. "It's just that there is nothing to see for miles; the horizon is empty."

Roly looked up at Sammy this time, his blues eyes twinkling.

'It is not far. Please close your eyes, all of you.'

They did as Roly bid. And then his voice chimed in their heads, echoes of panic in the tone.

'*Oh no, oh no, oh no. Noooooooooo!*' they heard him scream in their heads.

They all opened their eyes as one and gasped in horror at what they saw.

THE LAFEY TWINS had arrived at Jack's street just in time to see a flickering blue light at the house's downstairs window further down the street. They had been sauntering down the road, both of them fearful of what had happened the last time they were there and subconsciously dragging their feet. But they had broken into a run as they saw the lights flashing through the window down the street, like an indoor police strobe. They arrived at the house, panting and out of breath just as the light winked out.

"Mase, go and look through the window," gasped Tyler. "I'm done in."

Mason shook his head and grunted.

"Just do it," snapped Tyler. "A quick peek. Tell me if they're in there or not."

Mason reluctantly pushed open the gate as quietly as he

could and moved as silently as a six-foot lump of a boy could. He took a quick glance through the window, turned back to Tyler, and shrugged his shoulders. "Gone," he grunted.

Tyler felt his heart speed up a little as he felt fear shoot down his spine. The blonde woman had been quite specific. 'Go and make sure that they don't leave, and if they do, follow them.'

"I'm going to have to tell her that they're not here," he said to Mason and pulled out the phone. "And then we're going to ground. We're done with that crazy witch."

He called the number from earlier and waited, his breath catching.

"Dear boy. What news?" said the silky female voice.

"They're not there. Nobody's home."

"Okay...they will be back. I'll need you two to wait there for them to return, and then let me know."

"Lady, it's dark and freezing. We ain't staying out here all night, and you can threaten as much as you like."

"*You will do as I say!*" screamed Anastasia down the phone.

"*We will not!*" screamed back Tyler.

"Calm down, dear boy. You can wait inside for them. Get yourself well-hidden, though; I want to know immediately when they return. Then you can help us as needed."

"You want us to break in?"

"No, no, of course not. I'll come and let you in," said Anastasia and hung up.

Tyler looked at Mason.

"She wants us to stay here. She reckons she's going to let us in; must be in the area."

They were interrupted by the noise of the front door unlocking. It opened, and the blonde figure of Anastasia stood there.

"In. Quickly," she said, glancing up the street.

The twins stepped quickly inside, and Anastasia shut the door.

"What the hell, lady? You were there all the time?" said Tyler.

"Of course not, you little silly," cooed Anastasia, pinching Tyler's cheek. The twin brushed her hand off impatiently.

"Now then. To business. Your fee, of course," she said, handing over another roll of banknotes. "I want you to stay hidden here and update me when they are back. At some point, a gentleman, my dear Uncle Malchiah, will be calling. You are to assist him in whatever way he asks. Understood?"

"Stay hidden? How, lady? This place is tiny!"

"That is very much your problem. Do not get caught, and ensure that you keep me informed. While I am sure that my Uncle will not require any assistance, every little bit helps, as the saying goes. So just do as you are bid."

With that, Anastasia walked to the lounge door and pulled it closed. The twins watched her draw a strange symbol on it and then slap it, where it fell from the door in glittering sparks.

Pulling the door open, Anastasia looked over her shoulder. Her gaze was cold now as she stared at the twins.

"Do not let me down, boys. I will be furious if you do."

With that, she walked through the door and slammed it shut behind her.

"Mental, bruv, absolutely mental," whispered Tyler to Mason. "Where does she think she's going, eh?"

He pushed open the door to ask her and saw the empty room.

"What?" he exclaimed, looking behind the battered sofa and the curtains. She was gone.

"Mase, this is getting weird. I don't like this one bit. What do we do?"

"Hide," grunted Mason.

BACK AT THE MANSION, Anastasia called Malchiah.

"I have placed those louts in the house; they will give you information at the site that may be of use."

"Thank you, Anastasia. Can they be trusted?"

"No. But they will do what they are told. And they are expendable; do as you wish with them."

"I will," said Malchiah and hung up the phone.

As the friends opened their eyes, the first thing they saw about a hundred meters or so away was a huge wall made of the same wood-like material as Roly himself. It towered high into the air and stretched as far as the eye could see in both directions. They could make out cracks running through the whole structure even at this distance, a dim blue glow emanating from the jagged lines on the surface. Looking closer, they could see that the surface was curved, outwards towards them, with the bottom of the wall lying in slight shadow. But it was what lay in front of the wall that was the cause of Roly's anguish, the little tube's cries echoing in all of their heads.

Tubes. Thousands, no, millions of tubes, as far as the eye could see, lying scattered about on the floor in every direction they gazed. They looked like casually discarded toilet roll inners as they lay there, gently rocking in the slight warm breeze. They were all dark, an oily looking sheen glistening on them as they lay there in the red light of the sky like discarded rubbish.

Roly sprinted down the incline to where the tubes lay and lifted the first one with his stick-like arms. The tube was immobile like a block of wood. He placed it carefully back down onto the ground and moved onto the next one, shaking it. He continued to chime his anguish as he moved amongst the tubes, pushing, rocking each one he came to.

"What the grock is going on?" said Elsie, looking at the scene with horror. "Are those like him?"

"I think that they were once," said Fermy quietly. "But not now."

"So what happened here?" said Sammy. "It looks like mass murder or something if those tubes are supposed to be like Roly. Why are they all like that?"

Jimmy and Jack ran down the incline to where Roly was trying to rouse his kinfolk, stopping just short.

"Roly," said Jimmy.

The tube looked up at Jimmy with pure venom in his eyes.

'They're gone,' he spat chimed into their head. *'All of them. My people. All taken away from us, as the Focus has been taken.'*

"The Focus has been taken? What do you mean?"

'My people pass to the next phase when they are removed from the Focus. The Focus is gone; hence they are all removed. Look, you stupid boy. Look at them.'

"How do you know that the Focus is gone?" said Jack gently.

'Because the Focus pillar has gone.'

"I'm sorry, Roly, but I don't understand. What is the Focus pillar?"

'The resting place of the Focus. A great pillar; into the sky it rose, the centre of our existence and home to the Focus. Gone. Gone.' Roly broke down again in tears, the sobs echoing in their heads.

The boys glanced around them, looking for such a pillar, but there was nothing in clear view, certainly no object climbing high into the sky.

"Roly," said Jimmy. "How do you know? We can't see any pillar as you describe."

'It's there,' chimed Roly, pointing at the vast wall that stretched away into the distance. *'That was the great pillar. Destroyed, look at it. Lying there, smashed. By what, I do not know; that pillar has stood for uncounted darkness's and was the source of the Focus and the Cartulary. But I will find out.'* His eyes changed to a darker blue, almost purple, and Jack and Jimmy took an involuntary step back.

The others had made their way over to them during this time, and they stood in a small semi-circle around the little tube.

"What has happened, Roly?" asked Fermy, patting the tube. Roly ignored him and cradled one of the tubes from the floor in his arms, hitching a little as he silently sobbed.

"He says the Focus has gone. It was in that, there, but it's been destroyed," said Jack, gesturing at the wall.

"In that wall?" said Elsie.

"No. That was a pillar, which was the key to their realm. Something has destroyed it; made it collapse."

"Say that again," said Timothy, his face turning pale.

"Centre of their existence. A great pillar."

Timothy's eyes reeled back into his head, and he fainted, Dorcas just catching him before he fell onto the scattered tubes.

"Timothy? Timothy? Wakes up," she said, slapping his face. The scholar stayed out cold, his teeth chattering a little as if he was cold.

"What is going on?" said Sammy. "Why has Timothy..."

She didn't finish. From the corner of her eye, she caught movement. Glancing over towards it, she saw another tube, identical to Roly, limping towards them. It only had one leg and was hopping as it came, leaning on a small stick as it did so.

"Roly," she whispered and pointed.

Roly turned and looked. Then with a whoop, he was on his feet, his tiny legs carrying him at speed through his fallen people towards the tube limping towards them.

CHAPTER 4

The others watched as Roly gathered up the other tube in his little arms and swung him about in glee. They could hear a strange swooshing chiming in their heads from the two of them as they conversed rapidly in their own language. The noise was like the jangling of bells, blown in a strong gusting wind as it whooshed through their minds.

Roly set down the other tube and looked over to where the little group stood huddled together. He waved his arm, beckoning them to come over to him, jiggling about excitedly as he did so. Dorcas stooped down and lifted the comatose Timothy with her strong arms.

As they got close, his voice chimed into their heads.

'This is ...' the name was indistinguishable as it sounded like wind through the trees. *'He survived the destruction of the Focus. He survived it!'*

The other tube looked up at the friends. Its eyes were blue but not as deep or vivid as Roly's, more like a cornflower blue, pale. Its surface was the same warm wood colour as Roly, but it seemed more aged, tiny cracks running through the surface. It stood on its one leg, with what appeared to be a twig acting as a walking stick.

"Hello there, friend," started Elsie, bending down and extending her hand. "My name is..."

'Silence!' boomed a voice in their heads, making Jack and Jimmy duck involuntarily. *'I have no desire to know your ilk. Destroyers and thieves, the lot of you. If I had seen fewer darkness's, I would destroy you where you stand.'*

"Whatever do you mean?" said Fermy. "We mean you no harm."

'Not you, Fae,' boomed the tube again. *'Those tall ones.'* He gestured with his stick at the lifers, almost toppling over as he did so.

"Us?" replied Jimmy. "We aren't thieves, mate; we just got here. We're as shocked as Roly here to see the state of his home."

'Your kind comes with false promises. Friendship. And then you take what is not yours to take and bring great harm to the people.'

"Not us," said Fermy gently. "We mean no harm. We are at Roly's invitation, seeking a missing friend of ours."

'You are not welcome. Begone to whence you came!' the old tube hollered into their heads.

Roly put a reassuring arm around the tube, and the others heard the strange chiming and whooshing noise again in their minds as they conversed. The old tube listened, making strange little bows as he did so, and replying in the same manner. Eventually, he gave what appeared to be a nod and turned his pale blue eyes again to the friends.

'Your friend here vouches for you,' he began. *'And it appears that I was hasty in my judgement. I am told that you rescued the one you call 'Roly' here from enslavement. For that, I offer you my thanks and my apologies for judging you. Although I have good reason to do so.'*

"Can you tell us what happened here?" asked Elsie. "What could have wrought such a terrible tragedy to your people? And how did you survive when all these others were destroyed?"

'I can certainly share with you the terrible events. And if you could save Roly here, then perhaps you can also save the rest of my people?'

"What do you mean?" asked Jack. "Aren't these people gone?"

'No,' replied the old tube. *'They are in torpor, caused by the other tall ones and their actions on the Focus. They will all be within the Cartulary at this time but cannot be retrieved by the likes of us.'* He gestured at Roly and himself. *'They can only retrieve themselves. I would hear about how you rescued Roly here, as it may be that there is hope yet to release them.'*

"Of course, if we can help, then we will. But I am not sure about how exactly we rescued Roly here. He just sort of woke up after the fight with the Lisovyk," said Fermy.

'Describe to me what happened,' chimed the old tube, turning his pale eyes to Fermy.

The little Feeorin described the battle with the Lisovyk and Jack's bravery in killing the thing with the iron filings. Then Jack passing over the tube to him and Roly's revival.

'So, when the boy here passed over the tube, Roly started to come out of torpor?' said the old tube, looking up at Jack.

"Well, yes," said Jack with a shrug. "I didn't do anything special, just took him out of my jacket pocket."

'Could you please pick up one of my fallen brethren here?' said the old tube to Jack.

"Sure, no problems."

Jack stooped down and gently picked up one of the tubes. He held it in his right hand and then his left. Nothing happened.

'Now, place the brethren within your pocket, and mimic what you did before.'

Jack did as he was requested, placing the tube within the pocket and then extracting it with the same hand. Again, nothing happened, and Jack bowed his head in disappointment.

The old tube likewise had downturned eyes.

'Well, then, it must be something else,' he said, as Jack placed the

tube gently back onto the floor with the others. *'I had hope, but I can see now that I was a fool.'*

Dorcas has watched the goings-on quietly; something about the scene that Jack had just acted out wasn't quite right. She racked her brains for what was missing but came up blank. As was her custom, she started to fiddle with her dress when she thought hard, twiddling the hem. The voices of the others faded out. She studied the dress and noticed the dark spots that were dotted about it.

'Oh my grockles,' she thought, 'That's blood. This dress is ruineds now; I will's never get that outs properly. I coulds try Elsie's washing machinery things; that could do's it perhaps...' She trailed off as realisation hit her.

"Wait's!" she shouted out, making the others jump. "I know's what is missings."

The others turned at her outburst and stared at her.

"Jack," she said. "When's you gots the tube out, your noses was bleedings, wasn't it? From where the Lyso thingy got you?"

"Yeah," said Jack. "So what?"

"Did you have bloods on your hands?"

Realisation dawned on Jack's face. "I guess so; I'd been fiddling with my nose, wiping it away."

Dorcas turned to the others. "It might be the bloods that did it?" she said. "We could trys that?"

"Whoa," said Jack, taking a step backwards and holding up his hands. "I've shed enough blood for one day, thanks, and have the cuts and bruises to show for it."

The old tube looked up at him. *'It's worth trying, perhaps. If you would be willing?'*

Jack looked hesitant, but Elsie piped up.

"Here, I'll do it. I've got a pin somewhere in here; a simple finger prick should be enough." She started to rummage in her voluminous handbag and then produced a pin with a flourish.

"Right," she said, jabbing it into the meaty part of her thumb.

A bead of blood gleamed, bright red where the pin had pricked her. She bent down and scooped up one of the tubes from the floor.

"Okay, then. Here we go," she said and pressed the bloody thumb down onto the tube.

The other stood, apprehensive. And nothing happened. Elsie tried again on a different part of the tube, and still nothing.

"Well, that rules that out," she said, defeated, and gently placed the tube down on the floor.

"No," said Jack, a determined look on his face. "Let me try."

Elsie rummaged in her bag and produced another pin, which she handed to Jack. It was a good deal bigger than the first one.

"Hang on a minute," said Jack. "Why can't I have a smaller one? This one looks blunt."

"Should have gone first then," said Elsie. "Just do it. You got beaten up by one of the nastiest Fae ever a few hours ago. This should be a walk in the park."

Jack jabbed his thumb, cursed, and then jabbed it again. The blood bloomed at the end of it. He bent down, picked up another tube, and pressed his thumb against it. The effect was instantaneous; the tube started a strange thrumming noise and started to vibrate. Jack placed it carefully onto the floor and stood back.

As they had with Roly, the vibrations increased, snaking up into their bones as they stood watching. Just as it started to get painful again, they stopped, the tube changing from the oily black colour to a rich brown. Bright blue eyes opened, and little arms and legs popped out. The tube sat up.

The friends cheered as the bemused new tube looked around at them. The old tube sat awkwardly down next to it, and the whooshing chiming language filled their heads as he gave reassurance to his newly awakened fellow citizen.

"Got any more pins, Elsie?" said Jimmy, sidling up to her. "And any plasters? Think Jacksy boy here is going to need them by the time we've finished." He gestured at the field of tubes.

~

JACK MANAGED to revive thirty or so of the tubes before his bloody thumb became too sore to continue. They stood around the friends in a small circle, watching intently as Jack roused their fallen comrades from the torpor. Jack winced as he did the last one, and Sammy noticed.

"Right, that's enough," she said, putting a protective arm around Jack. "No more for now."

The tubes immediately began chattering, chiming in their heads, begging for one more friend or family member to be revived. They gathered around Jack, their blue eyes gazing at him, as they tugged at his trouser bottoms with their tiny hands. Sammy stared down at them.

"Look, I understand, I really do, but Jack doesn't have enough blood in his entire body to revive all of these people. It's futile to try. Maybe over time, he can help, but that's enough for now. We can try again in a while, but he needs a break."

"Why don't you tell us about what happened here while we give Jack a breather?" asked Elsie to the old tube, who had stood, leaning on his makeshift cane and watching proceedings. "I would be interested to know how you escaped the fate of the others here."

The old tube seemed to puff up at being asked to recount his story in more detail. The whispering, chiming noise filled their heads as he rapidly conversed with the others, who performed their funny little bows. Their conversation stopped, and he turned to Elsie.

'I would tell the tale to you if you would listen. My people here agree; it may be that the telling can help us all.'

"Would you wait a moment and see if we can wake my

friend here?" said Fermy. "He is a scholar of the Fae and very knowledgeable about all manner of things. I would like him to listen as well; he may well have a perspective on matters that we don't think about."

The old tube gave his odd little bow in acknowledgement, and Fermy smiled his thanks. He and Dorcas bent down to the comatose Timothy and started to shake him gently. Timothy gave a snore and didn't wake up. They shook him for a good minute with no results.

"I guess that we leave him," said Fermy in exasperation.

"Let me have a go," said Jimmy. He bent down and pinched the lobe of Timothy's small pointed ear with his nails. Timothy sat bolt upright and screamed with pain before clasping his hand to the offending ear. He looked around at the others, disorientated, and then focused again on the 'wall' that ran off into the distance. He gave a panicked gulp and said. "The oscillator was correct. It's the end of days." And burst into tears.

"Whatever do you mean?" asked Fermy. "The end of days?"

Timothy blubbered, "That, there. That fallen pillar. If that is what I think it is, then we are in serious trouble. The oscillator predicted times of great strife, but I couldn't get it more specific. I thought it was just another of its random throw-outs; I didn't ask the question, but the omens were all there."

"You're making no sense," replied Fermy. "Why would that pillar be the end of days?"

The old tube interjected into their minds with a polite, chiming voice.

'Your friend there may be correct. That pillar was a totem of great power; it is why we made it home to the Focus so many darknesses ago. It was here before our people came; the details are all within the Cartulary, our history from way before. I would recall it, but I cannot link to the Cartulary at this moment.'

"Why not?" asked Jimmy.

'Because I am disconnected from the Focus at the moment; it

happens with great age amongst my people. We lose connection; it comes and goes. It is the reason why I did not succumb to whatever the thieves did to the Focus when they took it; I was not connected to it. As part of our ageing, when we disconnect from the Focus, we eventually lose access to the Cartulary as well. It is peace in our end days, not having to maintain and manage the Cartulary. We earn the privilege over many years.'

"So there may be more of you advanced ones not affected by what happened to the Focus?" asked Fermy.

'Yes. And I have spent a long time searching here for them. But as you see,' he gestured at his missing leg. *'Being able to travel long distances is a problem for me. I cannot go where I once did. Without access, it is difficult to travel long distances.'*

Fermy nodded in understanding. "Perhaps you would tell us more of what happened then? Then Timothy can enlighten us as to why he thinks this is an omen of the end of days for us."

Timothy's sobs were diminishing now, and he nodded. "Yes, it would make sense to see if my theory is appropriate or not. Let us hear the tale, and then I will tell you what I believe."

The old tube stared off into the distance for a few seconds, gathering his thoughts. Then he began.

'When the lost, the missing, and the unwanted arrive here, they arrive within the area of the great pillar; this has always been so. The pillar is the beacon that draws them here from the other realms, and it is a constant stream, bathed in the light of the Focus. The area is a cavernous space, carved entirely into the land around the pillar, into which the items may arrive, safe and unbroken, for our cataloguing. Our role in the scheme of things is to place the items within the Cartulary, and they are saved. We do not know for what purpose, other than it just is and always has been. It is our responsibility to archive these materials for the good of those to come.

You may think, 'how do they do this?' Our people are tasked with removing these items from this realm to the Cartulary, which we do in our own manner. Our maker designed us to do this with this form; the power of the Focus flows through us, through our very bodies.'

The old tube bent forwards to show the hollow running through his body to the friends. The other tubes mimicked his bow, all of them showing the clean hole through their bodies from the top of their heads to the bottom.

"Who was your maker?" asked Fermy

'We know not, although we have searched the Cartulary for our history of this. We also have scholars who search for the clues to how we came to be here, performing this endless task.'

"So, how does the archiving work?" asked Timothy.

'May we show you a demonstration?' chimed the old tube.

"We've already seen one," said Jack quickly, thinking back to the damage Roly had done to the lounge.

'But only by a fledgeling, who is unskilled in our arts?' chimed the old tube. Jack shrugged.

"I guess so. Roly helped us to clear up, and it wasn't great," he said, looking at the little tube. "Was it? No offence."

'I'm over here,' came Roly's chiming voice, and Jack spun around.

"I'm really sorry, Roly, I thought that..."

'It is of no matter. I am aware that our uniqueness is inside, not on the outside,' chimed Roly, with a little bow. *'But the old father is right. Would you care to see a proper demonstration of our powers?'*

"Yes, please," said Jack, echoed by Jimmy and the others.

The tubes gathered together in a large circle and closed their eyes. A low hum started from the little group, which grew in intensity. The insides of all the tubes glowed the same bright blue, but this time no whirlwind appeared. They directed their lights into the centre of the circle, and as the light grew brighter, there was no swirling wind this time. As the light grew brighter still, the others shaded their eyes. And then, like a lamp switching off, the light winked out. In the centre of the circle was a huge hole, about a metre across, looking like a well but missing the rope and bucket. The others hurried over to the tubes and peered into the hole. They couldn't see the bottom of it.

"So, all of this earth and matter has been sent to the Cartulary?" asked Timothy. The old tube nodded his affirmation.

'Please, stand back now. We will retrieve what was removed; to leave such a hole would not be safe,' he said, gesturing for the others to move back. They did as he bid.

The tubes started humming again, but this time, there was just a bright spark of light, and the hole was gone. Fermy stepped through the ring and stamped on the ground.

"Amazing," he said. "Like it was never gone."

'Yes,' chimed the old tube. *'When we retrieve items, it is like they had never left. Such is the power of the Cartulary, as it works through our people when we stand together.'*

"But I don't understand," said Timothy. "You aren't connected to the Focus any longer, as it has been stolen. How are you able to perform these tasks still?"

'We are still one with the Cartulary,' replied the old tube. *'But with the Focus missing, we no longer function as one. We are individuals now and not together. Whatever the thieves did to the Focus has placed my people in this torpor. People were taken, for what purpose I know not. And things that are lost are no longer coming to our realm for archiving. So we lack purpose.'*

"I think that your people have been taken and put to wicked uses," said Fermy, with a thoughtful expression on his face. "Although I am still trying to determine what that purpose may be for. Tell us how the Focus was stolen from you and about your missing people."

The old tube gave his strange little bow and continued with his story.

'Our lives here in this realm are ones of order, and we perform our tasks as we have done for many darkness's. Things come here; we archive them. The only break in our routine is at the time of the Dark-

ness, which happens rarely. This is a time of great celebration, as we mark our time together, and archiving is stopped through the period in which all is dark. It has been this way for time immemorial. But some time ago, something strange happened.'

The tube closed his eyes, and the others felt a brief hum in their heads. He continued.

'My apologies; I had to take some energy. Our nourishment comes from the realm itself and the Cartulary. The strange situation was that a tall man came to the Focus area, although this alone is not unusual. We receive many lost strangers here from all the realms; Faeries, Men, and others besides whom you may not know of. However, when they arrive here, they are comatose; they do not speak or react to us. We will normally return them to their realm, or in extraordinary circumstances, bless them with safety in the Cartulary. This man, though, was different. He did not appear like the others. This man climbed through a door in a receptacle box, one in which we find garments.'

"A wardrobe?" asked Jimmy

'I know not the name, but it is a box. The man climbed out of it and was perfectly mobile, like you are here today. He was not like the others we have received here. Of course, the people who were archiving that day were shocked. We have never had anyone come here and be able to talk to us. The people fled in fear of this man.'

"Did you see him?" asked Fermy.

'I did not,' chimed the old tube. *'Not that first time. This part of the story is hearsay, rumours from my friends, but they had no reason to tell me falsehoods on this matter. My understanding is that the stranger was met by a delegation of scholars who came to see this curiosity for themselves. He stated that he was an ambassador from another realm and claimed to know why the lost and unwanted items came here. The purpose of his visit was to learn more about how to restore these items to their rightful owners. He also claimed to have travelled to our realm by learning of a unique key that allowed him to travel here.*

The scholars, of course, were in rapture. They have never been able to discuss with others from another realm; we knew of them, of course; we had to, given our role in things. But we have never travelled to see for ourselves. We have never had a requirement to do so. We are needed here. Therefore, to have a visitor from another place was of great importance to us.

A period of celebration was declared, and the scholars held great discussions with the stranger. They agreed not to archive the box, the wardrobe as you call it so that the stranger and others like him could return to our realm for talks whenever they so choose. The stranger was most insistent on that; he must have a door available to return to us. He promised many things, friendship, knowledge, and help to the scholars with their historical studies. The stranger was very knowledgeable about travel between the realms; they discussed it many times during his visits, which were often. He was hungry for knowledge about the Focus; the scholars showed it to him, our most sacred object, when he had earned their trust. Each time, the scholars allowed the people to be privy to the conversations that were had so that our understanding of our place in things could be better understood. And we all came to know Dr Cracklock, as he was called, very well.'

The others froze.

"Dr Cracklock, did you say?" said Elsie, staring at Fermy.

'Yes; that was what he called himself,' chimed the old tube.

"Malchiah," said Elsie softly.

'Do you know the thief?' chimed the tube, interested now.

"Yes, but he is no friend of ours. If he took the Focus, then we may be able to help you get it back. Can you describe it?"

'It is a wonderous thing,' chimed the old tube and was echoed by the other tubes in their heads. *'It is no bigger than my face, yet the power it contains is beyond reasoning.'*

"I understand. Can you describe its appearance?"

'Its appearance is of a bright light, pure.'

"Is it blue, the same colour as your eyes?" interrupted Sammy.

'Yes, for it is of the same essence as ourselves,' responded the old tube.

Sammy looked at Elsie, who nodded. The pendant.

Elsie looked down at the gathered tubes. "We know who has the Focus and where it is. We will be able to help you retrieve it, I think, although it will not be an easy task."

The tubes erupted, all babbling for attention in their heads, speaking in both their language and in words that they could understand. But it was all fragmented, as they talked over each other, and the others couldn't make sense of it. It was starting to get painful, and Jack had his hands clasped over his ears, his eyes screwed shut. Dorcas noticed and hollered. *"Quiets! You is hurtings us!"*

The tubes stopped in an instant, their eyes flicking to the old tube. He held up his stick-like arms in supplication and chimed in a much less sharp tone, *'Our apologies, but this is wonderful news for our people; the Focus has been missing for a long time now, and the people gone. With its return, we may be able to restore them and our lives.'*

"How?" asked Jimmy. "I mean, can the Focus do what Jack has been doing, with his blood? Can it call them back from the Cartulary thingy?"

'That, I do not know,' chimed back the old tube. *'This is a new circumstance to us, unprecedented. But the Focus is what binds us together. I believe that if the young gentleman there...'* he gestured at Jack. *'...would be willing to spare a little more of his essence for the Focus, we could wake up all the people at once. The Focus was presumably enchanted to place them into torpor; I believe that removing this curse would wake them again. And the boy is special, as we have seen.'*

"I wonder why that it is that only Jack's blood works," mused Timothy. "There must be something about it, something that sets it apart from others."

"I'd be willing to try if we can get it back," said Jack. "If I can help, then I will."

The old tube gave his funny little bow in Jack's direction, and the other tubes followed suit, mimicking the action.

"Can you please continue with what happened with Dr Cracklock?" replied Fermy, a dark look in his eyes. "We need to know everything; it may all be of help in formulating a plan to get the Focus back."

The tube bowed again and continued.

'On the last occasion, Dr Cracklock came with others. This time, I did witness his arrival; I was working within the area of the Focus, teaching the foundlings. He came through the door, and this time, he had others with him. Men larger than him, but not the same; bestial in appearance and carrying large containers on their shoulders and strange hose-like items. Apart from one, another younger man, like himself. This man was strange; he did not seem to have any awe of being in a new place. He giggled like a child in a high-pitched way as he followed the elder Dr Cracklock and even kicked one of the workers out of his way. Dr Cracklock did not acknowledge the people like he usually did, nor did he request to see the scholars. Instead, he led these others, in silence, straight to the chamber that housed the Focus. Those who are appointed attend the Focus at all times, but Dr Cracklock simply used enchantments on them, blasting them away to gain entry. His men took up position around the entrance to the Focus room at the great pillar base.

The scholars came to the scene straight away; they had been roused by the archiving disruption and had hurried to determine the cause. When they saw what was happening, they tried to gain entry and were repulsed violently by the men using the tube-like weapons that spouted fire. I saw it all. And when they tried to meet force with force, they were again repelled; our abilities are limited to the archiving, and I saw several scholars try to archive these men to remove them. To no effect, flames from their weapons destroyed them. The men could not be removed, and our people have never been threatened in this manner. We had no idea how to get into the Focus room; even en masse, we would not have stood a chance.

I know not what happened within that room of the Focus, but I do know that the people around me started to fall down. Darkness spread across them as they did so so that they became as you see here, left where they had fallen. My pupils, oh, my dear pupils, collapsed around me, clattering to the ground and turning dark. And the brutish men stood laughing as my people fell. Eventually, when all was still, Dr Cracklock came out of the Focus room with the younger man, carrying the Focus itself. Its light was diminished now, pale, and he carried it carefully in both hands. He glanced around at my fallen people and then nodded to the younger man, who produced a sack, and started to fill it, generous handfuls of my kin. This I could not take and stepped forwards to do whatever I could. I tried to speak, but Dr Cracklock simply looked at me and cast his enchantment. I was sent high into the air, to fall into the objects within the Focus pit, my leg snapping as I landed. Despite the tremendous pain, I pulled myself up through the objects to see Dr Cracklock gesturing to his men, who entered the Focus room themselves.

The younger man caught my movement in the corner of his eye, and he stopped gathering my people up. He came and stood over me, laughing at my misfortune. I will never forget what he said as he shook that sack containing my people, my friends, at me.'

"What?" said Jack, in hushed tones; all of them now entranced with the story.

A bright blue bead trickled from the old tube's left eye, and he wiped it away.

'He said, 'Enjoy the fireworks, little stick.' And with that, he was gone, bounding away over the forgotten items to the door in the box. I watched as the others came away from the Focus room and joined him. The door shut, and they were gone. With my people and the Focus.

But the horror didn't stop there. As I lay there, not comprehending what he meant by fireworks, there came a dull boom. Then the winds came; massive winds, flowing over me from the Focus room's direction, at the base of the pillar. I sought what shelter I could in the objects as the wind's speed and strength increased, howling it was, and all flowing towards the pillar and the Focus Room. There was another sound so loud it tore at my very being, and a huge bang. The world went white for me then.'

The others all stood, staring at the old tube, aghast.

'When I opened my eyes again, I saw the great pillar, as I have every single day of my life. But something was not well with it, and at first, I could not place it. It towered into our skies, as it has always done. Then it struck me; it was not straight! It was falling, moving slowly as it started to lean more and more as I watched it. It tilted slowly over, and then, with a rending that shook the whole of the Focus pit, it collapsed. The noise, my goodness, the noise as it crashed down onto the ground, shaking the earth as far as I could see. At this point, I closed my eyes and slipped away. I could not take it anymore.'

The old tube had a faraway look in his pale blue eyes as he relived that terrible day. The other tubes also stood, their brighter eyes weeping tiny beads of blue light, as they understood what had happened to them, to their people, and their realm while they had lain in torpor.

The strange whooshing noise filled the friend's heads again as the tubes conversed in their language, their grief evident, even though the words were not understood. The friends listened as they consoled each other, grim looks on their faces at what Malchiah and his cronies had done to these people, who had caused no harm to anyone.

When they finally grew silent, Fermy laid his hand on the old tube, careful not to overbalance him. He said gently. "And ever since this time, you have been here, alone, unable to help your people. How did you manage?"

The old tube's eyes narrowed. *'I wish I had been left alone, but it was not to be. That young man has been back here several times since that fateful day, each time to gather more of my people to take back to goodness knows where. I have tried to hide as many as I could from near the point he comes from, that damn box, but he just goes elsewhere and gathers them. I have tried to destroy the box, but it is impossible for me without the full connection to the Cartulary and enfeebled as I am. So he comes back and takes whatever he wants, and I am powerless to stop him. Of Dr Cracklock, I have seen no sign.'*

"How awful. How bloody awful for you," said Elsie, dabbing at her own eyes with a patterned handkerchief she had pulled from her sleeve. "Well, that can stop right now. We can destroy this wardrobe and anything else with a door, assuming that you can get us back to our realm?"

Roly, who had been quiet all this time, chimed slowly, *'I'm not sure that we can. I can return to this realm, but I don't know how to open the door to your realm. I was hoping that my people would know; that was my plan.'* He looked around at the other tubes, each of which echoed. *'I'm sorry,'* in the heads of the friends.

"Can't you travel back to Faery at will?" said Jimmy to the Fae. "Like you can from our realm?"

"Good point!" said Fermy. "Although if we try it, we aren't going to be able to get back here easily."

"Can't you at least try?" asked Jack.

"I will's do it," said Dorcas. She stepped apart from the others, close her eyes, and concentrated. Nothing happened. She screwed her eyes shut tighter, a grimace on her face, and tried again. Still nothing.

"Not's working," she said, opening her eyes and staring at the others.

"One thing at a time," said Fermy. "If there is a door, we can see if our travel glyphs work from here; I can see no reason why not if it worked for them. If they don't, then we worry. We will work out how to stop them from coming back here if we can leave."

He turned to the old tube and said, "Thank you for sharing your story with us, old father. I can see that it gave you great distress, but now that we understand the evil that those thieves did to your people, we will see what we can do to put this right. Starting with the Focus."

The old tube bowed again and then furrowed his eyes. He looked at Fermy and chimed, *'There was one more thing needed to complete my story. There was another who came.'*

"Another?" the friends said in unison.

The old tube looked surprised at their shock. He continued quickly. *'Yes, another. A man, he came via the same door, sometime after the great pillar fell, maybe two or three darkness's ago. He was different from the others.'*

"How?" said Timothy and Fermy together.

'He was respectful and seemed shocked and horrified by what he saw when he arrived. I was hiding at that time; I always hid when they came through the door after what they had done. I was fearful then; not so much now.'

"What happened?" said Fermy.

'The man was gentle and respectful; he did not step on anything that was on the ground. He slowly explored the area and paid great attention to the fallen pillar, examining it for a long time. He then followed the beaten pathway to what has been the Focus room. I followed him as fast as I could hobble.

I peeked around the Focus room door, and the man was examining the altar, where the Focus once lay. He was shaking his head in anguish, and I could hear him saying words like 'No' and 'those mad fools.' He was scribbling in a small item he held in his hand; he left part of it tucked into the altar.'

"What?" said Timothy and Fermy together again. "He left a note? Can we see it?"

'Of course,' chimed the old tube. 'I did look at it, but the markings meant nothing to me; I do not read your language. I hid it away in that room, lest those others find it.'

"Can you take us to it? Now?" said Fermy eagerly. The old tube nodded his assent.

"Old father," said Sammy quietly, "Can you describe this man to us?"

The old tube thought for a moment and then chimed, *'He was tall, of course, but you are all tall to my people. He had dark hair and wore glass over his eyes. I cannot tell you much more.'*

Elsie rummaged in her handbag and produced her purse. She opened it, rifled, and pulled out an old photograph, creased with age and wear from being in the purse. She bent down and showed it to the old tube.

"Is that the man you saw?" she said, tapping the photo of David and Sammy together on their wedding day, a beaming Elsie between them.

'Why, yes. That is the man. You know him well, I think; you seem very happy in this picture. We have seen such pictures before, and there are many in the Cartulary,' chimed the old tube.

Sammy looked at Jack, her eyes shining.

"Your dad was here, Jack. David was here. He left a note! And he's not trapped in this Cartulary thing."

"Please take us there. Right now," said Jack to the old tube, who nodded.

CHAPTER 5

The room that had housed the Focus was built into a hollow under what had been the great pillar. As a result, it was now open to the elements, but there appeared to be no rain in this realm, so it was dry and dusty. The altar of the Focus was a simple mound of earth, packed solid through years of use, so it was more stone-like than the earth of which it was composed. Its brown surface gleamed in the light as if polished. On closer examination, the many tiny hands who had attended it over the years had smoothed it. A simple circular indentation, empty now, showed where the Focus had once been carefully placed. The hole's rim was strangely darkened as if bathing in the light of the Focus had scorched it.

The old tube led the way across the room, hopping on his stick as he went. The others followed in a small group, the newly awakened tubes following up the rear. The old tube hobbled over to a pile of fallen rubble and grubbed around in it before pulling out a piece of dirty paper. He handed it to Fermy as the others gathered around eagerly. Fermy smoothed it down to remove the gathered dust and began to read.

"Timothy. If you are reading this before we have spoken, I am missing, and you have discovered the travel glyph for this realm that I hid in your library. Examine this fallen edifice. I believe it is a destroyed Realm Pillar and that the Cracklocks are behind this. I intend to travel to what I believe is another Pillar location and see if there is evidence of foul play. Check the Sichuan earthquake's timing in our realm and see if it matches events in Fae. If I am right, we are all in terrible danger, and the Cracklocks must be stopped AT ALL COSTS. Please keep watching my family; if the glamour holds, they will be safe.

Your loyal friend. David."

"He was here!" cried Jack, plucking the note eagerly from Fermy's hands. Sammy slung one arm around him as they read through the note again.

"That's your dad's writing, alright," said Sammy, her face beaming. "He was here, and if he's been here, who's to say where else he could be?" She hugged Jack close, the two of them beside themselves. Then they noticed the silence in the room.

The others were staring at Timothy, who had gone pale again, and was swallowing as if a lump was stuck in his throat. Fermy had also gone pale.

"Whatever does he mean, Timothy?" asked Elsie. "It's terrible what happened here, I know, but why does that mean we are all in danger?"

Timothy tried to answer, but his voice cracked. He slumped down onto the ground in a sitting position and looked up at the others. He closed his eyes, composing himself, and then gestured for the others to sit down with him. When they were settled, he started to speak.

"Realm Pillars are a hobby of David and myself; we have been discussing them for years, typically when we have enjoyed a drop or two of the hard stuff together. It started as curiosity, really; David asked me one day why we had to travel between the realms as we do and did I know what keeps them apart. I had to say that I had no idea. It has always been that way; we can travel between the lifer realm and the Fae realm as we wish, and lifers can also come to Fae if they are invited or able. We can also travel to the Realm of the Departed, but that is always a one-way travel arrangement. The other realms are, well... mostly beyond us, as you know. We knew of older Fae who may have been to other places, but their accounts aren't easily found, nor how they had managed to get there. But the question of what actually separates them? I have to say it intrigued me much the more I thought about it; most of the other scholars I discussed the matter with had given it no thought at all. One put it down to our magical nature, naturally keeping the Fae and lifer realms apart. None, though, really had much of an explanation that satisfied us. And you know David; when he gets the bit between his teeth, nothing stops him from investigating his little projects.

So David and I started looking in the libraries, the old texts mainly, and other scrolls and papers that have been written over time immemorial. And very slowly, from crumbling old records containing old Fae languages we had to translate, we concluded that the realms must be separated by something physical or metaphysical that holds them both together, but apart at the same time. Like the tiers on a celebration cake or the pillars that hold up the floors in a building. I asked the oscillator several times as we refined our research, and each time it confirmed that we were correct. Mostly, anyhow. We named them 'Realm Pillars' for want of anything better."

"So, these things hold the realms apart," said Jimmy. "How many are there? Must be a lot to hold apart worlds!"

"We don't know," replied Timothy. "But, as you say, there must be a lot."

"There are five," said Fermy quietly.

"What? How do you know?" snapped Timothy.

"I can't tell how I know; it is a secrecy matter of the Courts," said Fermy. "But it is known that there are five."

"Well, we could have just asked you," said Timothy crossly. "All that time wasted. Why didn't you say something; we discussed it often enough when you were there."

"Because I was sworn to secrecy as part of my previous role," said Fermy primly. "Believe me, if I could have said something, I would have. But looking at what has happened here, as they say in the Lifer realm, 'all bets are now off.'"

"I'm sorry, but I'm confused about all this," said Sammy. "So, there are five pillars or something that hold the realms apart?"

"No," said Fermy. "There are now four pillars that hold the realms apart if David is correct." He gestured at the fallen wall that stretched off into the distance.

"So, we're okay then?" said Sammy. "I mean, four more pillars are holding the realms apart. Nothing to worry about."

"Until they are all gone," said Timothy, his face pale.

"But what would happen if they are destroyed?" asked Jimmy. "I mean, this one has gone, but there is no noticeable effect, is there? Despite the horrors of what has happened here."

Timothy gave them all a sad smile. "The realms would collapse together, I would think, with nothing to hold them apart. I'm afraid, to coin a phrase from that book that the Cracklocks are so fond of quoting, it would be the 'End of Days?'"

"What?" said Jack.

"The End of Times. Ragnarök, Sermon of the Seven Suns, Judgement Day; take your pick," said Jimmy in a quiet shocked voice. "Dead rising, the end of life. All that apocalyptic stuff."

There was a stunned silence.

"So where are these pillars?" asked Sammy in a quavering voice.

"That's just it. Nobody knows," said Fermy. "Not even the Courts. But apparently, Malchiah found this one, so I am guessing the Cracklocks are familiar with them at least; they wouldn't just destroy something like this for the sake of it. Moreover, I now believe that they must know about the others. Why else would they steal the Focus if it wasn't to further their aims? But I have no idea though about why they are taking the people here unless it will help them somehow. Despite what we know the tubes are used for."

"But why would they try to destroy the pillars?" asked Elsie. "I'm afraid that I still don't get it. It makes no sense."

"What is the one thing that the Cracklocks want, above all else?" said Fermy.

"To destroy the Fae," Elsie replied promptly.

"And they have been waging that war for centuries. What better way to finish off the Fae once and for all than destroying their entire realm? And if it destroys everything else, who cares? The mad, mad fools!" cursed Fermy.

"By destroying everything?" replied Elsie. "They'd be killed along with the rest of us!"

"Remember, their damn religion is everything to them. I expect that they think it will grant them access to Heaven or something. Or they have some other plan to avoid the fallout from this."

"Do you think that this is what David suspected when he went missing?" said Sammy. "He did say that it could be the destruction of Faery."

"I think that he probably had a vague idea, yes, but not the full picture." Fermy shook his head. "I wish he were here now."

"We've got to stop them," said Jack.

"Well then," said Elsie. "Let's do a checklist, shall we?" She held up her hand and started counting off on her fingers. "Find David. Rescue the Focus. Rescue the missing tubes from whatever the Cracklocks are doing with them. Restore them and the rest of the good people here using the Focus. Find the Realm

Pillars, whatever and wherever they are, and stop the Cracklocks from destroying them. Did I miss anything?"

"Travel glyph for this realm," said Timothy. "David said he hid it in my library. I will have to ponder on that one; where would be safe? We scholars routinely swap books and documents..." he lapsed into thought.

"That's the summary," sighed Fermy. "Although where to start? And we will be playing catch up with the Cracklocks on all these things. They are way ahead of us."

"Plus, you do appreciate that I am technically retired and exempt? Saving the world doesn't come under my pension qualification," piped in Elsie, to which everyone laughed, the tension broken.

"Ahem," said Jimmy. "There's a common denominator here, pretty much. Anyone think of that?"

"Malchiah Cracklock," said Jack. "He's the key to most of this."

"So we get hold of Malchiah first, but that won't be easy," mused Fermy.

Sammy and Elsie were looking at each other again. Elsie nodded and spoke up.

"They want Jack badly. And Malchiah, well... he and I have history. I think that I can get him to speak to us. With a little bait."

"*No's!*" shouted Dorcas. "You's is not using my Jack-Jack as baits for those Cracklocks. Absolutely nots."

"Dorcas, it's fine," said Jack. "I'll do what is needed. We cannot let them get away with this, especially if they plan to do it again. They need to be stopped, and I will do what I can."

"Then I's will be with you," said Dorcas. "I's not losing you agains because of those Cracklocks."

"But they'll kill you, Dorcas," said Sammy. "They already tried."

"And how dids that work outs for them?" said Dorcas, defiantly, and slapped the rolling pin into her hand.

"We're all in this together," said Fermy. "Now then, this is what we're going to do..."

~

THE GROUP STOOD in front of the wardrobe in the pit of lost things, Timothy holding a piece of chalk in his hand. He drew the Faery travel glyph on the door, looked at the others, and mouthed 'here goes' before slapping it. The glyph fell from the door in its usual glittery spray, and they all sighed with relief.

"Looks like it works then," said Jack. "We should be able to get home, at least."

"We're not sure of the time difference here," said Timothy. "But we have to work with what we can. I will send word when I return to Fae. To which location?"

"Send it to Jack and Sammy's house if you would. That will be the first stop for us when we get back," said Fermy. Timothy gave a small bow, pulled open the wardrobe door, and smiled at the sight of the green flames flickering.

"Please," he said, holding out his hand to Sammy, who looked around at the others nervously.

"It seems like forever since I've been to Faery," she said.

"You'll be fine," said Elsie. "Stay with Timothy, and find that travel glyph. We need someone who knew David best to help Timothy figure out where the heck David would have hidden it."

Sammy gave Jack a brief hug, nodded to the others and climbed into the wardrobe. Timothy followed her in, pulling the door shut behind him. The others gave it a count to sixty and then yanked open the wardrobe door. The two of them had gone.

"Right then, our turn," said Fermy. "Elsie, if you would do the honours, please?"

Elsie pulled the marker pen from her bag and stepped up to the door. As she was raising the pen, a small voice chimed in their heads.

'I'm coming too.' Roly stepped out of the circle of the other tubes and stood with the others.

'No,' chimed the old tube, also stepping forwards. *'We have need of you here. There is a lot to do.'*

'I wish to assist these friends of ours,' insisted Roly. *'They may need our help with the Focus, and if they cannot find this travel glyph of which they speak, they will need help to return here. I have been to the other realm. You others have not.'*

'But you are a novice and know not the ways of the Cartulary,' chimed the old tube, and then the conversation switched to the strange whispery wind language. The others stood by, waiting for a resolution to what seemed to be an argument. It did not take long.

'Friends,' said the old tube, turning to the little group. *'The one you call Roly here wishes to act as our emissary in this matter. This is against our better judgement, but it is felt that his presence could best serve our contribution. However, he is not equipped to deal with the Cartulary, which is our main strength. Would you still take him with you?'*

"Of course," said Jack and Elsie together. "We'd be happy to have him with us."

'Then, would you allow us a short time to prepare our colleague? There is a ritual that could help; access to the Cartulary would assist you, we believe.'

"How long will it take?" said Fermy. "We need to get back and set our plans in motion. Every moment allows the Cracklocks more time to put their plans into action."

'It is but a short process. For a foundling to have access to and use the Cartulary effectively, it normally requires much time and study. It

makes the user more fluent with the usage and gain more respect for it. But there are ways, old ways, to bring a member of the kin into effective use when this is a requirement. It is bestowed on exceptional members, normally those who can be of use at a time of need. With the recent events, we believe that Roly here would benefit well from the ritual if it assists you with helping our people and making this right.'

Fermy nodded his understanding. "Okay, but please be as fast as you can."

'Fear not,' chimed the old tube. *'This will be fast. Please stand aside.'*

Roly moved away from the friends and stood proud. The other tubes, the old tube amongst them, stood around him in a circle, all bowing towards Roly, their tubes' tops pointing towards him.

'Friends, please cover your eyes. The light is bright, to shine the way for our young friend here,' chimed the old tube. The group did as they were bid and put hands over their faces. The strange whispering language started again in their heads, and a pale blue light started to seep through the gaps in their hands and their eyelids, dim in colour. Jack sneaked a peek through his fingers.

Roly stood in the centre of the circle, the top of his tube glowing with a pale blue brilliance. The other tubes stood around him, their tops wreathed in a brighter blue light, which pulsed as they chanted in their language. Jack watched a pulse of light leave the top of one of the tubes with a whoosh, to be swallowed into the light of Roly's, which grew instantly brighter. Another pulse of light left another of the tubes, and the light grew brighter still. Jack screwed his eyes shut; the light was starting to burn into his retinas.

The whispering in their heads grew louder and louder, and the whooshing sound of the light pulses leaving the tubes and into Roly intensified. It started as a monotone but got faster and faster until it was like a tap dance of whooshes going at speed.

Unlikely as it could be, it sped up again, the sounds like a woodpecker drumming on the branch of a tree, the 'rrrrrrrrrrrrrr' noise filling their ears. The noise became a single loud pulse, and the light was now almost too bright to bear, even through shut eyes and covering hands. The others all turned away from the circle, but the light was still bright as it reflected off the distant fallen realm pillar, dazzling them, despite their efforts to hide from the brightness.

And then it was gone. Blackness, but for residual lights dancing in their eyes as if they'd inadvertently looked at the sun.

"Is it safe?" Jack heard Elsie call out, and the affirmative chimed back into their heads. Jack uncovered his eyes and turned back towards the circle of tubes. They all stood looking at Roly, who stood in the middle of the circle, his eyes shut, tiny fists clenched. Then he opened his eyes, and they all gasped. His bright blue eyes were brighter than before, much brighter, an electric blue, almost radiant. He raised his eyes upwards to the sky, and a mighty shout echoed in their heads. From the top of Roly's tube, a bright blue pillar of light, the circumference of Roly himself, shot up into the sky as Roly screamed his shout through all their minds. His scream echoed off, and the pillar of light winked out of existence.

"Roly," called Jack. "Are you okay?"

'My friend, I...I feel different. Powerful. Like the whole cartulary is at my command. Ask me for something. Anything. Ask me.'

"Eerrm, I don't know," said Jack. "Chocolate bars?"

There was a flash of blue light, and a pile of chocolate bars appeared on the floor next to Roly. *'Yes!'* the tube exclaimed in all their heads.

Jimmy stepped forward, picked up one of the bars, shook his head, and held it up to the others. The brown wrapped bar with the blue writing on a white background was unmistakable.

"Marathon?" said Jack. "Shouldn't that say 'Snickers'? Is it some foreign brand?"

"No,..." said Jimmy with a smile. "These are just a little old, I think; I've seen them online. They stopped being 'Marathon' in the early nineteen nineties, as I recall."

'But they will be fine,' said the old tube. *'The Cartulary places things into torpor at the time of transition. There are no ill effects on those objects that are inanimate. It is the living where the issues lie; the body is in torpor, but the mind can still be awake. This is why we do not place living creatures into the Cartulary for more than a short period. It causes derangement.'*

Jimmy unwrapped one of the Marathons and took a tentative bite. "It's good," he said through a mouthful of chocolate. The others, realising how hungry they all were despite the earlier sandwiches, dived in as well, and they were all soon gorging themselves. When they had finally finished, Fermy wiped his mouth with a smile and looked up at the others.

"We need to go. Elsie, can you please prepare the travel glyph. To Sammy and Jack's house if you would."

Elsie stepped up to the wardrobe door and sketched the glyph onto it before slapping it again. She pulled open the door to see the dancing blue flames. She turned to look at the others and said, "Going to be a squeeze, I think," waved her farewell, and climbed in. The others followed suit, Roly riding on Jimmy's shoulder.

'Good luck,' chimed the voice of the tubes in their heads. *'And if we can help, then please, do not hesitate to ask.'*

Jack nodded and pulled the wardrobe door shut.

SAMMY AND TIMOTHY walked out of the pantry door into the untidy home, and Timothy bustled over to the large clock at the other end of the expanded room to check the time. Sammy stood, mouth open, looking up at the network of pipes and tubes that ran everywhere up to the cavernous ceiling. The high-pitched squeaking of the rodents inside the contraption was very loud.

"Ten thirty-three in the evening," called Timothy. "Now, where did I put that pointer; I need to calculate the time differential...Sammy, I wouldn't look up with your mouth open, my dear."

Sammy turned to Timothy just as a shower of tiny black dots fell from the top of the oscillator and rained down over the area in which she stood. Sammy jumped and started to brush the specks off her shoulders.

"Oh, for goodness sake!" she shouted at Timothy over the noise. *"I see you never solved that disgusting issue. And the oscillator has gotten a lot bigger, from what I can remember."*

"Sorry about the droppings!" shouted back Timothy. *"I haven't figured out a way to make the oscillator clean up after itself as of yet. Believe me; I've tried!"*

'It's still gross in here,' thought Sammy, sweeping more droppings off herself and stepping out from under the gantries and pipework. Timothy came back over to her, fiddling with the pointer as he did so. He was twisting it this way and that, and Sammy was reminded of a Rubik's cube as the little Fae manipulated it at speed.

"Okay. As far as I can tell, the differential between the tube realm and the lifer realm is only a couple of hours. Not that it matters, those tubes seemed to have no concept of time. Let me quickly leave a note for the others. Now, where did I put that paper?"

Sammy watched as Timothy rummaged through a pile of papers on the edge of the kitchen table, brushing off rodent droppings as he did so. Finding a blank page, he glamoured a feather quill out of the air and scribbled on the paper before turning to Sammy.

"Just a moment, please. I see no sense in both of us going; it will be quicker for me to go to the lifer realm without using the travel glyphs. Please wait here and make yourself at home. We will go to the library once I'm back and see what we can find. See if you can come up with any ideas while I'm gone."

Sammy glanced around at the enormous messy room and nodded. She had no plans to make herself anything in here; she had been here more than once and was acutely aware that Timothy's obsession with the rodents made things none too clean. Also, you never knew where the awful things were hiding; they had a habit of jumping out at you whenever you opened a door. Timothy bowed his head, stepped to the left, and vanished.

Sammy wandered over to the centre of the room to what she took to be the new and updated control panel for the oscillator. She smiled and tapped one of the glass tubes, the mice scurrying through it stopping at the noise to look at her with their ink-black eyes, before continuing their journey on whatever business they had within the guts of the machine. She idly flicked a couple of the toggles on the console backwards and forwards, not thinking about what she was doing. Her mind was wandering again, trying to think of book titles that David had talked about. He always had a book next to his bed, but he would read anything. Autobiographies of obscure rock stars, apocalyptic fiction, horror, thrillers, self-help books; the list went on. Nothing specific sprang to mind.

She jumped as Timothy popped back into existence a few feet away from her. He smiled and said. "Everything is okay at your home; nobody there yet, but there is no disturbance. I put the lights on for them and turned on the kettle thingamabob that you use for heating water. I figured that they would want a drink. Oh, excuse me, where are my manners? Would you care for tea?"

Sammy shook her head, looking at the liberal scattering of rodent droppings covering the floor around the oscillator. "I'm fine, thanks, Timothy. We should try to find this note from

David so that we can get back to the others. I feel odd to be away when they are planning to meet that Malchiah; it doesn't seem right."

"Oh, they will be quite safe if Fermy's plan works," said Timothy airily. "But I agree, the sooner we start, the sooner we will be finished. This way, please."

Timothy wended his through the various supporting beams that kept the oscillator's pipework above the floor, skipping neatly over the coiled cables and odd pipes that were everywhere at tripping level. Sammy followed, trying to avoid the occasional shower of tiny black pellets that fell from the machine. When they reached the other side of the room, Timothy stopped in front of a closed door and turned to Sammy.

"I try and keep the rodents out of here; they make such a mess with paper. There's a glamour on the room, so we shouldn't see any in there; I know that you are not a fan of my little friends."

"It's the tails," said Sammy, with a shudder. "Horrible scaly things, all warm and...yuck."

"Actually, the rodent's tail serves as a heat-loss organ," began Timothy. "It can't have any fur, entirely for that purpose. Did you know that the tail comprises only around five per cent of a rodent's surface area, but it can remove approaching twenty per cent of its body heat? Fascinating really, and also, when the body temperature drops..."

"Timothy. The library?" interrupted Sammy, remembering well how Timothy would talk about rats, mice, and Myomancy for hours if you let him.

"Oh, of course; I'm sorry. It's through here."

He opened the door and walked through. Sammy followed him and gasped. The dimly lit library ceiling was much lower than the previous room, but the room itself was easily as long. Stretched out along it into the gloom were bookshelves, crammed with books and papers of all sorts. There were books on the tables (of which there were at least seven that Sammy could see), books on the floor, books piled up along the walls' edges. Scrolls of paper, rolled up and tied with different coloured ribbons and strings, were interspersed between the books. Boxes of books were also stacked everywhere haphazardly.

"Please tell me you have a list of what is in here?" said Sammy.

"Oh, no, I'm afraid that I don't. This collection is my life's work; many many years, I've been collecting articles of all kinds of interest. I pride myself in knowing exactly where each volume is on any of the subject matters I've collected and can easily retrieve them." Here Timothy tapped the side of his head. "The list is right in here; just tell me which book you think it is, and I will fetch it."

Sammy looked at Timothy in exasperation. "How am I supposed to do that when I have no idea what books you have in here?" she said. "It could be anything; David would read whatever he could find. He had no favourites as far as I knew."

"But it must be something obvious," replied Timothy. "He's been in this library many times. He knows about how many books are in here; actually, he was pretty good himself at retrieving what he needed without my help."

"Well, I have no idea where we should start. What about books on realm pillars?" said Sammy.

"I would think that's a little obvious," said Timothy. "But why not? Every journey and first steps, as they say. Down this way, please."

Timothy glamoured a small floating light into existence, which hovered over their heads, cutting through the dimness of the library. He set off at a fast pace, twisting and turning between the overflowing racks as he did so. He finally stopped in front of one overloaded bookshelf that looked no different from the others and smiled at Sammy.

"Here they are; top three shelves. I normally have a little ladder to help me reach those, but with you here, if you can get the top two, I can reach the third one."

"What are we looking for? Will he have written in the books, or will it be a note or something."

"Oh, I would think a note. David would never dare to despoil any of my books. He is very considerate in that respect. Anyhow, most of these books are transcripts, some of which he wrote himself. So we will need to check carefully."

Sammy pulled a thick leather-bound volume from the top shelf, opened it up, and gave it a shake to see what fell out. Several pieces of thick parchment fell out and scattered across the floor.

"Please be careful," admonished Timothy. "Some of these books are extremely old; they were written well before I became into being."

"I don't think we have time to go carefully through each book," said Sammy, through gritted teeth, as she stooped to pick up the papers from the floor. A quick look through them showed them to be covered in an illegible scrawl and nothing like David's handwriting. While Timothy wasn't looking, she stuffed them back into the book and put it back on the shelf.

The two of them worked their way through all of the realm pillar books that Timothy held and then moved onto the scrolls on the same subject. There was no note that they could see, although Sammy did see David's writing on some of the scrolls, where he had carefully copied notes from goodness knows where. Her heart hitched a little at the sight of the familiar handwriting, and she realised again quite how much she missed him.

"Well," said Timothy, rolling up the final scroll and tying it neatly with a piece of string. "That's all on that subject. What do you think is next?"

Sammy blew her hair out of her face, noticing that a fair amount of dust went with it. "What subjects was he interested in when he studied with you? Perhaps we should look at those next?"

"There were many," replied Timothy. "Perhaps we can look at the poetry of the Fae? That was one of the later interests he was studying. It's an obscure medium, but I have some books on the subject."

"Whatever you think," said Sammy. "Lead on."

JACK, Jimmy, Elsie, Dorcas, Fermy, and Roly stepped out of the lounge at Jack's house, shutting the door on the blues flames behind them. Elsie looked at them and said. "I'll call Malchiah as agreed; set it up to meet him somewhere public. I think that the shopping centre here in town will be fine."

"Who's for tea's?" said Dorcas, going over to the kettle, where she stiffened when she put her hand on it. "This is still warms. Somebody has beens here," she said, groping for the rolling pin.

"It's fine," called Jack from the lounge. "There's a note from Timothy. He thinks that there is only a couple of hours' time difference between here and the tube's realm. Although he apologises, as he has had to calculate the time difference between here and there by extrapolation from the time in Faery."

"Typical Timothy," smiled Fermy. "Let's hope that they find that travel glyph; we can't rely on Roly to take us back each time; he may not always be here." The tube bowed in acknowledgement.

Elsie came through to the lounge, carrying what looked like a black plastic house brick and her battered address book.

Noticing Jack and Jimmy's look of horror, she stared at them and said. "Whatever is the matter?"

"Is that your mobile?" asked Jimmy, his face agog.

"Yes, it is. I've had it for a while now; very reliable and holds its charge very well."

"But it belongs in a museum," said Jimmy with a cheeky smile.

"Like me, I suppose?" said Elsie, swatting at Jimmy with the address book, a smile on her face. "It's fine; I can make a telephone call on it whenever I choose, and it costs next to nothing for me to run. Now quiet, please. I am going to arrange for us to meet Malchiah somewhere where there are lots of people." She started paging through the address book, looking for the number that she needed.

At the top of the stairs, shrouded in the darkness of the unlit landing, Tyler LaFey was leaning over as far as he dared to listen to the conversation. The twins had been hiding, if you could call it that, in the tiny bathroom which they'd dodged into as soon as they'd heard voices. The party downstairs must have come in through the back door, as the two of them had been observing the front door, ready to dart into hiding as soon as someone came in.

As Tyler listed, he noted that the conversation was certainly a strange one; it was one-sided by some of the participants as if someone was answering out of earshot. He could make out three separate people, certainly. An old lady, her quaverous tones carrying a cheeky note to them, Crackley and...Owen. Tyler bristled with anger as he remembered the earlier strange humiliation at the hands of that little worm, as well as a touch of fear; the situation had been odd all day since meeting that strange woman, and he didn't like it. But the sound of Jimmy's voice, happy and with his friends, made him angry. He was going to get it, even if it was the last thing that he did.

Moving backwards from the top of the stairs, he waved Mason back into the bigger of the two bedrooms and quietly closed the door. He nodded to his twin, pulled out the stolen mobile, and called the mad woman.

"They're here," he whispered as she answered.

"At the house?" Anastasia replied.

"Yes. Just got back now."

"Good," she replied and hung up.

Mason grunted, and Tyler nodded again. "See if we can get in that wardrobe. Once her Uncle gets here, we get out; see if we can lend a hand. I want that Owen kid to ourselves if possible; I'm gonna ask."

Mason grinned, his yellow teeth showing.

ELSIE DIALLED the number on the card that Malchiah had left at the hospital, squinting slightly at the small text on the card as she carefully punched in the numbers. The other they'd dumped in the bin of Elsie's hospital room; Sammy wanted nothing that that man had offered. She then held her hand up to the others to make them shush as she waited for the call to connect.

The number rang a few times, and then Malchiah's rich voice answered.

"Yes?"

"Malchiah. It's Elsie. I apologise for earlier; it was rude of me when you had made an effort to attend to me in hospital."

"Aaah, Elsie, Elsie, Elsie. Yes, you were rather rude, as was the wife of that dratted David. I simply wanted to enquire after your health and for you to hear my very reasonable offer. So, yes, you were rather terse with me. So, to what do I owe the pleasure of this call now?"

Elsie swallowed and said. "I've discussed what you wanted with Jack and Sammy; things were a little emotional at the hospital due to the shock of what happened to us. I felt that Jack should have the opportunity to speak to you himself; he's such a responsible young man, and I know that you don't represent your niece and her actions."

"That is true," crooned Malchiah. "My niece was a little overzealous in her dealings with you. I can assure you that such a discourtesy would not happen again."

"That is what I presumed. If it suited you, Jack would like to meet you to hear what you require of him. We would propose tomorrow, at the shopping centre in town. There is a coffee shop on the upper mezzanine. We can meet you there if you are willing?"

"The matter is rather pressing, Elsie. I would prefer it if we can discuss it this evening, despite the lateness of the hour. I would be happy to call on you at the hospital or the home of Jack and Sammy, of course?"

"We aren't at either of those places," said Elsie, keeping her nerve. "After this evening's 'happenings,' we have decided to stay at a small hotel; that way, we avoid having to tidy up tonight while we're tired. I was discharged but didn't fancy travelling overly much; it does so take it out of me nowadays, my age and all."

"Nonsense, you are as fit as a fiddle, my dear friend. I would be delighted to attend the hotel instead; where are you?"

"Not tonight, Malchiah, please. Tomorrow will be fine; Jack is already asleep. Will you come?"

"Yes, I will. Noon at the coffee house you mentioned; I will see you there." With that, Malchiah hung up his end.

"What did he say?" asked Fermy.

Elsie drummed her fingers on the table. "He will meet with us. But something's not right; he was too amenable to the whole situation."

"Perhaps we should go and find a hotel for the evening?" said Jack, a worried tone in his voice. "We need some rest, and we don't want to be caught unawares."

"I agree," said Fermy. "Get some things, and we can go. Jimmy, could you please call a cab if you would."

Taking the phone from Jack's outstretched hand, Jimmy started to say, "Sure thing; I think that we can go to the Draeburn Hotel; they always have..."

He was interrupted by a sudden loud bang from above. Jack dashed to the hall and flicked on the overhead lights, catching a glimpse of movement upstairs. A loud banging on the front door began, as well as the repeated pressing of the doorbell.

Dorcas twitched the curtain to one side and took a quick peep.

"Mens; lots of mens, and there is some Redcaps as wells," she said, pulling the curtain gap shut.

"Elsie, a travel glyph, quickly," said Fermy, cracking his knuckles and preparing to use whatever glamours were needed.

"No time. Out the back, quickly," hissed Jimmy, pushing past Jack and making for the kitchen. He stopped in shock when he saw the twins' prominent figures appear at the top of the stairs.

"Going somewhere, Owen?" said Tyler, a smirk on his face. "Go on then; answer the door. It is rude to keep visitors waiting. No manners, you, none at all."

They dashed past the stairs, and Jack pulled open the back door. A well-dressed man stood there, a bright blue pendant visible on his chest, and a group of others standing menacingly behind him. He smiled at Jack and Jimmy and raised his hat in greeting.

"Hello, gentlemen. Which one of you is Master Jack Cracklock?" asked Malchiah.

CHAPTER 6

"Oh, for goodness sake," said Sammy, slamming another set of books back onto the shelves in exasperation. "This is ridiculous. We are never going to find that message in here, with no other clues. What the heck was David thinking?"

Timothy carefully placed his own book back onto the shelf and rubbed his hands together. "Yes, I am afraid that I must agree. There was nothing in 'The Mating Habits of Gnomes', 'Domestic Glamours', 'Ancient Buildings', 'Ancient Building Techniques', 'Fae Couture', 'Legends of Lifers', or the Court's findings and readings. There are a few more subjects I can suggest?"

"My husband has weird reading habits, I know that, but as to where he would have hidden a clue for you to find, *I just don't know*!" Sammy screamed her frustration in the last few words and lashed out at a pile of boxes that were within reach of her foot. The wooden side of the box shattered inwards, and a slew of books skated out onto the floor.

"And now look. More books," she spat, stooping down and gathering them up. She handed them over to Timothy without looking at them and ran her hands through her hair in frustration.

Timothy sorted through the five or six books that Sammy had given him and gave a small chuckle as he did so. "How did you get mixed up in here?" he muttered to himself.

"What?" snapped Sammy as she scanned the shelves again. "Did you mistakenly file flower fairies in with goblins or something?"

"Oh no, no," said Timothy, ignorant of Sammy's sarcasm. "This book, here."

Sammy turned around and saw the brightly illustrated cover of a thin book. Moving closer, she snatched it out of Timothy's hands. She studied the colourful picture under the legend 'The Very Hungry Caterpillar'.

"Timothy, this is a children's book. How did it end up here?" she asked.

"I suspect that Jack probably hid it. He was always crawling away here in the library while David was distracted."

"Jack was in this library?" Sammy shot back, startled.

"Oh, yes, many times. David used to bring him here on days out. He used to make a terrible mess, quite distracting really, pulling books off shelves and things, but nothing that a simple tidying glamour couldn't fix. He loved it here, with all the things to get into mischief with."

"There's nothing dangerous in here, is there?"

"Of course not. Jack couldn't read at the time, and all the heavy books were well out of his reach."

"Well, that's a relief. He loved the library back home as well; we used to go there as a morning out. So much for him to look at, and he loved taking the books back home." Sammy smiled at the memory.

"Well then," said Timothy, taking the book back from Sammy. "Whilst I strongly suspect that Jack will not want this anymore, let's go and put it in the correct place, shall we?"

"What do you mean?" said Sammy.

"Jack's bookshelf. He had his own shelf for his little books. He used to go straight to it as well, scuttling along in his little crawl. Very fast, I always used to say to David."

"Do you mean to tell me that there is a shelf of children's books, belonging to Jack, hidden somewhere in the depths of this library?" said Sammy, the colour rising again in her cheeks.

"I didn't think it would be relevant. We are looking for a message from David; it stands to reason that he would have put..."

Sammy interrupted him. "Timothy, you may be one of the cleverest Fae I know, but you know bugger all about how us lifers think. We've spent hours going through these damned dusty obscure books, and now you tell me that there is a collection of Jack's books, here? And you didn't think to mention that? That's where the message will be; I'm sure of it. Show me this bookshelf. Now."

Sammy's palpable anger cowed timothy, and he gave a slight bow. "This way, please."

He led them towards the top of the library, near the door that they came in through. And there, on the bottom shelf of the stack nearest the wall, was a large selection of children's books. Sammy felt a lump in her throat as she looked at the collection, for the part of Jack's childhood that he had lost. She'd done her best, of course, but she couldn't help thinking that if things had been different, Jack would have had so much more. She felt a tear roll down her cheek.

Timothy patted her leg gently. "There, there, my dear. We all wish things could have taken a different course," he said, intuitively guessing the reason for Sammy's sadness. "But we are putting it right now, aren't we?"

"I hope so. I can't help thinking that he's in so much danger, though."

"Then," said Timothy gently. "Let's find this message and get back to him and the others. Strength in numbers."

Sammy swallowed again and nodded. "At least there's not too many to go through. I think that if we start at this end and..." She tailed off, her eyes fixed on a row of the books.

"I know which one it is," she said and pointed at a long row of thin white books, all of them numbered. They were out of number order, but it didn't matter. "Mr Men. By Roger Hargreaves." She sobbed again and started scanning them.

"Which one is it?" asked Timothy.

"This one," said Sammy, and she pulled a book from the row. She held it by the cover and shook it. A folded piece of paper fell out and fluttered to the floor.

"How did you know?" asked Timothy in amazement.

Sammy turned the book over and showed Timothy the title. A little orange man with glasses and a green hat started up at them.

"Mr Clever," Sammy explained. "He was Jack's favourite. He used to point at the cover and say, 'Timotee.' He thought it was you."

Timothy blushed as he looked at the book and gave a little swallow of his own. "Well, I never... I knew he liked me; he always had a big smile for me, but I had no idea quite how much."

The two stared at the book, the note entirely forgotten for the moment.

"JACK, GET BACK!" shouted Fermy, dashing into the kitchen, his hands glowing. He dodged between Jack's legs and hurled a glamour up at Malchiah. The bright red offensive glamour fizzed through the air towards his head, sparks dancing in the air and then changed direction to strike the blue gem pendant in the centre of Malchiah's chest. The gem winked once, a bright blue, and the glamour faded out.

"Ah, ah, ah, Fermerillion," said Malchiah, wagging one upraised finger. "That is no way to treat a visitor."

Fermy stood gaping at the ease in which his glamour had been negated. He raised his hands again, but lightning-quick, Malchiah's hands reached out, and a fine silvery net landed on the little Feeorin. Fermy screamed in pain as the net sprang shut tightly, encasing him in its mesh. He fell to the floor and started twitching like he was having a fit, shaking and shuddering as his eyes rolled back into his head.

There was a blur to Jack and Jimmy's left as Dorcas charged, the rolling pin held high above her head as she dashed at Malchiah. Dorcas was fast for her size, but Malchiah moved effortlessly to the side as the pin came down. The pin hit the floor where he had just been with a dull thunk, and Malchiah's foot stamped down on it, trapping it in place. Dorcas let go and aimed a massive swinging uppercut at Malchiah's groin, but again, seemingly without moving, he wasn't there when the blow would have landed. Another net sailed over Dorcas, snapping shut, and she reacted to it exactly like Fermy. She keeled over and started to twitch on the floor. Malchiah gave a little laugh and expertly flicked the rolling pin up off the floor with his foot. Catching it, he tucked it inside his overcoat.

"Stop it! You're killing them!" screamed Jack, dashing at Malchiah himself, his fists raised, anger surging through him. He threw a punch that the older gentleman neatly dodged and followed up by cuffing Jack so hard on the ear that he saw stars.

"Stand down, boy," he snarled. "I am not here for violence."

Jack shook his head to clear it as Jimmy got between him and Malchiah. "*Stop, stop, stop*!" he screamed at the top of his voice.

"Yes, stop it. Right now," said Elsie as she marched into the kitchen. "Malchiah, what the grock do you think you are doing here? This isn't right."

"Following up on our little call, a courtesy to you at this later hour. And for thanks, I'm attacked by your pet devils and this little thug here," said Malchiah, gesturing at Jack, who was being restrained by Jimmy and still lunging at him. Outside, the collection of goons were guffawing at the spectacle they had just witnessed.

Elsie looked down at her Fae friends, bound and helpless, and then back up at Malchiah.

"Let them out. You're hurting them."

"Pah," snorted Malchiah. "A mere lightning glamour net with just a touch of iron. They will be fine, and I am happier where they are. Fermerillion has had far worse in the past. The brownie, not so sure, but she looks tough enough."

"I mean it, Malchiah. Let them go," said Elsie, her eyes narrowing.

"Oh, please. What are you going to do? You need to appreciate the gravity of your situation Elsie. I do not like to be lied to, and I do not like to be attacked without provocation. The devils stay as they are. The quicker we conclude this sorry business, the quicker they will be released from their torment."

There was a snicker from behind them as the LaFey twins entered the kitchen. Malchiah looked at the large young men with keen interest.

"And who might you be?" he inquired.

"Tyler and Morgan LaFey," said Tyler. "The lady asked us to stay here and help you if you needed us to."

"Ah, yes, Anastasia's little helpers. Gentlemen, your help would indeed be appreciated. If you can assist my men by restraining the boys here, it would be useful."

Tyler nodded, and he and Mason stepped towards Jimmy and Jack, their eyes fixed on Jimmy. From behind Malchiah, three rough set men walked into the kitchen, and the group bundled the two boys out into the hall. Elsie noticed briefly that the goons had a dim blue light behind their deep sunken eyes that shimmered on and off. Malchiah glanced back and said something in a guttural language. A stream of Redcaps swarmed into the kitchen and stood over the bound forms of Fermy and Dorcas. They were jabbering away in their language with snarling laughs as they unleashed a few kicks on the helpless forms. A couple jabbed at them with their spears, not enough to puncture them but menacing enough. The creatures again had traces of blue light in their squinting little eyes.

Elsie looked helplessly at the scenario before her, knowing that she was defeated. "What do you want, Malchiah?" she said in a dull voice.

"Jack Cracklock," said Malchiah in a deep voice. "And I will be taking him with me. With yourself, of course, I want you where I can see what you are up to. Those two devils can come too; they may be of some use, given that Jack cares for them so. Benedict can have them afterwards for his little experiments." Looking back at Elsie, he said, "Who else is here? And I advise you to be honest. Where is that damned Sammy? Is she hiding upstairs? Actually, no matter, I will find out for myself."

Before Elsie could answer, he gestured to one of the remaining men outside. "Search the house, and be thorough about it. Bring anyone else who is hiding here into that pitiful sitting room of theirs. I want the whole crowd."

The thug grunted his acknowledgement and left the kitchen.

"Why are you so interested in Jack?" said Elsie.

"That's for me to know and you to find out," said Malchiah, his voice mocking. "Now, into that living room, please, Elsie. We need to make the arrangements to leave."

"Oh dear, oh dear, oh dear," came a silky voice, and Malchiah spun around quickly at the sound of it.

"Oh, Uncle, why so jumpy?" said Anastasia, leaning on the

jamb of the open back door, a sly smile on her face as she surveyed the scene before her.

"What are you doing here, Anastasia?" replied Malchiah, the anger barely restrained in his voice.

"I just wanted to meet little Jack-Jack," she said, coming into the kitchen. "And to make sure that everything was going to plan. Many hands make light work, Uncle, and I have a vested interest after the earlier festivities at this very abode." Smiling down at the two bound Fae, she suddenly delivered a vicious kick to the bound Dorcas, who whimpered and curled up as much as the netting would allow her.

"That devil is mine, Uncle. Payment for my part in this little charade."

"Leave her alone," said Elsie, stepping in between Anastasia and the bound brownie. Anastasia nodded, made to turn away, and then whipped around with cat-like quickness, shoving Elsie hard as she spun. Elsie stumbled backwards, scattering the watching Redcaps and tripping over her two friends, sitting down with a heavy thump that drove the air right out of her. The Redcaps erupted with braying laughter at the old woman's discomfort. Anastasia gave them a fake bow.

"Anastasia!" roared Malchiah, grabbing his niece's arm. *"Enough."*

"Oh, Uncle! You don't still carry a candle for that old battle-axe, do you?" said Anastasia, her eyes widening in mock shock. "You do, don't you? Well, I can tell you now, we won't be attending any nuptials, not to that anyhow." She started tittering behind her hand.

"Oh, there will be no nuptials, you psychotic witch," gasped Elsie, staring at Anastasia with hatred in her eyes.

Anastasia made to move towards Elsie, but Malchiah restrained her, pulling her back by the arm.

"You shall have the brownie. When its usefulness is at an end," he said quietly.

"Now, Uncle. That thing dared to attack me and rendered Benedict quite helpless."

"I said later, Anastasia, as we agreed before. Do not try my patience." The undertone in Malchiah's voice was tinged with menace.

Anastasia shook off his hand and raised both arms in surrender, wiggling her fingers as she did so. "Okay, okay, dear Uncle. Whatever you say. I can wait; it gives me time to make a few plans of my own." She smiled down sweetly at Dorcas, who shuddered.

A thug entered the room, interrupting them. "Nobody else here, Doctor Cracklock," he said.

"Fine, fine. Take these through to the lounge if you will; we need to be organised. And tell the others outside to disband; we can take care of things in here now."

"Very well, Doctor Cracklock," said the man subserviently and pulled Elsie to her feet. Malchiah gestured at the Redcaps, and they hauled Dorcas and Fermy up onto their shoulders and carried them off like a pair of captured animals. The man pulled Elsie along behind them, and Malchiah gestured for Anastasia to follow. She flicked her hair and did so.

Entering the lounge, Malchiah gave a satisfied smile. The two boys sat cross-legged on the floor, the bound Fae dumped unceremoniously next to them. Elsie sat perched on the armchair, a look of fear on her face. Around them stood various blue-eyed Redcaps and men, as well as the LaFey twins.

Malchiah glanced around the room and fixed on the two boys. "Okay, all present and correct. Now, I am assuming that the feisty one is Jack. But who might you be, young man?" he said, looking pointedly at Jimmy.

Jimmy stared back, insolence on his face, and said, "Pleased to meet you, Sir. I'm Daffy bloody Duck, and I'm..." A cuff to the back of the head silenced him, and upon turning, he looked up into the gloating face of Mason LaFey.

"His name's Jimmy Owen. Mate of Crackley's," Tyler replied to Malchiah, who nodded.

"Thank you," he said, looking again at Jimmy. "And what are you doing here?"

"Just love a party, me. After being chased through the streets by a giant made out of mud, what better way to relax than with an attempted kidnapping?"

Malchiah gave a small smile and nodded. "There is no 'attempted' about it. Your friend and his great aunt are coming with us, as are your little friends. I am assuming that you can see them?"

Jimmy nodded.

"As a lifer, you should not be able to see them or their world. You must be a transgressor yourself, making pacts with these devils. Still, no matter. You are not invited and can better serve us with another contribution. Hold him, please."

Two of the thugs stepped forwards and grabbed Jimmy, spinning him around and pushing him to the floor on his back. Malchiah stepped forward and pulled one of the tubes from out of his coat. Seeing it, Jimmy started to struggle.

"I said hold him," said Malchiah, bending down as the thugs tightened their grip. He looked into Jimmy's fearful face, reached out a hand and stroked his cheek as if trying to calm the stricken boy. He stopped as Elsie had a coughing fit behind him, spluttering out the words "No," and "Wait" as she did so. Malchiah glared at Elsie, who backed down, covering her mouth with her hand to stifle the coughing.

"I'm going to take your grackles now, Jimmy. We need as many as we can get, and your usefulness, I am very much afraid, is now at an end."

Jimmy went pale and said. "No, wait, please..."

Malchiah held Jimmy by the chin, clamping his mouth shut, and pressed the tube against his forehead. Jimmy's eyes creased in puzzlement and then screwed up, shut tight. He started to scream through his closed mouth, muted noises as the colour drained even more from his face. Thrashing his arms, he tried to struggle free, unsuccessfully, from the men holding him down.

"Stop it!" screamed Elsie. "Stop it, Malchiah!" Malchiah ignored her, focused on the task as he was. The tone of Jimmy's scream changed, becoming higher-pitched, and his face turned white. And that was when Jack lashed out with his foot.

Jack had sat watching the situation unfold, knowing that the moment he reacted, any efforts would be squashed by the sheer number of people in the room. However, watching his friend in such torment was too much for him. He felt the anger build up inside him again until he was powerless to stop himself from reacting. With a yell, he lashed out, kicking the tube out of Malchiah's hand and off his friend's forehead. It detached with a wet popping sound, leaving a scarlet red ring clearly imprinted on Jimmy's forehead as it flew through the air and out of sight. Jimmy stopped his screaming immediately, a little colour flooding back into his face.

Jack tried to get up in his rage but was forced back down into a sitting position by strong hands on his shoulders. Two of the Redcaps jabbed at him with their spears, pinning him into place with the threat of sharp points penetrating his flesh.

"Oh, what fun," jeered Anastasia from the doorway. "Little Jack has anger issues. That is something we can certainly help you with, my sweet."

Malchiah glared at Jack, a furious expression on his face. "You little idiot," he spat. "Where did it go?" The others in the room looked around on the floor and groped under the coffee table, but the tube had seemingly vanished. Malchiah upended the table in a rage and then stormed over to Elsie.

"Stand up," he commanded.

Elsie did as she was bid, slowly, and on the floor, just behind where her feet had been, lay the tube. As Malchiah went to snatch it up, his pocket began to sound with a jangling ring. He hauled out his phone, swiped it, and said, "What?" Listening, his face fell. "Yes, Mother. Right away."

Stuffing the phone back into his pocket, he turned and announced to the others. "We are needed back at the Mansion straight away. Mother was insistent that we returned as soon as possible; there is something gravely wrong apparently. It is not like her to be so rattled. Gather them up," he commanded, gesturing at the Fae and Jack. "And bring her as well," he said, gesturing at Elsie.

"What about the boy?" said Anastasia, pointing at Jimmy, who lay white-faced and panting on the floor, his eyes fearfully dancing between Malchiah and the twins.

"We don't have time now. Leave him here; nobody will believe what he says. Glamour him, so he forgets anyway."

"Please, Sir," said a voice, and Malchiah turned to see Tyler LaFey looking at him directly.

Tyler swallowed and said again in a completely alien polite tone. "Please, Sir. If we may, we can take care of Owen here; we owe him. We would be happy to use that tube thing on him if you wish and then return it to the good lady here when we're done? If it would help you?"

Malchiah considered for a few seconds and looked at Anastasia, who nodded. Staring at Tyler, he replied. "Why not? You have been useful so far, and if you fail me, we will take your grackles instead. Anastasia, please glamour the boy's hand so that he can use it. You others, with me, now." With that, he left the room, the party of brutes carrying and jostling the others along behind him.

Anastasia stepped forward, and without asking, grabbed Tyler's arm. There was a flash of reddish light around Tyler's hand, his bones becoming visible like an x-ray. Tyler shook his hand as if he had received an electric shock and then watched as it faded back to normal. Mason stood, his bottom jaw agape in a moronic pose.

"It feels...different. Stronger," said Tyler. "What did you do?"

"Enabled you to use the grackle tube," said Anastasia, her tone serious. "Simply hold it in the glamoured hand, press it against his head, and don't release it until you need to." Anastasia scooped up the tube from its resting place on the floor and placed it on the chair, ready for use.

"How will we know when to release it?" asked Tyler, and Anastasia laughed.

"You will know my little helper; you will know." With a smile, she turned and walked out of the room, following the others. Looking back over her shoulder, she said. "You boys have fun now, won't you?" She gave an evil laugh.

Tyler went to the lounge door and saw Anastasia following the others into the kitchen. She tipped them a wink and pulled the door shut behind her.

"Wait a minute, lady," called Tyler, dashing to the door and pushing it open. There was nobody there. He went to the back door and pulled it open as well; there was no sign of the party.

'Impossible,' he thought to himself, looking up and down the garden, 'Where the hell have they gone?' He heard Mason call his name in that unmistakable grunting tone of his and went back into the house.

In the lounge, Mason stood looming over an extremely pale Jimmy, who was sitting up now, eyeing the big twin with fear in his eyes. As Tyler entered the room, Jimmy's eyes shot to him, and he started babbling.

"Tyler, please, I'm sorry, I'm sorry, look, I'm sorry, I can pay you, I can do anything you want me to."

"Shut up," snapped Tyler. "Look at you, snivelling. Are you going to cry, Owen? Or pee yourself?"

"If you want me to Tyler, anything you want, just let me go, please, let me go, I won't tell anyone I promise," said Jimmy rapidly, swallowing as he tried not to let his tears flow.

Tyler squatted down on his haunches in front of Jimmy and cupped the boy's face in his hand as he had earlier. He stared at Jimmy eye to eye with a scowl on his face.

"You make me sick, Owen. I mean, really sick. Spoilt little rich boy, all the latest toys, and unwilling to share them with your old friends Mason and Tyler. And rude with it; always the mouth with you." Tyler patted Jimmy gently on the head, the menace of it causing Jimmy to recoil.

"Well, Owen, we're not going to let you go," Tyler continued. "My brother here and me, well, we're not sure about the little stunt that you pulled earlier, and there's been a lot of weird stuff going down over the last few days. But one thing I do know. We've got you now, and ain't nobody going to save you this time."

At this, Mason started to laugh, his grunting snuffles causing the tears that Jimmy was trying desperately to hold back to flow down his pale cheeks. He gave a slight hitch and a sob, which Tyler lapped up.

"Aawww, look, bawl baby is starting to bawl. Lie down, bawl baby," he laughed and gave Jimmy a hard shove, causing him to fall backwards and gasp as the air was smashed out of his lungs by the unyielding lounge floor.

"Pass me that tube thing, Mase," said Tyler, gesturing to the tube as he got to his feet. "Time to see what that little beauty can do."

"Tyler, please," blubbed Jimmy. "Please don't. It hurts so much."

"Don't you worry, bawl baby. We won't use it for long. We're gonna have some fun with you, and by the end, you are going to be begging me to use this thing. Hold him."

Mason lunged downwards, pinning Jimmy to the floor with

his full weight, his breath, rich with halitosis and cigarette smoke, panting into Jimmy's face as he leered over him.

"Please," Jimmy whispered, knowing what was going to happen and relaxing himself to accept the inevitable.

Tyler squatted down again, the tube in his right hand. He smiled at Jimmy and said. "I'll give you a short blast for now. Then we'll see about that arm of yours. The belt can come later."

He moved the tube towards Jimmy's head, and as the boy stared up at them, pinned in place and resigned, he saw a sparkle of blue on the side of the tube closest to him. A bright blue pair of eyes looked down at him, and as he watched, one eye closed and opened again—a wink.

'Get ready, friend Jimmy', a familiar voice chimed quietly in his head. *'I am not going to let these people do what they intend.'*

ROLY HAD BEEN SITTING on the arm of Elsie's chair when the doorbell rang, and the shouting started. As Elsie had jumped up from her chair, she had accidentally caught him with her elbow, knocking him off his perch and down the side of the chair. He was used to taking a tumble; the winds that came with the darkness often blew his people about, but he'd clipped the wall on the way down, and it had momentarily stunned him.

Once recovered, he immediately understood that something was very wrong; there was a great deal of shouting from the other room, and he could not see his friends. He watched two young men come down the stairs and go through to the kitchen. Getting out from the side of the chair was a squeeze, so he started to crawl under it towards the noises, mentally rifling through the Cartulary for something that might help. However, despite now having full access, he still had trouble locating items, and his inexperience of the layout showed as he rapidly skimmed through items, seeing nothing that he thought could help.

The shouting continued, and then some large strangers dragged Jack and Jimmy into the room and pushed them down onto the floor. Roly watched from beneath the armchair, desperate to do something but not knowing what. Those men could easily stamp on him, and judging by the noise, many more of them were in the other rooms.

The shouting died down from the other room, and Elsie was marched in and shoved into the chair that Roly was hiding under. Roly's eyes widened as the two Fae, bound in silvery netting, were also carried through and dumped onto the floor by some evil-looking things with long thin ears and squinting eyes, carrying pointed sticks. These they pointed at the two boys. Roly shrank back further under the armchair, so he was hidden in the shadows.

There was more discussion, and then the men pushed Jimmy down to the floor, and the man who seemed to be in charge pulled something from his pocket. Roly started in shock. It was one of the people, his people, and they were in torpor, dead-looking, in the palm of the man's hand. He bristled and prepared to burst out and try to do something, anything, to help his friends and the kidnapped kindred. As he pushed his way forward, he brushed Elsie's ankle, and she flinched.

'Help me,' he chimed quietly in Elsie's head, and he saw her leg tense. She tapped her heel twice, slowly. Roly didn't understand, and he tried to push past her, but she moved, hiding the motion that pushed him back under the chair. She doubled over, coughing and said, directed presumably at him. "No. Wait."

Roly watched the man press his kinsman onto Jimmy's head, not knowing what to expect, and then he felt it. A rush into the Cartulary that made him vibrate slightly with the force of it. He grasped the underside of the chair in shock, and the vibration he was feeling tore the lining, the fabric already old and brittle.

Focusing on what was happening in the Cartulary, he could sense Jimmy's life force flowing into it. Into a place where there was already a tremendous amount of life force, stored, swirling in chaotic patterns, held in stasis by the Cartulary itself. Roly was puzzled as he looked at the indices for this; there was so much. It was all new, recent by the standards of the people. Only a short time had passed, a few years by how these people measured it. It confused him; what was it doing in the Cartulary? To what purpose was it being stolen?

His thoughts were interrupted by a shout from Jack, and he pulled his mind from the Cartulary to see Jack kick the man's hand. His torpored kinsman sailed through the air between Elsie's feet and stopped just short of rolling under the chair where he hid. Elsie back-heeled the tube under the chair to Roly, who looked at it. He placed his tiny hands on it, and the same feeling as back in their realm came to him, not dead, but not here. Then he heard the man shouting again, to 'find it.' Roly didn't even think about it; he acted on instinct to protect his kinsman. He plucked it up and pushed it into the tear in the bottom of the chair, hiding it from view in the lining. He then lay down behind Elsie's feet and closed his eyes.

There was more conversation, and then he felt himself plucked up by a groping hand and opened his eyes just a crack to see what was going on. The man in charge was talking now; Roly was having difficulties making out what he was saying, something about leaving, but he could see Elsie. She gave an almost imperceptible shake of her head, and Roly said to her only in a low chime, *'I know. I will wait. I will come for you, somehow.'* He then felt himself placed down on the chair that Elsie had been warming.

Not daring to look, he listened to the conversation and then the quietness that followed. He opened his eyes a crack again and saw just Jimmy, pale, lying on the floor with one of the earlier young men, the ugly one, standing over him. He then saw the other one; the one with the stubbly hair on his top lip, come back in. And he heard Jimmy start to beg, the sounds pitiful. Roly started to feel anger himself.

"Tyler, please, I'm sorry, I'm sorry, look, I'm sorry, I can pay you, I can do anything you want me to,"

"Shut up," snapped the big one. "Look at you, snivelling."

Roly didn't listen anymore; he was back inside the Cartulary, looking for something that would help him best these two young men, and help Jimmy. The anger he felt actually helped his search, and then, with a sudden jolt, he had what he wanted. He gave a small smile to himself and prepared to release from the index what he'd found.

"Pass us that tube thing, Mase," Roly heard, and he braced himself, ready to react. He felt himself lifted into the air and passed to the lout with the hair on his face. Roly's body tingled in the hand of the youth, and he felt something trying to worm its way into his thoughts. It was weak, though, and with a mental heave, he shrugged it off and was ready.

"Tyler, please," he heard Jimmy say. "Please don't. It hurts so much."

He felt himself moving again, and he opened both his eyes to look down at Jimmy. He had seen the gesture of closing one eye and then opening it between the friends before, and he copied it now. He saw Jimmy's eyes widen, a measure of hope flowing back into them. *'Get ready, friend Jimmy'*, he directed at Jimmy. *'I am not going to let these two people do what they intend.'*

TYLER HAD SEIZED the tube in glee from Mason in the hand that the lady had done something to. Tyler didn't believe in magic, but he had to consider that there had been some extraordinary things going on today. Putting the earlier events to one side when a ghost had attacked them, there were the recent happenings to consider as well. He was sure that there had been something else in the house with them earlier, something that they could not see. Those blokes that had been with the man in charge had left spaces clear in the lounge as if someone was standing in them. Strange.

Tyler shook his head and came back to the present situation. He was going to enjoy this, whatever 'this' was shaping up to be. His right hand felt like he could crush rocks, a strange sense of power that jangled in time with his pulse. He looked down at Jimmy, smiled sadistically, and said, "Here it comes."

He pushed the tube down firmly onto Jimmy's head, as he had seen earlier. Jimmy wriggled under the pressure, but nothing happened; indeed, no instant reaction as had happened before. Tyler started to grind it into Jimmy's forehead when there was suddenly a flash of blue light, a light 'pop' sound, and then something hit him on the cheek with a thwack. The thing hurt—a lot.

"Oooww," shrieked Tyler, jerking both hands up to his head in pain. He could feel a small lump where the thing had hit him, and it was starting to throb. There was another 'pop,' and this time, Mason screeched, grabbing his elbow and letting Jimmy go in the process. Something landed on Jimmy's stomach, where it had rebounded off Mason, and he grabbed it. Opening his hand, he saw a brightly coloured, perfectly round stone. No, when he looked at it, it was a marble and an old one by the look of it.

Tyler dropped his hands, still clutching the tube, to stare at Mason, and there was another bright flare, and Mason howled again, this time grabbing at his face. Tyler looked down at the tube, which was glowing blue again, it gave another pop, and a picture frame shattered.

"*It's bloody firing stuff out of it*," he yelled and dropped the tube to the floor. As it fell, out popped legs and arms, and two blue eyes shot open. The tube landed on its little legs and stared up defiantly at the two LaFey twins. Roly stepped over so that he was in front of Jimmy.

'You do not use my kinsmen to hurt others. Do you hear me, youngsters?' thundered a loud chiming clanging noise in each of their heads. Jimmy gave a smile to himself as the LaFey's goggled at this thing in front of them.

"What the hell..." began Tyler, but stopped as a well-placed marble whined off his ear. He screamed again and grabbed at the side of his head.

'Jimmy,' chimed Roly, *'Pick me up.'*

"Are we going to get them?" asked Jimmy as he grabbed Roly.

'Oh, yes,' boomed the chiming voice, echoing in all their heads this time.

Tyler gestured to Mason, his hand still clamped to his head. "Grab him, and smash that bloody thing."

Mason lumbered forward, and Jimmy raised Roly, taking an involuntary step back as he did so; such was his fear of the larger twin. This time the blue light came on inside the tube, and a veritable stream of marbles was spat out at a high velocity. Jimmy could feel the tube vibrating in his hand, a rapid chattering noise like a machine gun. The effect on Mason was instantaneous. Marbles, travelling at high speed, stitched their way up from thigh to chin in a diagonal line, and Mason screamed in pain as the stinging pain registered in his dumb brain. Roly didn't stop in time and overshot; the marbles pinging off the wall and smashing another of the picture frames.

"Shot!" Mason screamed, not sure where to grab first, as his whole body was in pain. "Shot Ty, shot me!"

Tyler lunged at Jimmy, who turned Roly onto him. There was another blue flash, and Tyler was stopped in his tracks as a sticky yellow goop covered his entire head. He could feel it coating his hair and gumming his eyes shut. The sticky mass covered his face, and on his lips, he could taste sweetness.

'Honey, I believe you call it,' chimed Roly inside Jimmy's head. *'There's a huge reservoir of it in the Cartulary.'*

Jimmy laughed aloud; his stress and fear from earlier forgotten now. "What else you got?" he asked Roly, who chimed back a laugh himself inside Jimmy's head; his confidence in accessing the Cartulary was growing. *'Everything, Jimmy, everything. Point me at the one with the honey on him,'* he replied.

Tyler was now clawing at his face as he tried to clear the sticky mess from his eyes. "*Mase, Mase, where are you?*" he screamed. Mason was rolling around on the floor himself, hollering as he rubbed at his sore and bruised torso.

"Hey, sweetness," called Jimmy to Tyler, who staggered around at the sound of Jimmy's voice. "Hold still a moment."

Another blue flicker and a spray of finely chopped hair joined the honey sticking to Tyler's face. Jimmy laughed in delight; in seconds, the twin had been transformed into a pretty ugly werewolf as he scrubbed at his face desperately, mashing the substances into a congealed sticky mess.

Jimmy pointed Roly down at Mason as he thrashed around on the floor, the blue flash came again, and this time hundreds, no, thousands of tiny spiders flew out of the tube and covered the youth in a twitching black blanket of legs and eyes. Mason's screams went up a good few octaves, and he rolled around the floor in a frenzy, thrashing at the spiders, trying desperately to dislodge them.

Tyler finally finished clearing his eyes of the mess and forced his caked up eyes open to see Jimmy a few feet away, pointing the tube directly at him. There was a strange blue swirling light in the centre of it, like a mini hurricane.

"You had enough, or do you want some more?" asked Jimmy.

Tyler looked at his brother, who was sobbing on the floor, desperately brushing at the remaining spiders, the majority of which had now scuttled away into the darker recesses of the living room.

"I'm gonna..." he began, and Jimmy gestured the tube at him, its inner light flaring.

Tyler put up both his hands in surrender. "Alright, alright, enough."

"Good," said Jimmy, his face set. "Now get out. And take that," he gave Mason a little kick. "With you."

He then stepped back out of Tyler's way and motioned him towards the door, the direction of the tube never leaving his head. Tyler pulled Mason to his feet and guided his sobbing brother towards the front door.

As he pulled it open, he looked back at Jimmy. "You're dead, Owen. I mean it."

"Yeah, yeah, whatever," retorted Jimmy. "Roly, if you would?"

The blue light flared again, and this time a torrent of water, icy cold, jetted out of the tube. Jimmy aimed it at the twins, who yelped as its coldness soaked through their clothes, and they made a run for it, slamming the door as they went.

Jimmy looked at Roly, and the two of them burst out laughing together, hearty laughs that they both felt deep down inside. They were still laughing two minutes later when a yelling voice brought them back rudely to reality.

"What the hell has been going on here?"

CHAPTER 7

Jack and Elsie were locked in a small wood-panelled room that smelled strongly of dust. There was no sign of Dorcas and Fermy; they had been taken off separately by the Redcaps to goodness knows where. Two dusty old wicker chairs were the only furniture in the room, lit by the light of a single lightbulb covered with a moth-eaten old lamp-shade. The windows had shutters over them and were firmly locked; the thin streams of daylight shining through showed the dust swirling in the air around them. It wouldn't have mattered anyway if they could have got the window open; there were bars on the outside. Jack had pressed an eye to the gap in the shutters and confirmed to Elsie that they were high up in the mansion, so climbing out was not an option, even if they could have gotten through the bars.

When Malchiah's goons had first shoved them into the room, they had their pockets rifled through and emptied. They'd also taken Elsie's handbag from her, rummaging through it and laughing as they did so. Malchiah had fixed them with a glare after the men had exited with their property and said. "This room is secure. Travel glyphs do not work in here, and neither do glamours, so do not waste your time trying. I will send for you shortly." With that, he had left and locked the door behind him.

They had tried, of course, and Jack had opened up the scab on his thumb and tried the 'open' glyph using a piece of wicker snapped from one of the chairs as a makeshift quill for his blood 'ink.' Nothing had happened; the door remained firmly locked, so they had resigned themselves to being stuck here for a while. To pass the time, Jack had been tapping on the wooden panels, hoping for a secret passage or room until Elsie had snapped at him to stop with the rapping.

"What do you think they want to do with us, Aunty?" asked Jack as he slumped dejectedly into one of the chairs. "And what about Jimmy? Do you think the LaFey's will hurt him? What about Mum? Dorcas and Fermy? And Roly, for that matter; where did he get to? It's such a mess."

"I know, I know," said Elsie, patting him on the shoulder. "And I am very much afraid that I have no idea what they are planning for us all."

"Will they hurt Dorcas and Fermy?" said Jack anxiously.

"I don't know. The Cracklocks are against all things Fae, but they brought them with us rather than extinguish them directly. They must have plans for them, although as to what that could be, I only know that they won't be good."

"We need to rescue them," said Jack, jumping up for the umpteenth time.

Elsie motioned him to sit back down. "We'd need to get out of this room for starters, and I am guessing that that will only happen under guard. Our friends are on their own for now but do not underestimate Fermy. He was formidable back in his time before he left the service of the Courts. Do you know why he assumes the ferret form in our realm?"

"No idea, Aunty. Why?"

"It's kind of a joke. The name "ferret" is derived from the

Latin *furittus*, meaning 'little thief.' A lot of his work with the Courts was to do with acquiring items for them. He was more of a burglar than a secret agent, to be honest, if what little he's told me is correct, but needless to say, there is a lot more to him than first impressions would give."

"So, you think he'll escape on his own then?" said Jack excitedly.

"I wouldn't put it past him," replied Elsie, with a slight smile, "And then we can enjoy the havoc that will ensue afterwards."

"And he'll help Dorcas as well?"

"Dorcas is, well... Dorcas. She can take care of herself. But I don't think for one minute that Fermy would leave her behind."

"We still need to help them if we can," said Jack.

Elsie smiled a sad smile again. "We will do what we can, but for now, we bide our time and wait for our moment."

"I just wish they'd left us all alone until we were ready for them," said Jack, staring despondently down at his scuffed trainers. There were traces of mud on them, as well as on the bottom of his trousers—a souvenir from the Lisovyk.

"So do I, Jack, so do I," said Elsie and put her arm around the boy.

"What the hell happened here?" asked Sammy, looking around at the devastation that was her home. Roly and Jimmy immediately stopped laughing and stared at her. From around the back of her legs, the figure of Timothy peered at them, a piece of paper clutched in his hand.

"They came for Jack, Sammy. A load of men and some Faeries as well, I think; I couldn't see those, though. They took Jack, Elsie, and Fermy and Dorcas away with them."

"And you let them?" yelled Sammy, her face clouding with anger.

"Of course not," said Jimmy, smarting. "We had no choice in the matter; we couldn't fight so many."

"So why did they leave you here?" said Sammy sharply.

"They were going to take my grackles; they had one of Roly's people, and they tried to use it on me. They left me with the LaFey twins; they were supposed to finish me off."

"What?"

"When you press one of the tubes onto someone's head, it does something. It's like when you touch one of those electric fences that farmers have, it's like a painful jolt, but it just keeps getting worse. Sucks the life out of you."

"Ahem," said a small voice behind them, and Timothy stepped out from behind Sammy. "I believe that you are correct and that they were trying to remove Jimmy's grackles. May I?"

Timothy walked over to Jimmy and gestured to him to stoop down to his level. From out of his pocket, he pulled out a small wooden instrument, like a flute but a lot shorter. "Blow into this, please, Jimmy, if you would? Hard as you can."

"I haven't been drinking, officer," Jimmy joked as he took the flute and blew into it for as long as he could. As he did so, what he took for holes in the instrument started to light up with tiny yellow dots that winked on. When he had expelled all the air that he could, he dropped the flute back into Timothy's outstretched hand and inhaled loudly.

Timothy studied the array of lights on the tube and then looked up at Jimmy. "Bend down, please; I need to examine your head."

Mystified, Jimmy did as he asked. Timothy's small hands moved gently through Jimmy's hair before he nodded and stepped back.

"You have had grackles removed, I'm afraid, presumably by the tube, or Roly's kinsman if you'd prefer. There is no doubt about it."

"How can you tell?" asked Jimmy, interested in the gadget.

Timothy pushed his glasses up onto his nose and held out the device to Jimmy. "This is an ageometer. It measures age based on the user's grackle count. At this point, your grackles indicate that you are approximately twenty-one years of age."

"What?" exclaimed Jimmy. "Twenty-one? How... I mean, what... no, I..."

"Grackles are your life force. You lose them as you age or experience disease or trauma, all of which remove them. It dictates how long you lifers remain. Us Fae have far more grackles than you lifers, which again shows why we are much longer lived. Also, we don't do so many stupid things."

"So, what was the thing with my head then?"

"A simple test; I was looking for grey hairs. They are an indicator of grackle loss and should not be present in a boy of your age. You have several grey and white hairs now." Timothy replied politely.

Jimmy grabbed his head in shock. "So that tube thing sucked the life out of me? Literally?" He glanced at Roly, who stood watching the proceedings with his electric blue eyes. "Good job you switched, Roly, otherwise I'd be a goner. Six years in that short space of time. Jeez."

"But why would they do that? Why would they want to put your life force into the Cartulary?" asked Sammy, puzzlement on her face.

"I am afraid that I have no idea," said Timothy, shaking his head.

Jimmy was tapping his foot as he thought things through. Looking at Timothy, he asked, "What could you do with life-force if you were holding it in storage?"

Timothy thought to himself for a few seconds and then replied. "Not a great deal. From my learnings, I do not think it is possible to put grackles back into someone else, but I may be incorrect; this is unprecedented. There is certainly no 'Fountain of Youth'; we Fae would have found it by now if it existed. So, no, I don't think that your stolen life force could be given to someone else."

"What if there was a lot of that stolen life force available?" asked Jimmy. "Roly, can you check the Cartulary contents, please?"

Roly answered without hesitation. *'Yes, there is a large reservoir of these grackles, or life-force, in the Cartulary. It is contained.'*

"Where has it all come from?" asked Timothy. "Usually, life-force dissipates and then disappears completely when you move onto the Realm of the Departed. I have never heard of it being stored. This is really rather strange."

"I think I know where it's come from," said Jimmy, and he pulled Jack's phone out of his pocket, swiped it, and started tapping it. "Here," he said, holding it out to Sammy.

The online article was about the 'Boofs,' the strange epidemic that was striking down children worldwide. It featured a picture of one such child, wizened looking and grey, lying in a hospital bed unmoving. Sammy skimmed the article, her eyes widening as she did so.

"I reckon that they've been using Roly's kinfolk to extract the grackles from those kids," said Jimmy, tapping the article with a fingernail. "I've been reading about this a lot, as I am pretty worried; it seems to affect kids under ten, and my brother Sean is only six. The cases have been slowly increasing over the years. I bet that if we looked into it, it would all have started around the time that Cracklock bloke stole the Focus from the Roly's people."

"The younger children would have the most grackles," interjected Timothy thoughtfully. "It would make sense to target them. And Fae, of course. We have large amounts of grackles, although I would suspect it is difficult to remove them; it would take a long time, and the Fae, I would think, are very resilient to such attacks. Your children would be a lot easier to take from."

"But how are they doing it in such volumes?" asked Jimmy, more to himself than the others.

"The missing Fae," gasped Sammy suddenly. "I bet that's what they are using. That's what David thought, anyhow."

"What?" said Jimmy and looked in surprise as Timothy clapped his hand to his forehead and said, "Of course."

Sammy continued. "The day that we escaped from the Redcaps and that Hobyah thing. The day that David told us that he thought the Cracklocks had found a way to destroy Faery for the last time. What started him looking into it was the disappearance of some of the bigger Fae folk. I think that those folk are probably big enough to use one of Roly's people?"

"Yes," said Timothy. "And a Fae would always trigger a child's natural sense of curiosity; make them easier to be approached, rather than if a stranger approached them."

"Stranger danger," said Jimmy thoughtfully. "They teach it in all the primary schools."

"Yes," continued Timothy. "Your young lifers are raised on a diet of those moving picture things, so something like a Fae would bound to be of interest to them, and they wouldn't be scared. It would not matter if the Fae revealed themselves because the child will not be able to tell anyone afterwards anyhow. My grockles and grackles, those poor young lifers."

"We have to stop them," said Jimmy. "Even more so now. And rescuing Roly's people would be the way to do it, wouldn't it?"

'Yes,' chimed the little tube. 'My people would never willingly participate in such evil.'

"And we have to find out how the Cracklocks are controlling those Fae. I strongly suspect that it has something to do with that Focus," said Timothy. "We have to get the Focus, and we have to get Jack."

"Agreed. We need to rescue my boy and our friends and stop

that awful man once and for all," said Sammy. "Where is this Cracklock Manor, anyhow?"

They all looked at each other, and nobody spoke.

"Well?" said Sammy to Timothy. "Where is it?"

"I'm afraid that I don't know," said Timothy forlornly. "I have never been there, nor would I want to. That place has been responsible for the extinguishing of more Fae than can ever be truly known."

"Do you know anyone that would know?" asked Jimmy.

"No. Nobody has ever come back from there. I suppose that somebody in the Courts would know, but I do not know whom to ask. I do not have the contacts that Fermerillion has. Although I am willing to go and try, I fear it would take too long; I am something of a nobody at the Courts."

"So how do we go about saving our friends if we don't know where to go?" said Sammy, tears glistening in her eyes.

"I bet I know someone who can tell us where it is," said Jimmy quietly. "Jack's old friend, Mr Binks."

Sammy's lips set thin as she stared at Jimmy. Turning to Timothy, Jimmy said, "Timothy. Did you find the travel glyph for the Realm of the Lost?"

"Of course," said Timothy, producing David's note from one of his many pockets.

"Good," replied Jimmy. "Open a realm door to there, would you please? Roly, we're going to need your people's help."

THE CATACOMBS below Cracklock Manor were a dreadful place indeed. During cellar expansions in the eighteenth century, the masons had knocked through into a natural cave system, worn into the chalk-like rock by ancient rivers, long since dried up. The caves were linked by various tunnels, interspersed chaotically by the passage of the waters, and extending off in many directions from the main cave. The extent of them had never been fully mapped out; Jebediah Cracklock, the patriarch of the family at the time, had sent men to explore on more than one occasion. Several had never returned. Now the far reaches of the underground caves were being mapped by faeries under Malchiah's control; they were, of course, expendable.

Sparse electrical bulbs linked the separate caves, many of them burnt out, leading the way through the main areas in use. The light was dim, and a damp chill hung in the air, working its way into your bones if you spent too much time down there. While the extensive cellars were used to store the family's food-stuffs and alcohol collections, if you stepped through the secret door, cunningly disguised as a giant wine barrel covered in iron bands, and your eyes adjusted to the gloom, then the wretched place was revealed in all its glory.

There were workshops down here, where blacksmiths laboured away, as they had for generations, producing iron weaponry and objects. This area was hot and dry, dried out by the centuries of smelting kilns and fire as the raw iron transformed into the items the Cracklocks and their ilk used in their war against the Fae. The fires vented away through the natural chimneys, billowing the smoke through water-worn tunnels the diameter of a dinner plate to disperse within the cave complex further away. Racks of weapons and shelves of other iron objects filled the area, cages, nets, and even armour, all iron and heavy, and available to anyone who wanted to go up against the Fae.

Past the workshops was another large cave that functioned as the armoury where more conventional weapons were stored, all of which were illegal in the UK. Guns and explosives of all kinds were stacked neatly on shelving according to their age. Towards the back of the cave were old flintlock muskets and slow match pistols, as well as cannons and stacks of iron balls. There were wooden boxes of old TNT, sweating with age, white crystals covering their surface. Force glamours contained these in case of explosion, the air shimmering around them; they were too unstable to dispose of safely now. As the racks progressed towards the cavern entrance, the firepower got progressively more recent and modern, as did the explosives stored there. Ammunition, both conventional and iron-based, was stored in easily accessible racks. The armourer, a man employed solely for his knowledge of such weaponry, routinely maintained all of the arsenal, even the ancient ones, and he never left the catacombs. He had no desire to; his glamour had been in place for decades, and he had no free will left. These weapons allowed the Cracklocks to take what they wanted when it was needed and from whoever they needed it from. Nobody was able to stop them. The Lord's work was more important than the fancies of mortal men.

Past the workshops and the armoury, in a more dimly lit part of the complex, there was the gaol. It was no ordinary jail. It was a jail designed solely for the imprisonment of Fae, regardless of size. The Cracklocks often required subjects for testing new devices upon, and they maintained a steady supply. Lately, the captured Fae were utilised for other purposes, so the cells were only currently half-full. But there were still all kinds of folk trapped there; forlorn, desperate Faeries, devoid of hope and quietly sobbing, not the happy folk of legend.

The cells were more like cages, all shapes and sizes and stacked one upon the other. Constructed of steel, they had a fine band of neat iron running through the bars that crisscrossed here and there. The iron was enough to instil a faint feeling of unwellness in the captives without causing them to sicken and die quickly. Each cage was firmly locked with a single frontal lock system; there was no access from the inside to the mechanism, which was sophisticated and only opened by a specific key. Each cage was also individually Fae locked, as was the whole area with a secondary glamour; no travel to and from the area was possible at all. The cages were also glamour locked, a powerful enchantment that stopped the Fae's natural magical abilities. The Jailer oversaw the whole area; another individual dominated and glamoured by the Cracklocks to the point of extreme loyalty to the family. The man had a foul disposition; he was a thoroughly unpleasant individual who delighted in his charges' torment and anguish. His favourite thing was to keep them awake; bright lights flooded the cells on a timer, dragging the poor Fae from whatever uncomfortable slumber they could muster. And he kept them cold and wet with generously thrown buckets of water. The Fae feared the Jailer as he came stomping into the cells, his face covered by an odd-looking set of goggles that were actually hagstones strung together.

And it was here, locked firmly in cages, one atop the other, that Fermy and Dorcas sat, dejectedly looking up and down at each other as they pondered what they were going to do. The nets in which they had been trapped now lay discarded in the corner of the cellblock; the Jailer had simply tipped them out into a cage, slammed the door shut, and stacked them with the other Fae. Freed of their bindings, they'd quickly realised that there was little that they could do; no glamours seemed to work. They tried to talk to their fellow captives, but they were too despondent, lost in their own misery.

"Well, this is a fines fix," said Dorcas, plucking at the bars of her cage. "Whats are we's going to do, Fermy? Jack's and Elsie is upstairs with those evil Cracklocks. Jimmy's is most probably dead, and nobody knows where's we is."

"I know, I know," said Fermy as he was examining the lock on the cage he was imprisoned in. Tapping it, he said. "This thing is pretty much impregnable from this side. If I could get to it from the other side and if I had my stuff..." He tailed off and looked at Dorcas. "Where's your rolling pin?"

"Malchiah tooks it," said Dorcas sadly.

"Will it come back?" said Fermy excitedly.

"I'd don't know. I's try," said Dorcas and pulled herself to her feet, her head brushing the top of the cage as she had to stoop a little. She held out her hand and closed her eyes. Nothing happened. She opened one eye and tried again; nothing happened.

"It was worth a try," said Fermy, dejectedly.

"Why's did you want my rolling pin?" asked Dorcas.

"Eerm, well, you do know one of the handles unscrews?" said Fermy awkwardly.

"No's. I did not," replied Dorcas, fixing Fermy with a steely glare. "What dids you do to old Grannies rolling pin?"

"Nothing, nothing. Just put something inside it a long time ago that would be a huge help right now," said Fermy. "Kind of an insurance policy. I have many such policies; comes from working for the Courts. It doesn't matter, though, if you can't summon it."

They were interrupted by the sound of stomping boots coming down the corridor towards the room that they were held in. The frightful figure of the Jailer came clumping in, a bucket swinging at his side.

"*Oose talkin'?*" he shouted, glaring around at the trembling Fae before fixing onto Dorcas and Fermy, who were not cowering like the others were. He stomped over to them, squatted down, and peered into the cages through the hagstones, his eyes almost crossing as he stared at them.

"Newbies. Might 'ave known. Right. Listen here, you little buggers. I likes it quiet in 'ere. No talking, no wailing…" Here he bashed on the cage next to them that contained a weeping faun. "And no answerin' back. I make myself clear?"

"Why are we here?" asked Fermy, staring straight at the odd little man.

The Jailer did not respond. He simply upended the bucket he was carrying over the cage that held Fermy. Icy cold water drenched the little Feeorin and carried on down into the cage below, soaking Dorcas to the bone as well. The Jailer started guffawing at the sight of them coughing and spluttering, slapping his thighs at his own joke. As if someone had flipped a switch, he suddenly stopped and fixed them both with a glare.

"I mean it, you 'orrible little devils. I run a tight ship down 'ere, alright? Any of you little swines so much as put a toe or 'oof, or whatever it is that carries you about the world out o' line, and you're for it. The boss don't mind if a few of you go missin', and I've got plenty of toys to make that happen. Savvy?"

Fermy nodded, eyes downcast as he did so.

"Right. To make sure the lesson 'as sunk in, I'll be back in a couple o' hours with another bucket. Let you dry out a bit and think about things, eh? Then another soakin'll 'elp focus the mind. Any more rubbish, and I'll be sprinklin' you with defaeing powder an' all—the iron kind. *Now shut up*!" he finished with a shrill scream.

The Jailer stood up straight, grasped the bucket, and bounced it off a couple of the other cages for good measure, the occupants cowering back from the impacts. Laughing to himself, he stumped out of the room, leaving the door open as he left.

Fermy looked down at Dorcas, who was miserably wringing out her dress and shivering. "We have got to get out of here," he whispered. Dorcas nodded, her face set.

"Yes. And when we does, we's taking everyone with us. I's is going to deal with that Jailer bully man. Just watch me."

JIMMY, Sammy, and Timothy stood outside the gates of Twillington House in the dawn light, staring at the heavy iron lock that prevented their entry. In their hands were three of the tubes; Jimmy had Roly, of course; Sammy and Timothy wielding two of Roly's countrymen who, having been told what they'd figured out about the grackles, had gladly volunteered their help.

Sammy was nervously rolling her tube in her hand; its bright blue eyes fixed upon her. "Jimmy," she said. "How does this work again?"

"I'm not entirely sure, but with Roly, I just think of what I want to come out of the end, and he makes it happen by retrieving it from the Cartulary," Jimmy replied.

"And it works?" said Sammy doubtfully.

"Try it," said Jimmy. "But don't be too loud. He's in there, I'm sure, and he hasn't got the Lisovyk guarding the place anymore. He'll be wary."

'I will help you,' chimed the tube in Sammy's hand. 'Please try.'

Sammy screwed up her face and held the tube out at arm's length. There was a blue twinkle, and cascades of red roses fell to the ground in front of her. She gazed at them in awe.

"That is amazing," she said. "Totally amazing. And we can get anything, anything at all out of the Cartulary?"

'If it is there, then we can retrieve it,' chimed Roly. 'Or the closest thing to it that we can find. All items are linked, so we can easily find similar items.'

There was another blue explosion, and this time a chocolate Easter egg popped out of the tube in Sammy's hand and smashed on the floor.

"Okay, enough," said Jimmy. "Let's see how we are going to get this gate open. Oh, and does anyone have a hagstone? When we get in there, Sammy and I are going to be at a disadvantage."

There was a blue flash from Timothy's tube this time, and he neatly caught the two small objects that ejected from it. He handed one each to Sammy and Jimmy, who peered through the holes in the hagstones that Timothy had just retrieved. The tiny blue sparks on the gate were back.

"Nothing to worry about; it's just Fae locked," said Jimmy

knowledgeably, and he placed Roly against the lock and concentrated. The blue pulse of light came again, and he withdrew Roly from the gate. The lock was glistening with frost, and when Sammy pressed a finger to it, she yanked it back quickly as the cold burned her. Jimmy tapped the lock, but it stood firm. He held Roly a few feet away from the lock, concentrated, and was rewarded with a flash of fire. The lock now glowed a dull red. Without stopping, he repeated the cycle of cold, hot, cold, hot, cold, and then kicked the gate just below the lock. The lock shattered, and the gate swung open.

"Thermal stress," said Jimmy airily, gesturing them inside.

Inside, the shadows cast by the weak dawn sun were foreboding as they stared at the drive leading up towards the house, the trees overhanging it as before rustling in the slight breeze. Jimmy held up a hand for them to wait.

In a quiet voice, he said. "I've been in here before, but I can't say that I know the place. So we need to have a plan on how to draw old Binksy out. We can then question him, with the tubes' help if we must, but be aware of his little helpers; awful creatures they are. Jack reckoned he beat them up before, so hopefully, we can deal with them. I think that Sammy, as the adult, should do the questioning; Timothy and I will keep an eye out for anything else. Don't be afraid to threaten him, Sammy; he's a nasty piece of work."

"Jimmy, that man almost killed my son and then tried to kill you both by setting some sort of monster on you. I have very little sympathy for him, believe me, and we aren't leaving without that address."

"Good enough," said Jimmy. "Let's go. The easiest way to get his attention will be to get inside and make a lot of noise. I'm good at that sort of thing."

They trouped up the drive, Jimmy noticing that where there was once the elaborately crafted lawn and gardens, there was now only churned up earth and mud. He shuddered at the memory of finding Fermy buried there and the coming of the Lisovyk; was it really only a few hours ago? He wondered what other surprises Mr Binks might have in store for them in his oversized house.

Reaching the entrance porch and the overhanging pergola, they walked slowly over the tiles, careful not to make too much noise. When they got to the door with the big lion's head knocker, Jimmy again gestured for them to stop.

"Okay, this is it. If I remember rightly, there is loads of stuff in the foyer of this place; antiques and stuff. I propose to smash a few things, get his attention if getting this door open doesn't do that. Timothy, as we go in, keep an eye on the floor on the right-hand side. His helpers came out of a trapdoor there the last time we were here. Also, to the left is the door to the kitchen; they may come out of there as well. Blast them with something if you see them; they aren't friendly."

"What about this, Mr Binks?" said Sammy, a little nervous. "Isn't he an old man? Or something else?"

"I don't know," said Jimmy. "Jack reckoned there was something else inside him that swam into view every now and again, something monstrous, but I didn't see anything. He is strong, though; almost knocked the kitchen door off its hinges, and that was with us piling the counters and stuff up against it. So he's no ordinary old man if such a thing exists."

"Right," said Sammy, gripping the tube in her hand tightly as she steeled herself. "Okay. Open that door."

Jimmy stooped to examine the lock. Then, almost as an afterthought, he placed his hand onto the doorknob and gave it an experimental twist. The latch clicked open. "Well, that was easy," he whispered and pushed at the door, but it wouldn't open. He tried pulling it and was rewarded as the door swung quietly open under his hand. Gesturing for the others to stay put, he stuck his head in and took a glance around.

The foyer was in partial darkness, a couple of well-placed

lamps shining pools of light in the darker reaches of the room. Jimmy listened, his breath held until he had to exhale. All was quiet, and there was no sign of anybody that his straining senses could detect. He stepped over the threshold, gesturing for the others to follow him. Quietly they all moved along the wall to the right, keeping to the darkness.

Jimmy held up a hand to stop and then lifted a sizable ornate vase off a plinth. "Okay, here goes," he whispered to Sammy, lifting it above his head.

"Put that back, boy, if you know what's good for you," a voice suddenly boomed out of the darkness, and Jimmy nearly dropped the vase in shock as he and the others jumped in fright. With a sudden flare, all of the lights came on in the foyer, and as their eyes adjusted to the sudden brightness, the figure of Mr Binks came into view, standing resolute in the middle of the floor, his cane firmly planted in front of him as he leaned forward on it to glare at them. Jimmy raised the hagstone quickly to his eye and counted at least six of the nasty looking goblin things stood behind him, sinister smiles on their faces and murder in their eyes. Jimmy heard Sammy and Timothy gasp with shock behind him as they realised that they had walked into a carefully laid trap.

"Well, well, well," said Mr Binks, a smirk on his face. "Who do we have here? One thieving little sod and his friends, nicely caught in the act! Where's my Lisovyk, boy? Chomping down on your friend, eh?"

"Dead," said Jimmy, his eyes fixed on Mr Binks. "Not as unstoppable as you thought, eh, Binksy?"

The old man's face switched to a snarl of rage, and Jimmy caught just a glimpse of something behind the old man's face. "*What?*" he screamed.

"Turns out it wasn't so good at science," said Jimmy in a taunting tone. "Might have been big, but it was certainly as dumb as its owner."

The old man's face turned red with rage. "You killed my pet?" he asked in a quiet voice that shook with menace. "You killed my pet and my helper? You destroyed my only friend?" His voice rose as his rage built and built.

Trembling, his face scarlet, he motioned the goblins behind him forward. With a voice choked with rage, he muttered. "Seize them. Seize them all; we will take their grackles." The creatures started to move forwards but stopped when Jimmy stepped forward and held up his hand.

"You may find that a little difficult, Binksy, old boy. Remember what we found last time we were here?"

Mr Binks squinted myopically at the hand that Jimmy held up and then realised what he was holding in his hand.

"My tube," he screamed again. *"You have no right to that! Give it back."* The monstrous visage came clearly into view with his anger, and Timothy gasped in fright.

"Absolutely not," said Jimmy in a cheerful tone. "And you'll never guess what? It turns out that this tube can do so much more than suck the life out of people."

And with that, he pointed Roly at the nearest of the goblins. There was a bright blue pulse, and the creature was knocked soundly off its feet by the force of the bowling ball that hit it squarely in the stomach. It lay on the floor, clutching its belly and howling in pain. Following suit, Timothy and Sammy also pointed at the goblins nearest to them, and with their own blue flashes, dealt with them neatly. One went down, bound in what looked to be bramble branches; the other screamed and thrashed at the stinging jellyfish that covered its entire head. The other goblins, fear in their faces, took to their heels and ran for it, back into the depths of the house.

Sammy stepped forward with her tube pointing at Mr Binks, who took a step backwards with an unsure expression on his face.

"I want the address for Cracklock Manor. Or so help me, I'll set everything I can think of onto you." Her tube gave a slight blue glow, and Mr Binks twitched.

"I won't tell," he said in a surprisingly scared voice. "It's more than I'm worth. They will never release me if I tell you where they are."

Sammy flicked the tube, and with a gleam of blue, something dark and scaly landed on top of the hand with which Mr Binks held his cane. He registered it, screamed, and shook his hand violently. The scorpion dropped off and scuttled for the darkness underneath the cabinets that lined the outskirts of the room.

"I'll cover you in them," said Sammy, jabbing the tube at the old man. "Just try me. The address?"

Mr Binks seemed to sag visibly. "I can't. I cannot. Please don't make me; if they find out, then I will be in trouble. A lot of trouble. And not just me. I don't belong here." With that, he burst into tears, real genuine tears, not just acting.

Jimmy looked uncertainly at Sammy and Timothy. This certainly wasn't in their rapidly thrown together plan. Sammy raised her eyebrows, and Jimmy shrugged; he had no idea what to do next. Sammy took a hesitant step towards the sobbing old man, who continued to blub, oblivious now to the uninvited guests in his foyer. He fumbled in his pockets and pulled out a large spotlessly white handkerchief, which he set to his eyes as the tears rolled down his face.

Sammy reached over and patted the old man, who looked up at her with a defeated expression.

"What do you mean, you don't belong here?" said Sammy gently.

The old man pushed her hand off, and with a shift, the hideous monster face appeared again, overshadowing the old man's wrinkled face. Only this time, it was not snarling; it just looked pitiful.

"Lady, I don't belong here. I am stuck in this place, in this damned flesh, and I have no way to leave until HE says that I can," spat the man/monster thing.

"What?" asked Jimmy, lowering Roly. The tube chimed gently in Jimmy's mind, 'I think he is not what he seems, Jimmy. He is not of this realm.'

The old man-thing looked at Jimmy now. "As I said, boy, I don't belong here. In this body, in this bloody house and its gardens, or this whole damn realm. I am a prisoner here, bound to do the bidding of others, under pain of death for myself and my others."

"Sorry, but I don't understand," said Jimmy. "A prisoner? How? And why have you done the things that you've done? Who is making you?"

"Dr Cracklock," said the creature bitterly. "Him and that witch of a mother of his. They took me and mine as a fancy from our home and put me to work here. Bound me here, in this flesh. My others, I do not know where they are. They are captives, and if I do not do what I am instructed, they will be the ones to pay the price of disobedience. I have seen what the Cracklocks can do to people. I have no choice. This place is a power source for them; it is why we had to trap lifers and Fae alike here. 'You mind this place well,' I was told. And now you have come here, taken my tool, destroyed my beautiful garden, and my others will be the ones to incur their wrath."

"I thought you were a Fae?" said Jimmy, but Timothy interrupted him.

"I have never seen one of the folk quite like this gentleman if what he says is true. It is not possible to trap a Fae in lifer form, and it still hold both forms," he said, looking at the creature with renewed interest.

"I'm no damn Faery," said the old man-thing. "I hate the things personally, all happy and sprinkling damned magic dust about." Timothy tutted audibly at this and was about to say something cutting in response when Sammy interrupted him.

"Then what are you?" she asked. "And why can we see you through the hagstones? And what about these other Fae creatures that are here, helping you?"

"It doesn't matter what I am," said the creature snappily. "Just be happy that I'm not from around here, don't want to be here, and would rather be where I belong, which is not here. Nevertheless, I can't leave. As for those other 'helpers,' they were placed here by Dr Cracklock. To keep an eye on me, as well as help out with the damn things he tasked me with."

Timothy had stepped up to study the creature now, pushing his glasses up on his nose as he stared quizzically at the creature. He pulled a small red monocle from his pocket and looked through it at Mr Binks. "Most interesting," he muttered, more to himself. "Yes, most interesting indeed." He then used his tube, a dim blue light emanating from it, to examine the bemused creature that stood there and allowed him to do so in bewilderment. Timothy then put the red monocle away and turned to Sammy and Jack.

"I can't say for sure, but it would appear that this gentleman is some kind of astral entity; well, the part that is talking to us, anyway. The other part is the usual flesh and bone. It is really rather interesting how the two have meshed together."

"Yeah, yeah," snapped Mr Binks. "Those damn Cracklocks did it, bound me to this flesh thing as my punishment."

"For what?" said Sammy.

"For not fulfilling my part of our arrangement," he said. "And I'll say no more about that; I am ashamed of it, and I'll not discuss it."

"So now what?" asked Jimmy. "Can you give us the address or not?"

"I've already answered you on that," said the creature primly. "I will not risk my others on your account."

Sammy was just about to answer, her cheeks starting to

colour with anger again when Timothy put up a small hand to quieten her.

"Mr Binks. If I may be so bold, may I ask what you would do if you were to be unbound from this body you are trapped in?"

"Leave. Leave, go and find my others, recover them, and then leave. Go back to where we came from."

"And that would be your own realm, presumably?" said Timothy politely.

"Yes, yes, of course. Leave and never come back to this ghastly realm of yours, with all its limitations and awful souls. After a little payback to Dr Cracklock, of course." The creature gave them a hideous grin, its two faces intermingling as it did so.

"And would unbinding you be worth you sharing the address that we require?" said Timothy, a little forcefully this time.

The creature stared at Timothy, a puzzled look on its face before finally saying, "Of course. I would give anything to be free of this place. Anything that is within my power. But it is folly; only my captor can release me."

"Well, you see, that's not strictly true," said Timothy, pushing his glasses up on his nose again. "I believe that with the assistance of Roly and his colleagues here, we can extract you from the body you are in and place you within the Cartulary. We can then release you, and you would be freed."

"What?" said all the others at the same time.

"Oh yes," said Timothy in his learned voice. "I have been conversing with my friend here," holding up the tube. "And we are fairly sure that we can push you from the body if a few of us try it at the same time. If we then pull you into the Cartulary before the original glamour you carry returns you back into the body, providing that we take you far enough away, you should have the freedom that you seek."

The Mr Binks creature actually smiled, its lips struggling to find the expression. "You could? Do you reckon you could? Then do it, little man, do it. I'm ready!"

"I should warn you; it could be dangerous to you; my colleague here is not sure if it would work effectively."

"I don't care. Any chance is worth taking; I hate this place and everything in it. Do it! What do you need from me?"

Jimmy interjected. "Timothy, are you sure you want us to free this freak? He set that Lisovyk onto us, captured any number of your countrymen, and did goodness knows what to them."

The Binks creature suddenly bellowed. *"I had no choice! How many more times? What I did, I did against my will! Although I won't deny I received a small measure of pleasure on occasion; you people are all so irritating."*

"We need the address, Jimmy," said Sammy. "And if releasing this thing is how to get it, then I say we do it."

"Okay, but we need some promises first," said Jimmy. He turned to the creature. "Do you promise not to come after us, any of us, including Jack and Elsie, plus our friends Dorcas and Fermy?"

"Yes," replied the creature shortly.

"How do we know you're not just saying that?" said Sammy.

The creature bowed its head. "You will just have to take my word for it," it said in a quiet voice.

Timothy raised his hand again and said, "Actually, as the creature will be in the Cartulary, if it tries anything, we can just put it back in there in the event of any foul play. And there it will stay."

The Binks creature looked at the little Fae with narrowed eyes. "I think that will be enough of an incentive for me to keep my word," it said and tried another smile. It didn't look attractive, but the others nodded at this.

"We will need the address before we release you," said Timothy. "You will need to be plucked straight into the Cartulary for what I have in mind to work; there won't be any time for discussion once we've knocked you from that body you inhabit."

The Binks creature's eyes narrowed again. "My turn; how do I know that you won't just leave me here once you have what you want from me?"

"We're perfectly honourable, thank you," said Timothy in a prim little voice.

"I don't know you," replied the creature.

"Look," said Sammy. "Just write the address down and hold it in your hand. Once we've unbound you from that body, we can retrieve it from you. And if you've fooled us, then in the Cartulary, you'll stay."

"Agreed," said the creature and pulled a small notepad from its pocket, along with a pencil. Licking the point of the pencil, it scrawled something onto the pad, tore out the page, and then tucked the pad away again. It scrunched the paper up in its gnarled old man's fist.

"Now, do it," it said. "Release me."

"Please stand in the centre of the foyer," said Timothy, gesturing to a spot. "Sammy, Jimmy, you stand here, please; I will go behind him to catch him as he leaves. Direct your tubes towards him."

"You ready, pal?" said Jimmy to Roly. The tube chimed in his head in the rapid rushing language as Roly conversed with his colleagues, and then to Jimmy, 'Yes, friend Jimmy. We are all ready and understand what we must do.'

They got into position, forming a rough triangle with the Binks creature in the centre. They all pointed their tubes at the creature.

"Now remember, don't cross the streams," said Sammy, and Jimmy laughed. Timothy looked at them quizzically, and Sammy waved him away. "Just a lifer joke, from an old film. Don't worry."

"You lifers and your jokes," said Timothy with a grin. "Are you ready, Mr Binks?"

"Yes. Get on with it," said the creature in a subdued tone. It looked slightly scared.

The three raised the tubes, and Timothy counted down from five. When he hit one, Roly and Sammy's tube flared into life. A blue wind flew from them and buffeted the creature, who took an involuntary step backwards, its clothes flapping in the wind. It gave a loud howl and then steadied itself.

Sammy and Jimmy struggled to hold their tubes; they bucked and twisted in their hands with the power of the blasts coming from them. Jimmy grabbed his wrist with the other hand to steady it, and it helped. The beams of blue wind intensified as they harried the creature. Timothy stood, leaning forward in the twin blasts, partially shielded by the Binks creature but struggling against the forces that were battering him, his clothing flapping with the intensity. The piece of paper the creature held in its hand whirled free and disappeared under one of the display cabinets, but they did not stop.

And then, it started to happen. As the Binks creature howled, its voice started to tail off, slowly at first. A pale shimmering form was being forced back from the old man's body, a ghostly grey shimmering shape that looked like it was superimposed over the old man's body. The image shimmered and flickered as some mysterious force tried to suck it back into the body from where it came, and at this point, Timothy raised his tube and pointed it at the creature as well. The tube glowed a deep dark blue within itself, focusing onto the wind-buffeted figure before it. As it did so, more of the creature pulled free from the body, distinct features now present; the creature's face contorted in a hideous grimace as it fought to free itself. With a mighty tearing noise, the whole apparition suddenly left the old man's body and disappeared like a cobweb into a vacuum cleaner directly into Timothy's tube. The old man crumpled to the floor as if he had fainted, and the others pointed their tubes up to the ceiling. The howling blue wind winked out.

Panting, Jimmy said. "Did it work?" Roly closed his eyes and then opened them. 'The creature is in the Cartulary, in torpor,' he confirmed.

"Well," said Timothy. "That was interesting, wasn't it?" He smoothed his clothing down and then trotted over to the display cabinet, from under which he plucked the crumpled note. He opened it, nodded, and said. "He was true to his word. The address is here. And something else."

He held the note out to the others, who noted the address in Somerset, England. Underneath it, in surprisingly neat handwriting, was the following:

Do not release me until you meet Cracklock. I may be of assistance.

"He really doesn't like Malchiah, does he?" said Jimmy.

"Can you blame him?" said Sammy. "Now, I am guessing that travelling to Somerset isn't going to be a problem, with Timothy's help, but we need another plan once we get there on what to do next."

"How are we going to get in?" said Jimmy. "I assume that we can't just waltz up to the front door and knock?"

Sammy thought for a moment, smiled, and said, "Folks gotta eat..." to herself. Turning to the others, she said. "I think I know a way. Do you still have Jack's phone, Jimmy?"

"Yep," said Jimmy, tapping his pocket.

"What's the nearest town to that address?"

Jimmy tapped away at the phone before replying. "Looks like it's a place called 'Chard.'"

"Timothy," said Sammy. "Would you be so kind as to open a realm door to Chard, please? And you are going to need to work some glamours."

"What about the old feller, there?" said Jimmy, pointing at

the crumpled figure of the old man that now lay on the floor. "We can't just leave him there."

Sammy stepped over to the prone form and checked him over. "He's breathing well; just seems to be unconscious. Pass us some of those cushions there; we can lay him on those. He'll be fine."

Once the old man was secure, they stepped over to the kitchen door that was sporting the glowing travel glyph that Timothy had sketched on it. He slapped it, and as it faded away, he took a deep breath and said. "This adventuring life is really not for me."

CHAPTER 8

Jack and Elsie were dozing in the shabby chairs, exhausted by the late night and goings-on when their slumber was disturbed by the sound of a key scraping in the lock. Snapping awake, they stared at each other, disorientated as to where they were. They soon remembered as the door swung open and in strolled one of the goons carrying a tray, two glasses and a tall jug balanced upon it.

The heavyset man placed it on the floor next to their chairs with a grunt and stood back, folding his arms. He stared at them and then gestured to the tray. Elsie picked up the jug, took a long sniff, and then nodded to herself. "Smells like water," she said, plucking up one of the glasses and pouring the clear liquid into it. She took a long swallow and smacked her lips together. "Tastes like water, too," she said with a satisfied smile.

"But what if it's poisoned, Aunty?" said Jack, his dry mouth wanting some for himself anyway.

"That's why I'm drinking first," said Elsie with a smile. "But I very much doubt that they have locked us in this room for all this time if they are going to do away with us by poison. No, there may be a truth potion or something in here, but I can't taste anything. Give it a minute to see if I turn blue, then pour yourself some, sweetheart."

"You can pour yourself a glass now, young Jack," said a deep voice as Malchiah made his entrance into the room. "I assure you, it is nothing more than pure water. Here, allow me; I simply wished for you to be refreshed before joining Mother downstairs for our discussion. Unfortunately, she was detained this afternoon and has asked me to extend her apologies for not seeing you sooner. She is very keen to meet you, Jack."

Malchiah poured and then handed Jack a cold glass, which he gulped gratefully. Malchiah had taken a step back once he'd handed Jack the glass, and he looked at the boy thoughtfully. "Thank you for not throwing that over me, Jack; I appreciate that these are difficult circumstances. I am hopeful that we can put things right between us and start again. I have no wish for the Cracklocks to be at war with each other. There are other things more worthy of our antagonism."

"Oh Malchiah, I think we're a little beyond that now, surely?" said Elsie sweetly. "I mean, kidnapping us and leaving behind our friend to be murdered isn't the best way to endear yourself to a new family member, is it?"

Malchiah's face darkened. "That boy will live, or what passes for life following the removal. I will ask you, just this once, to keep your peace, Elsie Cracklock. You are here only because I wanted Jack to have a friendly face with him. I can arrange to have you removed quite easily if you would rather?." At this, the thug made to move forwards, but Malchiah raised a hand. "And while we are discussing you keeping things to yourself, I would appreciate it if you do not have your friends call me, pretending to be my mother. We could have left your residence earlier under much more pleasant terms without your little trick. Sammy, your mother, was involved, no doubt?" he finished, looking pointedly at Jack.

Elsie looked bemused. "I'm haven't the faintest idea what

you are talking about, Malchiah. And I doubt very much that Sammy would be involved either. Why would she want to call you and pretend to be your mother? She is more than aware of what you are, and you did drive her from her home all those years ago. Why would she ever want to speak with you; if nothing else, you were incredibly rude to her in the hospital?"

"I agree with Elsie," added Jack defiantly. "I want no part in any family that wants to hurt the Fae. Or any other races in their attempts to do so."

Malchiah frowned at Jack. "I can see that the devils have worked their charms upon you already. And so soon, following you re-joining us all from your little vacation from reality; they truly are the masters of deception. But I would make a small request that you hear us out with an open mind. Mother is most keen to talk to you and to explain. We need your assistance, regardless of what you think of us."

"The devils, as you call them, have worked nothing on me; they are my friends. Where have you taken them?" said Jack, getting to his feet and his temper rising. "Where are Dorcas and Fermy?"

"Enough," said Malchiah, again raising a hand as the large man stepped towards Jack. "Bring them."

He walked out of the room, and the thug gestured for them to follow. They did as they were bid and exited the room onto a large balcony, overlooking the main entrance hall. Two further guards moved into position behind them, both clutching handguns. Malchiah turned, stared directly at the pair, and gestured around.

"Unlike the room that you have just left, glamours will work within most of the house. Nevertheless, be under no illusion; if you try to cast one, or if we think you are trying to cast one, these guards will put a bullet in you without a second thought. No shield glamour in the world will be quick enough to prevent it; they are swift and well trained. I would rather not have to deal with the aftermath of that, so I would beg your favour not to try. Am I making myself clear?"

Elsie and Jack both nodded as they looked around open-mouthed. Even here, in a common first-floor corridor, the opulence was apparent. Gold gilt-edged furniture and stern-looking portraits were everywhere, documenting the Cracklock family through the ages. There was a smell of age in the air, of antiquities like an old country house, but no dust or cobwebs were present in the immaculately maintained area in which they stood. Jack stepped up to the balustrade, Malchiah gesturing to the guard to let him do so, and peered over into the grand reception area below. He gave a low whistle.

"This is all the property of the Cracklocks?" he asked in awe, entirely forgetting where he was as he took in the grand features and marbled flooring, along with the thick tapestries and curtains.

"Of course," said Malchiah. "The family's fortunes have been made as we travelled down the ages from the first, dearest old mother Philippa, until the present day. And your side could have been a part of it if you'd joined us in the Lord's work."

"Pah," scoffed Elsie. "Money isn't everything, and certainly not when it comes off the back of slaughtering such fantastic creatures. This is all just a testament to how corrupted your side of the family has become. To make yourselves feel better."

Malchiah turned to her, a vein standing out on his forehead in his anger. "I have already told you; I am not interested in your opinion. I am tired of it. Guards, put her back in the room if you would; Jack can meet Mother on his own."

"Absolutely not," said Elsie, stepping forwards and then stopping as a guard grabbed her by the bicep.

"I'm not going anywhere without Elsie," said Jack defiantly, clutching Elsie's other arm.

Malchiah fixed Jack with a steely look. "You have two choices, Jack. Either Elsie goes back in the room, and you behave and come with me willingly, or Elsie goes into the jail cells in the catacombs, and you come with me regardless. I would suggest that you choose wisely; it is cold and damp downstairs and no place for a woman of an elderly persuasion. Well, boy?" Malchiah folded his arms across his chest and stared at Jack.

Jack trembled with anger again, staring at Elsie, who gave him a stubborn shrug. "It's okay, Jack, go with him. Mark me, though; Agatha Cracklock is as much of a liar as her son here. Pay no heed to what she says; their life's mission is wrong."

"I know Aunty," said Jack quietly. Malchiah nodded, and the guards turned Elsie on the spot and frogmarched her back into the room.

"You do know how to make good choices then, Jack, my boy," said Malchiah cheerfully. "Now, let's see if we can convince you to make a few more. This way, please."

He led Jack down the curving stairs to the reception area, duly escorted by the remaining guard. Jack looked around him as he went, noting the forbidding iron items that were everywhere once you noticed them. The whole place was rigged to keep out the Fae in every way it would seem. Even the grand tapestries covered iron netting, artfully hidden beneath them; its dull silver touched with the red of rust. As they stepped onto the lobby's marbled floor, Jack also saw that what he took to be natural patterns in the marble was again iron, placed seamlessly into the aged tiles themselves. He shook his head and thought, 'This is really over the top.'

Malchiah led Jack through a large door at the side of the reception area and into another wide, brightly lit corridor, the portraits again staring down at them from along its length. He walked quickly along it before coming to a halt about halfway down outside an ornately lacquered door, brightly polished and inlaid with darker wood that formed intricate patterns. He knocked twice, two fast hard little raps, and then waited.

From within, a quavering voice called "Come." Malchiah swung the door open and then gestured for Jack to enter ahead of him. When he hesitated, the guard shoved Jack, and he stumbled into the room, an extensive library, glaring behind him at the guard as he did so.

"There, there now, there is no need to be manhandling the boy," said the voice, and Jack turned to look. Before him, partially hidden by a large cake stand that formed part of the afternoon tea laid out, was an old lady; the white hair that framed her face was partially covered by a small white head covering. Jack was reminded of Queen Victoria's old pictures in the school history books; this woman was of a similar build. The old woman stood, and Jack got a better look at her; she seemed to be incredibly ancient, which he supposed was about right; Malchiah was elderly himself.

The old lady gave Jack a broad smile that didn't touch her eyes, showing off some yellow-brown teeth as she did so.

"You must be Jack," she said. "Our erstwhile family member, finally back with us after all this time. I presume that you have been treated well while you have been our guest?"

"Not really," said Jack, rubbing his shoulder where the guard had shoved him. The old woman seized on his discomfort and turned upon the guard, her smile gone before Jack could say anything further.

"You damned fool. How dare you hurt the boy here? How dare you?" she screamed at the guard, her voice booming now and certainly not reflective of her tiny frame.

Jack jumped at the shout and said. "It's okay, really, he didn't..." He did not get to finish.

"Silence, Boy. I am dealing with this!" the old woman hollered at Jack and then came around the table. She was short in stature, only coming up to Jack's shoulder, he reckoned.

The guard was visibly shaking now at the old woman's rage, and he held up both hands in submission. "Ma'am, I'm so sorry,

I didn't..." He wasn't able to finish. She made a rapid gesture, her hands a blur, and the man's lips sealed themselves together. His hand flew to his mouth. Malchiah looked at Jack and tipped him a mischievous wink.

"Would you like to see me seal his nose as well, young Master Cracklock?" she cackled and made another gesture. The guard clawed frantically now at his face, his face turning purple as he gasped to draw a breath. His bulging eyes looked at Jack beseechingly.

"*Stop it!*" shouted Jack. "*Let him go!*" He made as if to dart at the old woman who was hooting with laughter and was stopped by the restraining arm of Malchiah. "Watch," he admonished.

The guard was now a bright red colour and had slumped down to his knees, the pawing at his face and throat becoming slower and weaker. The others stood impassively, watching the man's struggles. Finally, he crashed forward, face down, his body shaking. The old woman made another gesture, and the man's back contracted as his unconscious form pulled in a massive gulp of air.

"Remove him, have his mind wiped, and then throw him out. I do not want to see him again," the old woman said shrilly to another guard, and then, as if nothing had happened, turned to Jack and smiled again, a cold grin that didn't match her calculating eyes.

"Well, then, Master Jack Cracklock. You see now; I will have no harm done to our family. By anyone, and I do mean anyone. As matriarch, I will not allow it. Do you understand? Or would you like a little lesson yourself?"

"No, Mrs Cracklock," said Jack meekly, shaken from what he had just witnessed. These people were obviously extremely powerful.

"Oh, please," said the old lady with a wave. "I'll have no such formality here from an old member of the family. Please call me Agatha."

"Okay, Agatha," whispered Jack hesitantly, trying to keep the trembling from his voice.

"Now, come over here and sit next to your, well... Great, Great Aunt, I suppose? I hope that you're hungry; the chef has made a marvellous spread in your honour." Agatha patted the seat next to her as she sat down in the spot she had just vacated to work her mischief. Jack walked slowly over to the small table and sat down as indicated. Malchiah joined them and handed out cups of fine bone china, so thin that Jack was scared that it might well break when he picked it up.

"Help yourself, boy, don't stand on ceremony," said Agatha, pushing the cake stand towards him." I know that you're hungry, growing boy and all that." She tried another smile as Jack reached for a small triangular sandwich. As he went to take it, he remembered what Fermy had said back in Faery about eating Fae food and being bewitched by it. He withdrew his hand.

"Come, boy, eat," urged Malchiah, his eyes on Jack.

"I'd rather not if you don't mind," said Jack politely. "I am quite full from earlier on. Although I will take a cup of tea if that's okay?" He had seen Agatha slurping from her cup, having poured from the teapot, so took the gamble that that, at least, was safe.

"Of course, no matter. Don't know what you're missing though, lad," cackled Agatha, helping herself to some of the small cakes on the middle tier. With a gesture, Malchiah glamoured the elegant teapot to pour into Jack's cup and then pushed the milk jug and sugar cubes towards him. Jack took what he needed and stirred the cup with a dainty silver spoon.

"So then, young Jack," said Agatha, conversationally as she pushed a cream cake around her plate. "How have you been? More to the point, where have you been? We've missed you growing up."

Jack did not know how to respond. He figured that they

already knew what had happened to him, and while he didn't like these people at all, he was afraid that being rude to them would not be beneficial. He decided to feign ignorance for now. Taking a gulp of tea, he replied. "I'm not really sure. I mean, I know where I've been for the last few years, but it is only very recently that I found out about any of this. Before that, I was just a normal school kid, getting on with life."

"And now here you are, gallivanting all over the place with that fool Elsie and her devils. I have to say, Jack, you stink of Fae; it is most unpleasant." Agatha fixed him with a firm stare. "Have you been to the cursed realm yet? Elsie's side of the family, hexed as they are, are welcome there."

"What do you mean?" asked Jack, although he had an idea.

"Faery, boy, Faery, where those godforsaken things come from. Creeping here into our world, with their lies and deceit," spat Agatha. "Have you been there, boy? Have you been to the forsaken realm?"

"Yes, but just once," said Jack, draining his cup. "I didn't really see much of it, just a walk through it. The others kept me away from faeries and things while we were there."

"Thank you for your honesty, Jack. We are aware of your travels there; we have influence in many places, including that cursed land. And they would keep you away from others; it's how they work. They are ensnaring you in their wiles, but we may yet save you if we are forthright and strong. *'For I know the plans I have for you, declares the Lord, plans for welfare and not for evil, to give you a future and a hope.'* Jeremiah 29:11"

"But the Fae that I have met are all great," said Jack. He felt a little fuzzy, as if he had just woken up. "They are my friends; I remember them from my childhood."

"Yes, they like to take our childer whilst they are still young," said Agatha. "But that will stop when the devils are destroyed, and with your help, that will be soon."

Jack shook his head; he felt weariness creeping over him,

and the room was starting to spin a little. He focused on Agatha as she fixed him with an inquisitive look.

"Are you feeling okay, young Jack?" she asked, glancing at Malchiah as she did so.

"Feel strange," said Jack, and he noticed that his words were slurring. "Need some fresssshhhh aaiir." He grabbed the side of the table and tried to push himself up. He managed to raise himself and then slumped back into the chair again. It felt like a huge fluffy cushion, sucking him in. From what seemed like a long way away, he heard Malchiah, muffled.

"Looks like you were wrong about this one, Mother. The strickler venom does affect him. Disappointing. Very disappointing, I must say, after all the effort we have put in. It must be one of the others we discussed then, but who?"

"Wait," came the muffled response.

Jack shook his head and felt a little better. The world swam back into focus, and he could see Agatha and Malchiah staring at him. With what seemed like an immense effort, he pushed himself upright in the chair and said, "Whash yous mean wrong?"

"What, boy?" snapped Malchiah, the former friendliness now all gone.

Jack shook his head again. "I said, what do you mean you were wrong about me?"

Agatha shifted forward and stared into Jack's eyes. "How do you feel, boy?"

"What the heck did you give me?" asked Jack, his strength returning and pushing himself up from his chair.

"Hahahaha! I knew it, I knew it!" cackled Agatha, jumping up from her chair and clapping her hands together in glee. "He's immune. He is the one."

Jack eyed them both, starting to feel more like his old self again as whatever had affected him rapidly wore off. "What did you give me?" he said, feeling his anger rising again.

"Some of this," replied Malchiah, pulling a small box from out of his pocket and pushing it across the table to Jack. "Open it," he commanded.

Jack did as he was told and opened the box. Inside was a purple insect, resembling a bee but a little larger, lying dead in the bottom. He raised his eyebrows and looked at the Cracklocks.

"A strickler," said Malchiah by way of an explanation. "Well, actually, its venom was what you were kind enough to swallow on the sugar cubes. The strickler causes instant paralysis in normal people, and there is no natural immunity, as it comes from the cursed place. Indeed, my mother and I had to wear gloves to handle it. But you are far from normal Jack, Cracklock or not; you are quite different."

"Please indulge us, Jack, and lend us your forgiveness. We had to be sure that you were what we think you are," purred Agatha in a placatory tone as she saw Jack's colour rise in his face again. Jack stared hard at them both.

"As some sort of test for goodness knows what, you decided to try and poison me?" he said through gritted teeth. "So on top of kidnapping my friends and me, leaving my best friend to the mercies of those LaFey twins and threatening to lock my Great Auntie in your jail cells, you now want to add poisoning me with something from Faery to the list? You expect me to help you? I am done!"

Jack got up from the chair and moved towards the door. Almost without moving, Agatha was suddenly in front of him, her small ring-bedecked hand on his chest to restrain him. She smiled her sinister smile again, her brown teeth peeking over her withdrawn lips, and pushed Jack gently. The old woman's strength was far greater than her size, and Jack took a couple of involuntary steps backwards.

"Jack, Jack, Jack..." she consoled. "You were brought here to hear us out. At least give us the courtesy of listening to what we have to say. I assure you that you will learn something to your advantage here, something that will be of great interest."

"But, but... you people are crazy," Jack blurted out. Agatha's smile disappeared.

"Crazy? No, never. Driven, certainly, and if you knew the things that we know, you would be too. Please, take a seat and let me explain to you. If we can't change your mind, you will be free to go. We'll even help you leave if you wish."

"Really?" said Jack, a little hope blooming in his heart.

"Yes, really," said Malchiah from behind him. "Come and take a seat, boy."

Reluctantly Jack allowed Agatha to lead him back to the table. With a complicated hand gesture from Malchiah, the tea things moved themselves over to a sideboard against the far wall, leaving the table spotless. Agatha sat forward, crossed her hands, and stared intently at Jack.

"First of all, young Jack, let us talk about you. About why we think that you are so important to our cause. You are special, you see, more special than you could ever know. I would like to understand what you know so that I may fill in the blanks for you. Has the history of the family been explained to you?"

"Elsie and Fermy explained some stuff to me, yes, about the seven sects of Faery and the changelings and things. And how through marriages and stuff, Jeremy could see Faeries."

"It was Jeremiah, but yes, you are correct," corrected Agatha. "Carry on."

"And Timothy told me some other things about how Pippa, or someone, ran off and founded your side of the family."

"Yes, our founding Matriarch, Philippa, is to whom you refer. A great visionary," replied Agatha, pointing towards a large portrait that adorned the wall. A rather plain woman was captured in it; she wore expensive clothing and an expression as if she could smell something off.

"And that I got to be how I am because of my dad. He is a

Cracklock, and I inherited it from him, this ability to see Faeries and do realm travel and such."

"Again, quite correct," agreed Agatha. "Dear David, such a fool. He is a wanted man, you know, and not just by the Courts, God damn them. Others whom you would not expect are also keen to take him." Something in her voice made Jack think twice.

"What do you mean?" asked Jack, a shiver worming its way down his spine. "Who wants my dad?"

Agatha waved a hand in a dismissive gesture. "No matter, for now, Jack, no matter. Your father is long gone, and so it is of no concern."

Malchiah made a gesture, and suddenly above the table floated several various coloured spheres, tethered together with glowing golden strings. Jack was reminded instantly of balloons. Agatha gestured, and suddenly a dull blue bubble appeared at the bottom of the strings, the name 'David' shimmering on its surface.

"Jack, this is the Cracklock line, somewhat simplified, with your father at the bottom. And here you are." A light yellow bubble, the colour of white wine, with the name 'Jack' appeared, a thin golden string tethering it below the 'David' bubble.

"This you already know, albeit in a limited form. However, one thing that the scholars in the family do not consider is the other lines. For example, what history does your mother hide?" Agatha gestured again, and a light pink bubble with the name 'Samantha' appeared in it, also linked above the 'Jack' bubble by a golden string.

"You see, Jack, we Cracklocks are obsessive about our family history, so much so that we often forget that other family lines can contain their own wonders," continued Agatha. "And it was purely by accident I am ashamed to say that we discovered the fascinating history of your mother. The Cracklock scholars were developing the family tree further, and we asked them to look at the wayward family members once they had finished with the documentation of our own line. They made a discovery where your mother is concerned. An exciting one."

Jack's interest was piqued now as he looked at the two elder Cracklocks. "What did they find?" he asked in a low voice.

Malchiah waved, and some other spheres popped into existence, their golden strings leading down to the 'Samantha' bubble as they floated above her.

"Your mother, Jack, is from strong Romani stock and carries within her grockles the mysteries of those people. Mysteries that she has passed onto you. Abilities that are not present in any of the other Cracklock lines that we know about."

Jack stared at them both blankly. "I am sorry, but I have no idea what you mean," he said, looking from one to the other. "What is a rowmarnee?"

The other two looked at him solemnly. "Do they teach you nothing in those schools nowadays?" said Agatha, with a tone of irritation. "The Romani are a culture to themselves. Gypsies, I guess you would know them as, but the Romani are the true name for that nomadic culture. They originally came from India, the land of mysticism, and spread throughout Europe during the Dark and Middle Ages. They have their own powers, Jack. Surely you have heard of a Gypsies' curse?"

"I guess," said Jack with a shrug. "But most people nowadays think Gypsies are people with a bit of a strange lifestyle; there have been programmes on television about their weddings and things. Many people don't like them because of the mess that some of them leave everywhere. People are quite scared of them."

"Not travellers, you stupid boy," spat Agatha. "Authentic Romani. Although they have been diluted by marrying outside of their culture and leaving what they were behind, there are still some left in the world. They are often persecuted, after all. Here in England, they were banned from entering the country, and those living in the country had to leave or be executed. A number went into hiding, not unlike the members of our own family who were accused of being witches."

"But I still don't understand," replied Jack. "What's this got to do with mum? And with me?"

"What it has got to do with you, my dear boy, is that we believe that you have inherited the best of both worlds. The only member of our family to have inherited from two separate fantastical worlds. The Romani have all kinds of rumoured powers; they can travel through astral projection, touch things and know about them, make curses and blessings, and all kinds of innate abilities. They conjure or channel the spirits of the dead and talk with them. And they are extremely resistant to all kinds of magical attacks. As are you, it would seem, although your Fae blood enhances yours."

Jack started laughing at this outpouring. "I'm sorry," he said through his snorts. "But I'm no psychic; I can't do any of those things. You've got the wrong person."

In the fits of his laughter, he did not see Malchiah move. Before he knew what was happening, he was on his back on the floor, Malchiah's hand around his throat as the older man fumbled in his pocket. He pulled out one of Roly's people, this one in torpor; it's surface black and oily. Jack stopped laughing almost instantly and twisted, trying to worm out of Malchiah's grip, but he was too firmly pinned. He felt a cold rush of fear through him as Malchiah's unsmiling face loomed over him. He could see the cold light of the Focus shining through the man's waistcoat.

"This is a grackle tube, as you know," said Malchiah holding up the tube. "It is used to remove grackles from any living creature. You saw a similar one used on that loudmouth friend of yours. It hurts whilst it removes grackles." He pressed the tube onto Jack's forehead. As before, when Mr Binks had done similar, the tube seemed to suck onto his skin slightly, and then nothing happened other than the minor discomfort of having it pressed against his head. Jack squirmed a bit but could not get free. Malchiah pulled the tube from Jack's forehead and placed it back into his pocket.

The ringing of a little bell cut through the silence, and he turned his head towards Agatha. The door to the sitting room opened, and an enquiring face appeared in the gap.

"The earlier guard. Is he still on the premises?" barked Agatha.

"Yes, Ma'am. His mind wipe is just being finished now, and then we will dispose of him somewhere."

"Bring him back in."

"As you wish, Ma'am." The guard shut the door quietly and disappeared.

Jack squirmed again on the floor, but Malchiah kept his grip on. "You can stay there," he said. "And watch."

A few minutes passed before the door opened again, and the guard from earlier was brought back in by two other men. The man had a vacant expression and drool on his chin as his blank eyes stared straight ahead without registering them.

"Here please," said Agatha, gesturing to the chair that Jack had been forcefully ejected from. The two men steered the vacant man to the chair and pushed him down into a sitting position, pinning him by his shoulders. Agatha cupped the man's chin, raised his head, and stared into his eyes. She nodded to herself and pulled out her own tube.

"This is what should happen," she said to Jack, and with a small cackle of glee, pressed the tube to the man's head. As the contact was made, the man arched his back as if an electric current was flowing through him, and he started to scream. Jack watched in horror as the man's hair turned slowly white, and wrinkles formed upon his face, creasing it like crumpled paper. He was shaking and shuddering as the changes were wrought upon him, and Agatha's mouth was upturned in a horrendous smile as she kept the tube steady, firmly pressed against the man's head. The man appeared to age at a horrendous rate, his hair becoming fine and white and skin going from a healthy pink to parchment-like yellow in under a minute. The screeching noise he was making finally tailed off, and he stopped his shuddering. Agatha removed the tube from the man's forehead with a satisfied nod, and his unmoving form slumped forward in the chair. Agatha gestured to the two guards who had impassively watched the demonstration, and they snapped to attention.

"Get rid of that," she snapped, and the two men lifted the aged man from the chair and left the room.

Malchiah finally let go of Jack, who was shocked at what he had just witnessed. "It doesn't work on you because of your unique nature," said Malchiah. "But it will work on all of your friends. The devils take longer to drain of grackles, but we have the perseverance and blessing of the Lord. We are happy to take the time. Elsie and your mother, well, it'd be just as quick as that fool, I would surmise, although your mother and her Romani heritage may put up a little resistance."

Malchiah stood up and held out a hand to Jack to help him up. Jack allowed himself to be helped to his feet, but as he got his balance, he felt himself stiffen as a sudden, shocking paralysis set into his body.

"That was a freezing glamour," said Agatha from behind Malchiah. "It is usually impossible for lifers to break free from the paralysis. Those of Romani blood are more resistant than most lifers, but it still takes a while to free oneself from it. Get out of it, boy, if you can."

Jack strained against the glamour as he felt its binding powers, locking his muscles into place. Nothing… and then he felt it start to give a little. He could twitch his shoulders and then move his arms a little. The more he tried, the more movement he got back until after thirty seconds or so, he could move again.

"Would you like us to use some slightly less pleasant glamours, Jack?" asked Agatha with a sly grin. "See how you fare against something a little more painful? Or is our point proven?"

Jack held up both hands in surrender. "Okay," he panted. "I get it. I can shrug these things off easily. Because I'm special."

"Not that special, Jack, but certainly unique," said Agatha, a note of disdain in her voice. "Please keep that in mind. Now, if you will?" and gestured back to the armchair. Jack sat down again and looked at the two of them.

"Now then," said Agatha. "You have a better understanding of what you are. We would like to explain to you how you could help us. If you are willing."

Jack realised he had very little choice. These two were incredibly powerful, and he had very little to fight back with. He could throw off their glamours, that was clear enough, but he very much doubted he could attack them successfully enough to escape, and in any event, those guards looked like they would be able to eat him for breakfast. '*Bide my time*,' he thought and then nodded to the pair. "What do you want me to do?" he asked.

"Firstly, a little perspective," said Agatha. "I appreciate that you are not 'on board', as people say, with our position on the Fae devils, but at the same time, you have only just returned from your long jaunt of normality for a few days now. One side of the family only has told you everything you know. It is time for you to understand our position, as well. To have a balanced view, a person must have both sides of the story. Agreed?"

Jack nodded, and Agatha continued.

"What you need to understand, Jack is that the Fae are not your friends. They are indeed Devils in disguise and mean you mischief."

"That's not what I've found. Fermy, Dorcas and Timothy are

great and have been nothing but nice to me," said Jack carefully. "And all the others I've met, like those at Twillington House who were just scared, little people. They are not that much different to us."

"Of course they are different," said Agatha patiently. "But that is what they do. They deceive, they enamour, and then they glamour you. Then, when they are done, you are used for their own ends. It has happened many, many times throughout history. It happened in our own family for the Lord's sake; good children taken and replaced with Fae changelings!"

"But there must have been good reasons for that," said Jack. "Reasons we don't know about; they are lost in the history of the family. Unless you know better?"

Agatha flapped her hand impatiently. "I expect that the media and films have indoctrinated you, haven't they? Do you think that faeries are here to help humankind to better ourselves? That they are all good?"

"Well, yes, and those I've met have all been good and kind and ready to help," retorted Jack.

"But what if I told you that all the faery stories and all the accounts of people who have 'supposed' to have met the Fae show them to be dangerous to us. They always want something."

Agatha weaved her hands, and a large pile of books fell into the centre of the table. She pulled the stack towards her and tossed the top one towards Jack. "Here. Look," she commanded.

Jack pulled the book towards him. It was bound in blue leather, and in gold leaf on the front was stamped the legend 'The Blue Fairy Book.' He flipped it open to the contents page and saw a list of stories that the book contained. He was familiar with some of them as he skimmed down the page; 'Little Red Riding Hood' and 'Jack the Giant Killer' stood out. He looked up at Agatha, who nodded.

"Yes, those are fairy tales. But where do you think that they come from?" she said, her stare drilling into Jack.

"I don't know; the Brothers Grimm?" said Jack, looking at the book.

"People like the Grimm's indeed collected these stories, but they came from folklore, Jack. Folk tales going back for generations. An oral history of encounters with the Fae, embellished with each telling as the years go by, but always with one thing in common. Those featuring the Fae devils show that they always, always want something from us. And it is usually more than people are willing to give."

"I don't understand," said Jack puzzled. These were just fairy tales.

Agatha jabbed a gnarled finger at the book. "Look. Just look. 'Rumpelstiltskin.' He wanted the miller's daughter's first-born child. That story is supposed to be over four thousand years old. 'The Yellow Dwarf,' Kidnap and murder. 'Gulliver's Travels'; the little people wanted to blind him for no reason. It's all here."

She tossed another book at him, none too carefully, and it flopped to the floor. Jack picked it up; this time, it was the 'Yellow Fairy Book.'

"*Look,*" screeched Agatha. "*The Nixie of the Mill-Pond. Kidnap. Just one of many. And that's just in these books. The tales of their doings are scattered worldwide; we have many volumes in the library here that you are welcome to peruse. Think about it. Think about the tales you know from your childhood, and tell me the good in them. I ask you. Tell me!*"

Jack was getting a little scared now at the rant, but he volunteered, "Peter Pan?"

"A tale of child abduction, brutal treatment, and bewitchment," said Malchiah without hesitation.

"Pied Piper of Hamelin?"

"Grand-scale abduction. Those children were never heard

from again. In any of the legends. Taken for slaves in the mines of that cursed place."

"Cinderella. That one had a happy ending."

"Pah," snorted Agatha. "Yes, in the oh-so-twee Disney version, with its fairy godmothers and such rubbish. There is no such thing. That story is based on the history of Rhodopis, a Greek woman whose name means "rosy-cheeked." Captured, sold into slavery, and taken to Egypt, where she was sold to Pharaoh Ahmose. He was under the control of the seven Hathor's, supposedly representations of an Egyptian goddess, but in reality, Fae. The sirens of Greek mythology that we know are just nymphs. Everyone supposedly loves those damned 'Faery Godmothers.' I'd take the iron to them all."

Jack gave up. "But these are just stories."

Malchiah leaned over the table to look closely at Jack. "Yes, stories, but stories rooted in fact. The devils have been amongst us for centuries, for generations, and up to no good at all. All these stories; either the heroes outwit them, or they get away with it, don't they?"

"Well...I suppose so," said Jack, unsure. There was a ring of truth to this, but surely this was looking at just the bad? It was confusing.

"Exactly. If they were so good, then why do they need to be beaten, with wit or otherwise?" Malchiah sat back, a satisfied look on his face.

"But, the ones that I know are good. They told me about good and bad faeries; surely all these in the stories are bad?" Jack said, starting to doubt himself a little more.

"*They are all bad!*" screamed Agatha suddenly, banging her gnarled fists on the table and causing Jack to jump almost out of his seat. Tiny green sparks erupted from where her fists impacted and disappeared into the air. "*And mark me, boy, they need to be stopped.*"

Jack looked at her angry face, and thought 'Bide my time, bide my time.' He did not believe what they were saying; his own experiences, to his mind anyhow, didn't match what these two were telling him. But again, he'd seen evil Fae, the Lisovyk for one, and those goblin creatures. So perhaps there was something in it? And it was an interesting perspective on those tales, he had to admit. *'But,'* he thought, *'You can find the bad in any situation if you really try. If they looked for the good, it may well all have been so different.'*

"It's a lot to take in," said Jack carefully. "I ought to think more about what you've told me if you'll let me. I can understand your perspective, but I'm not sure it's right."

"But it is right, Jack. Moreover, our family has to stop these creatures from enslaving more of our fellow man; that is a given. Our mission comes from the Lord Almighty himself, and it is your God-given duty to assist us with cleansing our realm of these devils."

"I would really like to think more about it," said Jack, his eyes downturned.

"Of course, of course," said Agatha, all sweetness again. "You can ponder the whole thing while you perform the little task we've got for you."

"But you said that if you couldn't change my mind, I'd be free to go," said Jack a little more forcefully. "I listened to what you had to say, and I'm still not sure. My mind isn't changed. Yet."

"You are quite correct, Jack. We did say that you would be free to go. Of course, you are. Here, allow me."

Agatha seized the little handbell and rang it again, its shrill tinkling noise echoing through the room, louder than its size would indicate. The door opened, and a man's head appeared. "Ma'am, you rang?" he said.

"Take young Master Cracklock here to somewhere he can travel from. You can travel, can't you, Jack?"

"Yes, although I've not had much practice," said Jack. Agatha nodded her head and waved the man in.

"Certainly, Ma'am," said the man stepping fully into the room, his dress formal and butler-like.

Malchiah stood and offered Jack his hand. "It was good to meet you, Jack. I hope to welcome you back here to the ancestral family home once you have had the chance to ponder what we said. We are more than happy to answer any questions that you may have."

Jack gave the proffered hand a brief shake and got to his feet. As he turned to leave, Agatha said to the footman. "Once Master Cracklock has left, please bring Elsie Cracklock to us here. And those two devils she tolerates. Fermerillion and the fat one. They are in the Catacombs."

"What?" said Jack, suddenly on the defensive. "You said we were free to leave?"

"No," said Agatha, the sly look back on her face. "I said that *you* were free to leave. The others, well... they are ours. We will remove their grackles, as we will need them more than ever if you are unwilling to help us with our little task. Anastasia, in particular, is very keen to help with your friends, and I believe that Benedict would like the brownie?" Malchiah nodded.

"But you can't," said Jack. "You..."

Agatha cut him off. "We can do whatever we please, Jack. This is how it works. You don't help us; then, we help ourselves. Unfortunately, I cannot allow you to say goodbye; the dramatics would be rather unbearable. Now, please, get out of my sight." She nodded to the footman, who seized Jack's arm.

"Wait," said Jack as the footman pulled him towards the door. "If I do what you want me to do, will you let us all go?"

Agatha stopped the man with a wave of her hand. She cocked her head and looked at Jack.

"If you perform the task to our satisfaction, then we will consider releasing your friends. There will be terms, of course, as you would be a useful asset to us. Although I am sure we can come to some sort of mutually beneficial arrangement. Do you agree?"

Jack sighed inwardly; he was sure that no good would come of this. "What do you want me to do?" he said.

Agatha clapped her hands together again and rose from her chair.

"Oh, it's quite simple, Jack. We need you to find something for us."

"What is it that you've lost?" said Jack.

"It's not lost, well, not really," said Agatha. "It's just we don't know exactly where it is, and we need someone to go and check for us. And you are ideally suited to the task."

"Okay..." said Jack, uncertainly. "So, what is it?"

"A realm pillar, Jack. Specifically, the one that we know is located in the Realm of the Departed."

CHAPTER 9

Sammy sat behind the wheel of the 'Ocado' van, driving it carefully down the winding country lanes. Jimmy sat next to her in the middle passenger seat, with Timothy next to the window, the fresh air streaming in and over his rather green-looking face. The three tubes sat on the dashboard, excitedly chattering to each other in the chiming language that the others could hear faintly in their heads. Roly had confirmed that they had never been in a vehicle before, and they were enjoying the sights and speed as the van traced its course towards the mansion house where their friends were captive.

"You don't like cars then, Timothy," asked Jimmy to the petite Fae, who looked slightly sick.

"No, not at all," replied Timothy. "Awful machines, with their hideous gases and rocking movements. There are so many other civilised ways to travel. I yearn for the days when you lifers used the horse and carriage. So much more sedate."

"But not as quick," countered Jimmy. "And we need to get there and get the others out. Goodness knows what is happening to them in that place."

Timothy fixed him with a look. "If I wanted speedy travel, I can do it myself without this whole awful experience. However, we need to stay together. How much further is it?"

"About three miles," said Sammy, looking at the phone app that was tracing their route as they travelled. "If the directions were correct, that is."

"Talk us through again what we are going to do when we get there," said Jimmy, a determined look on his face.

"Okay," said Sammy. "Now, as we agreed..."

THEY HAD PREVIOUSLY ARRIVED in the small town of Chard directly from Twillington House, realm travelling to what they found out was the town's small museum. Exiting from the empty women's toilet was not the most glorious way to arrive, but they weren't seen as they came through the museum and out of the exit.

Once they were outside, Sammy had explained her plan to them. It was relatively simple; the intention was to locate and acquire a food delivery van, Timothy glamouring the driver as necessary, and then go to the manor with a view of talking themselves into the place as delivery people. Once inside, they'd stick together to try and find the others, hopefully not drawing attention to themselves as they did so. Sammy had explained what David had done before, and short of going in 'all guns blazing,' they all agreed that they couldn't think of anything better. The tubes would be held at the ready during the search.

"Ahem," said Timothy as they discussed where they were going to locate a delivery van from. "I can't go in with you."

"What do you mean?" asked Sammy. "We'll need your help."

"I mean that I am Fae. Given what we know about the Cracklocks, there is no possibility that a Fae can get into that place undetected. I would think that they will be alerted to my presence the moment I cross the threshold at the gate."

Sammy tutted. "Are you sure? There must be some way that we can sneak you in?"

"I very much doubt it," replied Timothy, polishing his spectacles on the edge of his robe. "I am sure that there must be all kinds of measures in place to stop Fae from getting in. The place is dedicated to the destruction of my kind. Why would they just allow me to waltz in through the gates?"

"But we could really do with your glamours," said Jimmy. "I mean, Roly's lot are pretty powerful, but it would be nice to have some different magical backup of our own. I mean, Elsie could do pretty impressive things, and Jack was just starting to learn. But I would think that those Cracklocks are quite tasty when it comes to that sort of thing. We wouldn't stand a chance."

"They are," said Sammy, with a shake of her head. "They used all kinds of things to come after us before David disappeared and that Anastasia had me at her mercy without breaking a sweat. We could really do with the help, Timothy."

Timothy shook his head sadly. "I think that I would doom our mission before it even began, loathe as I am to say it."

'We can assist,' a chiming voice rang in their heads, and Jimmy looked at the bright blue eyes of Roly peering at him from the dashboard.

"How?" said Jimmy, interested.

'Why don't we place friend Timothy here into the Cartulary? That way, we can enter this place and release him when we need to. He can help us rescue the others and obtain the Focus.'

Jimmy slapped his leg. "Of course! That could work. Couldn't it?" He turned to Timothy.

The petite Fae pondered this for a moment. "I believe that it would; I wouldn't be there, but somewhere else. But please tell me, you advised previously that living things were not so well kept within the Cartulary, particularly those beings of higher intelligence?"

'It would be acceptable for a short while. It is like a stasis; time would stop for you, although your mind would be free.'

"It would be interesting to see the inside of the Cartulary," Timothy mused.

'You would not see it. You would be compartmentalised until your release,' replied Roly.

"Well, that doesn't sound very exciting, but it could be a way around the issue," said Sammy. "What do you think, Timothy?"

"I agreed to help in any way that I could," Timothy sighed. "And if that solution would work, then it is acceptable to me."

"We will only find out during the actual run at it," said Jimmy. "But I say we try."

"Agreed," replied Timothy, and the tubes chimed their agreement. "Now, we must obtain this vehicle. What do you suggest?"

In the end, it was easy. After walking around the town's streets for a short while, they spotted an Ocado delivery van parked outside one of the more picturesque houses. The driver was unloading bags from a plastic pack in the back, an old lady standing at the door to receive them.

"What do we do?" asked Sammy to Timothy. The Fae sighed again and said. "I will bewitch them, although it is not something that I take pleasure in. The man can stay here while we borrow his transportation. Please wait for a moment."

Timothy walked over to the couple as they stood on the doorstep, making a complicated series of gestures as he did so. The two people froze, and Timothy beckoned Sammy to come over quickly.

"Tell them what you want them to do," he said, his hands still performing the gestures.

"Eeerm, can I have your high-vis, please?" said Sammy to the driver. "And your van keys?" Without batting an eyelid at this strange request, the driver slipped out of his yellow waistcoat and handed it to Sammy, along with the keys.

"Would you be able to invite this gentleman in for a cup of tea?" Sammy asked the old lady, who gave her a broad smile and pulled the door open wide. She gestured for the driver to enter and then pushed the door shut behind them as he disappeared from view.

"We should go," said Timothy. "That glamour will hold for a short while, but I did not want to enchant them for too long. I am not an entrapment Fae, and I fundamentally disagree with forcing you lifers to do things against your will."

The friends climbed into the van, and Jimmy tapped the mansion's address into the phone's map app.

"Down there and turn right at the roundabout," he said, pointing. Sammy shifted the van into gear, and they were off.

THE GUARD at the entrance to the catacombs sat nodding on his stool; the wine cask entrance securely shut behind him. Even glamoured as he was, the boredom from this duty was always overwhelming. Sitting in the semi-darkness, the smell of the furnaces wafting over him and the faint clinking sounds in the distance as the smiths plied their trade formed a white noise that always lulled him to near sleep. He was fully aware of what would happen to him if the lady or gentleman of the house caught him asleep at his post, but the atmosphere was hypnotic, and he couldn't help himself. Hence he was caught completely off-guard by a loud bang on the hidden door behind him, startling him to his feet.

Moving towards the door, the bang came again - a single loud thump on the wooden surface on the other side. The guard cocked his head. Sure enough, the same loud bang came again a few seconds later, like someone was hitting the door with a hammer. He pulled out his pistol and unsheathed an iron dagger. Something was definitely off.

Moving to the door, he called "Who is it?" and was rewarded with another loud bang. He listened, and it happened again. "Who's playing silly buggers?" he called out. No answer. Then the bang again. It was almost rhythmic now as it repeated itself every few seconds. The guard was in a quandary now. He was not supposed to open this door unless the person on the other side had the relevant password. But it could be someone in trouble out there. Not letting anyone through was a safety measure in case of attack from bewitched people, sent by the devils for whatever purpose - there was no way that any Faery would be able to penetrate this far into the manor house without being detected, but they had sent humans before to do their dirty work.

The door had a hidden lens in it, incorporating a small hagstone, to allow a limited check of whoever was on the other side. The guard pressed his eye to this but couldn't see anything. He then jumped smartly as the loud bang came again on the other side, echoing through the wood.

The guard's thoughts were somewhat subdued by the strength of the glamour on him, but he decided that he'd better check. He tucked his iron dagger within easy reach in his belt, and holding his gun, pulled back the thick bolt that held the door firmly shut. The door itself swung open easily, its hinges well-oiled, and the wood securely fitted. He put his head out into the wine cellar and looked left and right. Nothing. "Hello?" he called. Again nothing. Sighing to himself, he pulled the door shut, bolted it, and stood to listen; his head cocked to one side. No bang, no thud, nothing. He listened, alert, for a couple of minutes before giving up and slumped back down onto his stool.

What the guard hadn't seen while perusing the wine cellar for the phantom intruder was a small cylindrical object whirring over his head, spinning fast like a fan blade as it went. It banked in the air around the corner and set off at speed. The rolling pin was answering its summons.

~

DORCAS AND FERMY were wet and miserable as they sat, one above the other in their cages, their knees drawn up to their chins. The jailer had done as he had promised and given them another soaking. He hadn't spoken to them, just stumped in and tipped the bucket over them, ignoring Fermy's protesting shouts. Fermy had spent some time inspecting the lock again, but there was no chance of picking it with just his fingers. So there they sat, unable to do anything but wait to see what fate had in store for them.

Which was something neither of them was expecting. They didn't see the whirring object streak into the room, but they heard it as it glanced off Dorcas' cage with a dull clang and then dropped to the floor in the middle of the room. Roused from his melancholy, Fermy went to the edge of the bars and looked around for the source of the noise. And there it was, lying on the damp floor a way away from them—Dorcas' rolling pin.

"Dorcas," Fermy whispered urgently. "Your rolling pin. It came back."

Dorcas sat up, the clang having raised her from her miserable thoughts. "What's? My pin?" She scuttled to the side of the cage below Fermy and looked out.

"Shame we can't reach it," said Fermy.

"Ha," said Dorcas and held out her hand. The rolling pin shot into it from the floor, and they both gave a little cheer.

"Sshh," called one of the other Fae. "He'll hear you, and we'll all be for it."

Whispering urgently now, Fermy told Dorcas which end to

unscrew, and she did so. Secreted away in tiny space were some long thin wires and a tiny little file with a flat end.

"Hand those up to me," whispered Fermy. "And don't drop them." Dorcas did as he bid, and the little Feeorin tucked them into his waistcoat carefully. Dorcas did likewise, hiding the rolling pin out of sight under her damp dress.

"Right. Let's get out of here," he said and moved over to the lock again for another look. Using the file, he attempted to jimmy off the side of the lock, but as he put more strain on the tool, he could tell that it wasn't budging.

"Can you picks it?" whispered Dorcas, who could not see from her position. "Hurry ups."

"It won't go; I can't get it from this side," whispered back Fermy in despair. "It's too secure."

"What are we going to do's?" whispered Dorcas, the earlier hope she'd felt starting to drain away.

Fermy was silent for a moment, thinking. Then he looked down through bars at Dorcas.

"The only way for me to pick it will be from the front. Through the actual keyhole mechanism. And I can't reach it from this side; the angle is too difficult for me to do it." He sat down despondently and then jumped up again as inspiration struck him.

"I can't get at mine, but I could perhaps get at yours! We'd have to be quick, mind, and it would be extremely risky. And you'd have to take on that Jailer to get his keys if you think you could and assuming I can get your door open."

"That," said Dorcas, "Would be my pleasures. I have something for that jailer bully man's, and I's can't wait to gives it to him. What do we do's?"

"We're going to have to overbalance my cage so that it lands in front of yours," said Fermy. "And hope that it doesn't knock me out in the process. I should then be able to get at your lock, and I'll let you out. You'll have to get the keys from the jailer and let me and these others out."

Dorcas looked a little doubtful. She stretched to her full height and curled her fingers through the top of her cage, hooking them onto Fermy's cage above. She heaved with all her might, and the cage scraped forwards a little with a shrill screeching noise as the metal protested. Fermy set his feet against one of the bars, and they both tried again together. The cage shifted forwards a little more, the end now overhanging the top of her cage. Dorcas nodded in satisfaction to herself and looked back up at Fermy.

"I reckons I can move's it with your help. But it will make a bigs noise when it lands; I is not strong enoughs to slide it down. It is too heavy and awkwards from this angle."

Fermy frowned. "That noise will bring that awful jailer the moment it hits the floor. It's too much of a risk; we will only have one go at this, and I still have to pick the lock. I don't think that we can do it."

"Excuse me," came a timid voice, and they looked around to see the weeping faun from earlier, its tears now quite dry and a resolute expression on its face. "I hope that you don't mind me listening in, but if what you are planning is going to work, now would be the time. That awful lifer will be asleep now; he always is at this time. He gives out awful punishments if anyone wakes him during his naptime. I know, look." The faun turned around, and the friends recoiled in shock. Where its tail should have been, now there was only a mangled fleshy lump, scabbed over. "He took my tail when I cried and woke him up. 'To give me sommat to cry for,' he said. He used iron scissors on me; it's gone for good." The faun looked at them, its eyes glistening with tears again.

Dorcas's face clouded over with anger. She seized the cage with Fermy in it and heaved with all her strength. The cage moved forward a few centimetres. She moved back, seized it again, and pushed with all her might. More than half the cage was hanging over the edge now.

"Now holds steady," Dorcas whispered, as loud as she dared, and with one more mighty shove, Fermy's cage overbalanced and crashed to the floor in front of the door to Dorcas's cell with an almighty bang.

Fermy sat up, shook his head from the shock of the landing, and then was straight to the side where Dorcas's door was. From outside the cell room, a throaty scream, groggy with sleep, came, *"What are you 'orrible little swine's doing in there?'.*

"Quickly, unlocks me," said Dorcas, her eyes focused on the door to the cells.

"I can't reach it," shouted Fermy, panic in his voice, his arm stretched at full length but not touching anywhere near the lock. "It's too far."

In the distance came the sound of a horrible phlegmy cough and then another shout, *"I'm gonna kill you little devils. Wake me up, would yah? Where's me damn boots?"*

"Dorcas, can you reach me?" cried Fermy, holding out his arm. Dorcas stretched through the bars, but she couldn't fit her arm all the way through. "I can't Fermy's; I's too fat!"

The other Fae were at their own bars, watching the drama and shouting encouragement. Fermy looked around in despair. And then he saw the way.

"Dorcas. Throw me the pin. Quickly. I need it. Do it now."

Dorcas fumbled under the dress and pulled out the rolling pin. She poked it up between the bars and then threw it like a dart across the gap to Fermy. It clanged against his cage, and before it could roll away, he grabbed the handle.

"Oo wants the iron then?" came another yell from the room outside. *"Cos someone's gerrin it, you just see."*

Fermy wrestled as much of the pin as possible through the bars of his cage and then leaned on it with all his strength. *"Summon it, Dorcas,"* he screamed. *"Summon it!"*

Dorcas saw instantly what he was trying to do and held out her hand. The pin twitched, and then, dragging Fermy's cage with it, it made its way towards Dorcas. When it got close enough to her flailing hand, she grabbed the bars and pulled Fermy's cage in as close as she could.

"Okay, okay, okay," said Fermy in a breathless voice, inserting two of his lock picks into the lock. "Let's see." He forced himself to calm down as he set to the lock, feeling his way around the mechanism with the thin pieces of metal.

From outside the room came the sound of stamping footsteps, getting closer. Fermy swallowed and muttered to himself, "It's really complicated. Please, please, please..."

The door to the Jail room flung open with an almighty bang, and in stomped the Jailer. He held a vicious looking whip of many strands of what looked like barbed wire in his hand. Peering through his misshaped hagstone goggles, he took in the scene before him and gave an evil chuckle.

"Well, well, well. Bin havin a party 'ave we? We don't allow parties down 'ere. Not unless I'm the one throwin' 'em. Let's sort yer all aht, shall we?"

He started to stomp across the room to where Fermy's cage lay. Fermy focused on the lock, his tongue at the corner of his mouth, blocking out the impending arrival as he concentrated on the tumblers inside. He felt something give within the mechanism, and he delicately manoeuvred the wire into position again. He felt rather than saw the shadow of the Jailer fall over him.

"Ere, what do you fink you're doing, you little sod?" boomed the Jailer, and he bent down to grab the cage. And was then hit in the face by an accurately thrown stone travelling at high speed.

"Over here!" yelled a voice from one of the corner cages, and a gnome, its bushy beard matted and filthy, launched another stone which hit the Jailer on the top of the head. The big man rubbed the spot and glared at the offending creature.

"You first then. I'm gonna strip the flesh off yer back in front o' these 'ere. Be a lessun for all of yer," he snarled and fumbled at his belt for his keys. He stomped over to the gnome's cage, and the little Faery cowered backwards as the man loomed over him, key in hand. He put it in the lock, twisted it, and pulled the cage open.

Fermy's world had reduced to the lock and the picks now. He was calm inside as he felt the mechanism start to give, freeze, and then give again. "Hurry," whispered Dorcas, watching the Jailer haul the gnome from his cage and throw it onto the floor. He raised the hand containing the whip, and the gnome cowered, a weak hand held up to protect his head.

"*Yes!*" shouted Fermy triumphantly and twisted the two picks. There was a click, and Dorcas's cage door fell open. She didn't waste any time, pushing the door with all her might to make enough room to get out; the grating noise as Fermy's cage was shoved backwards causing the Jailer to pause and turn his head. He snorted with rage as he saw Dorcas scrambling out of the cage.

"*OOOIIIIII*!" he screamed. "*Get back in there if you know what's good for yer.*"

Dorcas cleared the cage and stood facing the Jailer. Her face was a mask of rage now, her eyes narrowed, and she held out her hand. The rolling pin plopped into it.

"*You's is a nasty evil man!*" she screamed back. "*And I is going to teach you a good lesson. AAAAARRRRRRGGHHH*!"

The Jailer was taken aback at the ferocity of the brownie as she came charging at him, screaming a war cry. These creatures had never, ever, stood up to him before; he was used to them being scared and compliant. So he was wholly unprepared for the rolling pin that caught him on the chin as Dorcas flung it at him, whirling away to return to her hand. He staggered back a step or so and shook his ringing head. Dorcas' next blow caught him across the kneecap, and he howled with pain as the audible crack echoed in his ears. Like a whirlwind, a second crack came across the other knee as Dorcas hit as hard as she could, her anger lending her extra strength. Behind him, the imprisoned Fae all cheered.

The Jailer staggered back a little, his bulbous belly quivering as Dorcas gathered herself for her next assault, the rolling pin weaving as she did so. However, like most bullies, the Jailer was a coward at heart, and he was scared. In his panic, he lashed out with a foot as Dorcas came at him like a bullet again, and, while she tried to twist aside at the last minute, her bulk betrayed her. The Jailers foot caught her on the hip and caused her to spin away, carried by her own momentum to bounce off the nearest stack of cages and end up on her back, her head hitting the floor with a thud. She shook her head, trying to clear it as her vision swam.

Seeing the brownie wasn't invulnerable, the Jailer felt a surge of confidence. Jiggling a little due to the pain in his knees, he hopped over and kicked her again in her big belly. Dorcas felt the air rush out of her, and the sickening stomach pain rocket through her whole body.

"You ain't so tough, are yer?" goaded the Jailer and raised his whip. He lashed down with it, but Dorcas rolled out of the way at the last minute, a few strands catching her and ripping her dress, blood welling through the cuts. She felt the sickening sensation of iron as she rolled back to her feet and crouched in a fighting stance.

The Jailer came at her again, growing more confident, and lashed out again with the whip. Dorcas took a neat step to the side and threw the pin at his head again. This time though, her throw was not as strong, the iron weakening her, and the Jailer ducked to one side as the pin sailing over his shoulder. He slashed at her again, and this time she was not as quick, the barbed strands catching her a glancing blow on the arm. Dorcas felt more iron and staggered a step or so to the side as dizziness overtook her.

The Jailer stood back and swung his arm about as if limbering himself up.

"I'm gonna flay yer alive, yer little scum. And then I'm gonna flay yer boyfriend," he spat. "And I'm gonna laugh the 'ole time I'm doin' it."

Fermy watched with horror as the Jailer stepped towards his friend. Then his analytical brain kicked up something. The goggles. Hagstones.

"*Dorcas*!" he screamed. "*The goggles*!"

Dorcas raised her weary head and looked at the Jailer. Hagstones. Over his eyes. And without them...

Dorcas shifted to the side so that she was directly in front of the Jailer, and jumped up, one hand hooking around the cages' bars. She pulled herself up, so she was almost facing the Jailer and held out her hand.

The rolling pin streaked through the air from where it had fallen and bounced off the back of the Jailer's head with a resounding thwack. The man saw stars and reached around to the back of his head instinctively, the pain rocketing through his skull as he howled in pain. As he did so, Dorcas launched herself at him and grabbed a handful of goggles; her weight tumbled her to the ground with her prize firmly grasped in her hand. She looked at the hagstone goggles and then tossed them into the shadows between the cages, out of sight. Her face set in a grim smile as she held out her hand for the rolling pin.

The Jailer, his head ringing from the blow, looked about for the brownie, but she'd vanished. As had all of his charges, the cages were all quite empty. He looked about in bewilderment and then clapped his hand to his face. His specs. His special specs. Gone! He glanced around the floor looking for them, and as he did so, an almighty blow struck him in the groin area, and he screamed.

"AAAARRRRGGGGHHHH, You little bugger! Where are yer? You come out and fight fair, yer little...OOOOWWWWW!" A further blow in the same area stopped him mid-sentence, and he sunk to his knees, clutching his wounded crotch with tears sprouting from out of his face.

Outside of the Jailer's senses, the Fae were all whooping with delight, banging and rattling on the bars as they watched their nemesis on the receiving end of some punishment for once. Dorcas wasn't being fancy about it; she walloped the man's outstretched hand, smashing his fingers as he groped blindly for her. As he snatched his hand back, she gave him a smash on his elbow for good measure and then brained him twice with the pin as he rocked backwards. The man was howling loudly in pain and trying to shuffle backwards out of his range.

Dorcas was not sadistic, and although she would happily have spent some more time punishing this foul bully for what he had done, she could see that all the fight had gone out of him. He lay huddled in a ball, crying huge snotty sobs as he cradled the various aching parts of himself.

"Alrights then," said Dorcas and hopped over to the side of the Jailer. With an expert downward swing, she clipped the man's jaw again, and he went out like a light. The fat bully lay there on his side, breath bubbling through his rubbery lips.

A huge cheer went up from the other Fae as Dorcas fished the keys from the man's belt and went over to Fermy's cage. It took a few goes, but she finally got the right one, clicking the lock open. The little Feeorin jumped up and hugged her.

"Well done, well done. I thought you were a goner then," he said, wiping away tears of happiness.

"I's nearly was until you's shouted," said Dorcas, leaking a few tears of her own. "I is getting too old for fighting nows. Time to hangs up my pin, I thinks. Thank you, Fermy."

"I'll believe it when I see it!" exclaimed Fermy and took the keys from Dorcas's hand. With a grim expression on his face, he said. "Okay, then. We are getting out of here. All of us. Including Jack and Elsie." He started to unlock the cages containing the other Fae, rapidly going through the keys as he released each of them.

"And we are going to 'elp yer," said the Gnome, coming over to them and holding out both hands. "Ta much for being so brave. I'm Gnorbitt, and please accept me thanks, gorgeous, for stopping that lout. I thought I was for it then." Dorcas stared at the gnome, not quite believing what she had just heard, and dismissed it.

"Thank you for intervening," said Fermy, shaking the gnome's hand. "We'd have never got the lock open without you."

Gnorbitt waved the comment away. "My pleasure; it were nice to get a bit of revenge on that evil swine. So, what are we doing next?"

Without missing a beat, Fermy said. "Tie up that brute, see what he's got that we can use, then get out of here and find our friends. If we can cause a bit of mayhem on the way out, all for the better. The guards will all have hagstones, I think, if that brute is anything to go by; the odd-looking spectacles like that monster wore. Take those away, and we even the odds. I don't think that this whole place is glamour locked; it can't be; it's too big. So we may be able to defend ourselves fairly well."

He tried a glamour gesture, but nothing happened. Hopping over to the main door that the Jailer came through, he tried again, and the ball of light flew from his hands, brightening the dim area. The other Fae cheered again, and they made for the door.

"Let's go and get Jack and Elsie," said Fermy. Slapping the rolling pin into the palm of her hand, a dark look on her face, Dorcas said, "Yes. Let's."

~

THE APP on the phone indicated half a mile to go, so Sammy pulled the van over and turned off the engine. She looked at Jimmy and Timothy and said. "I am really nervous about this. Will it work?"

"It has to," said Jimmy. "We need to get them out of that place. The plan is as good as it's going to get." He turned to Timothy. "Are you ready to go into the Cartulary?" he asked.

"As ready as I will ever be," sighed Timothy. "Do we need to get out of this awful vehicle?" Jimmy looked at Roly, who blinked his bright blue eyes and chimed. 'No, it will be fine. Friend Timothy, I will be gentle with your relocation. Please have no fear.'

"I am more concerned about being stuck in there for eternity," said Timothy in a small voice. "Please promise me that whatever happens, you will do your best to release me? I have over twenty thousand rodents to feed back in my laboratory."

Sammy gave a nervous laugh at this and then nodded. "Of course, we will do our best, always. We won't leave you."

"And you won't store me near that Binks character, will you?" said Timothy to Roly. The tube chimed a negative into their heads.

"Then, I am ready." Timothy removed his glasses and tucked them away into his robes. He closed his eyes and bowed his head.

"Very dramatic," said Jimmy and picked up Roly from the dashboard. He pointed the tube, there was a flash of blue light, and Timothy was gone. "Well, that was simple." He went to place Roly back on the dashboard with the other tubes, but Sammy held up her hand.

"Guys, I think you ought to get down from there now as well. I presume that there will be guards at the gatehouse or whatever, and they may be suspicious to see three brown tubes sitting on the dashboard. You may pass as novelties, but there could be trouble if they have seen one of you before. Plus, we may need you."

There was a brief exchange between the tubes, and then Roly chimed, "We agree. Please place us onto your persons; Sammy, you may take my countrymen here, and I will go with Jimmy."

With the tubes firmly out of sight, Sammy drove on. They soon came to an ornate set of pillars set on either side of a long private drive, curving off into the trees ahead. The phone app indicated the way, so Sammy turned, and they set off down it, tyres crunching on the gravel of the drive. Going around the bend into the trees, they shortly came to a set of substantial wrought iron gates, immaculately decorated with all manner of beasts and birds. Next to the gates stood a small brick-built building, and out of this came the security guard; although looking at him, he did not look like he would be able to stop much. He was old, wrinkled, and had a long grey beard bound into a plait. His eyes were hidden behind thick lenses, perched on a sizeable beaky nose, and he peered myopically up at them.

"What you lot doing 'ere today?" he said as Sammy wound down the window. "It ain't a delivery day."

Sammy faltered a little, but Jimmy smoothly took over. "Dunno, mate. It ain't the usual day, I know, but it's here on the job sheet, look." He gestured the clipboard towards the guard. "Bit of a pain, really; we were looking to finish early an' all. Coming out all this way. Still, customers are customers, and it's not like you lot don't spend a bit, is it?"

The guard eyed Jimmy suspiciously but nodded in agreement. "Reckon they're planning sommat; they order in extra then, like as not. Not that we see them much down here, any road, forget about us poor cousins they do. Open up the back, though; rules is rules."

Jimmy nodded and jumped out of the van, going round to the back. He pulled open the door to show the neatly stacked shelves of bagged up goods.

"Which is ours?" said the guard. "I need to have a look, make sure nothing's 'iding in there."

"What do you mean?" asked Jimmy, letting a puzzled note into his voice. "Nowt hiding in there, mate. No foreign spiders or ought like that."

"Just let me in, lad. Let's get this over with."

Jimmy stood to one side, and the guard climbed into the van. He took a half-hearted poke around the bags and then turned towards the front. He stood, his head cocked as he looked around. His nostrils started to flare as he took big deep sniffs. Then he froze and turned towards Jimmy slowly.

"Where is it?" he said in a slow voice.

"Where's what?" asked Jimmy, tensing.

"The Fae. I can smell 'em out, and you've had Fae in 'ere."

"What are you on about?" interjected Sammy. "What the heck is 'Fae'? Some kind of odour treatment? Only Fabreeze in those bags mate, or some other generic brands, I would think."

"Faeries. There's Faeries in 'ere. You glamoured?"

"I don't know what you're on about, you mad bugger," said Jimmy with a look at Sammy. "You gonna let us through or not?"

"Not," said the guard, climbing out of the van and making for the building. "You wait there."

"What do we do," hissed Jimmy to Sammy. "He's going to call for reinforcements."

Sammy opened the van door and jumped out. "Excuse me, Sir. Sir!" she called at the retreating figure.

The guard stopped and turned around to the beaming Sammy.

"Have you seen one of these before?" she asked, holding up her tube.

"Wot's that?" said the guard, stopping and looking at her quizzically.

"It's really rather exciting," she said. "Look."

There was a bright blue flash, and the guard was suddenly covered in a finely bound net. It was a tatty thing, covered in barnacles, but it covered him completely. The guard flailed at it in his shock, and it just tangled him further.

"'Elp. 'Elp," he started shouting. Jimmy ran over, pointed his tube, and with another blaze of blue, the enmeshed guard was surrounded by a clear zorb bubble, muting his shouts so that they could hardly hear him. Jimmy poked it with his finger, and it gave a little. Jimmy nodded. "It'll give, once he gets free of the net. So he won't suffocate."

"Well done," said Sammy. "But now what?"

"We roll him into those woods there, open up the gates, and drive up to the house."

"I do worry about Jack associating with you," said Sammy as she helped Jimmy roll the guard out of sight. "You think like a criminal. Very quick."

Jimmy gave a slight bow. "Why, thank you. Now, get in the van; I'll see if there's a way to get those gates open."

The building was laid out simply, with a very prominent dome-like button on one side of the desk. Jimmy pressed it and heard the whirr and clunk of the gates starting to open. He pulled the door shut behind him as he left, hoping that it would seem that there was no guard present if anyone should happen along.

The van rolled along the drive at a low speed, and Sammy whistled as the main house came into view. It was huge, a true mansion made from red and yellow brick. The gardens surrounding it were immaculate, as were the lawns as they drove slowly up towards the building. "Looks like the Cracklocks are worth more than I thought," she said to Jimmy, who was also in awe.

As they approached, they saw a sign, politely but firmly stating 'All trades and deliveries, this way,' with an arrow pointing in the direction that led around the side of the house.

"Good," said Jimmy. "Secret entrance. Better than the front door."

"Agreed," said Sammy, bringing the van to a halt next to a large, immaculately painted door. Jimmy jumped out and went to the large chain pull that was hanging down. He gave it a gentle tug and heard in the depths of the house the faint jingle of a bell. A few moments later, footsteps could be heard on the other side of the door, and it swung open. A woman, smartly dressed as a maid, stood and appraised Jimmy with a careful eye. "Yes?" she said.

"We have a delivery, Madam. For here, groceries and such," said Jimmy politely. The maid rolled her eyes and then stood to one side.

"Then you had better bring them in," she said in a haughty tone.

CHAPTER 10

"You want me to go where and do what?" spluttered Jack in shock.

"Into the Realm of the Departed," said Agatha patiently. "We want you to go on a little reconnaissance mission for us. We need to locate the Realm Pillar there. It will be easy enough to spot when you see it. Large, and you won't be able to see the top of it."

"A realm pillar?" said Jack, playing dumb.

"Oh, come now," said Malchiah. "We know that David knew what they were, and if he didn't tell his evil little devil friends, then I'll smile and kiss a pig. "

"It's not been mentioned," said Jack, trying not to look like he was lying.

"Well, no matter," said Agatha. "We just need to know where it is so that we can take a look at it ourselves. Find a large tower or pillar; that will do."

"But you have to die to go into that Realm!" said Jack. "Or if you don't, you will when you get there. That realm consumes grackles. I've been told about that place; people who are alive don't get to go there."

"Normal people don't, that's true. But you are far from normal, Jack, as we have discussed. We are hopeful that you will be resistant to the effects of the realm."

"But you don't know?" replied Jack. "I mean, I could die?"

"Maybe," said Agatha dismissively. "But that is a risk we'll have to take. Or you will."

"And if I won't do it?" said Jack, red spots of anger on his cheeks.

"Then we'll give you some more time to think about it. As you watch us drain the grackles from one of your friends. And if you need more time, we'll drain another, and so on. Starting with your Aunt. Make no mistake; I am not joking with you, boy, you are going to do what we want, or everyone that you love and care about is forfeit." Agatha glared at Jack.

"But what good will it do?" said Jack. "Even if I find it for you, then what?"

"Then others more suited to our requirements will go and complete the necessary tasks," said Malchiah quietly.

"Destroy it, you mean?" said Jack hotly. "And how do you intend to do that? You won't be able to go there, even if I find this pillar thing for you. And how will you know that I do find it?"

"Oh, we will be able to go there. The realm indeed extracts grackles at an alarming rate, but it is possible to venture there if you have sufficient grackles. Which we do."

Malchiah made a weaving gesture, and out of the air, popped a newspaper. He caught it and handed it to Jack.

"This 'Boofs' thing that the press is so fond of. It is our efforts to procure enough grackles to facilitate our entry into the Realm of the Departed."

Jack glanced at the front page and saw the black and white photograph of a wizened child, grey and wrinkled, lying in what appeared to be a hospital bed. His brow furrowed. Malchiah produced the oily-looking tube again.

"These devices collect grackles from their hosts, as you know. However, they also release those grackles collected at our command. The Realm of the Departed will siphon grackles from any living host, quickly making any living being part of that realm. In other words, departed. But we have determined that it will happily collect the grackles let loose from these devices, leaving the wielder unchanged for as long as those grackles are being made available. With these, we can enter the Realm and deal with the realm pillar."

"So, you have been draining people, children mainly, of their grackles to build up enough to be able to go and destroy another realm? And you think that's okay?" Jack's temper was rising again.

"It is a means to an end," said Agatha airily. "And once we have completed our mission there, then there will be no need to extract the grackles from any more children. Think of all the people you could be saving Jack, if you want to make yourself feel better?"

"But it's wrong. On every level!" shouted Jack, and to his satisfaction, the two Cracklocks recoiled slightly, Agatha recovering first.

"The devils are wrong!" she screamed back. *"And the price of a few children is worth paying to get rid of them once and for all. Make your decision, and for your friends' sake, it better be the correct one."*

Jack knew when he'd lost. If he didn't go, then his friends would be drained and gone forever. If he did go, he might be able to buy some more time to try to save them, plus something else might come up that could help them. He did not like it, but he knew he had no choice. He turned to look at the Cracklocks, his face set.

"I'll do it. But on the promise that you leave my friends alone."

"Agreed," snapped Agatha. "For now. Now come with me."

She led the way to the corner of the room, where a door sat

snug in the panelling. Pushing it open, she led the way through, then Jack next, followed by Malchiah. The room they entered was small with another more ornate door on the other side; intricate carvings around it. Against the sidewall was a large table, piled high with all manner of items, neatly stacked.

"You will travel from and return to here," advised Agatha. "Only come back when you have located the realm pillar and marked it."

Malchiah handed Jack a small metal sphere with a glowing red light at its centre; it looked like a fake eyeball.

"This is a positional marker. Please place it in the vicinity of the Realm Pillar, and it will enable us to travel directly to it when we enter the Realm ourselves. Once you have done so, you may return."

"But how do I get back?" asked Jack. "Are there doors there that I can use?"

"Yes," said Malchiah. "You will be able to find what you need; the scout we sent before briefly was able to confirm that at least. Waste of a good family member, due to you being unavailable, but there you go. Now, are you familiar with the travel glyph to return here?"

"Is it the normal travel glyph to this realm?" asked Jack. "I know that one."

"That will do quite nicely. You will need the glyphs for the Realm of the Departed, though; these were a closely guarded secret, but the Fae devils are so very careless. Please take this."

Malchiah handed Jack a smart-looking pen and a piece of fragile-looking metal, about the size of a playing card. Jack examined it and saw 'open' and 'unlock' glyphs etched onto its surface.

"We will not accompany you, although I will open the way for you. Once in the travel room, you will scribe the unlock glyph, go through and locate the Realm Pillar. It is imperative that you focus as you travel to get as close to it as you can. Once you have found it, place the marker, and then return here. Do not dally there; while we are sure that you will be resistant to the effects of the realm, we do not know how long you would be able to resist them. Are we clear?"

Jack nodded, too apprehensive to respond. He clutched the pen, ball, and metal card as if they were a lifeline.

Malchiah looked at Agatha, who nodded. He stepped up to the ornate door and quickly sketched the open rune upon it, slapped it, and watched as the golden dust fell away. He pulled open the door, and Jack saw silver and black dancing flames. They did not look welcoming at all.

"Off you go then, boy," barked Agatha. "And be quick. Your friends are depending on you."

Jack stepped into the small closet-like room, his heart pounding as he watched the flickering flames. He turned to the others, but Malchiah simply nodded and slammed the door shut. In the semi-darkness, lit only partially by the flickering flames, Jack studied the metal card and drew the 'unlock' symbol onto the door he had just come through. It did not work when he slapped it. Trying to quell his mounting fear, he tried again. And again, it didn't work.

Jack gulped, panic starting to well in him now. All he could think about was being trapped in this tiny waiting room forever until he starved. He tried the glyph again, and it didn't work. His heart was thumping in his chest, and his breath was coming in short gasps as the panic started to take over. And then, the quiet voice again in his mind, calming as it said in a low clear voice those same words as Jack had heard before.

"When you've got a problem, why not start at the beginning and see how to fix it?"

Jack took several deep breaths and looked at the metal card again and at his own artwork. It all looked okay, but...there! There was a missing line, short and almost invisible at the bottom of the diagram. Jack sketched the glyph again and added the line. He closed his eyes, slapped the glyph, and then opened them again. The golden dust was falling from the door this time, and Jack almost screamed with relief.

He pulled the door open and stared out into the blackness that met his eyes, strange lights swirling in the distance. Taking a deep calming breath, he closed his eyes and stepped through, the door clicking shut behind him as he did so.

SAMMY AND JIMMY had brought in a load of random shopping bags from the van and, under the maid's direction, had dumped them into the large larder off of the central kitchen. The maid spent her time tutting and looking at her watch, which was starting to get on Sammy's nerves as she unpacked the bags and lined up the goods on the large sorting table in the larder.

"Is she going to go?" Sammy hissed to Jimmy out of the corner of her mouth. Jimmy looked over his shoulder at the woman as she stood there, arms folded, and shook his head.

"What do we do?" whispered Sammy again. "We need to get in there." Jimmy looked around for inspiration and saw a receipt that had fluttered out of one of the bags. He grabbed it up, scanned it, and then turned to the maid.

"Excuse me, Missus, but there's a couple of items on here that we hadn't got in stock. You'll need to sign for them to say you didn't receive them."

"Not my responsibility," snapped the maid. "What is missing?"

Thinking fast as he pretended to scan the receipt, he replied, "Artichokes and snail caviar, Madam. These items are not something that we routinely stock, and looking at the notes, we had no idea what to substitute for them. The store is very sorry."

"Yes, well, your sort wouldn't know what to replace those types of items with, would you?" said the maid snootily. "And as

I don't know what Chef's intentions would be for them, you will have to have him sign for them."

"We'd be happy to," said Jimmy. "Whereabouts would we find Chef?"

"At this time of the day, he would be in the lower kitchens, I expect. Through that door there and down the stairs. Do you know where that is?"

"I think I've been there before once," said Jimmy, colouring a little at the lie. "And I suspect that you are super busy at the moment? We can go and get this signed off; save bothering you anymore. Would that be okay?"

The maid sniffed again and, looking down her nose at them, said. "Well... yes, this has been rather an inconvenience. Please go through that door there; you can see yourselves out when you're done." With that, she turned on her heel and left.

"Genius," said Sammy. "Where do we go now then? And should we let Timothy out?"

"We don't need him just yet. Not sure if it will set off some kind of alarm if he appears either; he seemed pretty certain it would. I suggest we give it a minute or so, then go in the same direction as that maid. We'll get Timothy out once we're properly inside."

"Okay. When David was here, he pretended to be a cleaner. Let's have a look about; see if we can see anything that could make us pass for the same."

The two of them rooted around in the various cupboards, coming up with a bucket each and few cloths as well as some bottles of cleaning products. They ditched the high-vis tabards they had been wearing and then followed the maid into the main house, treading warily as they went. They came to the servant's stairs at the end of the corridor, one flight up and one flight down. A large wooden door that presumably led into the main house stood next to the stairs.

"Where do you reckon they've got them?" said Jimmy in a low voice.

"No idea. Where would you keep prisoners? In a dungeon or something? Do mansion houses have dungeons in them?" replied Sammy.

"I don't think so. Personally, I'd prefer to check upstairs first and work our way down. Easier to do one if we are caught. If we are trapped underground in the cellars or whatever, they have us. More windows and doors upstairs, I think, easier to get out. Assuming that we can."

The two of them trotted up the stairs and opened the door at the top, Jimmy peering around the slight gap.

"All clear," he said and stepped out into the corridor. Again, they were taken aback by the opulence on display, gold gilding everywhere and foreboding portraits staring down at them. Expensive looking ornaments lined the corridor on plinths, interspersed between solid-looking wooden doors. The thick carpet completed the picture, soft underfoot and masking any footsteps that they made. They nodded to each other and walked up the corridor, clutching dusters in their hands in a vague attempt to augment their disguise. Jimmy hid Roly under his duster, ready to react in the event that they were threatened. The tube had chimed at the indignity of it but had then fallen silent at Jimmy's request.

"Let's check out these rooms," said Sammy in a low whisper. "I expect that the one holding them will be locked if they're up here. If it's open, then they're probably not in there."

"Agreed," said Jimmy and placed his hand on the handle of the nearest door. He twisted it, and the door clicked open. Looking at Sammy, Jimmy took a deep breath and pushed it open, ready to apologise to the occupant if there was one. He need not have worried. The room, a guest bedroom by the look of it, was empty. A bedspread covered the made-up bed, but the room smelled musty like it hadn't been used for a while. Jimmy pulled the door to, quietly, wincing a little at the click of the lock as it latched shut.

"One down, goodness knows how many to go," he said with a frown. Sammy nodded and moved to the next one.

The two worked their way along the corridor, trying each door, but all of them were in a similar state to the first one - unoccupied bedrooms made up and waiting for a guest to occupy them. They reached the end of the corridor and were about to move onto the next one, which ran at right angles to the first, when a voice called, "You, there. What are you doing?"

The two froze in shock, and Sammy groped for her tube in the inside of her jacket. Coming towards them was a tall, burly man dressed in an expensive-looking suit. Jimmy recovered first and gave a jaunty wave.

"Just getting some of these rooms shipshape, Sir. There are guests expected."

"Who are you?" said the man, his eyes flitting between the two of them suspiciously.

"We're from the cleaning agency, here to sort out some of these rooms," repeated Sammy. "Do you want to see our ID?"

"Yes," said the man, holding out his hand.

Sammy made a show of patting down her pockets and then gave the man an apologetic smile. "Sorry, I think I've left it in the last room that we did. Please, come with me, and I'll get it for you."

The man eyed her again and then turned to Jimmy. "You wait here. If this all checks out, you're good."

The man followed Sammy into the previous room, and she made a show of heading to the small ensuite bathroom that was visible from the door. "I took it out of my pocket while I was scrubbing the bath," she said. "Thing was digging in me." The man stepped further into the room, and Sammy went into the bathroom, pulling out her tube as soon as she was out of his eyeshot.

"Here it is," she called cheerfully and came back into the room, holding the tube in her outstretched hand. The man looked at it, not registering what it was until it was too late. There was a bright blue pulse of energy, and a cloud of white mist hit him full in the face. He went down like a bowling pin, crumpling into a pile. Jimmy flew into the room in time to see the man finish his fall.

"What was that?" he asked in amazement.

"Nitrous oxide, I think. The dentists used to use it to knock people out, from what I can remember. It's what I thought of anyway; I wasn't sure if it would work or not."

The man groaned and started to stir, so Jimmy gave him another blast with Roly. "We better tie him up; get those curtain ties down and one of those pillowcases. We can stash him in that bathroom for now. This is getting risky, Sammy. We can't keep this up; we need to find the others."

"I know, I know. I kind of panicked," she replied, trussing the man's wrists together behind his back with a curtain tie. Jimmy jammed a pillowcase over his head, and they dragged him into the bathroom, shutting the door on him. Exiting the room, they looked at each other. Jimmy had a brainwave.

"Roly," he whispered. "Are there any identification documents in the Cartulary?" The tube closed his eyes momentarily and then opened them.

"Yes, friend Jimmy," he chimed. "There are four billion, two million, three hundred and sixty-two thousand, four hundred and seventy-eight such documents within the Cartulary. Would you like me to retrieve some for you?"

"Sorry I asked," said Jimmy. "And no, thank you. We don't have time to try and find something appropriate. Let's go."

They turned left at the end of the corridor and continued down, checking rooms as they went, each time with no luck. Just empty room after empty room.

"I don't think they're up here," said Sammy as they

approached another turn in the corridor. "We should head downstairs."

"I think I agree with you," said Jimmy and then froze as he turned the corner. He ducked back quickly, gesturing for Sammy to stay put.

"What? What is it?" asked Sammy, trying to look.

"Wait," urged Jimmy. He took another glance, peering around the corner. Retreating, he said. "There's a man sitting outside one of the rooms just down the next corridor, reading a paper. The corridor opens up at the end; it looks like stairs to the main foyer area; it's very well lit."

"So we go back the way we came," said Sammy and started back down the corridor.

"No, wait. Why would a man be outside one of the rooms on this floor?" asked Jimmy.

"I don't know; perhaps he's…oh! He's guarding something?"

"Exactly," said Jimmy. I wonder what he's guarding."

"Let's go and find out," said Sammy, flexing the tube in her hand.

"Wait," said Jimmy. "I've got an idea."

THE GUARD FLAPPED his newspaper and turned over the page. The lead article on the "Boofs" was a recurring theme now, and he was tired of reading about it. However, it passed the time on this duty, which he felt was unnecessary – guarding an old woman who was securely locked up was not a true measure of his skills. Anyhow, he'd seen that classy blonde lady around earlier and was hoping that he'd get the chance to bump into her at some point. The woman was something else!

His senses twitched on immediately when a figure appeared at the end of the corridor, and his full attention focused on what looked to be a strange woman, grappling with an opponent who remained just out of sight around the corner. The assailant's arms that held the woman rocked her backwards and forwards, and then she was yanked out of view and into the corridor beyond.

The guard was on his feet before he knew what he was doing, his hand going to his pistol. He looked for his radio and cursed when he realised he had not bought it with him; this guard detail was pretty low risk, and he hadn't bothered. Moving to the balustrade, he looked over, hoping to see a colleague or another staff member, but there was no one there. He was about to shout when movement caught his eye. At the end of the corridor now stood a figure, human-sized but with a strangely distorted face. The guard squinted his eyes and saw that the figure seemed to have a bucket on its head. It dashed out of sight with a sudden movement, veering off the wall slightly as it went. The situation was extremely odd, but there were always strange things happening in this house, and he was sure that there were unseen creatures, despite what his better nature told him. However, his employers never put on any strange show without advising the guards in the locality first.

His training kicking in, the guard set off in pursuit, smart shoes slipping slightly on the thick carpet as he raced down the corridor. Reaching the corner, he slid to a stop and, with his gun raised, took a glance at the situation. He saw the crumpled figure of the woman lying in the middle of the floor, unmoving, but no sign of the bucket-headed assailant. The guard stepped cautiously over to the woman, crouched down, and shook her gently. She groaned, and the guard said in a low voice, "Are you okay, madam?"

Sammy fake groaned again and tried to roll over. The guard helped her do so, and as she flopped over onto her back, he noticed she was clutching a tube of some kind, the end of it pointing directly at his face. There was a blue flash of light, and he got a face full of acrid moisture, which made him feel dizzy.

He tried to bring his gun around but was suddenly covered by a large pile of netting, tangling him in his bemused state as he flailed at it. He stumbled over and hit his head on a large plinth, dropping down to the ground and not moving.

"Not much of a plan, but it worked," said Jimmy, stepping out of the room he had been hiding in and tucking Roly away. Checking the guard, he said, "Still breathing. Let's get this one hidden as well, and see what he was so keen to protect, shall we?"

Having repeated their earlier performance and leaving the guard thoroughly trussed up and out of sight, they set off down the corridor again to the room of interest. Jimmy took a quick look over the balustrade himself, gave a low whistle of envy, and then said to Sammy, "Nobody about. Should we knock, do you think?"

"I think we should just go in," she replied, gesturing to a small hook on which hung a key. "That should fit, I would think?"

Jimmy plucked it down, inserted it into the lock, and turned it. The click confirmed that it was indeed the correct key. Looking at Sammy, he raised a hagstone to his eye and said, "Get ready; if there's some monster in there, blast it."

He pulled the door open in one quick motion, and Sammy aimed her tube into the room, waving it from side to side as she did so. She need not have bothered. The figure sat in the chair jumped to its feet.

"About time," said Elsie. "What took you?"

Sammy flew into Elsie's outstretched arms, the tears starting to roll down her face as she hugged the old lady tightly. "Are you okay? Did they hurt you?" she said anxiously, patting Elsie up and down.

"Oh, I'm fine. About fit to die of boredom, but that's about it. Hi, Jimmy."

"Hi, Elsie. Glad to see you. Where is Jack? And the others?"

Elsie's initial joy drained from her face. "I don't know. Malchiah took Jack down to see his darling mother about two hours ago, and I haven't seen him since. I don't know what happened to Fermy and Dorcas; they whipped them off sharpish when we got here. They must be being held somewhere else, but where, I don't know."

"We'll find them," said Jimmy confidently. "We've already dealt with two guards."

"Where's Timothy?" asked Elsie. "He didn't come in with you, did he? I would have heard; this place is rigged with all kinds of anti-fae alarms on all the entrances."

"He's in here," said Jimmy, holding up Roly. The tube blinked his blue eyes and chimed into their heads, 'Hello, friend Elsie. It is good to see you safe and well.'

"Good to see you too, Roly; I see that you've fallen into bad company!"

'What do you mean? Jimmy and Sammy are good company,' chimed the tube with a note of puzzlement.

"Doesn't matter," said Elsie with a dismissive wave. "Just a lifer joke."

Turning to Sammy, she asked. "How did you get in here without being stopped? Moreover, how is Timothy inside the Cartulary thingy? Tell me everything."

Sammy and Jimmy quickly filled Elsie in on what had happened since she had been abducted, including what the tubes could do. Elsie had seen Roly retrieve the items from the Cartulary in the Realm of the Lost, but she was impressed that they could be used as a weapon.

"They're going to come in handy if we're going to get out of here. And you say that Timothy and that godawful Binks character are also in the Cartulary now?"

"Yes. We can let them out whenever. I'll release Timothy when we need him; we'll need all the help we can get to get out of here. Mr Binks...well, we promised to let him get at Malchiah, but I hope that we do not come to that; it depends on the whereabouts of the Focus. If we don't, then we can release him once we're clear of here. He can do his own thing."

"Sounds like a plan. Talking of which, what next? Who do we go for? Fermy and Dorcas, or Jack?"

"Jack," said Sammy without hesitation. "I want my boy."

Elsie and Jimmy nodded in their understanding. "Sammy," said Elsie gently. "I want Jack as well. But if he is with the Cracklocks, we will need as much help as we can muster to get him away from them. Even with Roly and his associates to help, it will be difficult; they have been waging war on the Fae for generations, and they have all kinds of tricks available to them. They are not to be trifled with."

Sammy considered the point and then nodded her head sadly. "I understand. I do. But I can't help but feel in my bones that Jack's in real trouble now, and we need to save him from them as soon as we can."

"I agree," said Jimmy. "But we stand more of a chance together. We still need to get the Focus if we are going to free Roly's people. That is a must. And to do that, we're going to have to overpower them, with Roly's help."

'Thank you, friend Jimmy,' chimed Roly quietly.

"Right then," said Elsie, cracking her knuckles. "Let's go find Fermy and Dorcas. Quickly. I expect that they will be in the catacombs that Malchiah threatened me with earlier; they must be down there if they aren't locked up here. That is where I'd put prisoners that I didn't really like. I just hope that the Cracklocks haven't extinguished them already, although I doubt it. They were holding them to keep Jack in line and do their bidding."

"We can go back the way that we came; down through the servant's quarters," said Jimmy. "Avoid any of those guards lurking around."

Jimmy cracked the door open of the room and peered

around to check that the coast was clear. He waved the women through and pulled it shut, locking it and replacing the key. "It'll pass at first glance," he said. "Hopefully, they will think that the guard has gone off to relieve himself or something."

Directly across from the door and against the balustrade were some low wooden sideboards, the dark wood immaculately polished, and vases of fresh flowers set atop them. Small doors concealed the contents. Glancing left and right, Elsie stepped over and opened one up. Nothing.

"What are you doing?" whispered Sammy.

"Those brutes took my handbag. I want it back," whispered back Elsie.

"Are you sure? Now really isn't the time," said Sammy as she watched Elsie work her way along the sideboards.

"It'll come in handy," Elsie replied, and then with an *'a-ha',* she pulled the bulky bag from out of the end sideboard and gave it a loving squeeze.

"Okay," she said. "Let's go."

They were halfway down the long corridor back towards where the servant's stairs were, hurrying as fast as they could when a sound caused them to freeze.

"YOOO -HOOOOO" came the loud shout. *"Elsie, Dearest. And Samantha too! How fortunate!"*

They turned, and cold fear ran down Sammy's spine. At the top of the stairs, coming from the main foyer, stood Anastasia. Behind her, Benedict grinned and wiggled his fingers in a grotesque wave.

"Where are you going, Elsie dear?" called Anastasia, stepping into the corridor.

"Run!" shouted Elsie, and the three of them ran for it. As they got to the end of the corridor, Jimmy pointed Roly back in the direction of the Cracklocks and concentrated. With a bright blue flash, all manner of furniture appeared; broken chairs, a three-piece suite, wardrobes, a table, and somewhere in the

region of one hundred large cushions. The furniture piled up in a heap, blocking the corridor and causing a shriek of rage from their pursuers on the other side.

"Well done, Jimmy!" screeched Elsie, and the three of them dashed for the stairs.

FERMY AND DORCAS led the released Fae captives into the dimly lit catacombs, continually checking for guards' presence. A few of the Fae had tried glamours and were visibly cheered that these still worked for them outside of the cells. A couple of them had also tried to travel away from the area, but it seemed that this was beyond them, for now. Despite this, they were in good spirits, even though they were still technically captives, and Dorcas had to shush them on more than one occasion.

On the rocky path away from the cells' area, the little group came to a crossroads. Above them, strung loosely from the ceiling, low wattage light bulbs stretched off in all directions. All three ways looked the same, equally daunting as they set off into the gloom cast by the bulbs.

"Which way to get out?" whispered a gaunt-looking Elf dressed in rags which looked to have once been expensive clothing, as she looked around in a slight panic. "There's no way to know. We can't get out! They'll capture us again!"

Her panic was infectious, and the other downtrodden Fae started to clamour as well as they cast about looking for an indication of which way they should go. A couple of them clutched at Dorcas as their saviour, and she pushed them away. Fermy stood slightly away from them, listening, and he held up a hand. The Fae ignored him. He tried to get their attention, but at only a foot tall, it was difficult as the panic was setting into them. In the end, Dorcas bellowed "QUIET'S!" and gestured at Fermy. The other Fae shut up and stared at the little Feeorin.

"Thank you, Dorcas. Now, listen." He cupped a hand behind his ear, and a number of the other Fae did likewise. And then they heard it. In the distance, the slight ring of metal on metal, dulled by the catacombs' rocky walls, but now they heard it, quite distinct.

"That way," said Fermy. "And be quiet. If we run into any lifers, take them out; if they're down here, they're up to no good."

The party progressed along the path, the metallic sounds getting louder as they did so. As they rounded a corner, Fermy stopped and gestured for them all to halt. Up ahead was an old man, fiddling with something on a table that stood outside what appeared to be a natural cavern opening. As the man turned, Fermy noticed that he wasn't wearing any of the hagstone goggles, just a pair of standard spectacles. Turning to the others, he said. "Wait here."

Fermy sprinted lightly down the path and up to the old man, who didn't acknowledge his presence. Jumping onto the stool next to the table, Fermy hopped up and studied what the man was doing. It looked like one of the lifer's weapons; a gun of some description was being repaired as it lay in pieces on the table. The old man was bent over, entirely focused on his task, and Fermy's glamour met with no resistance. The old man snapped to attention as a voice whispered in his ear, "Who are you?"

"The Armourer. Here to serve," the man replied.

"Which way out of here?" the voice whispered again.

"That way," said the Armourer, pointing in the direction the group had been heading. "Past the smiths and workshops. The exit is at the end of the pathway; it is a large wooden round door. It leads to the wine cellars."

"How many guards are down here?"

"It varies. Usually four. Sometimes less. I am not responsible for the guards."

"And how many other lifers?"

The man's brow creased. "Lifers?"

"People. How many more people?"

"Two blacksmiths. I don't know if there is anyone else."

Fermy pondered this and then glanced into the cavern. "What's in there?"

"The family arsenal. Munition and weaponry to be used for the glory of the great mission. I am its custodian."

"Really…" said Fermy, rubbing his hands together, a plan forming in his mind. "Thank you. You have been most helpful. Now, I would like you to head off back that way and see how far you can get before this glamour wears off."

"Of course. Thank you," replied the Armourer. He turned neatly and trotted off in the direction of the jail cells, the watching Fae moving to one side as he went past them.

Fermy gestured to the other Fae, and they came over at a run.

"There are around six more lifers down here. Find them, glamour them and send them off the way we came in like I just did. They need to be well clear of this area. And be careful; if they have those hagstone goggles on, they will see you. Once you've done that, get to the exit; it's that way over there; a round wooden door."

"What are you going to do?" asked a tiny sprite.

"I'm going to give the Cracklocks upstairs something to think about while we make our escape," said Fermy, a glint in his eye. "Dorcas, with me, if you will?"

Dorcas had been looking into the cavern entrance herself, and she turned, a big smile on her face.

"Oh, yes. Let's do that!" she said.

CHAPTER 11

As soon as the door swung shut behind Jack, he immediately felt a strange sensation all around him, like hundreds of tiny vacuum cleaners were pointing at him and gently sucking. He opened his eyes and looked at his arms, expecting to see his clothes ruffling, but his sleeves were quite still; indeed, there didn't seem to be any wind or even a breeze at all, although he wasn't struggling to breathe. There was just, well… nothing. No taste in the air, no odours, nothing. Just blackness in every direction apart from at one point in the distance, where a dim light could be seen, his eyes just discerning it from the void. And behind him, the door. Floating there in the blackness, its ornate surface no longer gleaming as it mirrored its surroundings. Jack twisted the handle and gave it an experimental pull, but it wouldn't open. Sealed shut. Jack gave up after a few tries. He assumed that it would open with the travel glyph; Malchiah had hinted at this.

Looking down, he couldn't discern any ground, although it felt like he was on a flat, stable surface of some kind, like hard marble. Jack stooped down to touch it, and his hand just carried on past his foot, as if it was going into a large hole just in front of where his trainers ended. He stood up again and tentatively took a step, placing his foot carefully down. It settled okay, and he took another step. Again, all fine. All around him, the strange sucking sensation continued. 'What is that?' he thought.

In the surrounding darkness, all Jack could do was aim towards where the distant light source was and set off. He had no idea how near or far it was; depth perception in the blackness was impossible. It was like walking through a dark ink that muffled all sound and external stimuli. Neither hot nor cold, just the black. As he walked, he played over the events in his mind, still wondering at everything that had happened in the space of only a few days. And he worried about his mum, and Jimmy, and Aunty Elsie, as well as his Fae friends. He had hoped that there would be something in this realm that could help all of them, but so far, nothing. No other people to ask, nothing but the endless darkness, the dim light ahead, and the door behind him.

'Where the hell is this realm pillar?' Jack asked himself. He had done as instructed and had focused on travelling to it when he drew the glyph. However, this was ridiculous; it was just nothingness as far as he could perceive, apart from the light. As he trudged on, it did not seem to get any nearer. Or any further away, just a constant in the distance, occasionally twinkling like a star. Jack walked solidly for nearly an hour, and absolutely nothing changed. He carried on for another hour, and still, nothing changed. The blackness still surrounded him; the sucking sensation went on, the door was there, and the lights stayed where they were. Strangely, Jack didn't feel tired, thirsty, or hungry; he felt the same as he had when he arrived. And no need for the bathroom either. Pondering on this, he came to a stop.

'It's like I'm not going anywhere, regardless of how far I think I've walked,' he thought to himself. 'And so, is walking really the answer?' He set off at a smooth jog, a theory forming in his mind. All he succeeded in doing was causing himself to pant a bit and work up a sweat, but he returned to normal almost instantly when he stopped. Nothing changed. 'That'd be a no, then,' he thought. Figuring it was pointless to carry on walking, he changed tactics.

"*Hello?*" he bellowed as loudly as he could. There was no echo; the sound seemed flat as he finished. He turned a full circle but didn't see anything. He cupped his hands to his mouth again and screamed, "*Heeeellllllllooooooo*!" for as long as he could, drawing it out until his throat started to hurt. He stopped and looked around again—still nothing. In the distance, the dim light twinkled. Jack was at a loss now what to do; he just wasn't getting anywhere. He would have to go back and tell the Cracklocks that he couldn't find the realm pillar and face the consequences. He knew that they would not be pleased at all and that his friends would also have to face their wrath. The options were, therefore, limited – stay here in this void until he faded away, assuming that the sucking was the grackles being pulled from his body, or go back and suffer at the hands of his captors. He was stuck.

Jack threw back his head and screamed as loud as he could, his frustration at the situation being vented in the power of his scream. When he finally stopped, he felt a bit better. He groped in his jacket for the fancy pen; he would go back, tell them he had planted the marker to try and buy a bit more time, and then see what he could come up with. Hopefully, they'd put him back in with Elsie; he'd see if he could get the bars on the window open or something.

He turned to the door and raised the pen.

"*FALSE BEACON, FALSE BEACON, YOU ARE NOT WELCOME*," a voice boomed all around him like thunder. Jack froze in his tracks, the pen almost touching the door.

"Hello?" he said tentatively.

"*FALSE BEACON, LEAVE*."

"Who is 'false beacon'?" called Jack.

"YOU ARE FALSE BEACON. YOU SHINE, THEY SEE YOU, THEY COME. BUT THEY STAY, THEY STAY. YOUR PURPOSE, FALSE BEACON? YOU HAVE INTERRUPTED THE BALANCE. YOUR PURPOSE?"

"I don't know what you mean," called Jack. "I'm here, because, well... because some people made me come. I don't want to be here, but I have no choice. If I can find what I came for, I'll go."

"I WOULD HEAR MORE OF YOUR PURPOSE. COME."

With that, Jack was suddenly at the light he'd seen in the distance. However, this close, it was almost blinding; the brightness of it scorched his vision, forcing him to cover his eyes with this sleeve.

"So bright!" he called. "What is it?"

"THE TRUE BEACON. THE PATHFINDER. YOU CANNOT SENSE THIS?"

"No," shouted Jack. *"It's just a bright light, blinding."*

He felt through his eyelids that the light was paling, and he tentatively removed his sleeve. He risked opening one eye and saw what appeared to be a colossal splotch of bright white light on the floor with several smaller splatters around it. At least it looked to be on the floor; it was difficult to tell, but his perception was that it was almost circular in appearance; it seemed to have width and circumference. But it was two dimensional; there was no depth to it. It looked like someone had spilt a pool of milk into the pitch black, and it was so white it almost glowed.

"Thank you," called Jack to the nothingness. "That's much better."

"I HAVE NO CONCERN FOR YOUR COMFORT, FALSE BEACON. WHY ARE YOU HERE? YOUR PURPOSE?"

"I was told to find a realm pillar that is supposed to be here. But I can't seem to find it; I have been looking for ages now."

"TIME HAS NO MEANING HERE, FALSE BEACON. THERE IS NO 'REALM PILLAR'; THIS IS NOT KNOWN TO US. LEAVE."

"I can't leave. The Cracklocks will kill my friends if I don't do as they say."

"YOUR FRIENDS WOULD BE WELCOME HERE. YOU ARE NOT, FALSE BEACON. YOU HAVE CHANGED THE BALANCE; EVEN NOW MORE COME TO YOU. THEY MUST NOT. YOU ARE NOT WELCOME HERE, FALSE BEACON; YOU DO NOT BELONG. LEAVE."

"What do you mean?" Jack shouted. *"Who are 'they'?"*

"THOSE WHO TRAVEL ON. YOUR BEACON DISTRACTS THEM, SHINING IN THE VOID. THEY ARE CONFUSED, LOST, AND UNABLE TO TRAVEL ONWARDS. YOU MUST LEAVE."

"I don't understand what you are telling me!" Jack hollered. *"I can't leave until I've found the realm pillar, don't you understand? They will kill my friends. Please help me."*

"IRRELEVANT. YOU MUST LEAVE. YOU ARE DISTURBING THE BALANCE."

"And if I don't?" yelled Jack. *"If I stay here and keep disturbing this balance. What then?"*

"YOU MUST LEAVE."

"I will not until I've found what I came for," Jack replied, his voice low, "So, can you help me or not?"

"I CANNOT ELUCIDATE. BUT I SENSE THAT YOU CAN KNOW. COME, BE."

There was a shimmering in the blackness, and then a figure-sized greyness coalesced. It was fuzzy at first, swirling like a grey mist as it gradually took a form—one that Jack recognised, although it had been a long time; six years in fact.

"Grandad?" he called, hope in his voice.

"Jack?" said the figure and stepped forward.

"Grandad," sobbed Jack, and flung himself at the old man, arms outstretched, but he passed straight through the figure of the old man. He gave a small sob and tried again, with the same effect.

"Jack, my boy, my brave boy. It is so good to be able to talk to you again properly. But you should not be in this place; it is not your time," said the old man, holding out his hands. Jack tried to grasp them, and his hand passed straight through them.

"Are you a ghost, Grandad? I can't touch you."

The figure laughed. "I am not a ghost Jack, no. No reason for me to hang around in the lifer's realm; I had a good life. More to the point, your Granny is here as well, so I have no reason to haunt anywhere. I am more of a, shall we say, manifestation."

"I don't understand?" replied Jack.

"Well, Jack, the void wants someone to explain to you about the situation, as it is struggling with the concept. Generally, those that come here do not wait around and ask questions. As someone you knew, it chose me. Your Granny and I, we have been watching you and Sammy from afar, trying to help where we can, so when the summons came, here I am. We have a closer bond than most."

"The voice in my head!" exclaimed Jack.

"Yes, that was me. You are sensitive to those that have left, Jack, and we can sometimes talk to you."

"Like those mediums on those television shows mum watches?"

"A little. But you are not like those. I am not sure that I am best placed to explain it, to be honest. The void bid me come, so here I am. Almost in the flesh if you like."

"The void? Is that what that voice is?"

"Yes, the void. It is nothing that exists here. Kind of a hole, I suppose; nevertheless, it has awareness, and it watches this space. And I am afraid that it doesn't want you here."

"Why, Grandad? I haven't done anything wrong. Other than come here to the Realm of the Departed to find that damned realm pillar, which I have to do, otherwise the Cracklocks will hurt my friends."

"This isn't the Realm of the Departed Jack. That realm lies through there." Grandad gestured towards the white lake in the gloom that stood behind them. "This is the void; the pathway to get to that Realm is through the light."

"So why am I here? I was supposed to go to the Realm of the Departed. Stupid realm travel doors."

Grandad looked at Jack sadly. "You can't go to the Realm of the Departed until you have departed, Jack. It simply is not possible for anyone alive to go there. The secrets of that realm are not for the living. As I'm sure, you know if you've watched any of those silly programmes that your mother likes."

"But they have the travel glyphs to get here; they said that this was the Realm of the Departed?"

"I'm sorry, Jack, but they are wrong. Whoever found how to travel here, I am afraid, was misled. This isn't the Realm of the Departed. It's the route to that place."

"Okay, I understand. But people who have come here before have lost all of their grackles as soon as they entered this place."

"Grackles?"

"Sorry, Grandad, I mean life force, or whatever you want to call it. People have travelled here and then been unable to get back because all of their life force has been taken away."

"So why hasn't your life force been taken away?"

"I don't really know. Something to do with the fact that I have Faery and Romani blood in me was what I was told."

"That would make some sense, although I don't know about Faeries. However, your Grandmother was of Romani blood; she could see and talk to restless spirits. It was quite frightening sometimes to come home and find her chattering away to someone who wasn't there."

"You never told me that," said Jack. "That would have been brilliant!"

"It's not the sort of thing you tell a child, Jack," replied Grandad gently. "If you'd shown any signs of being able to do the same, then we would have discussed it with you. But your mother never did, and, to the best of my knowledge, neither did you."

"No, I can't see any ghosts or anything. Just Faeries."

"I expect you got that from your Dad's side then; I have to say I'm not surprised at much nowadays. He was always off with the Faeries, used to drive your mum mad when they first started going out."

"Talking of Dad, you haven't seen him have you. You know, over there?"

"No. David is not in the Realm of the Departed, Jack. I know now that he vanished, but wherever he is, he isn't dead. He's not with us."

Jack managed a smile at that. "That is a relief; we were worried that he was dead. Nobody seems to know where he is."

Grandad looked all around him and beckoned Jack in closer. His lips didn't move, but Jack heard his voice clearly in his head. "He's still alive, Jack. But the question is, when? I will say no more."

Jack started to comment, but a ghostly finger was pressed to his lips. The voice in his head said quietly, "I cannot say more. Please do not ask."

Jack nodded his understanding, puzzlement on his face. Something else to ponder on then, to throw onto the massive pile of uncertainties that his life had become.

"Now then, Jack, tell me the full story of how you came to be here, and I will see if I can help you. I will also explain why you must leave. And soon."

"Where to start?" replied Jack. "It's been absolutely mental, Grandad," Jack told the shade of the old man everything he could remember, from the car crash to the trip to Faery, the Lisovyk (here, Grandad's mouth dropped), their journey to the

Realm of the Lost, and the capture by the Cracklocks. But most of all, about his new Fae friends and Aunty Elsie. When he had finished, Grandad was agog.

"So, the Cracklocks want to destroy these realm pillar things that hold the realms apart because it will destroy their enemies, the Faeries? And they don't care if it will destroy everything else?"

"The Fae, but yes Grandad. That's about it. We know that they have destroyed one of the five realm pillars. I presume that the one here will be the second one. I don't know about the other three, but there must be plans for those too."

"This is very concerning indeed. I understand what you mean now by a realm pillar. Something that holds the realms apart. Yes, I see now." The old man was thoughtful while he nodded his head, conversing with someone or something that was outside of Jack's perception. When he had finished, he turned to Jack.

"We cannot allow them to destroy this realm pillar, Jack, whatever we do. I find it difficult to understand how they could accomplish this, but from what you have said about all of the life force they've stolen, they could potentially enter this realm. And then they could wreak untold havoc."

"But where is the realm pillar, Grandad? It's not here, well, certainly not that I can see."

Grandad laughed aloud, great booming snorts. "You're standing in it, Jack," he said, once he had regained control.

"What?"

"These realm pillars, they're something to keep the realms apart, yes? The void does that; its very nothingness is the thing that you are looking for. The void itself is the realm pillar that you seek. It's why your travel door thingy spat you out where it did. You are in the pillar itself, but it is not a pillar. Does that make any sense? Cos I'm flabbergasted by the whole thing, to be honest!"

Jack shook his head, unable to take this in. When thinking it through, there was some sense to it, he supposed.

"But this place is huge, Grandad. There is no way that the Cracklocks would be able to destroy it, surely?"

"IT IS A POSSIBILITY, FALSE BEACON. THEY COULD," boomed the voice of the void, making Jack jump.

"How?" he called out.

Grandad stepped over to Jack and raised his hands. "I think that it would become clear if I show you why you need to leave as soon as you can; it will explain things in a way that words never can. May I place my hands on your eyes, Jack? What I will do won't hurt, and it will only be temporary, I promise."

"I trust you, Grandad. Do whatever you need to do."

Grandad placed his hands over Jack's eyes. Jack could see the bright light of the white blot through the misty grey of the old man's translucent hands, but then it suddenly faded in its intensity, a much duller white. It was still bright against the inky blackness of the void but diminished somehow.

Grandad stepped backwards and gestured to Jack.

"See yourself how we see you, Jack."

Jack looked down at himself and winced. His whole body was glowing with a bright white light, as bright as the lake before, almost blinding to him.

"What...why?" he stammered.

"Don't be afraid, Jack," said Grandad. "This is how the Journeymen who pass through the void see you."

"Who? What are Journeymen?"

"Close your eyes, Jack, and look again."

Jack again did so, and this time when he opened his eyes, the glowing light was just a dim blot in the far distance. Grandad stood next to him but obscured from Jack's view by something. Dark shapes had gathered around Jack, shadow-like in appearance. With a jolt of shock, Jack realised that they were clutching at him. He spun around, but they were everywhere, grasping and clawing at him with their shadow hands, a mob, surrounding him. They obscured the door that floated behind him, the wooden surface dimmed by their shadowy forms. Jack backed up a few steps, stepping through the forms as he did. They flowed around him, insubstantial like mist. Jack was reminded of the wraiths in the 'Lord of the Rings' films he'd watched.

"What are they?" he gasped, swiping at them as he tried to retreat, his hands passing through them. "Get them away."

"Don't be scared, Jack, please," replied Grandad. "They are the deceased, on their way to the Realm of the Departed. They cannot hurt you, for now at least. But look closely at your body, at the light that is surrounding you; tell me what you see."

Jack did as he was bid, squinting at the light as he did. By screwing up his eyes, he could cope with the light he was emanating, and he held out an arm for scrutiny. It was incredibly bright, but he could see tiny black lines like very thin hairs within the brightness when he looked more closely. Studying his other arm, he saw the same thing and on his torso. They looked like...

"Cracks! Grandad, this light is cracking around me."

"Yes, Jack. It is. And that is why you must leave, and soon."

"But I don't understand. What is this brightness?"

"That, Jack, is your life-force, the gracklies, or whatever you called them. You are alive here in the void, and the light you bring is attracting the departed who should go to the true light and onwards. The cracks you see are the departed starting to be able to drain your light, pulling your life away from you; that is what happens whenever someone alive comes here to the void. The light makes you a target for those who are lost and confused, as they flock to whatever light is nearest. They are trying to get through; it is instinct. And in those efforts, they drain the life force from those that they surround."

"But I've been here a while, and I don't feel any different."

Jack looked at the shadowy figures that continued to maul him with their insubstantial hands.

"That is true, Jack; due to your unique heritage, you resist better than most. Nevertheless, you will eventually succumb to their combined onslaught; despite your special nature, you will lose your life force to their efforts. This is inevitable, I am afraid. Those cracks will get bigger and bigger until you will be drained and become like these journeying souls."

"But why aren't you like them, Grandad?"

"I was, I suppose, but I don't remember it. As I say, it is instinct to pass to the light. Once you are through, I suppose you become like me. This form you see before you is not really how it is, but the most appropriate way for me to appear to you. I cannot tell you any more than that; those mysteries are not for the living, and I am prevented."

There was a subtle shift in Jack's perception, like a long blink, and then he was back again next to the glowing white pool in the darkness. Around him, the shadows were no longer mobbing him; instead, they were entering the brightness, which burned out their form as they waded into it. The odd one stopped to stroke their hands over his own glowing body, but they did not delay for long; the pull of the vast pool attracted them to enter the shimmering white light like insects to a bulb.

"I understand," said Jack. "I understand now why I am the false beacon now. However, I still don't understand what the Cracklocks could do to destroy this place; this entrance? This is something else."

"THE GATEWAY LIES IN BALANCE, FALSE BEACON, BALANCE BETWEEN THE LIGHT AND THE VOID. THE GATEWAY IS VULNERABLE, FALSE BEACON. THE BALANCE CAN BE INTERRUPTED, AS YOU ARE NOW. AND THE GATEWAY MUST REMAIN, OR DESTRUCTION FOR ALL." The voice boomed out of the blackness again.

Grandad was again listening to the unseen voices, nodding as he did so. He then looked at Jack and gave a sad smile.

"Jack, listen to me. The gateway here is very fragile, insubstantial even; it is a portal that is not intended to have the living enter it. If something were to happen to it that disturbed its delicate balance, then it would close. Which would be very bad. If someone were to come here with the intent to cause mischief, they would find it very easy. If enough of that life force you told me about were used to flood it, it would close. It is not built to accept outside forces like that. It has always been safe; there was no way for it to be disturbed. Until now, that is if those people intend it harm."

"What would happen though, Grandad, if it was destroyed?"

"This place would become a prison for the deceased Jack. Unable to go on. Roughly one hundred and fifty thousand people die every day in our realm, and that is not the only realm, as you know. The void is large, Jack, but even it could not contain all those souls over time. Think of a blocked up sink or a bath. What happens when you leave the tap on?"

"It spills over eventually."

"Exactly. And it would spill over into the other realms. That would be really what the effects of destroying this realm pillar would be. Unknown horrors as the spirits of the deceased lay claim to any life force they can find. In the realms of the living. It is unforeseen what would happen following such an occurrence, but it would not be good."

"'When there's no more room in hell, the dead will walk the earth,'" quoted Jack. "That's from this zombie film I watched. Mum didn't know."

"So, now you know. You must leave and never come back here. And you must stop anyone else, particularly those Cracklocks, from ever coming here."

"I need to get the Focus," said Jack. "It's the only way to stop them, I think. If we can get that, we can cut off their source of obtaining the grackles. If they haven't got enough already."

"You must go back, Jack. You must go back, get this Focus, and stop them."

"But what can I do?" replied Jack. "They have all the advantages. They are powerful, rich, and they are holding my friend's hostage. I am stuck. I can't just grab the Focus and run; they'd tear me to ribbons."

Grandad laid a translucent hand onto Jack's shoulder. "Your friends aren't hostages anymore, Jack. We here think that that will be enough. Now, you must go."

"But what about this marker, Grandad? I can't go back with it."

"Throw it away, Jack. They will never find it."

"Will I see you again, Grandad?"

"One day, Jack. Hopefully, a long time from now."

"But can I talk to you still?"

The old man was fading now. "Always," he whispered. "And I will answer when I can." He was almost gone now.

"I love you, Grandad," Jack called.

"And I you, Jack," came back a whisper in his mind.

"YOU MUST GO, FALSE BEACON," the voice around him said, quieter now, more subdued. *"YOU MUST LEAVE AND DO WHAT YOU MUST DO."*

Jack nodded, turned to the door, and pulled out the pen.

"FALSE BEACON. YOU MUST NOT RETURN HERE. HEED MY WORDS". The voice was softer now, but Jack could sense a subtle undertone of menace in the words.

"I understand," he called back into the black stillness, a slight shudder worming down his spine. He set to, sketching the glyph onto the door.

~

AGATHA AND MALCHIAH had planned to sit and wait for Jack in the armchairs opposite the small room from which he had left. One would keep watch at all times, taking shifts as they needed to, depending on how long the boy was away. Therefore, they were more than a little surprised as before they could even sit down, the door swung open, and Jack came back into the room.

"*What are you doing here, boy?*" shrieked Agatha, taken aback. "You were told what to do. Why are you back so soon? Go back at once, feckless child, and locate that realm pillar, or your friend's lives are over."

Jack looked as confused as they did. "What do you mean? You told me to come back when I had found it. So here I am."

"Boy, you have been gone no more than ten seconds," retorted Agatha. "Don't you lie to me."

"I found it," Jack insisted. "And I placed your marker. I did everything that you asked me to."

"*You lie!*" screeched Agatha, purple sparks dancing at the end of her fingers in her rage. "And resistant or not, you are going to learn a lesson about lying to me, here and..."

She stopped as Malchiah laid a hand on her arm. "Let's hear the boy out, Mother, shall we? We know that time shifts happen between the realms; take the devil's realm, for instance. People spend a few months there, but here, years can pass."

He turned to Jack. "How long do you think you were gone? And be honest."

"At least four hours, I think, but I don't know. Time has no meaning there; it's endless."

"And the pillar. What did it look like?"

Jack was worried about answering this question and had given it a little thought as he had stood in the waiting room. Taking into account what he knew from films about when you die, sprinkled with a little bit of the truth from his experiences, he had concocted a story that he hoped was believable.

Crossing his fingers behind his back, he said. "It's a huge

pillar of light, looks like a whirlwind, constantly shifting. Things are going into it; they look like ghosts."

Malchiah nodded, but Agatha continued to glare at Jack.

"And what is the realm like itself? Did you feel any ill effects? You don't look like you have aged any, but we didn't expect you to."

Jack continued with the fantasy he had created. "It's just black emptiness when you arrive there; nothing seems to exist there. No sounds, smells, or anything, but there must be air there because I could breathe okay. And there's this strange sucking sensation when you arrive, but you stop noticing after a while."

"And spirits, ghosts, etc. Where were they?" pressed Malchiah.

"I did see some things, but they weren't coming anywhere near me," Jack lied. "Just like spider webs, you know, immaterial, wispy things floating in the darkness. They were more interested in going to the realm pillar."

"Were there many of them?" snapped Agatha.

"Not loads that I could see," replied Jack, which was true. Initially. "But they went into the pillar thing, and I think that they disappeared, although it was difficult to tell – they all looked the same."

"Did you try to enter the pillar?" asked Malchiah.

"Well, I did try and put my hand in it. But nothing happened. It was like I was just waving it in the air, although I couldn't see it once it was immersed. It was very bright."

Malchiah studied Jack with a piercing gaze. Jack held it, looking into his eyes. When he was younger, he had staring competitions with the cat next door when it ventured into their garden to do its business, and he was pretty good at it. He just focused out and stared back, trying to look through the man. After twenty seconds or so of uncomfortable silence, Malchiah dropped his gaze and nodded.

"Your account matches closely what we already know. You are not the first we have sent to that Realm, but you are the only one so far to return unscathed. The other realms…"

"Are you sending people to other realms as well as this one then?" asked Jack, interrupting.

"My brothers are responsible for those, and anyway..."

"None of your business, boy!" shrieked Agatha over him, shrill and cutting, glaring furiously at Malchiah.

Malchiah paled visibly and bowed his head.

Agatha reeled on Jack. "Nasty, prying boy, poking his nose into things that don't concern him. I know your thoughts, you little idiot. You have no intention of thinking through regarding the Fae devils; you have too much of your father in you for that. And you think that we will spill our plans to the likes of you so that you can go crawling back, whispering to the devils about us?"

She slapped Jack hard across the face twice, his head reeling with the blows.

"And think yourself lucky that's all you're getting, you little toad. Get him out of my sight. Right now." The old woman was panting now, her lips wet with spittle.

Malchiah nodded meekly to his mother, grabbed Jack by the arm, and started to pull him towards the door to the main house.

"You can go back in with Elsie until we decide what to do with you," he said, his face red.

Jack's cheeks were stinging from the force of the slaps, but he found the courage to say quietly, "But you said…"

"I don't care what we said," snarled Malchiah. "You did what we wanted, and now you can wait until we need you again. While you do so, I would strongly suggest that you ask yourself a few questions about the morality of your dealings with those devils. Your immortal soul is at grave risk. Nevertheless, you may yet be redeemed if you correct your course."

Malchiah hauled Jack over to the door and pulled it open. He flung the boy out, none too gently, into the corridor and gestured to the guard there.

"You. Take him back upstairs, and lock him up with the old woman. And nil by mouth for them tonight; a little hunger may focus the mind."

"Yes, sir," said the guard and started to reach for Jack. However, as he grasped him, several things happened almost at once.

First was the start of the racket at the end of the corridor, just out of their line of sight. There was a series of small bangs, followed by shouting and then what appeared to be smoke drifting lazily from the other corridor that ran perpendicular to the one they were standing in. Sprinting around the corner away from the noise came a figure. Jack recognised him instantly.

"Jimmy?" he said to himself. Then. *"Jimmy!"* he bawled at the top of his voice, Malchiah flinching at the noise.

Another figure came round the corner, closely following the first and holding something emitting bright blue flashes of intense light. The figure recognised Jack and screamed back, *"Jack!"*

"Mum?" yelled back Jack and shoved at the guard who was holding him. A third figure came around the corner, handbag swinging as she threw glamours back at the unseen assailants. And then a fourth one, small, the height of the old lady's waist, also throwing glamours back in the direction they had just come from.

"What madness is this?" boomed Malchiah. *"Where did you all..."*

Before he could finish, there came the noise of a muffled explosion from beneath their feet. A second later, the whole house shook on its foundations, vases crashing from their plinths, and a shower of dust fell from the plaster as zig-zag cracks appeared on the ceiling overhead. A series of shorter explosive bangs followed, muffled by the floor but no less fierce in their intensity, the vibrations rising through their entire bodies. They winced as the screeching of a piercing alarm suddenly started to sound throughout the house, deafening in its volume. The floor shook again beneath them, and the guard let go of Jack in confusion. Malchiah stumbled and grabbed onto the doorframe to steady himself. His waistcoat twitched open, and Jack saw his chance.

He threw himself at Malchiah and grabbed the Focus as it dangled on its chain. He yanked it hard, snapping the chain and causing Malchiah to yell out in pain as the links cut into the back of his neck with the force of Jack's efforts. With the Focus in his hand, Jack turned and dashed down the corridor towards his friends.

CHAPTER 12

Fermy walked through the Armoury, studying the various shelves and looking for something familiar. In his previous life, working for the Courts, he had been inside many weapons storage places. Evil places they were and the stored items were used to create so much harm to others. Usually, his role was to look for items that could cause damage to the areas densely populated by the Fae, the natural places. Destruction of these areas was detrimental for both lifers and the Fae, so Fermy and the others were responsible for stealing secrets and sabotaging such items before they could be deployed. They had only one major failing - the awful material the lifers called 'Agent Orange.' The Courts had no choice but to intercede on that one once the damage was done, subtly glamouring the relevant lifers to ensure that their laws meant that it couldn't be used ever again. Fermy still bitterly regretted that one, and he shuddered at the memory, but his passing knowledge of lifer weapons meant that he hoped to find something that he could use.

Dorcas was also rooting through the shelves and boxes.

While she had no actual knowledge of the things themselves, she did have a lot of experience watching movies with guns and bombs and cars crashing. Dorcas loved those movies and wished that they had the moving pictures in Faery when she was back there. Elsie was a massive fan of 'action films', as she called them, and Dorcas liked nothing better than to sit with a massive bowl of salted buttery popcorn and watch the mayhem unfold. Elsie had had to explain a lot to start with, but Dorcas had studied the movies hard, stuffing her face as she did so, and nowadays didn't have to bother her housemate with 'loads of inane questions' as Elsie called them.

Something caught her eye as she moved in the dim light of the Armoury, a small wooden box tucked away on one of the bottom shelves. She prised the lid off it and gasped when she saw the small metal pineapples nestled snugly in their foam nests. She plucked one out, looked at the ring detonator and smiled to herself. '*Grenade bombs. Me is liking these, BOOM!*' she thought, reaching to take another when Fermy's voice called out to her.

"Dorcas, come here, would you? I've found what we're looking for, but I need some help. It's too big for me to manage."

Dorcas trotted in the direction of Fermy's voice and found him standing next to an old-looking box that shimmered slightly with the glamour that surrounded it.

"Look at this," he said, a smile on his face. "This is dynamite. The lifers use it for causing huge explosions; we can use this to cause some mischief, no doubt about it. It has a protective glamour over it, though, look. I wonder why?"

Fermy made a series of gestures and then reached out a hand to pluck the glamour away. It came away from the box like tearing cellophane, disappearing as it did so. Dorcas leaned over to take out a stick when Fermy slapped her hand away.

"Look at it. It's covered in little crystals. This is ancient stuff, unstable and will explode really easily if we fiddle with it. Best that we don't touch it," he advised.

"Then what's are we going to do's with it?" asked Dorcas.

"The best thing for us to do is to blow it up here. Look around. There is so much explosive stuff in here. Those rockets there and all kinds of bullets and things. If we do this right, we can destroy the lot and hopefully cause a bit of damage to the Cracklocks in the process."

"How will we blows it up?" said Dorcas, looking at the pile of glistening sticks.

"We'll need to use something else and make that explode. There must be something…."

"Would this do? It's a grenades," said Dorcas knowledgeably, pulling the grenade from her pocket. Fermy snatched it from her.

"Where did you get this? These are incredibly dangerous."

"I know's. I see's it many times in the movies. *Boom, bangs*!"

"Well, this would do it, but you have to pull out the pin and then throw it. But I don't know how long we'd have before it explodes, and this box is right at the back of this place. We would have to throw it from the entrance and then run. Given how much stuff is in here, when it goes off, it will really go bang. I don't think we'll have enough time to get away; there will be lots of flying iron in the explosion; this place is riddled with it. We just need some way of setting it off at a distance. They have delay timers, but I don't know how they work or what one looks like nowadays."

The two friends stood in silence for a minute or two, thinking about it, looking about it as they did. Fermy gave a little start as he had another flash of inspiration.

"Dorcas, give me your rolling pin, would you?"

Dorcas obligingly handed over the pin, and Fermy examined the grenade again. He looked at the loop on it and smiled to himself.

"This comes back fast when you summon it, doesn't it?" he asked.

Dorcas shrugged. "Very fast; it's just comes to my hand's straightaways, assuming it can get's to me. Why's?"

"Because we can set it all off with this. Look. If we pull the loop pin almost all the way out of the grenade and then wedge it in the box, we can push the rolling pin's handle through the loop. Then, when you summon it, it pulls the pin and...*BOOM*!"

Dorcas clapped her hands in glee. "Ooohh, yes. Just likes the movies. Let's do it."

"And let's make sure that it's going to be a big explosion as well. Help me stack a few other things around this box, but *BE CAREFUL*. We don't want to jar the box and set the whole thing off."

The two Fae set about stacking whatever looked explosive around the dynamite, careful to avoid touching the box as they did so. Rocket-propelled grenades, what appeared to be a missile warhead, and all kinds of boxes of things labelled with the explosive symbol were wrestled into place. When they had done, their efforts resembled a bonfire, proud and ready to be lit. Manoeuvring his way carefully through the stacked items to the gap he had deliberately left, Fermy gently placed the grenade into place next to the box of dynamite and then weighted it down with a smaller heavy box. He jiggled the loop until it was almost free of the grenade, holding his breath whilst he did so, and then carefully slid the handle of the rolling pin into place. Backtracking slowly, he finally let out a deep breath once he was clear.

"Okay, that should work. Now, let's get out of here. Where are the others?"

They exited the cavern that contained the Armoury, being careful to avoid the iron weaponry. As they left, they were met with a line of lifers marching smartly past in the opposite direction to the way out, their eyes glazed and distant. At the rear came Gnorbitt, a smile on his face as his small legs jogged to keep up with them. He came to a stop as he saw Fermy and Dorcas.

"Got 'em all, I reckon. Easy as pie; none of them had the goggle fings on, so didn't see us coming. I'm sending them as far as they can get before the glamours wear off. I 'ave to say though, I am a bit worried about 'em. I take it you're gonna do a bit of damage? These lot could be trapped down 'ere for the foreseeable in the aftermaff."

Fermy's eyes were dark. "I know, and I don't want to hurt lifers. But these lot are partially responsible for everything that has happened down here to our kin. As far as I am concerned, we are doing them a favour, letting them go. There is plenty of air down here; this place is huge. They should be able to find their way out. The main thing is to get them out of our way for now. So don't feel too sorry for them."

Gnorbitt nodded his understanding, and the three of them stood for a moment, watching the glamoured lifers head off into the gloom.

"Where are the others?" asked Fermy eventually.

"By the big door, waiting fer us. We had better 'urry; we don't know if anyone else is gonna pop out of the woodwork. If they do, we'll 'ave to glamour 'em and send 'em this way as well."

"Let's get out of here fast and find Jack and Elsie," agreed Fermy. The three of them set off at a jog, Gnorbitt leading the way along the winding path. They saw the door in the distance, and the distant figures of the Fae prisoners gathered around it. From one of the side alcoves, the flickering of fires came and the smell of melting iron, causing them to veer away.

When they got to the others, they clamoured around Fermy and Dorcas, chattering away, until Fermy held up his hands.

"Listen, listen. We've rigged the lifer's armoury to explode, and once we're clear, we'll set it off. However, I don't know how big the explosion will be; there's a lot of horrible lifer weapons in there. You will all need to get well clear before it goes off. You may be able to travel once we are clear of this place, but it is more likely to be fae-locked inside the house. You need to get outside, and even then, I'm not sure if you'll be able to get away. If anyone wants to stay and help us rescue our friends, we will be grateful for the help. But don't feel like you have to; you have all been through enough."

There was a lot of muttering amongst them before the gaunt elf stepped forwards. "I am sorry, but I just want to return home," she said. "I have been trapped here, tortured, and starved for such a long time. And although I thank you for releasing us, I cannot stay any longer." Most of the other Fae nodded their accord.

Fermy smiled up at the elf and patted her gently on the leg. "I completely understand, and there are no hard feelings. When you can leave here, do so." The elf smiled sadly and nodded.

There was a polite cough, and Gnorbitt said, "Well, I'll be 'appy to stay and give you an 'and. Always a pleasure to 'elp out a pretty lady." He stared pointedly at Dorcas, who uncharacteristically blushed and turned her eyes away. "Ain't nobody back 'ome for me any'ow, and besides, I always pay me debts. You'll 'ave to point out 'oo we're rescuin' though, cos I won't 'ave a clue!"

"Thank you, thank you," said Fermy effusively. "We need all the help that we can get. Let's get this door open."

That was harder than it looked, as the iron bolts were way out of the reach of any of them and were extremely stiff. In the end, with Fermy standing on Dorcas's shoulders, torn pieces of cloth wrapping his hands as he tugged at them and the others using opening glamours, they managed to get everything unlocked. Hopping down, Fermy pulled the door open and took a quick glance around.

"All clear. Let's go." The Fae scuttled out into the extensive wine cellar and regrouped. Fermy waved them on. "Go to the end, near the stairs. We'll be following you at a run; there is going to be one big bang if it all goes to plan."

Turning to Dorcas, he said, "Ready?" and the brownie nodded her agreement. Fermy pushed the door shut as far as he could, but with enough room for Dorcas to poke her arm through. "The minute it's in your hand, run for the stairs. I'll try and push the door shut, but I may not have time. I will be right behind you.

Dorcas nodded again, twisting herself so she was facing the stairs. She closed her eyes and summoned the rolling pin. Fermy was facing the gap where he saw it whirling towards them and thunk into Dorcas's hand. As it did so, a flash lit up the gloom. It was followed moments later by a dull 'whumpf' sound, which expanded into a full-blown loud whipcrack that hurt their ears.

Dorcas pulled her arm through the gap and ran for it. Fermy tried to press the door shut, but on seeing the expanding cloud of flame in the distance rolling rapidly in all directions, he gave up and took to his heels. He was just in time as he reached the bottom of the stairs; the concealed door behind him slammed open with terrifying force, rebounding off the wall with a mighty boom. Anyone standing there would most certainly have been squashed flat by the power of it. A sheet of flame sprayed into the room, rocking the shelves of wine bottles and causing multiple bottles to fall and smash on the stone flag floor. The cellar ceiling absorbed the blast; plaster and dust rained down on them as they fled up the stairs. Jagged cracks appeared all over the walls and ceiling above them, lit by flickering flames as some of the wooden shelving burst alight in the expanding heat.

"Time to go!" yelled Fermy over the noise, herding the sprinting Fae up the stairs and onwards down the short corridor towards the wooden door at the end. They wrestled

the door open, and the influx of fresh air caused the flames downstairs to grow in their intensity, the shadows flickering madly on the walls as they surged with the fresh feed of oxygen. The muffled pops of bottles blowing reached their ears in the racket, clear over the continuing explosions that still rang out in the distance from the Armoury.

Slamming the door shut, the Fae gave a muted cheer to themselves as they panted and leaned against the walls of the room they had just entered, getting their breath back. However, as they paused, a shrill alarm started sounding throughout the house, klaxon-like as it rose and fell. Fermy looked around for the source and then realised that it was because of them. The Fae had triggered a magical alarm by entering the main house through a monitored door, alerting the occupants to their presence. 'Wonderful,' he thought, 'As if things aren't going to be difficult enough.'

Visible cracks ran through the walls up here as well; the mansion's foundations had taken a pounding from the explosion, and the doorframes seemed to be leaning slightly now at an angle. Another door flung open, and a fancily dressed man in black and white clothing dashed into the corridor, the sound of yelling behind him. He made for the door that the Fae had just left through.

"Do...not...let...him...open that door," gasped Fermy, and the man was hit with half a dozen glamours, locking him into place. Regaining his breath, Fermy yelled, "That door needs to stay shut; we can't let that fire spread until we've found the others. Get that chap out of here; send him into the grounds where he'll be safe along with anyone else you come across. Time to get out of here if you're going and take any lifers you come across with you if you can."

They could feel the heat now coming through the closed door; in the gap at the bottom, the flicker of flames could be seen; fiery questing fingers were feeling their way into the corridor.

"This should give 'em somefink to worry about while we find yer mates," said Gnorbitt. "And I think that we should get goin'. This whole place is probably gonna go up."

The Fae pushed through the door that the man had come through and into a large kitchen. On the other side of it, a door stood open, daylight streaming through it. Several men and women were dashing around frantically, seemingly at a loss of what to do. They all froze on the spot as the Fae's glamours hit them, and they started marching towards the open door and freedom.

"Good luck, friends," said the Faun, as he and the other Fae made their way towards the door. "May fortune smile on you."

Fermy nodded to them with a small smile. "Get yourselves safe. We'll see you again soon."

Turning to Dorcas and Gnorbitt, his face was grim.

"Jack and Elsie. And nobody, repeat, nobody is going to stop us. "

They pulled open the other door out of the kitchen and looked up the short flight of stairs ahead of them.

JIMMY, Sammy, and Elsie took the stairs two at a time in their haste to get away from Anastasia and Benedict. Behind them, they could hear the sound of the barricade that Jimmy had hastily thrown together being smashed apart by the pursuing Cracklocks; Anastasia's screams of frustration and Benedict's hoots of delight were evident over the noise of destruction.

"Where to?" gasped Sammy to Elsie. "Any ideas where they took Jack and the others?"

"I have no idea, my dear. Although I suspect that if Malchiah had taken him to see that witch, Agatha, it would be on the ground floor somewhere. Some kind of reception room or something. Unlikely to be in the basement or the servant's area."

They burst through the door at the bottom of the stairs into the servant's corridor and almost knocked the maid there flying.

"Oi, who are you lot?" she said, a furious look on her face. "What you doing down here?"

Jimmy slowed to a stop, conscious of their pursuers but still able to turn on the charm.

"I'm awfully sorry, Madam. Lady Cracklock sent us to escort Mrs Cracklock here, and I'm afraid that we got a little lost. We weren't sure which room she was staying in, you see. And now we're very late, and the Lady of the house will be frightfully angry. Just trying to make up some time. Can you remind me; whereabouts is Lady Cracklock currently? I'm in rather a dither, it must be said."

The maid's expression softened a little. "Well, we don't want you to get on the wrong side of Lady Cracklock now, do we? She's in the library with her guest, taking tea. Just through the door, there, the second corridor on the left. The room is clearly marked."

"Many thanks, Madam; that is most helpful. And we will try to be more careful, I promise," said Jimmy.

They set off at a slight jog, avoiding the door in the centre of the corridor while trying not to draw attention to themselves. They were about two-thirds of the way down when the door for which they were aiming opened, and two men stepped through, deep in conversation. The friends stopped and looked at each other in a mild panic.

"I'll handle this," said Elsie. "I'll just..."

But before she could finish, the door behind them burst open, and Anastasia and Benedict stormed through, Benedict skittling the maid again.

"There you are!" screamed Anastasia. *"Stop!"*

The two men up ahead were instantly alert, their hands darting into the insides of their jackets as they stared at the three people ahead of them in the centre of the corridor. "Stop right there," one of them called out, his hand out in a 'halt' gesture as they sprinted towards the little group.

"Errrr, what do we do?" whispered Jimmy, glancing uncertainly from Elsie to Sammy.

Sammy glanced from one end of the corridor to the other, and then, her jaw set and face grim, shouted, *"Get them!"* She raised her tube in the direction of the two guards, and with a blue flash, a powerful jet of water, dirty brown, streaked out of the tube with all the strength of a firefighter's hose. It bowled into the two guards, soaking them and knocking one directly off his feet.

"Oh, my grackles!" screeched Elsie as she gestured, her shield glamour springing up just in time to deflect the two glamours aimed at the group by Anastasia and Benedict.

"Ding, ding, round two then eh, you old bat?" yelled Anastasia. *"See how it works out for you this time, shall we?"* She pitched another glamour that dissipated in a shower of purple sparks from Elsie's shield, but this time it did not weaken any. Elsie's face was set with determination as she sent a shimmering red glamour back in response at the two Cracklocks.

Jimmy pointed Roly around the edge of Elsie's shield, and with a blue pulse, several golf balls fired at them with high velocity, glancing off of Anastasia's shield. Jimmy gave a cackle and shouted back at them, *"I've got millions of these; most lost item ever."* He fired another volley, and as one ricocheted off the shield, it caught Benedict a blow to his jaw. He howled and redoubled his efforts, a sickly yellow, glittering glamour catching Jimmy on his elbow as he ducked back behind the shield.

Jimmy screamed as his whole arm erupted into blisters, turning scarlet as it did so. The pain, like the sting of a thousand nettles, raced up his arm, and he stumbled a little. Elsie caught him as he nearly fell and yelled, "Sammy. A little help, please." Her shield wavered as another barrage of crackling glamours hit it.

Sammy has pretty much finished off the two guards that she was tackling; they were flapping around on the floor in the filthy water, covered in netting and what appeared to be tar and flour. They were clawing at their faces, trying to free themselves, unsuccessfully, of the gunge that covered them. To finish the job, the tube flashed one more time, and the two of them were covered in a twisting mass of small insects. They started to scream as they set to, the insects biting at all the exposed areas they could find in their anger.

"Fire ants," said Sammy with satisfaction as she turned to the others. "Saw it on that Australia programme, with those two Geordie presenters."

"Lovely," shouted Elsie. "But I need to fix his arm. And if we don't slow them down, we're in real trouble; I'll have to drop the shield to do it."

Sammy nodded and then had an idea. Pointing behind her, she yelled, "Timothy," and with a flare, the petite Fae stood there, blinking in surprise as he fumbled his glasses on. He took in the two fallen guards, gulped, and said, "Oh, my goodness. Whatever is going on?"

"Timothy, help us!" screamed Sammy. The Fae turned around and saw the snarling face of Anastasia instantly at the other end of the corridor. He paled and then saw what had happened to Jimmy. His resolve stiffened, and with a few gestures, a considerable shield glamour sprang into place, pulsing with orange light. Elsie dropped her shield and grasped Jimmy's arm as the boy wailed, tears on his face. She passed her hand up and down

the injured limb, muttering as she did so, and relief washed over Jimmy's face.

"Sorry," he gasped. "Hurt's so much."

"Don't worry, dearie. I've been on the receiving end of that one myself. It'll be fine in a moment."

Anastasia had been screaming incomprehensible abuse as she'd thrown glamour after glamour at the friends in her rage, Benedict hollering alongside her. Noticing movement behind the drifting coloured mist that resulted from their efforts, she slowed to a halt, shield charm in place, and peered at her targets. She counted one, two, three, and, wait, a fourth? A short figure partially obscured. Surely not? How dare they?

"*Who is that with you?*" she screamed. No answer. The drifting mist cleared further, and Anastasia spotted the diminutive figure of Timothy behind the shield.

"How dare you? How dare you bring a filthy devil into our ancestral home, uninvited? I will kill you for this, I swear!" Anastasia was apoplectic with rage at the sight of a Fae walking freely about in their historical home. She threw a handful of more fizzing glamours at the shield Timothy had generated but with no effect.

"Ha," gloated Sammy. "Bit stronger than you, eh? Not so tough when you have someone who can fight back, are you?"

Timothy tugged on Sammy's leg. "Please don't antagonise them. Let us just get away from them. They are on home territory here, and this place is a death-trap to the Fae."

There was a blur through the air, passing through Timothy's shield, and an iron throwing knife buried itself in the wall just above Timothy's head.

"*No matter,*" screamed Anastasia. "*We can do this any way you want. You are mine!*"

The two of them fumbled into their clothes for more weapons, but before they could grasp anything, Jimmy stepped forwards. With a blaze of blue light, gallons of yellow liquid streaked through the air, spraying off Anastasia's shield but still coating the two of them in its backwash. The floor was coated in the stuff, and a strong fatty smell of oil wafted through the air.

"You little idiot!" howled Anastasia. *"What is this stuff? How dare you, how dare you?"* She fumbled a blade out of her soaked clothing but then screamed with frustration as it slipped through her fingers. Benedict had more luck; his blade was raised above his head, ready to throw, but as he bought his arm down, his slippery hand released it before he was ready, and it clanged off the wall a few metres away from him. He cursed, took a step forward, and the oil on the floor skidded his feet out from under him quite nicely, landing on his backside with a bone-shaking thud.

"Castor oil," said Jimmy to the others, backing up but never taking his eyes off the two figures who were slipping and sliding about, trying desperately to keep their balance. "That should keep them occupied for a moment or two."

The four of them dashed towards the far door, jumping over the prone guards as they did so. Sammy risked a look back through the shield that Timothy was maintaining and saw Anastasia, her eyes closed and chanting as she moved her arms in concentric patterns. Behind her, Benedict was now back on his feet and had positioned himself well back from them, his eyes crazed.

"What is she doing?" she asked herself as they fled up the corridor. Hearing her, Elsie also turned to look as she retreated. A look of shock passed over her face, and she sped up. "Come on, come on, move it."

"What is it?" asked Sammy.

Timothy took a glance and gulped. "I don't know, but that's old Fae glamour gestures. It won't be good. Just go, come on before it's..."

There was a creaking and crunching noise, and the door in

the middle of the corridor seemed to blow itself apart. The pieces stopped in mid-air, like someone had hit the pause button, and then retracted back into themselves apart from one long plank-like piece that seemed to plant itself into the corridor. The door pulled itself away from its hinges with a rending crack, forming itself into a roughly humanoid shape as it did so. The exploded pieces zoomed back in to form a crude head, jaws snapping with splinter like fangs and eyes resembling sunken pits. Splintered arms ended in a facsimile of hands, jagged wooden claws scratching at the air. Its crunching jaw made a strange creaking noise, like the rocking of a wooden swing, and Anastasia replied to it with a similar noise. It bowed its head to her.

Timothy saw the creature emerge, and he paled, his shield wavering as he did so. Elsie noticed and shook him. "What is that thing, Timothy?"

"It's a...it's a... it's a wood golem. An old enchantment. Those things are incredibly resistant to glamours. Run!" he finished in a shrill voice, and dropping his shield, he ran for the door. The others followed, infected by his panic. Anastasia's booming laughter followed them down the corridor, and as they reached the door; slamming it shut behind them, they heard her screech, *"Kill them! Kill them allllllll!"*

The four of them sprinted up the new corridor, Timothy, despite his short little legs, leading the way as panic helped his flight. They turned the corner as the door they had just come through smashed open, and the golem pushed its wooden body through. Spying them, it gave out a loud creaking scream and bashed its way into the corridor. On its long wooden legs, it gave chase, bounding down the corridor after them.

"We've got to stop that thing," gasped Jimmy. "It's gaining on us."

"We can't," panted Timothy. "There's nothing we can do. It is glamour proof and incredibly tough despite being made of wood. A long time ago, we used them as labourers, but they were banned in Faery when we realised that they could not be controlled. The control glamour wears off them, you see; they are so resistant to any kind of magic they just shrug it off. When they do, they do as they please. And they are vicious."

"Sounds like the Lisovyk," replied Jimmy. "And we did okay against that thing. Well, Jack did. Using something from the physics lab, I found." Jimmy thought for a moment and muttered, "Physics. Of course! Right, stop running."

"Are you crazy?" shrieked Timothy. "We can't stop it."

"No," replied Jimmy. "But we can slow it down so much as to render it ineffective. To quote Karate Kid part three, if your enemy can't stand, he can't fight."

He stopped dead and pointed Roly at the floor. The blue light pulsed, and thousands of tiny round objects flew out of the end in a torrent.

"*Marbles!*" he yelled. "*Help me.*" Sammy threw a tube to Timothy, and the three of them poured marbles, ball bearings, and a whole host of small balls into the corridor. The floor was soon thick with them, and as the golem came charging around the corner, its long wooden leg planted in the carpet of them and shot out in front of it. The creature almost did the splits as its other leg was anchored on the floor, and it hit the ground with a tremendous crash. It tried to right itself, pushing up with its jagged hands, but the balls underneath them just rolled away, and it went face down again, its creaking screech voicing its frustration.

"It's made of wood," suggested Sammy. "We can burn it. "

"Fire doesn't work on them," replied Timothy. "It's one of the reasons why we couldn't stop them back in Faery."

"So, what did stop them?"

"They were lured into a trap and left for nature to take its course on them. Weathering weakened them enough over the years to allow the Fae to deal with them. It took a long time."

"We haven't got a long time. What else?"

"Axes, termites, sunlight?" suggested Elsie. "Will water will warp it?"

"Won't work," said Timothy.

"Then what will?" screamed Sammy as the creature tried again to unsuccessfully get to its feet. Its head came up, and it stared at the little group. While it had no discernible features, they could sense the malice as it glared at them. It fumbled about in the balls on the floor with one outstretched hand as it did so and then suddenly buried its arm in the lake of them. With a colossal swipe, it threw the balls everywhere, revealing the carpet underneath. It planted the same hand down and, now unhindered, started to push itself back up. As it looked up at the friends, its dull wooden face seemed to be mocking them. Thrashing with its legs, it managed to clear more of the balls and get some footing under it.

"We've got to go!" yelled Timothy. *"Come on!"*

The golem finally pulled itself to its feet and stood staring at the floor. It used one foot to sweep the balls out of the way with a careful, almost delicate gesture. It took a step into the cleared spot and creaked its delight in its awful voice.

Jimmy looked on with dismay; if what Timothy was saying was true, destroying it was impossible. They would have to run, and chances were that it would catch them eventually; they couldn't leave without Jack and the others. They would not abandon him to the Cracklocks, not ever.

'Leave,' he thought, 'Leave. Leaves.' Despite the severity of the situation that they were in, Jimmy's mind flung itself back to a time a couple of years ago when he and his little brother Sean played in the garden. They had been swinging on the big branch of the pear tree, something that their dad had expressly asked them not to do. That tree was their dad's pride and joy; he doted on it and spent most of the summer finding ways to keep the wasps away from the fruit, usually unsuccessfully. Jimmy's mum used to joke that that tree was their dad's other wife, although she didn't really mind him pottering in the garden to relieve the stresses of work. He remembered they had been laughing as they swung, and then the shock as, with a huge cracking sound and a shower of leaves, Jimmy had ended up on his backside in the dirt. The big branch had cracked under their weight along the base, causing a massive split in the trunk. Their dad had gone mad at them over that; they had both had a thrashing from his hard hand (which was unusual; Dad never slapped them) and been sent to cry in their rooms. Mum had come up to them and explained that Dad was fond of the tree because his mother's ashes were sowed there, and that was why he was so mad. The tree was his way of keeping his mum's memory alive. And they had probably killed it.

But they hadn't. Instead, Dad had bought some special glue-like material and had painted it all over the gash in the tree. He had then bound it up tightly, using a winch and some thin rope to form a kind of bandage around it. And while the yield that year of the delicious juicy pears that the wasps were so fond of was tiny, the following year, the tree had bounced back to total health. Dad had carefully cut away the rope, and while there was a scar, the trunk and branch were fine. The boys never swung on it again.

But the rope and the glue had fixed it. Fixed it. And then Jimmy knew what they had to do to beat the golem.

He was roused from his thoughts by cackling laughter, and Anastasia and Benedict appeared at the end of the corridor behind the golem. The creature turned at the sound to face the two and took a step towards them. Anastasia stared at it with a puzzled look and then said something in the creaking language. The creature replied and took another step towards them.

"Not us, you foolish thing; them!" shouted Anastasia, pointing. The creature took another step towards them.

"Get back!" screamed Anastasia and pitched a glamour at it, which dissipated without harming the creature.

"I am your master. Do as you are bid."

The creature gave what sounded like a braying laugh in its creaking voice and took another step.

"It's broken their hold over it," said Timothy. "It's out of control now. It'll kill them."

The pair threw more sparking glamours at the creature, but they were equally as ineffectual as the first one; bleeding off the creature in zig-zags of red light. Anastasia and Benedict started to back off as the creature stalked towards them, fear in their eyes. Benedict threw one of his knives, and it stuck in the creature's chest, quivering. The golem looked down at it and simply brushed it away.

Anastasia performed a complex series of gestures in the air, and a wall of fire sprung up, separating them from the creature. The creature took no notice of it and simply grabbed through the flames to where they had been before. A shrill scream followed.

"Ha!" called Elsie. "See how you like having a monster after you, eh?" and clapped her hands in glee.

The golem whipped around at the sound of her voice, its dull eyeholes seeking the source. It casually batted out the flames on its arm and turned its body towards them. Lowering its head, it chattered out in its creaking tongue and started to move towards them again, sweeping the balls aside with its feet as it did so.

"Oh dear," said Elsie, as the others glared at her. "My bad. Eerrm...what do we do?"

"Listen," said Jimmy frantically. "We can stop it with Roly and the gang. We need glue. Lots of glue and as much thin fabric as we can throw at it. You good with that, Roly?"

'Yes, friend Jimmy,' chimed the tube. *'We understand exactly.'*

"We need to layer it, wrap it up so much that it can't move. Glue, fabric, glue, fabric. Follow?"

"A plan that can work!" said Timothy, gesturing with his tube. "Let it get closer; I'll get behind it."

"And I'll go for its head first; see if we can cut off its vision," replied Jimmy. "Sammy, be ready with fabric; I'll glue. Timothy alternate the two from behind."

"And me?" said Elsie.

"Stay back, goad it for us. It needs to have its attention focused everywhere." Elsie nodded and started to rummage in her handbag for anything that would help.

The golem cleared the balls, and with a war cry, Jimmy ducked under its thrashing arm and sprayed it in the face, Roly spewing out a thick stream of grey-coloured thick liquid. Sammy blasted it a split second later, and what looked like a towel hit it in the face and stuck fast. Timothy hurried around the back and coated one of its legs, following it up with a sack-like material. The golem clawed at its face, removing the towel, which clung to its hands, stuck in the glue. It creaked loudly and shook its arm, but the towel stayed put. Jimmy got it again in the face, as did Sammy, and it thrashed ineffectively as the glue and cloth obscured its vision. Jimmy went for the other leg this time, and Sammy followed suit. The creature flailed at its head again with its other hand and succeeded in pulling the cloth free, frantically shaking its hand as it did so. The cloth flew clear, leaving the hand free, although still caked in the glue.

Sammy got too close, trying to aim the cloth at the spots that Jimmy was hitting, and the creature plucked out its free hand and grabbed her arm. It hoisted her into the air easily, dangling her by one arm. Sammy screamed.

"Aaaaarrrrggggghhh, it's got me! Help, help!"

Jimmy and Timothy looked on helplessly as the creature swung Sammy backwards and forwards. It tried to grab her with the other hand, but the towel-wrapped appendage couldn't get a grip on her.

"It hurrrrrttttss. Help me!" Sammy screamed.

"Stand aside!" came a yell, and Jimmy looked back just in time to see Elsie dash past him, something in her hands. Something long and pure black. Elsie lashed the object at the arm that held Sammy, jumping to do so and the black object wrapped around it. Sammy fell to the ground, the severed arm of the golem still holding her. Its hand relaxed, releasing her, and she backpedalled quickly out its range, a look of horror on her face.

Elsie ducked as the golem swung at her with its towel wrapped claw, and with a backhanded slash, wrapped the object around the other arm and pulled, severing that arm as well. The golem screeched a tremendous creaking yell, lashing out with its hindered legs but not making contact with anything.

"Portable hole," gasped Elsie. "I don't know why I didn't think of it sooner. Doesn't work on living flesh, but anything non-living...."

"You genius!" yelled Jimmy.

Elsie stretched the hole again to its full length and fixed the hindered golem with a stern look. *"And now I'm going to take you apart,"* she cried.

Moments later, the golem was lying face down on the floor, its legs missing, rocking backwards and forwards on its torso, unable to move. It was giving out a low creaking croon as it pitied itself.

Sammy went over to Elsie and said. "May I?" holding out her hand for the hole. Elsie gave it to her, and Sammy straddled the creature, looping the hole under its misshapen chin and snapping it shut at the back of its neck. The head rolled away, and the torso stopped moving. Sammy handed the hole back to Elsie, who squished it up back into its box.

The four friends looked at each other and started to laugh. "You never know, finding Jack and the others could be really easy from now on," said Jimmy, wiping his sweaty face. It was getting hot in the corridor.

"*Very clever, I'm sure,*" came a shout, and the friends wheeled around. The walls at the end of the corridor were on fire now, lazy flames wafting in the breeze, presumably from the fire shield Anastasia had conjured but was now gone. She and Benedict were strolling towards them, avoiding the parts of the carpet that were smouldering and the scattered marbles. Behind them, several guards followed, guns drawn and aimed at them.

"But now it's time for you to stop. And for your little devil friend there to be extinguished," she continued, tossing a knife from hand to hand. Benedict held a similar knife in each hand.

Timothy's shield glamour shot straight into place, and he glared at Anastasia. "Why don't you just leave us alone, you anger-ridden witch?" he spat. The others looked at him momentarily stunned; the mild-mannered Fae rarely used such language.

Anastasia threw a pitch-black glamour, and it all went off. The friends fought a retreat, bullets glancing off the shield with clouds of sparks, Jimmy and Sammy firing off all kinds of missiles from the tubes back at them, and Elsie and Timothy throwing glamours as fast as they could. The corridor was wreathed in smoke now, and all the combatants were coughing in the thick hot air.

They finally reached the end of the corridor and turned onto the next one, Jimmy leading the way. He launched a cricket ball at their assailants and was focusing on the next when a voice behind him bawled, "*Jimmy?*"

Sammy dashed around the corner at the sound of the voice and saw the distant figure, held between two men. She could hardly believe her eyes at who it was, and she screamed, "*Jack.*"

"*Mum?*" screamed back, Jack. They watched him shove at the guard who was holding him, and then there was a massive explosion from somewhere deep underneath the mansion, causing them all to wobble as the explosive force rocked the floor beneath them. Around them, cracks zig-zagged up the walls and across the ceiling from the blast, and plaster rained down onto everyone. Then followed the sound of a loud alarm that rang through the house, rising and falling in a wailing tone.

Jimmy saw Jack tussle with the second man who was shouting something. And then his friend was sprinting up the corridor towards them, something swinging in his hand.

CHAPTER 13

Agatha shot from her seat in shock as the explosion rocked the house beneath her, staring in disbelief as cracks appeared behind the bookshelves, several of the tomes falling to the floor. When the Fae alarm started braying as well, she realised that there was serious trouble brewing.

"Malchiah!" she screamed. *"Devils in the house!"* She dashed to the corner bookshelf, pulled a book, and the shelf swung outwards, canting slightly as it did so as the wall behind it cracked further. The motion revealed a hidden rack of iron weapons, and Agatha wasted no time snatching up some throwing knives, stuffing them into her dress pockets. She plucked down a sword as well and dashed for the door, her speed belying her age.

Yanking it open, the first thing she saw was her son clutching at his chest, a look of disbelief on his face, and the guard picking himself up from the floor. The smell of smoke drifted into her flaring nostrils, and to her right, at the end of the long corridor, partially hidden by the swirling smoke and dust, was the retreating figure of the boy, running towards others shrouded from her sight.

"What is going on?" she demanded of Malchiah, who simply pointed at the retreating figure of Jack.

"Get after him!" she screamed at the guard, who nodded and sprinted in the direction Jack had taken. Seizing Malchiah, Agatha shook him and cursed, "What in the Lords' name is happening?"

Malchiah had recovered from his shock, and after several coughs, he croaked. "Explosion below us; something must be wrong in the catacombs. And he…he took the control stone. Snatched it from me."

"What? Why? How could he know about the stone?" Agatha screamed in his face. *"It is not possible!"*

Malchiah pushed her away gently. "I don't know mother, but he took it anyway. And I'm going to get it back." He started up the corridor at a sprint and then screeched to a halt as a blue flare in the smoke erupted, and the guard came flying back down the corridor, his feet off the ground. He collided with the wall and slumped to the floor in a crumpled heap. Malchiah turned towards Agatha, whose face was a mask of rage.

"If you want something doing..." she muttered and ran down the corridor past Malchiah, the sword raised above her head.

FERMY, Dorcas, and Gnorbitt popped out of the door at the top of the stairs into the main mansion and tried desperately to get their bearings. Behind them, they could hear the roar of the flames as the inferno consumed the entire wine cellar. Wisps of smoke were drifting under the door behind them.

"Which way?" asked Gnorbitt.

"I don't know; I can't think over the noise of that damned alarm," said Fermy, who stood, his head cocked to one side. "I guess that we'll have to do a…."

Another door being flung open further down the corridor

interrupted him, and four men came through at a pace. They had their guns drawn and were clutching what looked like daggers. However, what was more disturbing was that they all appeared to be wearing the misshapen goggles. Fortunately, they didn't see the three Fae and set off in the other direction at speed.

"I have a feeling that they are going where we need to be," Fermy panted, fear in his eyes. "Follow them."

The three of them kept a careful distance behind the guards, following them as fast as possible. The guards seemed to notice something ahead and sped up, sprinting away from them. The three friends redoubled their efforts, but their smaller legs could not keep up, and they fell rapidly behind.

"Shall. . .we's...travel?" gasped Dorcas. "Can't ...keeps...up...this...pace."

Gnorbitt seized her hand, and Dorcas was so shocked, she didn't pull it away. "I'd be 'appy to try it for you, gorgeous," he said with a smile. He grasped Fermy's hand with the other, and then, with a sensation like they were being sucked down a tube, they were much further down the corridor, the guards not too far ahead.

"It works in here then," replied Fermy. "Good to know in a pinch." However, as he spoke, Gnorbitt fell to the floor in what appeared to be a dead faint. Dorcas was immediately kneeling next to him, patting his face.

"Gnorbitt, what's wrongs?" she said and leaned over to place her pointed ear next to his mouth. "He's breathing."

The gnome's eyelashes fluttered, and his eyes opened. "Ohh, me 'ead," he muttered. He pushed himself up into a sitting position and looked around. "What 'appened?"

"We just travelled a short distance, and then you dropped to the floor," replied Fermy. "Wait one second."

He performed a series of gestures, and then the entire corridor shone a pale green and then faded.

"It's one of the traps here, for the Fae," he confirmed. "A strong glamour. Designed to stop Fae from leaving and to make them vulnerable. I guess that it is designed to make sure that we cannot leave this evil place easily; it gives the damn Cracklocks time to extinguish us. For grocks sake!"

They pulled Gnorbitt to his feet and followed the guards again as fast as they could. However, as they got towards a branch in the corridor, Fermy's keen ears picked up something over the alarm's braying, and he gestured for the others to stop. He approached the corner of the wall and peered sneakily around it.

The four guards had stopped and were receiving a briefing; one stood with his hand to his ear. He blinked a few times, a grim expression on his face and said, "Understood. Over." He then turned to the others and gave a jerk of his chin. "Dr Cracklock and the Lady of the House have got the intruders cornered in the East Wing. All reinforcements are to meet there. The boys are to be taken alive at all costs; the women are expendable. They have a devil with them; terminate it with extreme prejudice. Understood?" The men all nodded.

Fermy's eyes widened as he understood the implications. Women and boys; it could only be their friends, particularly if there were a Fae with them which must be Timothy, however surprising it was that the bookworm was here. He gestured the others forward, frantically.

"Elsie, Jack, and the others are in trouble. We need to help them. This lot are on their way there now; we need to take them out before they can make any trouble. Then we will see how best to intervene. You ready?"

"Ready's," replied Dorcas, brandishing the rolling pin. Gnorbitt swallowed nervously and nodded too.

They followed the guards at a short distance; fortunately, they were focused on their task and were not checking behind them as they sprinted across the lobby and into another corridor. The friends could now hear the sounds of a battle happening in the near distance, and not allowing these guards to join it was the priority.

"*Get them!*" hollered Fermy, and the rear guard swung around at the sound of the deep voice. He gave a double-take, his eyes bulging behind his goggles as he saw the three devils streaking towards them.

"*Contact,*" he yelled. "*Cont...*"

He was silenced as a well-flung glamour by Gnorbitt froze him in place, the gun and dagger dropping from his fingers. The other guards had also spun round at the shout and reacted more quickly, guns coming to port. Fermy's hands flashed as he performed a rapid glamour which ripped the goggles from the three remaining guard's faces, their targets winking out of their line of sight as the goggles disappeared.

"Where did they go?" asked the youngest guard as he tried to sight his gun. "They took the devil lenses," said another. "They're still here."

"Back to back," said the one who seemed to be in command, and they formed up into a loose triangle, frantically tracking backwards and forwards, nerves on edge. They reeled as one as a vase crashed to the floor to the left and let fly with a volley of bullets, the youngest one emptying the weapon in his panic; his eyes darted crazily around.

With a sudden shriek, another guard dropped his gun and jammed his fingers in his mouth to try to stifle the pain of his cracked knuckles. Then he locked up, a stunned look on his face as he toppled to the side. His two colleagues had time to glance at each other before they met the same fate, falling wordlessly into a stiff pile in the centre of the corridor.

"Well done," said Fermy, kicking the guns out of sight under one of the cabinets. He went to kick the daggers away as well and then winced. "Iron," he said. "Leave those; nothing we can do about them. Let's go and join our friend's party."

They glanced around the corner again, just past the comatose guards. At the end of the long corridor ahead, the sparkling of glamours was visible through the swirling smoke, the combatants hidden from view. Nevertheless, what was clear was the two people making their way hastily towards them. Fermy's eyes narrowed.

"Malchiah and Agatha; I'd know that wizened crone anywhere. We better get involved; this is going to get intense."

JACK RAN into the smoke and straight into Sammy's arms. "Oh my goodness, you're alright. What did they do to you? I'm going to..." she snarled.

"I'm fine, mum, really. I'll tell you later, once we get out of here."

"Speaking of which," said Sammy, resolve in her voice, and blasted another set of random objects from the tube back down the corridor at Anastasia's group.

"*We can't get back this way*!" yelled Elsie. "*There's too many of them. This house is going to collapse!*"

As if the mansion could hear her, there was a sudden judder, and a wall between the two battling parties collapsed inward into the corridor. Plaster dust and powdered mortar swirled into the smoke, making it even more challenging to see what was going on. Timothy reinforced his shield, trying desperately to keep the blindly thrown glamours from hitting anyone in the little group. He extended it across the walls and over them on instinct and was just in time. There was a rending crunching sound, and the ceiling along the whole corridor collapsed. Wails came from their opponents, who were not quick enough to get out of the way.

"*I can't hold it*!" screeched Timothy as the weight of the collapsed masonry pressed down on the shield. "*Help!*"

Elsie added her own glamour to the shield, and Timothy's pinched face eased a little.

"Lovely to see you, Jack, my boy, but we need to get out of here now," she said over her shoulder to Jack in a breathless voice. "You haven't seen Fermy and Dorcas have you? I am assuming that they are the ones who have set off that dreadful alarm?"

"How do you know it was them?" gasped Jimmy, firing another volley around the shield glamour. He was rewarded with a scream of pain, followed by bullets pinging off the shield that protected them.

"Because..." Elsie gestured a little, and the shield expanded again. "Fermy has a way of wriggling out of most situations. Now, as nice as it is to chew the fat, can we go, please? This ceiling is really rather heavy."

"We can't go back that way," replied Jack, looking back through the smoke. "The Cracklocks are down there; they'll be waiting for us."

He had barely finished his sentence when a figure loomed out of the swirling dust and grabbed him. Malchiah's face was a mask of rage as he thrust Jack up against the crumbling wall.

"Wrong, boy, we're right here. Give me the stone. Now." he spat into the boy's face.

Agatha materialised out of the swirling smoke as well and placed the tip of her sword against Jack's open throat, just above Malchiah's hand.

"No!" screamed Sammy, aiming the tube at her, but Agatha simply cackled and snapped her fingers. The tube flew from Sammy's hand and disappeared.

"I don't think so, devil lover," she goaded. "Stop, or sweet little Jack here becomes a pin cushion. Back up, and let down your defences—all of you. Otherwise, I will run him through. *Do it. Now."* Turning to the swirling smoke, she finished, *"Anastasia, stop. We have control,"* yelling down the corridor. A coughing response, unclear, came back through the dirty air, and the glamours stopped sparking on the shield.

Elsie stared at Agatha. "If we let down this shield, we'll all be buried under this rubble here, you mad old dog."

"Silence!" screeched Agatha. "You will keep your glamour and your tongue in check, Elsie Cracklock. The devil that you saw fit to bring here, into my home, will step forward."

Jimmy dropped Roly to the floor next to his feet and raised his hands. Timothy swallowed, his eyes wide behind his glasses, and let down his shield. He took a tentative step towards Agatha, who sneered and spat at him. She glared around at the others.

"You weak-willed fools, allowing these devils to blind you with their wickedness. You shall see, oh, yes!"

"It is you who is blind, Agatha," said Elsie quietly. "The Fae are not what you think they are. They mean no harm."

"You will be re-educated after today, Elsie Cracklock. To quote Proverbs 12:26, *'The righteous is a guide to his neighbour, But the way of the wicked leads them astray.'* We are truly the righteous, and these creatures shall all die in hellfire when the Lord passes his judgement."

"Well said, Great Mama," came a voice, and the others watched Anastasia emerge from the smoke, Benedict behind her, his inane grin in place and backed up by a couple of surly-looking guards. They were covered in plaster dust, and Anastasia had blood on one cheek, but her face was alight with the thrill of the battle. She glared at Timothy and gestured Benedict forward. "Come here, little devil, or the old bag gets this," she said, the blade of a dagger visible in her hand.

Jimmy watched with dismay as Timothy took faltering steps towards Anastasia, the horror on the little Fae's face apparent. As he did so, he felt a slight tug at the bottom of his trousers. Roly stood there on his tiny legs, blue eyes looking up at him. He made a shushing gesture, one finger to where his mouth would be if he had one. The tube started to climb up Jimmy's leg towards his open hand, and with a glance across at Sammy, he saw the same thing was happening with her discarded tube. He steeled himself.

Malchiah tightened his grip on Jack's throat, and with the pressing of the sword against him as well, Jack started to choke.

"The Stone. Give it to me," hissed Malchiah. Agatha stared at Jack, her eyes crazed.

Benedict came from behind his mother and squatted down on his haunches, so he was at eye level with Timothy. From behind his back, he produced the taser he had taken from the police car.

"Do you know what this is, little devil?" he crooned, the blue electric arching between the things 'arms'. Timothy nodded, and a tear rolled down his cheek as Benedict started into his eyes.

"I'm going to flatten the battery on you, little beast. And then we'll see what other fun we can have. You're going to have a busy night." He giggled like a schoolboy and slapped Timothy lightly on his cheek.

"You will take that devil elsewhere, please, Benedict," commanded Anastasia. "And you can have your fun once this mayhem is under control. But keep the noise down this time. We don't want to hear."

Timothy stared beseechingly at Sammy as Benedict grabbed his arm and yanked him off his feet, almost pulling it from its socket.

Jack was turning a bright shade of red as he gasped for air. He grabbed Malchiah's wrist and tried to wrench it away, sliding down the wall as he did so. Agatha moved the sword back to get a better angle, and as she did so, it was suddenly wrenched from her grasp by an unseen force, twirling off into the dusty gloom. At the same time, an object whirled out of the smoke and ricocheted off the side of Malchiah's head. He shrieked and clutched instinctively to the spot, loosening his grip on Jack as he did so. Gulping for air, Jack used the wall behind him to push off, and he shoved Malchiah hard. The man tottered backwards, arms pinwheeling before sitting down on the floor with a thump.

Agatha whipped around at the disturbance, words forming on her lips when the rolling pin twirled up from the floor, fetching her a good one on the back of the head as it returned to the hand of the figure who dashed out of the dusty smoke. Two other figures weren't far behind.

"Dorcas!" yelled Elsie. *"Help us!"*

But she spoke needlessly. Fermy and Gnorbitt backed Dorcas up, and the two of them sent simultaneous wriggling green glamours at Agatha, the dual force of them causing the old woman to stagger backwards past Elsie straight into the arms of Anastasia. Sammy and Jimmy launched attacks at the remaining two guards simultaneously, tubes flaring with blue light; the men fell to the ground as a stream of bricks pelted them viciously.

Benedict, his face contorting with anger as he spied Dorcas, dropped Timothy and launched himself at the brownie. Anastasia tried to grab him as he went past, sensing that their advantage had been lost but failed. With a snarl, he charged directly at the brownie, the taser raised and lightning arcing, but he didn't get far. Glamours slammed into him from both Fermy and Gnorbitt, and he went face down on the floor, an anguished howl issuing from his lips.

Elsie started to walk slowly backwards now, keeping the glamour shield angled up at the ceiling. Beads of sweat stood out on her forehead with the effort of keeping it in place, pieces of the ceiling twitching on top.

"I can't hold this much longer," she gasped. "Get clear." The opposite wall gave a menacing creak, and more plaster fell away from it. The friends shuffled back down the corridor, the menacing glares of Anastasia and Agatha following them.

"You can't escape!" screeched Agatha. *"You cannot leave."*

Dorcas clipped Malchiah across the head with the pin as the party moved backwards and stared back at them. "You will leave my Jack-Jack alone from nows on. Is that's understoods?" she spat at the two receding figures. "Otherwise, I will make's sure that you's never can walk again to comes after him."

"I strongly suggest that you get clear," called Elsie. "This is coming down in a moment."

As they reached the end of the corridor where it turned to the left, Elsie squinted through the murky air. There was no sign of the four Cracklocks that she could see, so she dropped the shield. The ceiling fell with an enormous crash of wooden lathes, plaster, and items from the floor above joining the mess. They watched in horror as, following a grinding sound, the floor of the corridor in which they stood also tilted to an angle.

"The whole house is going to collapse!" shouted Jimmy. "What did you do?"

"Blew up a load o' stuff in the cellars," said Gnorbitt.

Jack and Elsie blinked at the gnome in puzzlement, unsure as to where he had come from. Gnorbitt blushed slightly and gestured with his thumb at Dorcas and Fermy. "I'm wi' them there."

"Who are you looking at?" said Sammy. "Is someone there?"

"A gnome, I think; looks like Dorcas and Fermy made a new friend," replied Jack.

"Well, you're very welcome," said Elsie. "But we need to go." There was a resounding crack, and the floor of the corridor in which they stood shook beneath them. *"Now!"* Elsie finished with a shriek.

"Follow me!" yelled Fermy. "This way. We can realm travel out of here, but we need to get clear of this wing before it collapses. There are doors everywhere down this way; we'll use one of those."

They raced down the corridor towards the main foyer,

feeling the heat through the floor when, with a grinding noise, cracks appeared in the walls on either side of them. The floor started to tilt downwards behind them, and they found themselves running up an incline that became steeper by the second. A gaping hole formed at the bottom, and licks of flame came darting up as the inferno in the cellar below them finally found its way into the main house. The flames grew higher as the air fed them, and the walls and ceiling started to smoke.

Gnorbitt started to slide down the ramp that had become the floor as it tipped further. He grabbed out as he slid and managed to grasp onto Jimmy's leg. Jimmy felt the tug and recoiled, "*Something's got me!*" he yelled above the roar of the fire.

"*It's Gnorbitt,*" yelled back Fermy, "*Help him.*"

The floor canted again, and all of them started to slide down towards the inferno behind them; the flames hungrily reaching through the hole. Sammy screamed, and Fermy looked around at them desperately.

"We'll have to travel. Take care of us; this is going to hurt." He grabbed Elsie, and Dorcas threw herself at Jack. Timothy grabbed at Sammy as he went sliding past and managed to seize her outstretched arm. The eight of them disappeared with a flash and reappeared in the mansion's foyer, the four Fae lying pale and unmoving on the floor. Behind them, the floor of the corridor continued to tilt upwards until it almost touched the ceiling. They could see the eager flames below licking along the bottom of it, and dark smoke poured out of the gap as oxygen fed the fire below. With a grinding noise, the floor disappeared into the flaming pit.

"What's happened to them?" cried Sammy, bending down to Timothy as he lay there.

"I don't know," responded Elsie. "But whatever it is, they are still alive at least. Pick them up, and let us get out of here. There, that door will do."

She gathered up Fermy, and the others did likewise, Jimmy

looking for Gnorbitt through a hagstone before picking up the little gnome. Hurrying over to the door, Elsie plucked her pen from the handbag and sketched the travel rune on it. She slapped it and pulled open the door a second later; the dancing blue flames in the corridor beyond a welcoming sight.

"We'll go to mine and re-group!" shouted Elsie, as part of the foyer floor started to crumble into the hungry fire below with a thunderous crash. She hurried through the open door, carrying Fermy, and Sammy followed with Timothy in her arms. Jimmy went through next, Gnorbitt under one arm, and Roly grasped firmly in one hand, scanning for any kind of trouble. Finally, Jack struggled over, carrying Dorcas's dead weight with some difficulty in his outstretched arms.

"Help me, someone; she's really heavy," he gasped. Jimmy placed Gnorbitt carefully onto the floor among the blue flames and, tucking Roly under his chin, reached out across the threshold and took Dorcas under her arms. He lifted her gently from Jack, and as he took her total weight, gasped a little as something clicked in his back. "Oww!" he exclaimed, moving his head, and as he did so, Roly dropped to the floor and rolled towards Jack.

"Gotcha, buddy," said Jack and scooped him up. "Let's get out of he..."

He was interrupted by a scream of absolute malice behind him. He whipped around to see the four Cracklocks emerge out of a door on the other side of the lobby, the soot smearing their faces not able to mask the looks of absolute rage as they stared at the friends in the act of leaving.

"Come on, Jack!" screamed Jimmy, reaching to grab the back of his friend's jacket and haul him in. Across the foyer, Anastasia threw a wild glamour. It flew across the room in a red streaking arc and struck the glamoured door. The door swung shut with a juddering bang, Jack still in the foyer clutching Roly, and his

friends in the waiting room, waiting to travel onwards to their next destination.

~

"*JAAAACCCCKKKKKK*!" screamed Sammy as she grabbed at the door, the dancing blue flames lighting them up all around her. It wouldn't open, of course.

"Get back," said Elsie, barging her out of the way. She quickly sketched the 'unlock' glyph onto the door, slapped it, and pushed the door open into her tiny kitchen.

"Get them out," she said, gesturing at the unconscious Fae. "We'll go back. Hurry!"

They hauled the four Fae out of the pantry and laid them quickly on the floor. Elsie sketched the 'open' glyph on the pantry door, slapped it, and pulled the door open. She saw her own well-stocked shelves but no blue flames flickering.

"Hurry up," gasped Sammy. "Get that door open!"

"It's not working," said Elsie in exasperation, slammed the door, redrew the glyph, and slapped it. The golden dust drained away, and she yanked the door open again. Again, the same shelves, but no dancing blue flames.

"You must have made a mistake," said Jimmy, equally as anxious. "Try it again."

"What's happening?" said a hoarse voice from behind them, and they turned to see Fermy sitting up, looking a little dizzy.

They bought him quickly up to speed while Elsie tried, unsuccessfully, a third time to open the travel room.

"I don't understand it," said Elsie in a panic. "It should be working."

"Unless the doors to Cracklock Manor are glamoured to prevent access," Fermy said, fear in his voice.

Sammy whirled round on him. "But they took you all there directly from my house. They must work."

"Maybe for them," said Fermy. "But not for everyone; that house is too well guarded. Would they just let people turn up unannounced? Think. When you went to the house, was there anywhere we could use?"

"No, we went to the nearest town," said Sammy.

"The guardhouse," exclaimed Jimmy. "That had another door in it, a toilet, or something. It's a way from the house, but it might work."

Elsie nodded and sketched the 'open' glyph again. This time when she yanked the door open, the blue flames were dancing.

"Quick," she said, and Sammy, Jimmy, and herself bundled themselves into the pantry. Fermy tried to stand but tottered, reaching out to steady himself.

"Stay here," said Elsie firmly. "You aren't in any fit state to help anyhow. We'll be back."

She slammed the door, sketched the 'unlock' glyph on it, slapped, and jerked the door open as quickly as she could. To be faced by her kitchen and the three Fae friends on the floor.

"*Nooo!*" yelled Sammy. "*Make it work; make it work!.*"

Elsie shook her head sadly. "I can't. We are getting bounced each time. The protection is too strong; I can't break it."

"There must be something we can do," Jimmy croaked, tears in his eyes. "We can't leave him there with those...those maniacs."

Sammy turned on the Fae. "You lot, you can transport us there, right?"

Fermy looked at Dorcas and Gnorbitt; their downcast eyes told their own story and then turned to Sammy. "We can transport ourselves to places, but carrying a lifer restricts the distance we can travel. It would take many hops to get there from here. Plus, that place is Fae locked; it's impossible to get into from the outside by travelling. I don't think that there's anything we can do to get there in time."

"We must be able to do something!" Sammy yelled at the group. *"We need to help Jack!"*

"We'll rescue him, I promise," Fermy choked. "But we need to think about how. For now, there's nothing we can do but hope. He's got Roly; he may still be able to escape."

"He doesn't know how to use the tubes; he's never done it," retorted Sammy.

"Roly will help him, Sammy, I promise," said Jimmy. "But think about what we can do. Think!"

JACK YANKED the door open quickly, but, as he already knew, the others were gone; the realm travel room was no longer visible. Another corridor stretched off into what must be the west wing of the manor and seemed to be surprisingly untouched after the chaotic events in the east wing. He ducked through it as another glamour hit the wall close to his head, the force of it cracking the plaster and shattering the lathes behind it. The four Cracklocks were sprinting across the foyer towards him now, Benedict in the lead as his younger legs outpaced the others.

'*Run, Jack, Run*!' boomed Roly in his head, and Jack did just that. He sprinted down the corridor into the west wing, the curses of the Cracklocks ringing in his ears as he did so. As he ran, carelessly thrown glamours shattered ornaments and ripped through the portraits along the walls, showering him with bits of porcelain and debris as he weaved his way at top speed. He risked a glance over his shoulder and saw that he was outdistancing them a little, the fear lending him the strength to his flight. Benedict was still in the lead, his dirty face flushed red as he sprinted after the scared boy, and the others were a little further behind him, their faces set in grim determination.

As Jack came to the middle of the long corridor, a side door suddenly opened, and a gaggle of grim-looking Fae emerged, goblin-like with sharp teeth and little red hats. The Redcaps gave a start at the boy charging at them, the crowd of people close behind him, and levelled their spears at Jack. He slowed down in fear as the creatures chattered together in their snarling language and then started to jab the spears in his direction.

"Capture him" came a command from behind him; *"He is the enemy!"* The creatures dashed at Jack and gathered around him quickly, snapping and snarling as they did so.

Roly chimed quickly into his head. *'Friend Jack, look at their eyes. They are under the influence of the Focus.'*

"How does that help?" said Jack quickly.

'You have the Focus, do you not? See if you can command them. Quickly now,' chimed Roly. *'They are almost upon us.'*

'Nothing to lose', thought Jack, and thrust his hand into his pocket, curling his fist around the Focus. He felt a tingle run up his arm, and the Redcaps stared at him curiously.

Facing them, Jack said clearly. "I am not your enemy. Those people there are. They have taken you from your homes and placed enchantments upon you. I only want to release you and all the Fae that they have captured." He felt the stone thrum in his hand as he finished speaking. Two of the creatures shook their heads, ears flapping, and then stared up at him.

Jack gestured towards the Cracklocks. "There are your enemies. Stop them," he commanded.

The Redcaps chattered in their language briefly and then pushed past Jack and headed at Benedict at a sprint; their spears levelled as they charged. Benedict screeched to a halt, and with a small scream, ran back towards his family members in panic.

"How dare you set these devils upon us?" screamed Agatha, and the four Cracklocks stopped in a loose formation, fumbling inside their clothes for iron weapons.

"You were happy enough to set them on me!" yelled back Jack and set off at a run again, not waiting to see what happened.

The sounds of an affray soon reached his ears as he turned right at the top of the corridor. A door on his left was marked with a brass plaque with the words 'Kitchens'.

"Let's get out of here, Roly," said Jack and pulled out the fancy pen that Malchiah had given him earlier. He quickly sketched the 'unlock' glyph, slapped it, and pulled open the door. The corridor ahead was ethereal and lit by the dancing blue flames. "We'll get to Elsie's and find the others. And never come back to this awful place." Roly chimed in agreement, and Jack stepped through the door. He reached for the handle and started to pull it shut, but as it swung closed, strong fingers curled around the edge, pulling it open again. Jack took a few steps backwards in shock as Malchiah came into view, his filthy face sporting a large cut that bled down his cheek. His dishevelled clothes bore signs of other slashes as well, and his face was like thunder.

"Give me back the stone, you beglamoured wretch!" he screamed and lunged for Jack. Jack turned on his heel again and ran for it into the flickering blue flames. He heard the sound of the door slam behind him and the rapid thud of Malchiah's feet as he gave chase. He tucked his head down and ran, looking desperately for somewhere to hide and give him time to use the 'open' glyph. But no such luck. He tried pushing at a few of the doors as he ran, but they were all sealed shut; the waiting room was just a reflection of the real world, and there was nowhere for him to hide. He started to despair, and then something hard hit him in the middle of his back, throwing him forwards. Jack crashed to the floor face first, and before he knew what was happening, a tight grasp had him and was hauling him to his feet.

Malchiah spun him around, grabbed him by the lapels, and slammed him against the wall. He looked crazy in the dancing light of the blue flames, and he stared Jack in the eyes, seeming to pierce his thoughts.

"You little fool," he spat. "You are dabbling with things that you can't possibly understand. Give me the stone."

Jack had been kidnapped, coerced, and beaten over the last twenty-four hours, and the events of the past day were starting to catch up with him. His indignation at how he'd been treated turned to real anger, and his eyes grew dark as he felt rage rise inside him. He reached out his arms, grabbed Malchiah by the lapels in a similar fashion, and hauled him in close.

"I do understand," he said in a quiet, dangerous voice, his face an inch from Malchiah's snarling visage. "I understand more than you know. I understand that your side of the family is pure evil, dressing it up somehow as the Lord's work. I understand that you took what was not yours and enslaved the race to whom it belonged when they dared to try to stop you. You used what was not yours to damage children, young, trusting children, in order to conduct an act of mass murder against a race of creatures you know nothing about. I understand plenty."

"You do not," said Malchiah in an equally dangerous voice. "You think you do, but your dealings with those devils colour your views. They are not what you think. You are a fool."

"And yet, you've been unable to change my mind with anything convincing," said Jack. "And it stops now. I am taking the stone, and you are not going anywhere near the Realm of the Departed. That realm pillar, and all of Faery, will remain untouched. Do you understand me?"

With that, he thrust Malchiah away from him, the strength in his arms causing the man to hit the opposite wall and slump to the floor.

"Now, stay away from me. I am going home," said Jack, staring at Malchiah, who, for the first time, felt real fear at the look on the boy's face.

Jack had gotten a few steps when Malchiah's laughter rang in his ears. He turned to the man sitting on the floor amongst the dancing blue flames as he chuckled with laughter. Malchiah fixed Jack with a narrow-eyed stare, and the look of sheer malice chilled Jack to the bone. "It matters not. Take the stone. One pillar alone cannot hold the realms apart. The result will be the same."

"What do you mean?" asked Jack in a menacing tone, taking a step back towards him.

"What I mean, you little idiot is that once the other realm pillars are destroyed, the outcome is guaranteed. It is of no matter that the Realm of the Departed remains intact. A single pillar will not be enough to hold the realms apart and prevent the cataclysm. We shall prevail. My brothers even now grow closer to the destruction of the others. Nothing can stop them. Not even your meddling father, despite his best efforts." Spittle ran down Malchiah's chin; his composure truly gone now in his rage.

"Others are doing this? And what did they do to my dad?" yelled back Jack, shock in his eyes now.

"Of course, there are others," laughed Malchiah insanely. "This is truly a family affair. Mama and I cannot do it all alone, you fool."

"So what did these 'others' do to my dad?" snapped Jack, taking another step forwards.

"They tricked him into going somewhere that he can never escape from. So gullible, like father, like son," said Malchiah in a dangerous voice as he got to his feet.

"So, he's still alive?" asked Jack.

"Oh, yes, you little fool. Not that I care; he is out of our hair." Jack's heart gave a little leap at that, but the gravity of the situation dragged him quickly back to reality. Malchiah's face was hideous in the shadows cast by the flickering flames. He continued.

"The Lord's work will continue, and there is nothing that you and your little friends can do to stop us. The fact that I could not complete the destruction of the departed pillar is not an issue. We will prevail, as I said. And besides…" Malchiah pulled an iron dagger from out of his shirt, an evil sneer crossing his face. "There is nothing to say that I won't be able to complete my part anyhow. I am not going to glamour you, Jack; we both know that it does not work. However, I will take back my stone of control, and I am going to leave you in this realm corridor forever, be it dead or alive. Nobody will ever find you here, that I promise you. Fitting really; two lost Cracklocks, gone forever in a place nobody will ever find them."

Jack eyed the dagger, fear worming down his spine as Malchiah advanced on him. He could do nothing; he was a fifteen-year-old schoolboy again, with no weapons and no glamours at his disposal. Apart from the remembering one, which was pretty basic and not much use in this situation to protect himself unless he could get Malchiah to remember not to attack him and leave him alone, which seemed unlikely. He could try it, he supposed, but…

Inspiration suddenly hit Jack, and he whispered to Roly. "I need to slow him up a bit; I've got an idea. Help me."

'Yes, friend Jack. Point me at him and think of the object. I will retrieve the most accurate approximation from the Cartulary,' the response chimed in his head.

Jack took a few steps backwards and pointed the tube at Malchiah, who did not flinch. There was a flash of blue light, and a rock hurtled through the air, where it glanced off the invisible glamour shield that sprang up in a shower of orange sparks. Jack stepped back and tried again, with the same result.

"Try again. Try harder," goaded Malchiah and threw his own dull red glamour, which Jack only just dodged, hitting the wall as he did so and gashing his head. It would appear that the waiting room still obeyed some of the laws of physics concerning solid materials, at least.

With a rapid series of blue pulses from Roly, Jack fired whatever came into his head at the advancing figure. None of which hit Malchiah; his shield was too strong. The mocking laughter echoed in Jack's ears as Malchiah closed in on him.

"No glamours of your own, Jack? Pity. That thing there is no match for the secrets of the family. Now, your last chance. Give me the stone, and I will make it quick for you. If you don't, while I do not doubt that you can throw off whatever I put on you eventually, the pain of it will drive you quite mad." He gestured again, and his glamour hit Jack full in the chest this time; it was so fast there was no time to dodge. The sensation of a thousand needles forced into his skin caused him to scream, and his legs gave way, Roly dropping from his hand as he did so. He sat sprawled on the floor, the pain coursing through his body as Malchiah loomed over him. He held out his hand.

"That is just the start. *The stone*," he commanded.

Jack forced one trembling hand into his jacket pocket that contained the stone and made his fingers try to close around the Focus there. He could hardly clutch it, the waves of pain causing his muscles to twitch in spasm as he jerked and twitched involuntarily. But then, with sudden relief, the pain started to subside, and his head cleared as the glamour bled off him. Nevertheless, he knew when he was beaten; he had nothing left. He pulled the Focus from his pocket and looked up at Malchiah. He felt something running down his head and wiped what he thought was sweat away with the back of his hand. When he glanced down, though, he saw the back of his hand was bloody; his head was bleeding from the knock he had taken earlier. He looked thoughtfully at it.

'Do not give it to him, friend Jack, do not,' chimed Roly urgently in his head. *'You will doom my people for all time if you do. And your own.'*

"Give it to me; there's a good little boy," sneered Malchiah and leaned in to take it.

Jack stared at the man towering over him and smiled; it

didn't touch his eyes. "You can take it from me once you've done your worst. But you won't be able to use it."

And with that, he pressed the Focus on the back of his blood-slicked hand and covered it up with his palm.

"Just give it to me, you little idiot, you are finished. Don't make this any..."

Malchiah did not finish his thundering threat as the chiming of what seemed to be many bells suddenly filled their heads, distant at first but growing louder as if rushing towards where they stood. Underneath Jack's hand, the Focus started to glow, a vibrant deep blue light that shone first through the cracks in Jack's fingers and then through his hand itself; Jack's bones visible in the intense blue light.

"What are you doing?" screamed Malchiah and grabbed at Jack's wrist. Jack scooted back on his backside out of reach.

"Releasing all of the creatures you have enslaved with this thing!" he screamed back at Malchiah. *"Your control is done."*

A dull boom echoed through their entire bodies, and the chiming intensified until it felt like their skulls would split. Malchiah sank to his knees, his hands over his ears, as did Jack; the Focus dropped on the ground in front of him, entirely forgotten. It quivered on the hard floor, little jittery bounces as flashes and arcs of blue light streaked off it. Then, with a final pulse that blew all of the flickering blue flames of the waiting room sideways, it went out. The blue gem lay there on the ground, back to a brilliant blue but no longer glowing.

Jack recovered first and said, "Roly?" There was no answer. He grabbed the Focus and stuffed it back into his pocket as he got to his feet.

"What...did...you...do?" quavered Malchiah as he removed his hands from the side of his head. "I can't feel them anymore."

"No, you won't," said Jack. "I've released them all. Everything that you controlled with this thing is free now. And I am taking it back to where it belongs."

'Friend Jack,' came the chime into his head, weak, no more than a whisper. *'I can feel my people again. Thank you.'*

"Roly, where are you?" said Jack, looking about him. He saw the tube on the floor and plucked him up. The usual bright blue eyes were squinted, and the tube was dormant.

'Fading Jack, the Focus is fading me for now. The effects...so strong...' the chime stopped mid-sentence.

Malchiah got to his feet as well, slightly shaky. *"You don't know what you've done, you and your damned mixed blood,"* he cackled, his eyes wide with rage. "Your actions have doomed us all."

"I don't think so," Jack retorted. "Now, leave me alone. We're going."

"You are not!" screamed Malchiah suddenly and lunged at Jack. He had lost the dagger, but his groping hands grasped Jack's throat, and he started to squeeze. Keeping a firm grip, he swept Jack's legs out from under him and pinned him to the floor.

"You think that you are going to just leave? I am going to end you for what you have done. Our home! Our plans! And you think you get to walk away? Never!" he screamed. Jack recoiled and grabbed at Malchiah's hands, but he couldn't pry him loose.

"And then, when we're done, I am going to find your friends, and I am going to end them as well," Malchiah spat into his face. His grip tightened, and Jack started to see black spots in his vision as he strained for air. He struggled with the hands, but they were too strong; Malchiah, in his rage, had him in a grip of steel. Instead, Jack groped within his jacket for something, anything, which could help him. His questing fingers were looking for the pen, but they brushed the metal card with the glyphs for the Realm of the Departed. The black shadows were closing in now at the sides of his vision, and he pulled it out as a last resort, clenched it between his knuckles, and jabbed his fist at Malchiah's bright red face. The man screamed and relaxed his grip slightly as the card scraped open the wound on his

cheek from earlier, bright red blood blossoming again from the cut.

Jack managed a single strained gasp of air before the hands clamped down again. His eyes rolled in his head as his lungs choked for air, and then he felt something against his hand. It was Roly. He lagged into semi-consciousness as the ringing insane laughs of Malchiah echoed from far away. He looked at Roly, whose eyes were closed. The tube chimed weakly in his head. A single word. 'Binks.'

Jack forced his fingers to curl around the tube, and he whispered as his air left him the name of the thing which had started all of this. "Binks."

There was a bright blue flash, and suddenly Malchiah was off of him. Jack swam back to consciousness as air entered his tortured throat in huge gasps. He opened his eyes to see the sight of what looked like a ghost rolling on the floor with Malchiah, the thing screeching as it did so.

"Where are they, where are they, where are they?" the thing screamed as it battered at Malchiah with its fists. It reared up and hovered above Malchiah, its body composed of insubstantial wispy parts, like cobwebs floating around it, its face a mask of evil before diving back down again at the prone figure. It grabbed Malchiah by his throat and started to try to choke the life out of him as he had Jack. Suddenly the creature shot up into the air, hitting the ceiling as Malchiah cast a glamour to protect himself, and it stuck there, pinned.

"Give me back my others," it screamed from the ceiling, grabbing all the time at Malchiah as is struggled against the force that held it.

'Now or never,' thought Jack and weaved the only glamour that he knew. He pitched it at Malchiah, and it hit home, although whether it did anything or not, Jack did not know. However, it gave the Binks creature enough disruption to escape from the ceiling, and it swooped down and started grappling with its adversary again; Malchiah trying desperately to keep it from his eyes.

Jack tucked the silent Roly into his pocket and limped back down the corridor until he was far enough from the battling pair. He pulled out the pen that Malchiah had given him earlier, sketched the 'unlock' glyph onto a door, and slapped it. As the golden dust fell away, he was suddenly aware of the fact that the noise had stopped. He turned to see Malchiah sprinting towards him, the ghostly figure of Mr Binks lying suspended in mid-air as if paralysed.

Jack yanked the door open to the welcome sight of Elsie's kitchen; the others all stood there with their mouths open at Jack's sudden reappearance. Sammy reacted first, shrieking, "*Jaaaccckkkk*!" and stepping forward to grab her son, his dishevelled state and dark bruises on his throat clear for all of them to see. The others were fixated on the sight of Malchiah coming towards them like a steam train, battered and bloodied but not any less dangerous.

Jack jumped through and tried to slam the door shut, but just as it was closing, dirty fingers again curled around the edge, and a muffled curse came as the door trapped them. "*Help me,*" he screamed at the others. "*We can't let him through.*"

Rage giving him strength, Malchiah hauled the door open and stood there on the threshold, madness on his face and his fingers sparking with whatever glamour he had in mind. He threw his arms wide and cackled, "*Now you are all mine.*"

Then he crumpled from multiple glamours thrown from Elsie, Fermy, Gnorbitt, and Timothy, a carefully aimed rolling pin and what appeared to be a chunk of masonry from the flashing blue tube held by Sammy. The force of the combined attack pitched him backwards down the blue flame lit corridor, and he landed on his back a few yards from the open door.

Amazingly, he started to push himself up, groggy and his

eyes unfocused. As he pulled himself together, he glared at Jack, who stood with his hand on the door.

"WE WILL NEVER STOP, BOY," he thundered, the power of his voice somehow amplified in the corridor. *"I AM COMING STRAIGHT FOR YOU WITH EVERYTHING I CAN MUSTER. YOU WILL NEVER ESCAPE."*

Jack smiled back at him, but his eyes were hard. "Maybe. However, you are the one that will never escape. When it comes to understanding, I may not know a lot about Faery and our abilities yet. But one thing that I do know is that you need two glyphs to realm travel, correct? Both 'open' and 'unlock'?"

Malchiah looked puzzled now. "I know a hundred glyphs, you little fool," he sneered. "As soon as you close that door, I'll be back to Mama, and then we'll find you."

"No, you know ninety-nine glyphs. And one piece of rather grubby blank paper, I think. I'm sorry for that; I was under some stress when I glamoured you," replied Jack in a calm voice.

"You glamoured me? What are you talking abou..." Malchiah tailed off as understanding dawned, and his eyes widened. "How could you...The unlock glyph...how?"

Jack cut him off. "Enjoy your time in the waiting room, won't you? As you said earlier, fitting really, two lost Cracklocks, gone forever in a place nobody will ever find them. Although that will be only one soon, as we will find my dad."

"No, wait," called Malchiah in panic. "You can't. PLLLLLEEEEEEEAAAAAAAASSSSSSEEEEEEEEE..."

"See ya," said Jack, slamming the door and cutting him off. He turned to his friends and shrugged. "I only know the remembering glamour. All that that maniac remembers about the 'Unlock' glyph for this realm is a blank piece of paper. That is how it works, right? Trapped forever if you can't get out?"

Elsie burst out laughing and clapped her hands. Sammy and Jimmy grabbed Jack and hugged him to them, Dorcas and Fermy wrapping their arms around Jack's knees and shins, respectively. Timothy and Gnorbitt stood with huge smiles on their faces until Elsie gathered them up in her arms and danced a little jig.

Jimmy pushed Jack away and held him by the shoulders. "That'll do, Jack. That'll do," he said with an entirely serious face, and then both he and Jack burst into peals of laughter.

CHAPTER 14

TWO WEEKS LATER

"...*And in other news, the victims of the unknown wasting disease continue to make good progress following what some are saying to be a miraculous worldwide recovery. Public Health's Centre of Infectious Disease Surveillance and Control are still at a loss as to why the victims are now making what appears to be a return to total health, and further research goes on in the area. In the meantime, children are being released from observations to complete their care under their parents' and guardians' watchful eyes at home.*"

Elsie clicked off the television and looked across at Fermy, who was fiddling with the brim of his hat on the other sofa.

"So, asking the Courts to help put this right worked then?" she asked.

"Yes," said Fermy. "They were most interested in my report on what the Cracklocks have been up to, although most of them disbelieve it, of course. They simply do not comprehend what we are telling them, although visiting the Realm of the Lost and seeing the pillar swayed a few. And the testimony of the tubes helped, of course."

"Were there many volunteers to try and help the lifer children?" asked Elsie.

"More than I expected, if I am honest. My fellow citizens really care about you lifers, you know, even some of the Unseelie members volunteered their time. Moreover, of course, all of those that were under the control of the Focus wanted to put right what they had been involved in. They were dismayed that they had been used in such a manner. Putting the grackles back into the children, though, is taking some time; it is a slow process, but the tubes are extremely helpful. It took a little experimenting to get the process right, but it's working now."

"No ill effects, though?" asked Elsie.

"None that we can see; as you know, we Fae are extremely resilient to glamours overall. The Fae will be fine. As will the children, although I expect there will be some nightmares and exhausted parents for a while yet."

"All good then."

Fermy looked at Elsie with a sad smile. "Are you okay, Elsie? About Malchiah, I mean. With your history…"

Elsie cut him off. "As you say, that is history. And with what that man has both done and tried to do, he isn't the person I knew back then. So, yes, I am fine with it."

"Okay, then. If you're sure."

Elsie nodded and gave a small smile. "I better get the dinner on. Sammy will be back from work soon, and Jack has gone to fetch Jimmy. Shame that we aren't in the same town anymore, but it doesn't make too much difference to those two; Jack just goes to fetch him. And I am assuming that Timothy will show up when he's ready, assuming that he isn't side-tracked with that infernal machine of his."

"Isn't Dorcas cooking tonight? She'll be angry if you mess up her kitchen."

"Ah, I forgot you've been away on this lifer matter and aren't up to speed. Dorcas isn't here tonight. She'll be back later," said Elsie with a smile.

"Where is she?"

"That's the strangest thing. She has gone off on a date. With Gnorbitt."

"A Date? Dorcas?" Fermy's voice was incredulous.

"Yes, it seems that the Gnome is smitten with our little brownie and has been trying his best to woo her for a while. Anyhow, it turns out that there is a new action film at the cinema in town. He said he'd steal some popcorn for her if she'd go with him."

"Well, I never," said Fermy, shaking his head. "After all this time…"

"You mustn't tease her," said Elsie firmly. "This is a big thing for her. You know how she is."

Fermy mimed zipping his lips and throwing the key away. He smiled.

"I guess that I better help you then if we're having guests over. They'll want something edible after all."

"You cheeky little bugger," said Elsie with a chuckle and made to swat him. "You're on peeling duties for that. And no glamours allowed."

Fermy cursed under his breath and followed her out of the room.

JACK EXITED the walk-in wardrobe in Jimmy's bedroom to find his friend sitting on his bed. Jimmy looked up and smiled as Jack stumbled into his room.

"Alright, mate. How's the throat?" he asked.

"Much better, thanks. Having the grackles choked out of you really takes a toll, though."

"Try having them sucked out of you by some master maniac followed by two giant bullies and then come and complain to me," smiled Jimmy.

'Friend Jimmy, my brethren deeply regrets that action,' came a

familiar chime in their heads, and Jack looked at the bed closely. Roly appeared from behind Jimmy on his stick-like legs, his blue eyes looking up at Jack.

"Hey Roly, you recovered from the Focus then?"

'Yes, thank you, friend Jack. And my countrymen have requested that I spend some time in this realm to learn more of your customs. For our archives. Friend Jimmy here has kindly offered to show me around.'

"Well, if you like gaming and looking at stuff on the internet, you're in the right place," said Jack with a laugh.

"Oy! I resent that. I have a whole series of things lined up for us, actually, including a trip to London. Educational like. Wanna come?"

"I can't," said Jack sadly. "We are back into semi-hiding again; the Cracklocks are still out there somewhere."

"How did you wangle the new place so quickly? Must have been expensive."

"Well, it turns out that Great Aunt Elsie doesn't always practice what she preaches when it comes to glamours. She has been using them to cheat at gambling in casinos. The 'harmless old lady' routine."

Jack stopped and gave a very impressive imitation of Elsie's voice, "*Jack, the secret is not to be too greedy. That way, they don't twig to it. But no harm in making a little money, is there?*"

The boys fell about laughing at this. When they had recovered, Jack continued.

"Anyhow, it turns out she's got a tidy sum stashed away; been doing it for years. So finding another place that the Cracklocks don't know about was a doddle for her. And having the necessary papers to support the rental agreement...well, again, no point being what we are if we can't get a few fake documents together, is there?"

Jimmy nodded his understanding. "Just a shame you're not around here anymore, though; I can't just pop in and see you."

"Just message me whenever you fancy a visit, and I'll come and get you like today. Alternatively, one of the others will. You're part of the family now. Mum says you're like the brother I should have had if Dad hadn't gone missing."

"Good to know," said Jimmy. "What about school? Take it you'll be switching to one near you."

"Not sure yet. Mum wants me to carry on here for now and go back in; it should be okay if I'm careful. Couple of conditions, though, one of which involves you. She wants me to go from your house. You okay with that?"

"Of course, no worries. Although explaining to my mum about how you got here without knocking might be a problem. And Sean's a nosy little git."

"Thought I'd come through the shed. That alright with you?"

"Yeah, that'd work, I guess, until we get caught. Mum probably won't notice, though, and Dad's normally away pretty early. What's the second condition?"

"I have to have a chaperone with me. It was going to be Fermy, but you never guess what? That gnome, Gnorbitt, volunteered to do it."

"Is he alright?"

"I think so; Dorcas seems to like him. He took me to one side and told me not to worry; whatever I'd got 'going on,' he'd turn a blind eye to it, so no reporting me to Mum and Elsie, like Fermy probably would. He's just going to hang around and make sure that I don't get into any trouble."

"All good then. Shall we get going? Don't want to be late for tea. I'm the only one in, so we can go out the same way as you came in if you want?"

"Ah, we can't. Elsie asked me to pick up some ice cream for pudding for her and stash it in the freezer. She's supposed to be baking something, but she says she's a bit rusty."

"Isn't Dorcas doing it?"

"Nah. Dorcas is out on a date."

"What?"

Jack laughed. "C'mon. I'll tell you everything on the way to the shop."

Ten minutes later, the minimarket was in sight, and the two of them were messing about, without a care. As they approached the shop, two hulking figures sidled out of the alleyway further up the road, their backs to the two boys. Jack spotted them first and put a hand on Jimmy's shoulder.

"Look. The LaFey's," he said and pointed. Jimmy paled visibly.

Seeing his friend's distress, Jack said quietly. "Let's go somewhere else, come on. We'll go to the Metro on the high street."

Jimmy looked at him and smiled. "No. We are going here as we planned. Aren't we, Roly?"

The tubes little arms appeared at the top of Jimmy's shirt pocket, and Roly pulled himself into view. He saw the two figures in the distance, and the blue eyes narrowed.

'Yes, friend Jimmy. We are going wherever you want to go. And that's a fact,' came the chiming into their heads.

Jack looked at the resolution on the two's faces and started to chuckle to himself. He almost hoped that the LaFey's spotted them.

ANASTASIA SAT in the darkened bedroom of her home, seething quietly as she observed her Great Aunt. The old woman was snoring now, whistling gasps through an open mouth, revealing her brown teeth. Anastasia was glad that she was finally asleep; she was incredibly demanding during her waking hours, ringing that damned bell and expecting instant attention to her every need. Anastasia eyed the pile of embroidered cushions that propped up Agatha, thinking that just one was all she would need. But no. She couldn't. Great Aunt Agatha was the key to their success.

In the two weeks following the destruction of Cracklock Manor, she had returned to the site a couple of times to oversee the removal of any of the goods that could be salvaged and stored here in her own home. The mansion itself was completely unliveable now; half of it had sunk into the giant pit that had formed when the armoury had blown up the weak chalk rock underneath it. The other half was extensively fire damaged; the fires had ripped through the historical wood that had centuries to dry. It had taken some work to glamour all of the staff and the authorities; work that she had had to do herself as her Uncle was still nowhere to be found, and Benedict was next to useless. Nevertheless, she had managed it; the reports were of an unexpected gas explosion from underneath the mansion, and the media had soon forgotten about it; it wasn't a tourist attraction anyhow. Her Aunt had sent for her other Uncles to assist, but they had yet to show; they were engaged on 'important family tasks' as Agatha had put it to her, which were at a critical point. And of course, the old lady herself was too grand to go and perform the necessaries, choosing instead to languish in bed, recovering from her injuries. Which were minor; Anastasia and Benedict had to fight off the Redcaps that day, while their great aunt had cowered at the back shouting commands, and Uncle Malchiah had set off after Jack and whatever fate he had subsequently met.

However, she tolerated her Great Aunt, as she had promised to let her into the 'great plan', as she called it, for the destruction of the devil's realm. Anastasia was intrigued at the concept of it all, mainly as they had valid proof in the form of one of the pillars already lying destroyed. Her other Uncles, Malchiah's brothers, were apparently working on the others, and they were all finally due to report to Great Aunt very soon. She would be present during their briefing of what the situation was. 'A shame they couldn't be here to help me before,' she thought bitterly but pushed the thoughts to one side.

The old woman snorted in her sleep and then called out, "Malchiah." Anastasia patted her aunt's hand, and she settled again, resuming her snoring. Anastasia went back to her seething, as the one thing that bothered her above all else was the fact that Elsie and her lot had bested them and then disappeared, taking her Uncle with them. She had tried to find them but quickly determined that the Fae slaves they usually utilised had all gone missing. All of them, along with the control tubes. Therefore, she had no way to track them down other than by using glamours, which did not work (Elsie was wily enough to know how to avoid these) and regular private investigators. Anastasia had employed a number of these, but so far, nothing. They had spotted the brat, Jack, a couple of times, but there was no sign of the others, and the boy was too quick for them to follow. Moreover, it was difficult to get at him in the school now that they had no devil slaves to use. 'Something else I will have to take a hand in, I suppose,' she thought bitterly.

There came a polite rap at the bedroom door, and Anastasia called "Enter" in a quiet voice. The calming figure of Nigel stood there.

"Ma'am, there is a visitor for you. At the front door."

"The front door, you say. How did he get down the drive? Who is it?"

"I'm afraid I don't know, Ma'am. The gentleman had an American accent, though."

Anastasia fixed Nigel with a puzzled look. "I am not expecting anyone. Show him through to the Reception room, please. I will greet him there."

Nigel cleared his throat again and looked at his mistress.

"Yes? What is it now?" snapped Anastasia.

"Begging your pardon, Ma'am, but if you'll permit me to

speak out of turn, something does not feel right with the gentleman in question."

"Whatever do you mean?"

Nigel hung his head. "I don't know, Ma'am. But please be careful."

THE DINNER at Jack's that evening was just what they all needed, full of laughter and jokes, most of which were at the expense of Elsie's cooking, although Fermy accepted part of the blame. It was edible for the most part, but Jack was glad that he had bought the ice cream earlier, as the smell of burning pastry still hung in the air in the kitchen. Elsie had finally glamoured the smoke alarm to stop its noise; the machine was hanging from the kitchen ceiling by a single wire following repeated jabs with the broom handle to silence it. The roast she had served up had been passable, though, and both Elsie and Sammy were onto the third bottle of wine, helped along by Fermy and his small glass. Jack and Jimmy had been permitted a glass each with dinner, but of course, had stolen more when people were not looking and were quite giggly themselves. Timothy had noticed what they were up to but had decided not to say anything. Elsie had asked him to confirm, in writing, that he had no rodents about his person before he sat down, and he was still smarting slightly at that.

There was a click of the front door, and Dorcas strode into the dining room, her cheeks a little flushed, followed closely by Gnorbitt. The gnome's change was wonderful to see; his matted beard nicely combed out, and his potbelly started to show again under his clothes. He beamed at the others with a massive smile as he entered the room.

Dorcas stood sniffing and then said. "What is burnings?" causing the others to start laughing again. Jack smiled down at his old nanny and friend and said. "Better you don't ask, Dorcas. I think that the pan is rescuable, though."

Dorcas sighed and rolled up her sleeves. "I's go and see's to it," she said, but Elsie called her back.

"Oh no, you don't. Come and have a drink with us. I'll sort it out later. Pass me a glass, Sammy, would you? Gnorbitt, can I tempt you?" she said, gesturing with the bottle.

"Have you got any beer?" said Gnorbitt, rubbing his stomach. "All that salty popcorn gives you a right thirst. Well, what little bit I managed to get of it, any'ow." Dorcas went even redder and cuffed him on the back of the head lightly.

"I think that there may be a bottle or so of it in the fridge, yes," said Elsie. "Sit down, sit down. I'll get it for you."

She got to her feet and was on her way to the kitchen when she heard a ringing sound coming from her voluminous handbag. She looked at the others, puzzled.

"Is that my phone?" she asked. They listened, heads cocked, and then Sammy said. "It's coming from your bag, I think."

"Oh, for goodness sake," said Elsie and rooted about in the bag, before pulling the phone free. She looked at the number on it, a puzzled look on her face.

"I don't recognise that number. Seems too long," she said and showed it to Sammy.

"Odd," she replied. "Looks like an international number. Are you going to answer it?"

"I guess so," said Elsie. "This place is well protected; even those clever men in the government won't be able to trace this phone with the cell phone mast thingies."

Elsie pressed the green 'answer' button and said, "Hello?"

A female voice, seemingly flustered and with an American accent, said, "Missus Cracklock? Missus Elsie Cracklock?"

"Why, yes. Who is this, please?" said Elsie politely.

"Oh, thank the Arcadians!" said the voice, and it cracked a little "I'm sorry to call you like this, Missus Cracklock, really I am, but I have nowhere else to turn. This number is what Gramps told me to call if things went south. Which they have, big time."

"I'm sorry, dear, but who are you?" said Elsie.

The voice gave a sob down the phone. "My name is Alice. Alice McBride. I am so sorry to call you, but I didn't know what else to do."

"I'm sorry," said Elsie gently. "But I'm afraid that I have no idea who you are."

"I know, I know," said the voice, tears now evident in the voice. "I am just some kind of weirdo, calling you out of the blue like this. But Gramps said you'd be able to help me, us, if he got took by 'them.' Which he has been; I don't know where he is, and neither does Popple and..." She broke off in tears.

"Oh, dearie," replied Elsie soothingly. "Who took him?"

"The Dark Men is what Gramps called them. They tried to catch us at the graveyard, but we got away. But they came again, and that time they got Gramps. It's the reason why we had to leave home; they're after us, and I'm so scared."

"Where are you at the moment, my dear?"

"In Nebraska, USA. But I don't know what to do or where to go." More sobs.

"But I'm not sure what I can do to help you, dear. You do know that you are calling England, don't you?"

"Sure I do; Gramps told me that that was where the family is still mainly. Only we offshoots are out here in the US."

Elsie's ears pricked up. "You have family here in the United Kingdom?"

"I guess; that's what he always said. Where the family started."

"And your family's name is McBride?"

"That's my name. Gramps's is the same as yours. Cracklock."

Elsie clutched her chest and sat down suddenly, the others staring at her.

"You're a Cracklock?" she whispered.

"Sure, I am. Do you want proof? Gramps said to tell you that Nathaniel was Bartholomew's brother. And to speak to Popple. One second."

There was a rustling sound, and a kindly voice, light and airy, came on the line.

"Can you hear me?"

Elsie's heart leapt at that. "For certain, my dear."

"Listen, if you can really hear me say 'McDonald's.'"

"McDonald's."

"They're Cracklocks alright," said the voice, and then Alice came back on the line.

"Can you help me? I don't know what to do, and those men are around here somewhere, looking for me."

"Is this a mobile number?"

"What? I don't know what that is."

Elsie slapped her forehead and said. "Is this a cell phone you are calling on?"

"Sure. But I don't know if I can keep it on; they may be tracking me with it. You know, like those detective shows?"

"I do. Turn it off for now, and turn it back on in thirty minutes. I have an idea, but I need to talk to my friends here to see if it could work."

"Okay, but please call me back. I don't know what to do, and I'm scared."

"I will, dear, I will; have no fear. We never leave a family member behind. Stay safe."

The call rang off, and Elsie turned to the others who were sitting silent, listening.

"You get all of that?" she asked

"Some," said Jack. "Is that an American Cracklock?"

"I don't know. The evidence is convincing, though. It looks like we may finally find out what happened to Nathaniel after all this time. But first, we need to help that poor girl, she's scared, and there are people after her."

"What can we do?" asked Jimmy. "It's not another one of Agatha's traps, is it?"

"I don't think so," said Elsie. "Something about the second person who came onto the call. If that wasn't a Fae, well, I'll clean up this messy table naked."

"No need," said Jack hastily. "How can we help her?"

"Well," said Elsie. "Do you think that this could work...?"

He sat in semi-darkness in the room, lit only by the light of his computer screen as he read the encrypted email for the third time. As if by sixth sense, he looked up a few seconds before a single rap at the door came. "Come," he called.

The suited man entered the room and stood, waiting for permission to speak.

"Have you located her?" the sitting man asked.

"Yes. She made a call, just like you said she would. We know the approximate grid she's in now."

"Good. Make it happen, as we agreed. Tell the others that we are now in motion. The old man will talk once we've got some leverage. David Cracklock is as good as ours."

The person nodded and left the room.

TO BE CONTINUED IN THE CRACKLOCK SAGA BOOK 3 – ALICE AND THE MIRROR GLASS.

ACKNOWLEDGMENTS

To my family first and foremost. For their encouragement and criticisms and everything else. And a special thank you to Sam, who helped me with all the electronic stuff that I am so awful at, but she dances around like it's her own glamours in action. Thanks, Sammy!

To my beta team. You guys showed me that one pair of eyes is never enough. Thanks for all that you caught. And special thanks to Angela, who has kicked me along when I needed it.

To the professional folk, the team at SR Press LLC. A brilliant editing team, and you couldn't hope to meet nicer, more helpful folks—my thanks.

And to you. The reader. Thank you for taking a punt on this book. Time is so precious, so the fact that you have chosen to spend some of yours with the Cracklocks makes me feel very humble. I hope that you think it is time well spent.

ABOUT THE AUTHOR

I live in the East Midlands, right in the centre of the UK, and when I'm not writing or working, I'm with the family or walking the dog in the local woodlands seeking those ever-elusive Fae. Or sitting, pint in hand with the good friends I grew up with. Some of them are hidden in the books themselves; quite a few characters are based on the people I know and love.

Publishing wise, I am a mere fledgling writer, having had a few short stories published to date but always trying for more. Check out other published works at:

- Spooky Tales From The Pub: Volume Two (https://www.amazon.co.uk/Spooky-Tales-Pub-M-Smith-ebook/dp/B08LV4JZ2W)
- Written Tales Magazine Volume 2: Night Terrors (https://www.amazon.co.uk/Written-Tales-Magazine-Night-Terrors-ebook)

And so, to the Cracklocks... "The Cracklock Saga" series of books came about from reading some pretty awful fairy books to my daughter over the years – she's 13 now and has now (with more than a little relief, I have to say) left those behind. But I always wondered what would happen if someone didn't like fairies, what they would do about it, and could anybody stop them? This idea grew, and the Cracklocks were born. I liked the idea of people who hated the Fae and everything they stood for. And who knew just how wicked those people were? I certainly didn't until Anastasia and Agatha got their claws into me!

The Cracklock Saga is my first series, and I have huge plans for it. The shadowy Tobias is begging for his tale to be told, and this will be forthcoming. Plus, I want to know more about Fermerillion, Dorcas and the rest of the good guys – where did they come from? And what really happened between Elsie and Malchiah all those years ago? I think I know, but they all have a habit of surprising me when I'm scribbling. More than you will ever know.

You can keep up to date with the happenings in the Cracklock world by visiting www.thecracklocksaga.com and signing up. I won't bombard you with spam as I'm not too fond of that sort of thing myself.

So, I do hope that you'll want to come along for the ride. You would be most welcome...